THE ENDEX

A NOVEL

LL FOX

LL FOX BOOKS
NASHVILLE, TENNESSEE

LL FOX/LL Fox Books
email: llfoxbooks@gmail.com
www.llfoxbooks.com

Ordering Information:
Quantity sales. Special discounts are available on quantity purchases by corporations, associations, and others. For details, contact the "Special Sales Department" at the address above.

The ENDEX/ LL Fox. -- 1st ed.
ISBN : 978-1-0878-7950-5

Contents

For Mary Frances

Prologue

Forty Years in the Future

Few could remember life before the collapse; most could only imagine. To those who survived it, nothing felt the same.

The couple sat together on the porch swing, watching the children play in the front yard. It was mid-summer, and the afternoon temperatures were approaching 90 with humidity to match. But the children didn't notice as they were caught up in a game of tag with the trees in the yard as the safe spots. The couple, now in their 60's, talked and turned from time to time to watch the children as they ran.

"You're it!" a boy shouted at his cousin.

"No, I touched the tree first! You're still it!" she argued. The grandparents smiled as they watched them play.

The house, an old two-story farmhouse, was in the country surrounded by forest and fields. Half the house was freshly painted white while the other half was spotted with places that had been scraped, awaiting a fresh coat of white.

An old pickup truck, that decades before had been red but was now mostly rust, sat to the side of the house. A strange contraption with a smoke stack and coils of copper tubing occupied the bed of the truck. Someone who didn't know what it was might have mistaken it for a mobile still. The road and the drive were gravel and badly needed more rock as there were more potholes than road. Grass grew in the middle of the drive and in places on the road. There was very little traffic to keep the grass down.

"Joe had lemons at the store," said the woman to her husband as the swing slowly swayed. "I got them for the children, so we could make lemonade. Joe said there's a ship making the run from South America to New Orleans! With the train service improving to Nashville, he said we might even get bananas in a month or two. Can you imagine, bananas! I try to remember what they taste like, but I can't." Her husband smiled and reached over to take her hand.

"I hope the store gets our paint in soon," the man said. "It drives me crazy to have the house half painted. We've been waiting for four months. Do you remember Home Depot? I could buy as much paint as I wanted in thousands of different colors." His wife smiled at him with a look that said, *Be patient. At least we can buy paint now even if it takes a long time, and the only choice is white.* "OK, you're right. And I am grateful. Things are better. It's much easier than it was. How 'bout you go start on the lemonade, and I'll gather the kids on the porch."

The woman, wearing a beige, print dress with a design of tiny flowers, went in the house, gently closing the flimsy, wooden screen door so it wouldn't slam when the spring pulled it shut. The husband walked down the steps, his legs stiff from having sat too long. He had a slight limp from a gunshot wound in his right leg, but that was long ago. His red plaid shirt and jeans were both too big for him, and a .45 Colt 1911 pistol sat on his right hip in a worn, leather holster.

"Kids, come on up to the house," he called, waving to the children. "Grandma has a treat for you. Something you've never had before!"

"What is it, Grandpa?" asked a little, blonde-headed girl of ten.

"Your grandma found lemons at the store this week," he explained. "She's in the kitchen getting ready to squeeze them to make lemonade."

"Lemonade?" asked one of the grandsons. "I've not heard of that. Is it good?"

"I guarantee you're going to love it," said the grandfather. "The lemons came in on a ship from somewhere in Mexico or South America. When I was your age, we had lemons all the time. We could have lemonade anytime we wanted, so we didn't even think it was that special. But it was. We took it for granted. I can't wait to taste it again. And I want to see your faces when you taste it."

"Grandpa, can you and Grandma tell us about before? Tell us about the cabin! We want to hear the story again," said the second oldest granddaughter.

The man looked at the children gathered around him and smiled. He knew it was a miracle any of them had survived. "Yes, we'll tell you the story again. But first, you girls get in the kitchen and help your grandmother. You need to learn how to make lemonade. And boys, go out in the barn and bring the wood chips for the gasifier. Fill up the hopper in the truck so that when it's time to take you home, the truck is ready. The girls happily ran up the steps to the porch as they heard their grandpa warn, "Don't let the screen door slam!" The boys ran to the barn and quickly emerged, each with a bucket of chipped wood.

They sat the buckets on the tailgate of the old truck then jumped up in the bed. Taking the cover off the hopper, they poured the wood chips into the machine. "You two go back and get more wood," said the oldest grandson to the two youngest, and they ran back to the barn. "Grandpa says that before, all these cars and trucks ran on gasoline. It was sold at stores called gas stations," said the oldest boy. "Do you see the little doors on the side of all the old cars and trucks? That's for the gasoline."

"It seems strange to think that trucks could run on something besides wood gas," said a middle grandson. "I wonder if someday there will be gasoline again?" The two, younger boys returned with the wood chips and handed them up to the older boys who filled the hopper and replaced the cover. Then the boys ran to the front porch and sat down, waiting for the girls to bring out the lemonade.

"Everybody, take a glass and sit down," instructed the grandmother as she came out on the porch with two pitchers of lemonade. Two of the girls had trays with glasses, handing them out to the boys and their grandfather. Then, one by one, the grandmother filled every glass. "OK, kids, this is your first lemonade. For your grandpa and me, it's the first time we've had it in 40 years," she said, raising her glass. All the children followed suit.

"Here's to lemons and the ship that brought them to us!" toasted the grandfather. And with that everyone took a first sip.

"Oh, that's sour!" said the youngest girl, making a face.

"No, it's sweet and sour," said the oldest boy. "I like it!"

The man watched his wife close her eyes and slowly take her first sip. A smile came across her face as she opened her eyes and saw her husband. Savoring the taste on her tongue, she gave him a look that said *Go ahead, try it. It tastes just like it did a half century ago*. He took a drink, and the taste triggered memories of long ago. "So, what do you think?" he asked his grandchildren. They all chimed in and agreed it was delicious, except for the youngest granddaughter who still thought it was too sour.

"Did you drink lemonade every day before you went to the cabin?" asked a grandson.

"No, not every day," answered the grandmother. "Sometimes iced tea, sometimes coffee, then there was a drink called *Coca-Cola*, and sometimes just water. Oh, my! Coffee," she sighed, looking at her husband. "Do you suppose coffee is still grown in Central America? I wonder if the ship that brought the lemons will bring coffee someday."

"Tell us what happened, Grandpa," pleaded a middle-sized girl. "Why did everything change? How did you know to hide?"

"Well, the world was very different, kids," he answered slowly, taking another drink of lemonade. "There were lots of people, many more than there are today."

"What happened to them? Where did they go?" asked a younger granddaughter as the oldest grandson looked over to her, already knowing the answer. He had heard his grandparents' stories before.

"They died, honey," said the grandmother.

"We don't know how many. We don't know how many people are alive today. Perhaps in a few years we can have a census," the grandfather explained. "But most people died. Most people here in the US didn't make it. I believe from talking to folks on the radio that the same happened in other countries as well."

"But why did they die?" asked the inquisitive granddaughter.

"Lots of reasons, sweetheart," said the grandmother.

"I doubt if anyone understands it," said the grandfather. "In the years leading up to the collapse, everything just got worse. People were killing people for no reason. Crazy people would run into a school and start shooting. Fanatics would set off bombs in the cities, killing hundreds. Remember how we told you about September 11th, 2001, when airplanes were flown into the twin towers in New York City? Well, things like that continued, and it got worse. But that was just part of it. We had machines called computers. More and more, these machines controlled things. They became so complicated that when they would malfunction, no one seemed to know why." The children sat silently on the porch, sipping lemonade and listening.

"But I guess what pushed everything over the edge was when the servers quit working. Those were machines that stored data for almost everything. There was a huge company that owned almost all the servers. We don't know for sure how it happened, but something malfunctioned at that company. When the servers stopped working, everything stopped. The electricity went out. The warehouses couldn't function. Neither did the airports, the railroads, and cell phones. The cash registers in the stores wouldn't work, so they closed. Everything stopped.

Then the rioting started. Across Europe and here in our country, people started rioting in the cities. I've never understood why because what's that going to help? But they rioted everywhere. There weren't enough police to contain them. Then, the police were afraid to leave their own families unprotected, so there were effectively no police. When the criminals discovered there were no police, there was chaos. Everyone was afraid to leave their homes. If people don't go to work, there are no nurses in the hospitals. There are no men driving trucks delivering food to grocery stores. If the folks who work at the water department don't show up for work, the water stops. No food, no water, no medicine, no police. Bad people started setting buildings on fire in the cities, but there were no firemen. It was mayhem."

The children sat in silence, trying to picture a world

unlike anything they had ever known. A world with billions of people, electricity, clean running water from every tap, freeways, computers, and lemonade every day.

"But you and Grandma escaped. You didn't die. Because of Uncle Matt? Right, Grandpa?" asked the oldest granddaughter.

"That's right... because of your uncle," said the grandmother. "We are here because of him, and Mary Frances. I am sure we would have died, too. But, thank God, our paths crossed. Thank God, I took that job, met Mary Frances, and then your grandfather. And thank God, for that blizzard."

"My mother was born there at the cabin, wasn't she, Grandma?" asked the oldest boy.

"She was," the man said. "But Sam and Hannah were the first children. Your grandmother and I adopted Sam, and Uncle Matt and Aunt Mary adopted Hannah. That happened unexpectedly just before we left Nashville. Then James was born in the sixth year after we returned. And two years later, Steven. And your mother, of course, is your aunt's and uncle's daughter."

"You and Grandma had three children. How many did Aunt Mary and Uncle Matt have? A dozen?" asked a middle boy.

"Well, I guess they did," laughed the grandmother. "You see your aunt couldn't have children. But when we returned, there were lots of orphans. Children whose parents had died. Your aunt just started taking them in. I remember your uncle saying, 'Mary Frances, not another one! How are we going to feed all these children you keep finding?' All those children would have died if your aunt and uncle hadn't taken them in."

"So, were you at the cabin for five years?" asked a middle girl, Elizabeth.

"That's right, five years," answered her grandfather.

"And no one ever found you?" asked the oldest boy.

"No, no one ever did," answered the grandmother. "It's not surprising. We were so far from anything. We were so hidden. It was as if we just disappeared."

Sitting together on the porch, enjoying lemonade, the time passed as the grandparents retold the story. To the children it seemed like a grand adventure, but to the grandparents the memories were very real. They recalled the parts they had played and how it had resulted in bringing them all together now, 40 years later. The sun moved across the sky, and the afternoon passed.

"It's time for me to take you kids home now. Boys, go fire up the gasifier like I've showed you. When you see the blue flame coming out of the stack, switch off the torch valve and open the valve to the engine. Give it 20 seconds or so, then start her up," the man instructed. "Don't forget to thank your grandmother for the lemonade." The boys jumped up and hugged their grandmother and then ran to the truck to carry out their grandfather's instructions.

"Grandpa, can you tell us about the journey to the cabin next time?" asked the middle girl as she gathered empty glasses from the porch.

"Sure, sweetie," said the woman as she and her husband watched their grandchildren with love and affection. The girls carried the glasses to the kitchen while the boys piled in the pickup truck, some up front and the younger ones in the back with the gasifier that was generating the wood gas that ran the truck's engine. When the girls ran out the kitchen door to the truck, there was pushing and complaining as the girls all wanted up front in the cab with their grandfather. But ultimately, some of them had to ride in the back with the younger boys.

"I'll be back soon, Dagny," called the grandfather, waving to his wife, as he walked around the truck to the driver's seat. Standing on the porch, Dagny leaned against a column and waved as the truck drove away. She could still hear their laughter as the truck disappeared from view.

Chapter 1
Nashville
The Beginning - 40 Years Earlier

Dagny Bennett turned on her directional signal and checked twice before changing lanes. She was nervous, both from the traffic and the prospects of her new job. She was from Sparta, Tennessee, a small town about an hour from Nashville. Sparta didn't have the job opportunities that Nashville offered, so she did what thousands of other young people did and moved to the city. Dagny had just arrived the previous weekend and was staying with friends, other young people from Sparta, she knew from high school. She was welcome to sleep on their couch until she found an apartment.

Almost all the jobs back home were minimum wage, but the pay in Nashville was much higher. The only problem, as Dagny was discovering, was that the cost of living was also much more. She knew she wouldn't be able to afford an apartment on her own, so finding a roommate to share the expenses was a necessity. Dagny would never have admitted it, but she wanted a roommate for another reason. The city frightened her. Back home, she had known almost everyone. But in Nashville, she knew practically no one.

Then, there was the traffic. Nashville had grown so rapidly in recent years that the highways could hardly handle it. Rush hour was a nightmare, especially for someone who thought a traffic jam was more than three cars at a stoplight. Dagny had been worried that she would be late for work on her first day, so she had made a trial run on the Sunday before to learn the route-south on Interstate 65, exit at Old Hickory, left after the Jaguar/ Land Rover sign, then right to the Veritas Strategies building on the left. There had been no traffic when she had practiced this on Sunday afternoon, but Wednesday, three days later, was a different story. *I must get over to exit on Old Hickory*, she thought as she kept glancing to the right looking for an opportunity to change lanes. Soon, someone let her in, and she sighed in relief.

Dagny pulled into the Veritas parking lot in front of the imposing six-story building. The sun was shining, and the weather was pleasant for December. Driving slowly, she looked for a spot to park and finally found one on the left side of the building by a small lake complete with a fountain. The thought crossed her mind, *Why would someone build a lake with a fountain right here? I guess just because it looks pretty.* Early for her appointment at HR, she sat watching the people walk across the parking lot to the front door of the building. *Uncle John was right*, she thought. *This is the big city. I've never seen so many beautiful women. They look like they all stepped off the pages of a magazine.* Then, she noticed the men. Back home, men rarely wore suits, and when they did they seemed uncomfortable in them. But, these men seemed very comfortable in suits. *I guess it's because they wear them every day*, she thought.

Dagny's Uncle John knew the head of maintenance at Veritas, and he had told her they were hiring for the cafeteria. Starting pay was higher at Veritas than anyone made after decades of doing the same work back in Sparta. Two weeks ago, her uncle put in a good word for her, and she got the job with just a phone interview. Of course, she didn't have the job permanently until she passed her six-week probation. Dagny was excited to get the job and called her uncle as soon as she hung up the phone with the Human Resources department at Veritas. After thanking him, she realized she didn't know what kind of company Veritas was. She googled it. Reading the description on-line, she still didn't understand. All she knew was it had something to do with investments.

Dagny looked at her iPhone and decided it was time to go in. Dagny called her mother before getting out of her car.

"Hello, Mom," she said, as her mother answered. "I'm here. I'm getting ready to go into work. There are so many people. I'm pretty nervous."

"Now, don't be nervous, honey," her mother replied. "You'll do just fine. Before the day is done, I'll bet you'll have made some new friends."

"I hope so, Mom," she answered with a sigh. "The people here seem different. But, I'm going in there, and I'll do my best."

"That's the spirit, Dagny," said her mother. "Give me a call this evening when you get back to the apartment, and tell me all about it. And Dagny, pay attention to the weather. There's a front coming in from the West, and it could snow."

"Thanks, Mom. I'll call you tonight." And with that, Dagny got out of her car, carefully locked it and joined the others who were headed into the Veritas Strategies building to start another day's work. *OK,* she thought, *HR Department, third floor, Mrs. Martin. Stand up straight, Dagny. Be confident.*

A tall, young man with a leather computer bag slung over his shoulder crossed the parking lot and fell into rank next to her. "Good morning," he said. "I don't believe I've seen you before. Are you new?"

"Yes, first day," Dagny answered, thinking, *My goodness he's cute.*

"What department are you in? ETF's?" he asked. "I'm in international ETF trading."

"No, I'm afraid I don't even know what that is," she said. "I'm in the cafeteria. I guess my job is to feed you, so you can do whatever it is you just said you do."

He smiled and said, "That's probably the most important department in the whole building! We've gotta eat. The cafeteria's pretty good. It's not a profit center for the firm, so they run it at cost. It's very reasonably priced. I eat there almost every day. Sometimes I'll take lunch back to my desk if I'm running behind. We do lots of different things here, but ETF's are a major focus. Because the supply of ETF shares must expand and contract with demand, sometimes I'm very busy and sometimes not. If there's lots of net buying or selling, I buy or sell the underlying positions. On days like that, I'll eat at my desk. We run some closed end funds here, too, but the guys in that department don't have to contend with that like I do. So maybe I'll see you in the cafeteria. My name's Jack. What's yours?"

"Dagny. It's nice to meet you, Jack," she responded, thinking, *I have no idea what he just said. It sounded like English, and I didn't understand a word, but he sure is cute!* As Dagny walked through the heavy glass doors into the lobby, everything suddenly felt different. Even though there were lots of people, it wasn't noisy as everyone spoke quietly, almost like in a library. She was more aware of the click, click, click of high heels on the gray marble floor than what was being said. The gold signage on the wall behind the receptionist read **VERITAS *Strategies***, with Veritas in block letters and Strategies in script. Making her way onto the elevator full of people, she was glad to see that someone had already pushed the button for the third floor.

Dagny stopped at the receptionist for the HR Department and told the young lady, "Dagny Bennett to see Mrs. Martin."

"Just take this hallway to the third door. That's a waiting room for Patricia... Mrs. Martin. A couple of other new hires are waiting already. I believe there are three of you today. Shortly, Mrs. Martin will come for you when she's ready. Dagny thanked her and started down the hall, passing an open area with four desks where four young women were taking off their coats and turning on their computers. Another office was occupied by a man in his forties who was on the phone having a heated discussion with someone on the other end of the line. Arriving at the waiting room, Dagny entered to find the other two already there.

"Hello, I'm Dagny," she said, nervously.

"Hello, Dagny. I'm Sandra," said the first young lady.

"And I'm Ginny," said the second. "What department will you be working in?"

"I'm in the cafeteria," said Dagny, immediately thinking, *Oh, no! They probably have important jobs like Jack, and I won't understand a thing.*

"I'm Compliance. Specifically, Dodd-Frank and DOL compliance for the broker dealer," said Sandra. Then noticing

Dagny's confusion, she added, "Just trying to keep everyone legal, so we all have a job."

"And I'm Operations," said Ginny. "All the IMA's, individually managed accounts. I keep everything straight for the clients at their investment firms. Like the dividends, foreign taxes, mergers, splits, and 1099's. All that operational stuff."

"Wow, that sounds complicated!" said Dagny. "Everyone here is so smart. I had no idea what y'all did here. Truthfully, I still don't understand what y'all do, but it must be very complicated."

"Oh, we're not that smart," laughed Ginny. Sandra started laughing, too. "Acting confident goes a long way!"

Soon, Mrs. Martin called the three women into her office and began the process of officially hiring them which entailed a lot of forms and signatures. Then they went to a small conference room to view a video about the firm. Dagny was sure the other two understood it all much better than she did. When the video ended, the three returned to Patricia Martin's office.

"Ladies, you are ready to go," said Mrs. Martin. "Soon, someone from each of your departments will be here to take you to the area where you will be working. I want to officially welcome you to Veritas Strategies. You may not realize it, but we are fortunate to work for such a generous company. Perhaps you noticed that your medical insurance premium is completely paid for by the firm. Your 401(k) match is extremely generous. I don't know of another company like Veritas. It is so rare to find a company like this today. One more thing, the CEO, Mr. Borland, will probably find you sometime today and personally welcome you. He likes to do that. If he's too busy today, he'll find you tomorrow. He's very nice, and you'll enjoy meeting him. We have just over 600 employees, and he does his best to know everyone by name."

In no time, Ginny and Sandra said goodbye as they were taken to their respective departments. Dagny was alone and patiently waiting, wondering who would be coming for her. When she looked up at the young woman standing in the doorway, she couldn't believe her eyes. Dagny thought, *She looks like me, only a few years older.*

"You must be Dagny," she said. "I'm Mary Frances. I'm

here to take you to the cafeteria." Dagny stood and shook her hand. The two young women looked at each other both thinking, *We could be sisters.*

"Good luck, Dagny," said Mrs. Martin as Mary Frances directed her out into the hallway.

"Thank you, Mrs. Martin," Dagny replied over her shoulder as she followed Mary Frances out of the office.

Mary Frances was 5'5" with dark brown hair and a light complexion. Dagny was 5'4" also with dark brown hair and a similar complexion. Both had brown eyes. Mary Frances was dressed in a chef's uniform of white pants and white coat. The coat was starched with perfectly ironed creases. On the left breast was embroidered in blue, her name, *Mary Frances*. "After we speak with Mrs. Joiner, I'll take you to the locker room and find you a uniform," she said, glancing at Dagny as they walked. "I think we're about the same size. You'll get uniforms with your name embroidered on them once you've passed the probation period. Mrs. Joiner, she's the food services manager, will give you her orientation speech."

"Thank you," said Dagny. "I don't know if you can tell, but I'm really nervous."

"I know you are," replied Mary Frances, "but don't worry. I think you're going to like it here. I do. A word of warning on Mrs. Joiner. Just smile and agree with her when she gives her speech. She's a good boss, but she can be a little intense. Simply nod your head, and agree with her. I'll explain later. So, where do you live, Dagny?"

"I'm living with some friends temporarily until I can find an apartment," Dagny explained as the two young women got on the elevator. "And I probably need to find an apartment with a roommate. Rent is way more expensive here than back home."

"Really! I'm looking for a roommate," said Mary Frances. "I live at The Grove. That's north and a little west, back toward Nashville. It's nice! Gated. Two swimming pools. I have a two-bedroom, two-bath apartment. We should talk more. Maybe we could be roommates. We could car pool and save gasoline since our schedules will be the same."

"That would be wonderful," said Dagny as they exited the

elevator. "Yes, let's talk about that." *I like her,* thought Dagny. *I think we would get along just fine.*

"Yes, let's do that. But first, Mrs. Joiner's office is right down this way," Mary Frances said as they walked through the cafeteria. "Mrs. Joiner?" said Mary Frances, knocking on the cafeteria manager's open door. "I have Dagny Bennett, our new employee."

"Come in, come in," said Mrs. Joiner, motioning to the two chairs in front of her desk. "Sit down, both of you. This won't take a minute, then you can get her a uniform and to work.... OK, Dagny Bennett," Mrs. Joiner said sternly, "Listen up. Here, in this cafeteria, I am God! You will do exactly as you're told. If you work hard, we'll get along fine. If you're lazy, you're gone. Do you understand?" Dagny nodded her head in agreement. "You must know your place. This building has six floors, and you, young lady, are on the bottom. The only thing lower than you are the catfish in that lake out front. So, don't forget it. There will be no fraternizing with men on the second, third, fourth, fifth, and, well, this would never happen, but God forbid... on the sixth floor. There is no company rule against dating other employees, but there should be. Here in my cafeteria, it's forbidden. You leave the men alone. I don't want any of my girls coming up pregnant!" Dagny looked at her new boss with wide eyes and nodded. "Do you understand? I can't hear you!"

"Yes, ma'am!" Dagny answered loudly.

"Good, so now that you understand everything, get moving. Mary Frances, work her hard. No slacking!"

"Yes, ma'am," answered Mary Frances. With that, they left Mrs. Joiner's office.

As they walked down the hallway to the locker room for Dagny's uniform, Mary Frances said, "I'm sorry. I hope she didn't scare you too much."

"Wow, you warned me!" said Dagny. "What does she mean about men on all the different floors?"

"The sixth floor is the executive floor, Dagny," explained Mary Frances. "They even have their own chef and executive dining room. They make the most money, of course. As you move down the floors people make less money. And we're here on the bottom floor, the very bottom of the ladder. She means we should remember our place. Of course, she's right, no vice president from the sixth floor is ever going to notice us, much less ever ask us out on a date. You never even see them unless you cross paths on the parking lot. You can sometimes tell who they are by the cars they drive. The higher the floor, the more expensive the car."

Mary Francis looked through a stack of uniforms until she found the right size for Dagny. "Gosh, this reminds me of high school," said Dagny. "At my school, there were places in the gym for everyone to sit as the buses arrived in the morning. There were no signs. It was just understood. It was all divided by where you lived. If you lived in one of the small, poor places outside of town, you sat in that section. If you lived in an expensive subdivision in town, you sat in another. You would never dream of going out with someone not from *your* section.

"What was that all about... getting pregnant?" Dagny asked. "That was unexpected."

"What Mrs. Joiner was referring to, is that someone on the sixth floor, one of the vice presidents, has gotten several girls pregnant," explained Mary Frances as Dagny changed into her uniform. "He seduces girls on the floors below him. They're flattered, of course, to have his attention. Then after he gets what he wants, he dumps them and goes on to the next conquest."

"Oh, my," said Dagny. "What's his name?"

"I don't know," said Mary Frances. "I've just heard him called *the guy on the sixth floor*. But don't worry, Dagny, neither one of us need be concerned about him. We're not his type. Besides not being on the right floor, we're missing other requirements. We're both too short. We're not blonde. And we don't have enough *personality*, if you know what I mean." Both girls laughed and went out into the cafeteria after Dagny had put her clothes away in a locker. Mary Frances showed her how to check all the condiments, napkins, knives, forks, and spoons in the cafeteria. Then, they reported to the kitchen manager.

"Mary Frances, we're kind of slammed right now with the pasta," said Mrs. Klein, the kitchen manager. "There's a delivery back on the dock. You must be Dagny. I'm Mrs. Klein. Welcome aboard. Mary Frances, take Dagny back with you and teach her how to check in a delivery. Have you heard anything on the weather? Someone was talking about snow." The kitchen manager walked away quickly to the stoves, not waiting for an answer to her question.

"Come with me," said Mary Frances, and Dagny followed her through a storeroom filled with racks of canned goods. When they got to an industrial garage door, Mary Frances pushed a button, and the door slowly opened. "Oh, that's cold!" she said as the door opened to the outside. "It wasn't this cold when we came to work this morning. The temperature has really dropped."

"Hello, Mary Frances," said the Sysco driver as the door opened all the way, exposing the back of a semi-trailer. "I've got an order for you. Can we do this quick? I just got a call from our depot. Bad weather is coming, and they want us back as soon as possible."

The driver handed Mary Frances an invoice that she placed on a clipboard, as he started the process of bringing in boxes on a two-wheeler. Mary Frances began counting and checking them off the invoice. Dagny watched as Mary Frances explained what she was doing. Soon the order was off the truck and checked in. The driver hurried back to his truck and on his way. Mary Frances looked up at the sky as the automatic door was closing. "It does look like some bad weather is coming. The sky almost looks angry," she said.

"Thanks for checking in that order, Mary Frances," said a young man who started moving the cases of food to their places on the various racks. "Mrs. Klein needs you both back in the kitchen." With the order checked in, the two hurried back to the kitchen.

"Mary Frances, start moving food to the warming tables. Dagny, you help her. Let's go, people! We're about 10 minutes behind today," warned Mrs. Klein. "First hungry people will be here in less than an hour!" There was a flurry of activity as all the kitchen staff stepped up the pace to have everything ready for lunch.

Outside the kitchen in the dining area, Mary Frances and Dagny made sure all the warming tables were on and set to the appropriate temperatures. Then as the trays of food started coming out, they were placed in the correct location per the plan-o-gram from Mrs. Klein. "Dagny, make sure the placards are in the right places. The fried chicken and alfredo are switched."

Dagny stopped as she looked up and saw a distinguished-looking gentleman in a suit walking across the cafeteria toward her. As he came to a stop in front of her, he asked with a smile, "Is lunch about ready, Dagny?" Mary Frances turned around to see Mr. Borland, the CEO, addressing Dagny.

"No, sir. The cafeteria won't be open for another 15 minutes," said Dagny. "We'll see you then."

"Mr. Borland, how nice to see you," said Mary Frances. "Dagny, this is Mr. Borland, the CEO of Veritas Strategies."

Oh, no! I just told the CEO he'd have to wait for lunch, thought Dagny. "I'm sorry, Mr. Borland. I didn't know who you were. Of course, we're open for you."

"That's OK," he laughed. "I was guessing you were Dagny Bennett because there isn't a name on your uniform and because Mrs. Joiner said Mary Frances was training you today. I just wanted to stop by to introduce myself and welcome you. But I stopped by at the wrong time because I can see how busy everyone is. There will be a few more customers today, Mary Frances. Jean Claude is off, and the weather is getting bad outside, so it's likely that more people from the sixth floor will be joining you today for lunch. I'll leave you to your work and come back in 15 minutes when you're open."

"Thank you, Mr. Borland," said Dagny. "It's very nice to meet you."

"Nice to see you again, Mr. Borland," said Mary Frances.

"Yes. See you soon," said the CEO as he turned and walked out of the cafeteria.

"I can't believe I did that," cried Dagny. "You don't think they'll fire me? Was he mad? I am so embarrassed."

"He's not just the CEO, Dagny. He's also the majority stockholder," chided Mary Frances, trying hard not to laugh. "You just kicked the man out of *his* cafeteria."

"Me and my big mouth!" cried Dagny. "I'm not going to say another word to anyone! I always get myself in trouble. I'm always doing that."

"It's OK, Dagny," said Mary Frances. "He wasn't mad. He's very nice. The sixth floor isn't all bad. But... I'll never forget when you told him to leave and come back in 15 minutes! I was biting my tongue so hard." Dagny looked at her new friend who was struggling to keep a straight face. Together, they finished setting up the serving line, and soon the hungry employees started flooding into the cafeteria.

When Mr. Borland came through the line with another gentleman from the sixth floor, he said, "Brian, this is Dagny Bennett. This is her first day on the job here at Veritas. Do you know she made me leave the cafeteria this morning because it wasn't open yet?" Brian laughed, and Mr. Borland did, too. "We're never going to let you live this down, Dagny," he smiled as the two men moved on down the line.

"Mary Francis, who was that with Mr. Borland?" asked Dagny.

"That was Brian Eastman," answered Mary Frances. "He's our chief economist. He's a good friend of Mr. Borland. Mr. Eastman is a big deal. He's on the financial programs on TV and sometimes speaks to Congress in Washington, DC."

"I guess Mr. Borland isn't mad," Dagny said, "But I wish he wasn't telling everyone what I did. I swear I'm going to stop talking." Mary Frances smiled at her new friend, certain she would fit in just fine. After the lunch rush, the kitchen crew worked hard to get everything cleaned up before starting on preparations for the next day.

Mrs. Klein returned to the kitchen from Mrs. Joiner's office. The weather conditions were deteriorating. "Attention, listen up!" she called. Everyone stopped their work and gathered around Mrs. Klein. "OK, girls and boys, stop all prep for tomorrow. Here's the scoop. I've just talked to Mrs. Joiner. The weather outside is not good, and the forecast is for bad weather... really bad. In a few minutes, the announcement will be made to all employees that Veritas will be closing at 3:00. The prediction is for over a foot of snow tonight with even more tomorrow. Mr. Borland is planning on not opening tomorrow, and maybe not Friday. He wants to give everyone a head start on getting home because of the storm, so that's why we're closing at three. Let's close up this kitchen like it's a Friday and get out of here. Drive carefully, and we'll see you when we see you. Everyone will be updated by text."

Mary Frances looked at Dagny, "Quite a first day for you, Dagny! First you insult the CEO, then we all get to go home early! I've only been here six months myself, and I've never heard of closing early. This must be some storm. Let's get everything ready for tomorrow, whenever tomorrow is." Throughout the building, employees were preparing to leave. Some were packing up laptops so they could work from home if they were employees with time critical functions. The text came through with the official announcement of closure. Soon it was three o'clock, and people started heading for the elevators. The kitchen employees went to their locker rooms and changed into street clothes.

"I should have worn warmer clothes this morning," said Mary Frances. "Honestly, I just didn't pay any attention to the weather."

"Mary Frances, let's exchange phone numbers," said Dagny. "That way if we're snowed in like they're saying, we can talk on the phone about maybe being roommates." Mary Frances agreed, and the two exchanged cell numbers as they walked through the foyer and out into the cold.

They weren't prepared for what they saw. The ground was already white with snow, and it was falling rapidly. The wind was blowing hard, and the temperature felt like it was already into the 20's. Cars were beginning to be completely covered in snow.

"Drive carefully, Dagny!" shouted Mary Frances as she got in her car, and Dagny walked on across the parking lot.

As she started her Toyota, Mary Frances considered the possibility that she might be snowed in. *What if I can't get out for two or three days? Well, I think I'll cook. I can work on that new recipe I've been wanting to try. I'll just swing by Publix and pick up a few things before I drive home.*

Chapter 2
Blizzard

Already a good two inches of snow had accumulated on the ground, and in true Nashville fashion, drivers were having difficulties. Snow wasn't something they encountered often. *This is slick,* thought Mary Frances as she slowly made her way down Old Hickory Boulevard. *I don't want to slide and hit someone.* She carefully made her way into the supermarket parking lot and began the search for a parking spot. Everyone in Brentwood had the same idea, swarming the store in preparation for the storm.

My shoes are wet, and my feet are freezing, thought Mary Frances as she walked to the front door of the supermarket. *I should have paid attention to the weather and worn more sensible clothing.* Inside, the store was chaotic. Mary Frances grabbed a smaller-sized shopping cart and quickly entered the store thinking, *I must get the ingredients for my recipe and get out of here quickly.*

"Mary Frances!" called a voice behind her. Mary Frances turned to see another employee from Veritas waving at her.

"Hello, Gretchen," said Mary Frances as her friend caught up with her.

"What are all these crazy people doing?" asked Gretchen. "And what kind of shoes are those, Mary Frances? You need boots!"

"I do," said Mary Frances.

"And that light jacket won't do with this wind," said Gretchen.

"I just didn't realize we were going to get snow. And these crazy people are doing the same thing we are." The two laughed and quickly went on their way.

OK, I need lamb chops. I have olive oil and port. I need shallots, dried cherries, maybe some lettuce for a salad, cherry jam, and I'm going to do mint instead of parsley. That might give it that extra, little kick I'm looking for. And a nice Cabernet Sauvignon. Oh, I'm out of cardamom. Mary Frances moved quickly finding the items from the list in her head. She completely skipped the bread aisle where the mob of customers had stripped it bare. *I'll just make some bread from scratch,* she decided. Soon, she had checked out and was carrying her bags to her car. The wind was blowing even harder, and the snow was coming down sideways as she began to shiver. *Where is my car?* Mary Frances thought as she looked around the parking lot. Everything was white. The wind-driven snow stung her eyes, and she blinked and squinted, trying to see. When she finally found her car and got in, she was wet, cold and exhausted. *My goodness!* she thought as she started her car and fastened her seat belt. *This is a blizzard! It will be tricky getting home!* Grasping the ice-cold steering wheel, she thought, *I wish I had my gloves.*

As Mary Frances eased her car out of the supermarket parking lot and onto Old Hickory Boulevard, she glanced in the mirror and saw that her hair was covered in melting snow. *I'm a mess,* she thought. Then she heard the pinging on the windshield and thought, *Oh, great, it's turning to ice.* Tiny beads of ice bounced off the glass, and freezing rain started to stick to the windshield.

Mary Frances was grateful to be moving even though it was slow going. She leaned forward and peered through the windshield in an attempt to see better. As the glass began to fog up, she carefully reached down. Fumbling around, she finally located the defroster button. When both hands were back on the steering wheel, she realized how hard she was gripping it. Seeing another vehicle off in a ditch increased the tension she was feeling. *Oh, gosh, I wish I could stop to help, but I might not get going again,* she thought.

Mary Frances was moving at 20 miles per hour when the semi-trailer truck roared past her on the left. Her car shook as ice and snow shot up from the truck's rear tires, covering her windshield and leaving her completely blinded. The next few seconds were a blur as she lost control. Seeing nothing but white, she felt herself spinning and falling. Expecting a crash, she held tight to the steering wheel that no longer seemed to steer. The spinning and falling seemed to occur in slow motion until finally the car came to rest.

"What happened?" she asked aloud, feeling disoriented. "Where am I?" Mary Frances looked around and couldn't see the road. Inside the Toyota, she was surprised to see her groceries still on the seat where she had placed them. Becoming aware that her hands were trembling, she didn't know if it was because of the cold or from fright. She touched her arms and legs and felt no pain. *I think I'm alright,* she thought, *but I've got to get going.*

In the shelter of the car, Mary Frances could hear the wind howling outside. *Where's the road?* Then trying to open her door, she found that she couldn't. Mary Frances unfastened her seatbelt and leaned over to try the opposite door only to find it wouldn't budge. Trying to roll down a frozen window didn't work either. *Am I trapped? What am I going to do? If I can find my phone, maybe I can call for help.* While retrieving her purse from the floor to get the cell phone, she heard a voice. A big, gloved hand was sweeping snow off her window.

"Are you alright?" came the voice from outside.

Thank God, someone has found me, she thought. "Yes, I think I'm OK," she answered. "I just can't open my door."

"Hang on, we'll dig you out," the voice said. "Give us a minute."

Mary Frances watched as the man dug and moved snow with his hands, making an opening in the snow that would allow her door to swing open. Another set of hands began clearing her windshield. Then, a third set joined in sweeping the snow off the passenger side.

"Three people!" Mary Frances said out loud. *Three people have found me. Thank you, God! For a second, I was afraid I might die here, frozen to death.* She watched the three, two men and a woman. The man working to open her door was wearing a big, green parka with a fur-trimmed hood. *He is a very, tall man,* she thought as she watched him work. The woman clearing the windshield smiled and gave Mary Frances a thumbs-up with her gloved hand. Soon she heard her car door crack and groan as it slowly opened.

"Hey, are you OK?" came the voice as she saw him. "Are you hurt?"

"I don't think so," she answered, the bitter wind now blowing into the car. "I don't know what happened. I lost control."

"It was that semi that passed you and blew you off the road. You slid down this hill. But we need to get you out of here, now," he ordered, feeling the urgency of the situation. Helping her out of the Toyota, he got Mary Frances on her feet and soon she was standing by her car that was almost invisible under the snow.

"My groceries, I need my groceries," she said.

He started to tell her that her groceries were irrelevant when the woman said, "We'll get them, Matt. You get her up the hill to the Rover, and we'll bring her groceries for her."

Mary Frances started up the snowy hillside, but quickly found the ballet flats were more like ice skates. Suddenly, her feet were out from under her, and she was sliding back down the hill. *Oh, no!* she thought, *I'm going to knock down* the *people behind me.* The tall man quickly grabbed her arm and helped her to her feet. Putting his arm around her, they struggled together up the incline while the other man and woman came behind with four plastic bags of groceries and a purse.

"Where're your boots?" he asked. Mary Frances didn't answer, not sure if he was serious or kidding. The three rescuers brushed the snow off Mary Frances and got her in the backseat of the SUV. Then Fredèric took the groceries and put them in the back while Sophia got in the back seat with Mary Frances. Finally, Matt got in the driver's seat with Fredèric in the copilot's seat.

"How is she?" asked Matt. "She's shivering hard."

"She's very cold," answered Sophia, rubbing Mary Frances' hands.

"Her heated seat is on, and I'm turning up the thermostat," said Matt. "Shivering is good. It's when shivering stops that I get worried."

"Hi, I'm Sophia. Sophia Steiner," said the woman, introducing herself. "What's your name?" she asked. Sophia was trying to make Mary Frances comfortable, but she was also trying to be sure she wasn't injured.

Mary Frances sat in the back seat, a bit in shock. She was aware of two things, the warmth of the heated seat and the three faces watching her intently. "Mary Frances Foster," she finally answered.

Looking at her from between the two front seats, the driver said, "Mary Frances Foster, we have a real blizzard here. Where do you live?"

With his fur-trimmed hood pulled back, Mary Frances thought, *Do I know him*? "I live at the Grove. But, my car."

"Mary Frances," he began, while thinking, *She looks familiar somehow.* "You're going to have to leave your car for now. With this weather, there's no way you can get a wrecker. The Grove is too far in the wrong direction. I can't get you there and then get the three of us back to my house before the roads become impassable. I'm taking you home with us."

Mary Frances' eyes were big, processing what he had just said. Her shivering had stopped as she was starting to warm up.

"What Matt means," said Sophia, giving Matt a look as her husband Frederic turned around and chuckled. "What Matt means is that this is really a bad snow storm, and we don't want to get stranded like you were. Matt is offering to take you home with us. You'll be very safe and comfortable there. In a few days when this is over, we'll arrange for a wrecker. Then we'll come back and help get your car back on the road. Isn't that right, Matt?"

"Of course," Matt replied. "I'm sorry. I want to get moving because the snow is piling up. I shouldn't have told you what you were going to do. I should have asked. So, Mary Frances, would you come home with me and my friends from Switzerland?"

"It will be fine," said Sophia, holding Mary Frances' hands. "I promise, we'll take good care of you."

"OK," said Mary Frances, cautiously, realizing there was no other choice. "Thank you for helping me."

“Great, let’s get moving,” said Matt, putting the SUV in gear and maneuvering onto the highway. The snow had not let up but continued to fall at a steady pace. With the wind, the whiteout conditions made driving precarious. The temperature on the dash data display had dropped to 25 degrees. Still, the SUV made 30 miles per hour.

“I live south and east out in the country. Well, it used to be out in the country, but Nashville keeps growing so much that it doesn’t feel as remote as it did at one time,” Matt explained to Mary Frances as they navigated through the blizzard. “These are my friends, Fredèric and Sophia Steiner. They’re from Switzerland. They like to laugh at us and how we struggle with snow in Nashville. This little blizzard is nothing to them.”

Fredèric and Sophia smiled, and then Fredèric explained, “Matt and I are old friends. I’m the CEO of a private bank back home. I was in the States for a conference in New York and decided to bring my wife. When the meeting ended, we flew to Nashville to visit Matt for a few days before flying home.”

“You were also going to meet with Brian so you could write off the flight to Nashville,” said Matt, laughing.

“Yes, Matt works with an important economist here in Nashville. I always enjoy talking to him and getting his opinion on things economic,” Fredèric explained.

Brian... economist.... Brian Eastman? Mary Frances wondered. *Oh, no! That’s how I know him. Matt works at Veritas. I’ve seen him in the cafeteria but not often.* Then before she could stop herself, she blurted out, “Brian Eastman?”

Matt immediately looked in the rear-view mirror and sat up a little straighter to see Mary Frances’ face. Fredèric turned around to look at Mary Frances sitting behind him. “Do you know Brian Eastman?” he asked.

“No, I don’t. But I know he’s an important economist,” she answered, carefully. “I saw him on CNN, I believe,” she added. *That’s all true. I’m not lying. If Matt works with Brian Eastman, then he’s on the sixth floor. What have I gotten myself into? What if he’s that guy on the sixth floor? I can’t ask his last name.*

“Are you from Nashville originally?” asked Matt while he thought, *She is so familiar. And her name, it’s like I’ve seen it somewhere. But where?*

"No, I've only been here six months. I'm originally from Charlotte, North Carolina," she said, then attempted to divert the conversation by turning to Sophia. "Thank you, Sophia, for getting my groceries and my purse. I'm going to get my phone and text my mother just to let her know I'm alright. She's probably watching the weather and worrying about me," said Mary Frances. But she didn't text her mother. Instead, she found a coworker's number in her Contacts:

Jane, the VP on the sixth floor who got those girls pregnant. Is his name Matt?

No, his name is Lynn Hanson.
Matt is Matt Archer, VP of research.
Why?

No reason just curious

Like I believe that. So why r u asking about Matt Archer?

I'll tell you later. What do you know about MA?

Not much.
MFF what r u up to???
Quiet. Smart. NOT MARRIED

Thanks, Jane!

So, he's not that guy, she thought with a sigh of relief. *I should admit I work at Veritas. I don't want to deceive him.*

"Are you OK, Mary Frances?" asked Sophia as she had been watching her text.

"Yes, thank you," she responded. "I'm fine. I'm just tired .... and cold."

"Sophia, we're getting close to home," said Matt. "Let's put Mary Frances in the bedroom next to yours. Check her for frostbite. Put her in the bathtub. Not too hot at first, gradually. Then some hot tea."

"Yes, Matt, I know what to do," said Sophia. "He's just concerned that your core temperature is too low," she whispered, patting Mary Frances' knee. "You'll feel much better once you've warmed up." Mary Frances felt much better having Sophia there.

"I'm thinking I'll make my famous razorback chili tonight," said Matt. "Doesn't that sound good for a night like this with the blizzard?"

"Do you have plenty of firewood, Matt?" asked Fredèrick. "I expect a big fire in that fireplace."

"Of course I do, Fredèric!" said Matt. "It's ready to go, and I'm lighting it as soon as we get there." Matt turned off the road and onto a one-lane drive that disappeared into the woods.

Should I be afraid? Mary Frances wondered. *These people are strangers, and I'm letting them take me someplace in the woods where I have no idea of the location.* Sensing her concern, Sophia reached over and patted Mary Frances' hand.

The Range Rover moved effortlessly through snow that was over two feet deep in places. The wind had caused drifting. Soon it would be dark. When the house appeared, Mary Frances caught a glimpse of where she would be spending the next few days. Through the snow, she could make out a structure of some sort. The driveway continued past the front of the house and then around the side where a garage door was opening. Soon, the SUV was safely inside, and the garage door was closing behind them.

"We made it, everyone!" said Matt, relieved.

"Was there ever any doubt?" kidded Fredèric.

"Sophia," asked Matt, getting out of the car, "could you loan Mary Frances some clothes after you get her warmed up? I don't have anything she could wear."

"I have plenty of extra clothes in my suitcase," Sophia answered. "We're close to the same size. Mary Frances smiled at Sophia again, grateful for her presence.

The four walked across the garage and through the door that led into the kitchen. Mary Frances wasn't prepared for what she saw as she looked around the room. *This is a log cabin. But it's more than just a log cabin... Oh, my goodness! Look at that!* Mary Frances thought when her eyes landed on the blue and copper range nestled in a stone niche. *That's a La Cornue Chateau range!* she thought. A copper, farmhouse sink complimented the hewn stone countertops. Wide oak planks covered the floors. Overhead, massive log beams formed the ceiling with more wide planks above. The kitchen space had a rugged beauty and rustic charm. *This kitchen is a dream come true!* she thought.

"Mary Frances," said Matt, watching his guest as she stared at the range. "Sophia is going to take you to your bedroom. You have your own bathroom. Let me know if you need anything."

"Thank you," replied Mary Frances, snapping out of her trance. "I'm sorry. It's just that .... You have a La Cornue Chateau. It's beautiful."

"Thank you," Matt replied, smiling at her again with curiosity. "So, you know what that is. I'm impressed. Most people don't. They just call it the blue stove." He studied her as she tried to straighten her hair. "Go get warmed up. When you return, you can help me with my razorback chili .... on the La Cornue."

"Yes, thank you. I will," she said as she followed Sophia.

Walking around the stone wall that contained the range, Mary Frances found herself in the great room. Its focal point was a huge fireplace of Tennessee fieldstone that was the opposite side of the kitchen niche. The high ceiling and great beams exuded the cozy cabin feel. The main entrance was opposite the fireplace in a foyer. Heavy, wrought iron hinges supported the massive, oak entry door, a perfect entrance for the grandeur of the great room. Taking in her surroundings, Mary Frances was drawn to the massive chandelier made of deer antlers. It hung above the leather sofa and chairs sitting in front of the fireplace.

"This is beautiful," she said to Sophia as they crossed the room.

"Isn't it!" said Sophia. Fredèric and I always enjoy staying here when we visit Matt." Upon entering Mary Frances' bedroom, she added, "I'm sorry if Matt scared you. He can be a little direct at times and doesn't think about how someone may take it. I could tell he scared you a little. You're safe here. He's very nice.

"Now, I want you to go in the bathroom and run a hot bath but not too hot. Make it warm enough that you can stand it. Then as you warm up, add more hot water. Fredèric is bringing in our suitcases. I'll find you something warm to wear. Close the bathroom door, and I'll close the door to your room. I'll be back in a bit."

Mary Frances thanked her and stood looking around at what possibly would be her room for the next few days. The walls were log, and the floor and ceiling were hand-hewn beams just like the rest of the house. She walked to the window to peer outside into the December darkness. The glass felt cold against her forehead and hands. Outside, the wind howled, and the air was filled with more snow. Turning her attention to the bed, Mary Frances ran her hand along the Hudson Bay blanket that lay folded on the comforter. *This is so welcoming, and the bed is going to feel so good tonight,* she thought. *How did I end up here!*

Mary Frances took off her coat and removed her cell phone from her purse. Entering the bathroom, she noticed the vanity top was made of stone just like in the kitchen. The shower had been built into a stone niche. Finally, she caught sight of the white, claw-footed bathtub. *My, what a bathroom! I might just enjoy being snowbound here.... with that fireplace, and the kitchen... and the owner.* She began to wonder about him. He had certainly been kind to her. Being rescued in a blizzard was turning out to be fun. *But no, Mary Frances, you know you can't think like that.*

She turned on the water and took off her clothes as the antique tub filled. Turning to the mirror over the sink, she saw a tangled mass of dark, wet hair. *Mary Frances, look at yourself. I'm surprised he'd even let you in the car!* she thought. Slowly, she put a toe in the warm water and eased into the tub. Adding more hot water as Sophia had instructed, she started to feel warmer. Mary Frances washed her hair with a shampoo she'd never heard of before, Xapayul. It smelled heavenly. Finally feeling warm and clean, she lay back in the tub and relaxed for a moment before reaching for her phone.

Her first call was to her mother, but she could only leave a message. "Hi, Mom! It's Mary Frances. We've had a blizzard here in Nashville. I just wanted to let you know I'm OK. The storm was so bad that I had to catch a ride with some friends from work. So, I'm staying with them. We may be snowed in for a while. It hasn't stopped snowing yet. But I'm fine. Love you!"

Her second call was to Dagny.

"Hello, Dagny! It's Mary Frances."

"Hey, how are you? Did you make it home OK?"

"Well, that's a long story. Did you make it back to your friends?"

"I did. We're all hunkered down for the duration. I hope we don't lose power. What do you mean, that's a long story?"

"Dagny, I had a wreck. A semi ran me off the road, and I ended up at the bottom of a hill."

"No! Are you alright?"

"Yes, I'm fine. But my car is still there and completely covered with snow."

"Where are you, Mary Frances? Did you make it to your apartment?"

"No, I'm not at my apartment. You're not going to believe this, Dagny. I was rescued by a man and his friends from Switzerland."

"Switzerland?"

"Yes, and Dagny, you won't believe this either. He works at Veritas, and I remember seeing him in the cafeteria."

"No!"

"Yes, and he works on the sixth floor. He works with Brian Eastman. The people from Switzerland know Mr. Eastman, too."

"Mary Frances, he's not the guy from the sixth floor, is he?"

"No, I texted Jane since she knows everybody and everything. He's not the same man. His name is Matt Archer, and he's Vice President of Research."

"Mary Frances, is he cute?"

"Yes, Dagny, he's very handsome. And kind. He couldn't be treating me any nicer."

"Mary Frances, I'm not believing this. You're going to be in so much trouble with Mrs. Joiner."

"Dagny, this is not a date. He just rescued me when I went off the road. That's it."

"Is he single?"

"Dagny, stop it! Yes, he's single."

"So, what's his house like?"

"It's an amazing log cabin. Everything is wood and stone. There's a huge fireplace in the living room. He's lighting the fire now. Then he's going to make dinner for all of us."

"Where are you right now, Mary Frances?"

"I'm taking a bath in a big, white claw-footed bathtub. Do you know the kind I mean... like they had a long time ago?"

"Mary Frances, I haven't even known you 24 hours. Are you telling me the truth? You're snowed in with a handsome, single man in a log cabin. He's lighting the fire in the fireplace, and you're soaking in the bathtub. You're killing me! Why can't this happen to me?!"

"Dagny, I need to go. The lady from Switzerland will be back with something for me to wear in just a minute. I'll call you tomorrow. And be thinking about being my roommate."

"Yes, I'll be your roommate. You have the most exciting life. Maybe some of your luck will rub off on me."

"Dagny, my life has never been exciting. Until now. But this is not a date! He's just being kind."

"OK, whatever. I'll talk to you tomorrow. Stay warm!"

Mary Frances relaxed in the warm tub and closed her eyes, savoring the feeling. She said a silent prayer, thanking God for protecting her when she'd gone off the road and for the kindness of the people who had rescued her. She realized it easily could have ended very differently. She had eased out of the tub and was drying off when she heard the knock on the bathroom door. Quickly wrapping the towel around her, she responded, "Come in."

"Hey, Mary Frances," said Sophia, bringing in some clothes. "Are you warmer now?'

"Yes, I'm feeling much better," she replied.

"Good, here's a gray hoodie and sweatpants. They're fleece inside so they're nice and warm. Sorry, no underwear, but we won't tell anyone. We'll put your clothes in the washer and you'll be good to go for tomorrow. And here's a pair of flannel pajamas for tonight."

"Thank you, Sophia. You're so kind," said Mary Frances.

"And there's a hair dryer in one of those drawers," said Sophia. "Also, I'm not sure about shoes. Because my feet look bigger than yours, you probably wouldn't want to wear my shoes. Here's a pair of heavy socks. They'll make do."

"Thank you, I can do that," Mary Frances answered, looking out the window. "On a night like this, I am so grateful to be safe and have the comfort of a warm bed."

Sophia nodded in agreement and said, "When you're dressed, join us by the fire. Matt has it going, and it's wonderful. There's nothing quite like sitting by a warm fire."

Mary Frances went to work trying to make herself presentable. When her hair was dry, she put it in a ponytail to the side that hung over her left shoulder. While the gray hoodie and sweatpants were warm, they were a little big. Mary Frances was very aware that she was completely naked underneath. *Don't I look sexy!* she thought sarcastically, as she looked at herself in the mirror. *I hope it's not noticeable that I'm not wearing underwear.* Finally accepting the situation, she walked out into her bedroom and put on the heavy socks. *It doesn't matter. Why am I concerned about how I look?* Then she opened the bedroom door and immediately saw the roaring fire in the great room fireplace.

"There she is!" said Fredèrick. "Sophia, let's get Mary Frances something hot to drink." Mary Frances walked to the fireplace where everyone was seated. Sophia and Fredèrick went to the kitchen.

Matt got up from his oversized, leather chair and taking a folded blanket from a stack of blankets by the leather sofa, he spread it and said, "Here, sit down. Are you warmer now?" Mary Frances sat on the blanket thinking, *He is very considerate. He's so worried that I'm cold.* Then, he wrapped the blanket around her as Sophia returned with a steaming mug of hot tea.

"Thank you so much," Mary Frances said as Sophia and Fredèric took their seats and held their mugs of hot tea. Mary Frances took in the whole moment as the four of them sat around the fireplace, watching the fire and listening to it crackle. Mary Frances held the warm mug between her hands taking small sips of the savory, jasmine tea. *I don't know these people, but I've never felt so safe and warm,* she thought. For a moment, she became a bit emotional but blinked back tears. Mary Frances looked up at the big, wooden beams and the deer-antler chandelier to distract herself.

"So, Mary Frances, are you exhausted?" asked Matt, taking a sip from his mug as the firelight illuminated his face.

"Yes, I guess I am, but I feel much better," she answered. "I want to thank you all for helping me. You've just been terrific."

"We didn't do anything," said Fredèric. "We wanted to just leave you there, but Matt insisted we dig you out."

"Fredèric!" scolded Sophia. "Don't listen to him, Mary Frances. He's kidding. But Matt is who you should thank. We just happened to be along and helped a little."

"Mary Frances, are you too tired to help me make chili?" asked Matt. "You seemed to like my range. By the way, we brought in your groceries and put them in the fridge."

"Oh, yes, I'd love to," she answered. "You must be a very good cook to have such a range."

"Well, not really," he answered, smiling. "I'd like to be, but I'm not. I enjoy cooking, and maybe someday I'll have more time to practice and get better."

The two walked into the kitchen, and Matt started getting out the ingredients for the chili. "Have you ever had razorback before?" he asked, getting a big casing of sausage out of the refrigerator. "I shot it myself. Razorback can be tough, but ground up into sausage, it's very good."

"No, I haven't had razorback. That's a wild hog, isn't it?" she asked, thinking, *He's a vice president of research who lives in a log cabin with a La Cornue range and hunts wild hogs .... and he's handsome. What an unusual and interesting man!*

"Yes, that's right," Matt answered as he opened the razorback sausage and emptied the contents into a copper frying pan. "Do you like to cook? I'm guessing you do since you seem to know your ranges. And I couldn't help noticing your groceries as I was putting them away. That's not the typical grocery list someone buys at the supermarket before a snowstorm."

"Would you like me to brown the meat?" Mary Frances asked. "Yes, I like to cook. If we're still here, I'd love to do the lamb chops for dinner tomorrow. There's just four of them. Ideally, I'd like everyone to have two each, but I didn't expect this would happen."

Matt went to the French door that opened onto a covered porch. Turning on a light outside, he said, "Mary Frances, come here and look at this." She walked to him in her sock feet and looked out. The snow had drifted all the way up and over the deck. Standing very close she to him, she thought, *My, he is tall.* Her mind went back to how he had rescued her. The snow continued to come down hard.

Matt said, "The snow must be a foot and a half by now and still coming down. We should turn on TV while the chili is cooking and get a weather report. So, yes, from the looks of this, we're likely to be here for dinner tomorrow. Lamb chops sound great!"

As Mary Frances was browning the meat, Matt was opening cans of tomatoes and jalapeños and dumping everything into a big, copper pot. Mary Frances watched him, thinking, *I should tell him now. He's going to find out, so I must tell him.*

"Mr. Archer, there's something I need to tell you," she said cautiously as she stirred the frying pan. Matt looked up, hearing *Archer* and remembering he had never told her his last name.

"When I first saw you... there in your SUV... after I could see your face, I thought I recognized you. But I wasn't sure until you were talking about Mr. Eastman. I don't really know him, but I do know he had fried chicken for lunch today, and Mr. Borland had the alfredo." Matt stopped opening cans and watched her with a serious look. *I hope he's not mad at me,* she thought.

"I know that because I work at Veritas Strategies. And I realize now that you do, too. That's why you looked familiar. I've seen you in the cafeteria."

Mary Frances stood frozen, waiting for his reaction. His serious expression slowly turned to a smile, "Mary Frances in the cafeteria! Yes, I thought you looked familiar, too. And your name, it's embroidered on your uniform," he said, touching his finger to his chest where her name would be. "Jim .... Mr. Borland was just talking about you this afternoon after lunch," Matt said, laughing. "He was talking about a new girl who told him to get out of the cafeteria because it wasn't open yet. And he said the girl who was training her, *Mary Frances*, looked mortified when her trainee told him that."

"Oh, my goodness, does everyone know about that?" Mary Frances sighed, shaking her head while she resumed stirring the meat.

"No. Well, yes. He found it hilarious," he said. "Jim said the look on your face was priceless. He wasn't angry. Did you think he was angry?"

"I wasn't sure," Mary Frances said. "But I didn't think he was. My trainee, Dagny, was afraid she'd be fired on her first day."

"No, no, it was just funny. And you're Mary Frances Foster, the same Mary Frances I dug out of a car half-buried in snow," Matt said, laughing.

"Mr. Archer, I wanted to be upfront when I realized we worked at the same place," she said.

"You have to stop calling me Mr. Archer," he said. "I insist you call me Matt." Then walking around the corner of the stone wall that separated the kitchen from the great room, he called out to his friends, "Fredèric, Sophia, guess what! Mary Frances works at Veritas, too. That's how she knows Brian." Mary Frances breathed a sigh of relief as she added a little olive oil to the pan and turned down the burner to let the browned meat simmer.

Matt turned on the TV and tuned in to the local weather. The storm was indeed a blizzard with snowfall approaching two feet. The temperature had dropped to 19 degrees. The governor had declared travel illegal on roads in Middle Tennessee for everyone except emergency and essential services. No power outages had been reported, but the weatherman's concern was for the next day. The snow was to stop by midnight, but Thursday had a possibility of ice. "We may not be able to leave on Friday," said Fredèric, after turning off the TV. "Ah well, we'll need to call your parents, Sophia, and let them know. Sophia's parents are taking care of the boys back in Switzerland while we're away."

"Why would the power go off?" questioned Mary Frances.

"Ice accumulates on power lines and can bring them down," explained Matt. "Our utilities are all underground here, but a downed power line miles away can still cause us to lose power. But it's nothing to worry about. We can heat with wood. Our hot water is gas, and so is the range. We'll be just fine."

"If you must be snowed in and lose power," said Sophia, reassuring Mary Frances, "this is the place to be."

When the chili was finally ready, the four sat around the island and dug in. "I'm starved," said Matt.

"Me, too," said Mary Frances. "Your razorback chili is very good. And I'm in love with your La Cornue range." *That didn't come out right,* she thought. *Why did I say it like that?* Sophia glanced at her husband and their eyes met as Fredèric slightly smiled.

After dinner, everyone moved back to the great room where Matt threw more logs on the fire. The evening was spent around the fire, enjoying its warmth. Most of the lights were off, and the fire cast its flickering light as they talked and laughed. *This is just so wonderful,* thought Mary Frances. *What a day I've had!*

"Well, I don't know about anyone else, but I'm tired," said Matt. "There are plenty of blankets, more in your closets if you need them. Mary Frances, if you need anything just ask me or Sophia. There should be new toothbrushes and toothpaste in a drawer in your bathroom."

With that, everyone said good night and started to their bedrooms. Mary Frances turned to Matt, "I just wanted to thank you again, Matt, for saving me. You did save me. And for your kindness taking me in."

"You're welcome, Mary Frances from the cafeteria. It's my pleasure," he said. "See you in the morning. Sleep tight." Matt turned and went to his bedroom.

"Good night, Mary Frances," said Sophia as she and her husband headed to their bedroom.

"Good night, Sophia. Good night, Fredèric," she said. Reaching her room and closing the door, Mary Frances changed into the flannel pajamas Sophia had loaned her. Having spread the Hudson Bay blanket, she turned down the bed. Once in and snuggled under the covers, she turned off the light on the night table. *This is a day I will always remember*, she thought before peacefully falling asleep.

Chapter 3
Snowbound

As the morning light found its way through the snow on the bedroom window, Mary Frances opened her eyes. She began to recall where she was and what had happened the day before. *It wasn't a dream after all,* she thought looking around at her surroundings. *I slept all night. I must have been exhausted,* she thought. Getting out of bed and wrapping a blanket around her shoulders, she went to the window. The world was white with snow; all detail of the ground was gone. Mary Frances was sure her car was completely buried. She shivered for a second considering what might have happened if she hadn't been found. *Where is everyone?* she wondered. Turning from the window, she walked across her bedroom and opened the door, stepping into the great room. Fredèric and Sophia were in front of the fireplace and a roaring fire, coffee cups in hand. "Good morning, Mary Frances, come join us," said Sophia. "Would you like some coffee? Cream? Sugar?"

"Yes. Cream and sugar, please," Mary Frances answered. Sophia disappeared around the corner to the kitchen while Mary Frances sat down on the sofa, wrapping the blanket around her.

"Did you sleep well?" asked Fredèric.

"Gosh, yes," answered Mary Frances. "I didn't wake up one time. Have you looked outside? Have you seen how deep the snow is?"

"We are truly snowed in," said Sophia, returning with Mary Frances' coffee.

"Thank you," she said, taking the mug from Sophia. "Where is Matt? Is he still asleep?"

"Oh, no," said Fredèric. "He's been up for hours. He's been out in the workshop, and now he's outside measuring the snowfall."

"A workshop? Is he making something?" asked Mary Frances.

"No," answered Fredèric. "He's just getting ready in case we lose power later today." Mary Frances took a sip of coffee and wondered what he could be doing in preparation for a power outage. Fredèric smiled and said, "That's just how he is. As you get to know him, you'll understand." Then, the French door in the kitchen opened, and Matt came in stomping his feet to knock off the snow. "Close that door," shouted Fredèric. "You're letting all the cold air in!"

Matt laughed and shut the door. Walking into the great room, he went directly to the fire to warm up.

"Good morning, Mary Frances," he said, rubbing his hands together. "Did you sleep well?"

"Oh, yes. Thank you. The bed was so comfortable," she answered. "How much snow do you think we have?"

"Good question. Hard to say exactly," Matt answered. "We had so much wind there are high spots and low spots. The least I measured was 12 inches, but other places are three feet deep. In more protected places, the average seems to be around 20 inches. This is the biggest snow we've had around here in years."

"Mary Frances," said Sophia. "I washed and dried the clothes you were wearing yesterday, but feel free to use the sweat suit if you want. It's probably warmer than what you were wearing."

"I checked on the weather. It all looks good until this afternoon when another front is supposed to pass through. This one may be ice rather than snow," said Matt. "I'm going to make bacon and eggs for breakfast. I know how y'all like yours," he said, looking toward Fredèric and Sophia. "But how about you, Mary Frances?"

"Scrambled would be great," she answered. "I'm just going to get ready. Then, I'll be right back to help."

When Mary Frances got to her bedroom and closed the door, she quickly made her bed then went to the bathroom to shower. Glancing at her phone, she saw two text messages. The first was from Veritas officially announcing that the company would be closed until Monday. The second was from Jane.

Mary Frances,
Matthew Archer, 33 years old
Brentwood High School
University of Tennessee, Knoxville
Finance Major, Magna Cum Laude
Vanderbilt MBA, Magna Cum Laude
US Army, Lieutenant, 75th Ranger Battalion
Afghanistan, Airborne Sniper (don't piss him off MFF)
Member Brentwood Baptist Church
Placed 1st in his division of US Outdoor National Archery Competition (considered for US Olympic Team, but was in Afghanistan)
Speaks English, Spanish and Arabic
Vice President – Research at Veritas Strategies
5% owner of Veritas Strategies, Inc.
I can't find anything on him in the female dept.
Dates occasionally, but no steady girlfriend
You're welcome!!!

Jane, I didn't ask you to get all this information!

MFF, yes you did and you're welcome.

Thank you, Jane.

So WHY did you want to know about Matt Archer??

No reason. I just saw him in the cafeteria.

Hmmm. I don't believe you.
We'll talk more Monday. Enjoy your 4-day weekend!

Mary Frances got in the shower, fuming. *I guess maybe I did ask, but I didn't want all that detail. I just wanted to make sure he wasn't that guy on the sixth floor.* Mary Frances stood under the warm water and looked around at the rough stone walls of the shower. *This is kind of like taking a shower in a cave. I like it.*

I like everything about this place. Once she was out of the shower, she picked up her phone and called Dagny.

"Hey Dagny!"

"Mary Frances, how are you! Is everything alright?

"Yes, I'm fine. In fact, I can't believe how much I'm enjoying this. It's like being on vacation."

"OK, Mary Frances. Talk to me. How is he? I looked him up on Facebook. Mary Frances, he's gorgeous. Have you found out anything else on him?"'

"Dagny, no. I don't know anything else. He's very nice, and he's being very kind to me. But that's it, Dagny. You must stop this."

"OK, if you insist."

"I'm afraid someone's going to find out I got snowbound with a man from the sixth floor, and Mrs. Joiner will come unhinged. No one knows about this except you, so don't tell a soul. OK?"

"OK, I promise, but I can't believe this. He's got to be smart. And he's not a jerk?"

"Dagny! Yes, he's very accomplished, and he's not a jerk."

After the two friends said goodbye, Mary Frances dried her hair and tried to make herself presentable. *Sophia's right. The sweat suit is so warm and comfortable. But I can't wear it every day! At least today, I have my underwear*. Putting the finishing touches on her hair, she returned to the great room and on to the kitchen. Everyone was seated at the island for breakfast.

"I'll do the dishes when we're finished," said Mary Frances, feeling guilty for not having helped with preparing breakfast. Everyone enjoyed bacon and eggs with orange juice while Matthew and Frederic talked about a sailboat race out of Malta. When the story was finished, Mary Frances said, "Matt, I've been at Veritas for six months now, and I'm still not sure what we do. Could you tell me what you do? What do you research?"

"Well, it's a good thing we have several days because it could take that long to explain," Matt said as Frederic smiled. "But, I'll try to give you the short version. First, we invest money.

We take money that clients place with us and try to make more for them. Sometimes we do that directly when a client gives us a lump sum, say $1,000,000, and we invest it in various ways. But another department at Veritas is the ETF division. That's an acronym that stands for Exchange Traded Fund. An example is Fredèric, who through his private bank, also runs portfolios. Let's say he's decided he wants a 5% exposure to Emerging Markets in a $1,000,000 portfolio. That's only $50,000. You can't get much diversification from $50,000, so he uses our Emerging Markets ETF. You could say we *manufacture* ETF's and maintain them. Then there's me. The money managers and the folks that build the ETF's all need research, so my department follows all the various economic indicators in the world. We look for anomalies, correlations, and causations in all those numbers. We can't exactly predict the future, but we can manage risk with that knowledge. Does that make any sense?"

"Maybe, a little," Mary Frances said. "I've heard people talk about building a portfolio with so much stock, and so much bonds, or so much of what did you call it .... emerging markets? It reminds me of a recipe. A cup of flour, a tablespoon of vanilla, four eggs."

"Yes! It's sort of like that," Matt said, pleased with her analogy. The only difference is that a great recipe in the kitchen will always be a great recipe. But a great recipe in a portfolio is always changing." Matt watched as she pondered it, intrigued by her inquisitive mind.

"So, we're snowed in folks," said Fredèric. "What would you all like to do today?"

Refilling her coffee cup and heading to the fireplace, Sophia said, "Well, for starters, I want to sit by the fire some more." The others also poured up another cup of coffee and moved to the great room, sitting down while Matt threw on more firewood.

"I'd like to take a hike in the snow," said Sophia, "but Mary Frances doesn't have the right clothes. She almost froze to death yesterday, and we don't want to repeat that today." Then Sophia smiled, teasing her new friend.

"You all go ahead," said Mary Frances. "I don't mind. Don't miss out because of me."

"I tell you what," said Matt. "Fredèric, you and Sophia go on the hike, and I'll stay here with Mary Frances. You remember where the trail is, don't you?"

"Are you sure?" pleaded Mary Frances. "I hate to make you miss out."

"No, it's fine. I want to stay and find out more about you," said Matt.

"Is there anything you need done, anything I can do, perhaps in the workshop to prepare for a power outage?" Mary Frances offered.

Matt laughed and asked, "Now, how do you know about my workshop and preparing for a power outage?"

"Fredèric told me that's what you were doing this morning," she answered.

"OK, I'll show you the workshop while the Steiners are out hiking on the trail," said Matt.

Then addressing the Steiners in the kitchen, he said, "The snowshoes are on the wall in the garage. You probably have a few hours before any bad weather starts. We'll eat lunch when you get back." Fredèric and Sophia suited up in snow gear, said their goodbyes and headed out the door to the garage.

"Don't get lost and make me have to come find you!" Matt called after them. Mary Frances could hear them laughing.

"OK, let's finish our coffee then I'll show you the workshop," Matt said to Mary Frances as they sat by the fire watching the flames.

Mary Frances said to herself, *He wants to know more about me. I'm sure that will bore him to death.*

"So Mary Frances, tell me about yourself," Matt said. "Did you say you're from Charlotte?"

"Yes, I'm from Charlotte," she answered, "born and raised."

"Family?" Matt asked.

"I'm an only child. My mother lives in Charlotte. My dad passed away 10 years ago," she said, quietly.

"I'm sorry," he said. "So, how did you get to Nashville from Charlotte? And what brought you to Veritas?"

Mary Frances held the coffee cup, feeling its warmth, trying to figure out how to tell him. *Am I about to get myself fired?* she wondered.

"Mr. Archer, and I know you've told me to call you Matt, but you've asked a question that calls for me to be more formal." Matt looked at her curiously. "You're an important person at Veritas Strategies. I know you're friends with Mr. Borland. I'm afraid answering the question may cost me my job, but I don't want to lie to you."

Mary Frances watched Matt's face for any sign of emotion. She saw nothing, but she had his attention. Taking a deep breath, she continued. "I went to school in Charlotte. Then I went to college there, too. My bachelor's degree was in culinary arts and food service management. After that I worked at a restaurant in Charlotte. Then I went back to school and got my master's in Food Service Management."

"Mary Frances, you have a master's degree in Food Service Management, and you're frying chicken in our cafeteria?" Matt asked in astonishment. "You should be running the cafeteria!"

"No, I don't think so," she said, shaking her head. "You see... I've lied. I've worried about this for the last six months. And now I'm snowed in with you, and you've asked me; I can't lie to you."

"What are you talking about, Mary Frances?" Matt asked.

Mary Frances took another deep breath. "After I graduated, I wanted to start over, to move somewhere where no one knew me," she explained. "It seemed that Nashville was the place to be, and I knew there would be lots of job opportunities. So, I moved to Nashville. I didn't think I'd have trouble finding a job, but I was wrong. I didn't understand until someone was honest enough to explain it to me. It was my education. I had more education that the individual who would be my boss. I didn't have experience, but I had the degrees. I think there were people who were afraid I might take their jobs in the future. So, I changed my resume. I removed my degrees. Instantly, I could get a job. No problem. So, you see, I lied on my application at Veritas."

"Unbelievable," Matt said, shaking his head. "I've never even thought of the possibility of something like this happening."

"Are you going to tell Mrs. Joiner or HR? Please don't. I know it was wrong to understate my qualifications, but I really like my job. Veritas is a wonderful company, and I want to stay there," she pleaded.

"So, you think that Mrs. Joiner wouldn't have hired you if she'd known?" asked Matt.

"I really like Mrs. Joiner," answered Mary Frances," but no, I don't think she would have."

"Well, then your secret is safe with me," he said, studying her closely. "Mary Frances from the cafeteria, you're just full of surprises."

"I don't want you to think I lie," she said. "I don't. I hate lying. I would rationalize it to myself when I'd start worrying about it, by telling myself Veritas was getting a real deal with me because of my salary versus my education. I know that's wrong. And maybe someday when I have more experience and Mrs. Joiner retires, perhaps I could move up. But then I'd have to admit to my deception on my application."

"Oh, don't beat yourself up too much," he said. "Things have a way of working out."

"Are you upset with me?" she asked, thinking, *I don't want him to be disappointed in me.*

"No, I'm not upset with you," Matt responded, continuing to think about what he'd just been told. Finishing his coffee, he changed the subject, "I believe you wanted to see the workshop. You know, I don't believe anyone has ever wanted to see my workshop, particularly a woman. But if you're interested, come on."

Taking their empty coffee mugs to the kitchen, Matt led her down a hallway. "This is the laundry room," his said, pointing to a door on the left. "And this is the workshop," he said, opening the last door, turning on a light.

Mary Frances wasn't sure what she expected, but she was surprised. The workshop was much bigger than she'd anticipated. Across one end was more firewood than she had ever seen- all neatly cut, split, and stacked seven feet tall. Then she saw a strange contraption adjacent to a large rack of batteries. "What is this?" she asked.

"Well, it's several things," he said. This part is a boiler. It has a chimney that goes up through the roof. It burns firewood to make hot water and steam. Then, this part is a steam engine," he said, pointing to a green and red colored engine with a big flywheel. "The steam from the boiler powers the engine. The belt on the pulley on the drive shaft powers the alternator. The alternator in turn charges this battery bank. If an ice storm causes a power outage, we will still have electricity. This battery bank of 20 D8's will run the house for several days. That is, if we don't run the oven or hair dryers... things that take a lot of electricity. The lights are all LEDs that use very little power. Since the house is AC and the batteries are DC, the electricity is run through this device called an inverter to change the DC to AC. When the batteries start to get low on electricity, we'll just fire up the steam engine and recharge them."

Mary Frances looked at everything in amazement. She thought, *This is what Sophia meant. If you have to get snowed in and lose electricity, this is the place to do it.* "I've never seen a steam engine before. Is this like the steam engines that were used a long time ago?" she asked.

"It is," he said. "In fact, this type was very popular around 1900."

"Where in the world did you buy such a thing?" she asked.

"I didn't buy it," he answered. "I built it."

"You built this?" she asked, more than surprised. "But how?"

Walking over to the workbench where all the tools were, he pointed out two machines. "With these," he said. "This is called a lathe, and this is a milling machine. I took castings and machined them down. Then, I assembled it."

"This is amazing," she said. "And what is this?" she asked, pointing to a green machine with a flywheel.

"That's a flour mill," he said. "I tell you what... if the power goes out and we have to fire up the steam engine to recharge the batteries, we'll mill some flour and bake some bread. All I do is switch the belt from the alternator to the mill."

"If you say so," Mary Frances said, still amazed. *And to think, I was concerned about the electricity going out!* she thought.

"You were a little worried about the electricity going out, weren't you?" he asked.

"Yes," she admitted, wondering if he could read her mind.

"You'll hardly know if it does," he said. "There will still be hot water because that's from propane. The range is gas, too. We'll heat with wood. We can even watch a movie if you like." He watched as she looked at the mountain of firewood, the battery bank, and the steam engine. "Let's go back to the fireplace. Frederic and Sophia will be back soon."

Mary Frances followed Matt out of the workshop and back to the great room. *Dagny will never believe this!* she thought. *He just builds machines and makes his own electricity.*

"I'm glad you like your job as Veritas," he commented as they walked down the hall.

"Yes, very much," she said. "Food management is interesting, as well as practical and necessary, but what I really like is cooking. I like experimenting and coming up with new recipes, new tastes, new ideas. I'm looking forward to dinner tonight, although I am a little nervous because this will be a variation on my lamb chop recipe. I normally try it first myself before I serve it to someone."

"I'm looking forward to it," said Matt. "You helped me with the chili, maybe I can be your assistant tonight. Just don't give me anything too complicated."

"Oh, I don't think you would have a problem with something complicated," she said and then thought, *Mr. I'll just build my own steam engine and make some electricity*!" Matt smiled at her poking fun at him. "But you can help me," she said. "I had a half bottle of port at my apartment for the sauce, so I didn't buy any. Do you have any port I could use?"

"No, I don't, but you're welcome to use anything here," he said, opening the doors to an antique, mahogany liquor cabinet in the great room. It held an extensive inventory of liquors.

"This is tricky, changing more than one variable at a time," she said. "I'm already switching mint for parsley." He watched as she considered the various bottles in the liquor cabinet. *This girl is very smart*, he thought. *I like the way her mind works. Does she know how smart she is?*

"This may be a complete disaster, but may I try the Disaronno?" she asked.

"Of course," he answered. "Be my guest."

"I think I'm already your guest," Mary Frances smiled. "Now I'm bumming liquor from you!" As the two laughed together, Fredèric and Sophia came back in.

"I'm starved," called Fredèric from the kitchen. "Where's lunch?!" The foursome gathered in the kitchen, and Mary Frances helped Matt get deli meat and cheese out of the refrigerator.

"How was it out there?" asked Matt.

"Cold!" said Sophia. "I don't know how it's possible, but it feels colder here than it does back in Switzerland."

"No ice yet?" asked Matt.

"Nothing yet," said Fredèric. Everyone made a sandwich as the Steiners recounted their hike around Matt's property. "Here's an idea for this afternoon," said Fredèric. "Matt, you know how to play pinochle, don't you?"

"Maybe. I think I remember. It's been a long time," Matt responded.

"How about you, Mary Frances? Do you know how to play pinochle?" Fredèric asked.

"I'm like Matt," she said. "I've played with my aunt and uncle, but it's been a long time. I'm not very good."

"That's great!" Fredèric exclaimed. "Sophia and I are challenging the two of you to a game of pinochle. The losers have to cook dinner."

"Actually, Mary Frances is in charge of dinner tonight," said Matt, "so this would be dinner tomorrow night."

"What *is* today?" asked Sophia. "Between jet lag and being snowed in, I'm not sure."

"This is Thursday, and Mary Frances is doing dinner tonight. You will prepare dinner Friday night when Team Steiner loses," he said, winking at Mary Frances. "And maybe we'll dig out by Saturday, Sunday at the latest." Mary Frances gave Matt a look that said, *I hope I'm good enough. They will probably beat us.* "But I have a feeling that if we lose, Mary Frances is up to the task for Friday night, too," Matt said.

Chapter 4
Pinochle

Disappearing from the kitchen, Matt quickly returning with playing cards. The women had begun clearing the table. Fredèric was loading glasses in the dishwasher.

"Are we playing single or double deck?" Matt asked the group.

"We can beat you at either," teased Fredèric.

"Ignore him, Mary Frances," said Sophia.

Matt paused to see if Mary Frances had a preference. She smiled and said, "I've played both."

"Double deck it is," replied Fredèric. While he and Matt went to the great room to arrange a spot to play cards in front of the fireplace, Sophia and Mary Frances finished up in the kitchen.

When the women joined the guys in the great room, Mary Frances took a seat across the table from Matt; Sophia sat across from her husband.

"Before we begin, can we go over the rules?" asked Mary Frances. "I need to refresh my memory a bit. And would someone make a cheat sheet for me? I'm unsure about the point values."

"Prepare to lose," Fredèric said to Matt.

"Ignore my husband," remarked Sophia again. "I'll make that sheet for you."

Quickly, Sophia wrote out the information Mary Frances needed for bidding. Matt briefly reviewed pinochle rules as he was accustomed to playing. Offering to deal first, Fredèric shuffled the cards.

"One last question," Mary Frances said as the dealing began. "Are the *nines* used in this game?"

Fredèric displayed a huge grin, and Sophia answered. "No, not in double deck pinochle," she said, trying to make eye contact with her partner.

Once the cards were dealt, it was up to Matt to begin the bidding process. He was seated to the dealer's left. "I'll open with 50," said Matt. The bid moved to Sophia who gave a bid of 52. Then, it was Mary Frances' turn.

Studying her cheat sheet, Mary Frances said, "Pass." It was Fredèric's turn.

"53," said Fredèric, and the bid returned to Matt. In the end, Fredèric won the bid naming spades as trump.

As the four players put down their meld, Mary Frances also lay down a run in spades. "How 'bout that, Fredèric," said Matt who was now the one grinning.

When the last round of the first hand came, Mary Frances took the trick which was worth two extra points. "Hey, hey, that's my partner," said Matt.

It was Matt's deal. When the bidding came to Mary Frances, she did not pass this time. As it turned out, she won the bid, naming trump for the second hand. Throughout the hand, Matt observed Mary Frances. She always seemed to know what to lead when it was her turn. And when Matt had the lead, she threw a counter his way whenever possible. *This girl is good,* Matt thought.

Play after play, Matt paid careful attention to his partner. Hand after hand, Mary Frances often took the last trick. It was almost as if she knew what cards each player held. *She's incredible,* Matt thought. It took a little longer for the Steiners to realize what was happening, but eventually they caught on, too.

"What do you mean you're not very good?" Fredèric asked. "How is it that you're always taking the last trick?"

"Leave my partner alone," intervened Matt, laughing. "She won't be sharing any secrets with the other team!"

The game stayed close between the two teams. Mary Frances took the bid for what would be the decisive hand. She named hearts as trump, laying down a run in hearts.

"We've got you now!" said Fredèric, also laying down a run in hearts. "You'll never make your bid. You're set." He smiled from ear to ear.

Then, Mary Frances added to her meld... aces around and double pinochle, putting her team's score over 500 and winning the game. Fredèric's face fell. He'd been so sure he and Sophia would win... he couldn't believe it.

"Sorry my partner smoked you," Matt said, pointing to Mary Frances.

"She did not *smoke* us!" Fredèric said, indignantly.

"My cabin, my rules, my definition of *smoked*," said Matt, laughing at his embarrassed friend.

I hope they're not too angry with us over losing, Mary Frances worried. Then she said, "Do you hear that? What's that noise?" Everyone stopped talking to listen. It was a steady, pinging sound.

"That's ice hitting the windows and the metal cap on the chimney," Matt said. "Sounds like the ice that was predicted has started."

Curiously, Mary Frances and Sophia walked to the window to look out. Sleet was falling, peppering the glass. "The sound is mesmerizing," said Mary Frances.

"Isn't it," replied Sophia. "I love it."

"I'll help you with dinner tomorrow night," Mary Frances whispered to Sophia as they continued watching the ice come down. "I don't know what all Matt has, but I'm sure we can figure something out."

"Thank you," said Sophia, smiling. "I may take you up on that because Fredèric can't cook. He was very certain we would win. You're quite a pinochle player, Mary Frances." Mary Frances smiled.

"Here we go, guys," said Matt. "If we're going to lose power, it will be soon. I'm thinking about a cappuccino. Does that sound good to anyone else?"

Everyone chimed in in agreement, as Matt threw a log on the fire and went to the kitchen. Mary Frances excused herself for a moment. She went to her bedroom, closed the door and phoned Dagny.

"Hello."

"Hi, Dagny!"

"Mary Frances! How are you? Are you believing this weather?"

"I know, and now it's raining ice. Are you getting ice? Do you still have power?"

"Yes, it's icing here, but we do have power. Mary Frances, are you serious about a roommate? If you are, I'm willing to hike through this blizzard right now and move in. Rooming with these girls is driving me crazy. Plus, I'm sleeping on the sofa, and didn't you say I would have my own bathroom? I would give anything to have my own bathroom!"

"Yes, Dagny, I'm serious. And yes, you would have your own bathroom. As soon as this storm is over, you can move in."

"Thank God! I'm going nuts here. How is it there?"

"Oh, Dagny, it's not bad at all. In fact, it's beautiful and peaceful. Matt's cabin's perfect. There's a fire in the fireplace all the time. I'm preparing dinner tonight for everyone, lamb chops. We just played pinochle. Matt and I beat the couple from Switzerland. I wish you could see my bedroom and bathroom. They're to die for!"

"Mary Frances, tell me about Matt."

"Oh, Dagny, Matt is wonderful. He has every reason to be arrogant and pretentious, but he's not. He's been very gracious and considerate, and he's funny."

"Mary Frances, you like him, don't you? I can tell."

"Yes. Who wouldn't? But it's not like you're thinking. He's very different, Dagny. If the power goes out, we'll still have electricity. Matt actually built a steam engine to make electricity for emergencies!"

"Mary Frances, I've seen his picture! And you're talking about steam engines? He's gorgeous!"

"Dagny! Nothing is happening here, and nothing is going to happen. Don't forget, we're on the first floor, and he's on the sixth floor. Besides... Mrs. Joiner would shoot me if anything did, and it won't. I should go now. My phone is about dead. Hang in there with those roommates, and I hope you all don't lose electricity."

No sooner than Mary Frances had plugged in her phone, the lights went out. *We lost electricity,* she thought as she hurried back to the great room. Matt was just placing the four cappuccinos on the coffee table, and the Steiners were seated comfortably in front of the fire. "Did you see, Matt? We just lost power!" said Mary Frances.

"I noticed," Matt answered, calmly. "I got these cappuccinos done just in time." Mary Frances took a seat on the leather coach and picked up her coffee mug, savoring its warmth as she held it.

"Shouldn't the emergency power have come on automatically?" asked Mary Frances, puzzled.

"Mary Frances, when we finish our coffee, I want you to come with me, and I'll show you how we switch everything over to battery. Then I'll show you how we're going to keep the cabin toasty."

Mary Frances nodded. *He's so calm,* she thought. *I would be worried we would freeze to death. But he's planned for all this. Oh, no! Poor Dagny. I wonder if her power went out. How did I get so lucky to end up here in this blizzard?*

"So does this mean no more cappuccinos, Matt?" kidded Fredèric.

"No, buddy, you know better than that. We'll just make them on the stove," laughed Matt.

Gathering the empty coffee mugs, Matt said, "Come with me, Mary Frances." She got up and followed him to the kitchen.

"I'll grab a flashlight so we can see," he said, taking one from a drawer in the kitchen. Matt led the way as Mary Frances followed him to the workshop. Making their way across the pitch-dark workshop, Matt shined the flashlight to guide them. When Mary Frances stopped in front of the breaker box, Matt put his hands on her shoulders to gently move her over. "Scoot over here, so I can get to the breakers." Being in the dark with Matt and his hands on her shoulders, Mary Frances felt a tingling sensation ... one that also felt safe and warm.

"First, I throw the main breaker," he said. "That will cut us off from the grid, the grid that currently isn't giving us any electricity. Next, I'll turn off all the breakers in the 200-amp service box. Then, I'll turn on the inverter and thrown this switch." Mary Frances watched the flashlight beam as he explained what he was doing. "Now, I'll turn on all the breakers that I've premarked with a blue dot. Those are the essential circuits." Matt flipped the light switch, and the lights in the workshop came on. "Voila!" he said. "Now, let's go see about heat."

I don't understand what he just did, but the lights work, Mary Frances thought as she followed him down the hallway back to the kitchen. Once in the kitchen, Matt opened a door to the walk-in pantry and motioned for her to enter. *What is he up to*? she wondered. The pantry was lined with well stocked shelves, everything needed to run a kitchen. Matt shut the door behind them. He reached under one of the shelves, and Mary Frances heard a click. The wall swung open, revealing a wooden staircase that descended between stone walls. When Matt turned on the lights, she could see it was much deeper than what she would expect for a basement. Matt started down the stairs then turned and said, "Come on down." Mary Frances paused at the top of the stairs, suddenly hesitant to follow him. *What's down there? It looks like a dungeon or something,* she thought. "Mary Frances, what's wrong?" Matt asked as he walked back up the stairs to her."

"What's down there?" she asked, cautiously. "Why do we need to go down there?"

"It's my heating system," he answered, puzzled at her concern, "a wine cellar and storage. I wanted to show you how it works. It's another one of my inventions." *Why is she so scared? Why would this frighten her?"* he wondered.

Mary Frances gave a cautious smile. *What is wrong with you, Mary Frances*? she thought. *He's not the creep on the sixth floor. Surely, he doesn't have a torture chamber down there. Of course, he doesn't.... he might. I need to read that book.*

Matt took her hand and led her down the long staircase. The walls on either side were roughhewn stone. Overhead were heavy beams. At the bottom of what was a very long descent was a built-in bookcase. He continued down a hallway that doubled back through a stone passageway ending in a room of wine racks. There was a small, wooden table with two chairs in the center of the room.

"This is my wine cellar," he said, still holding her hand. "I'm not sure exactly why you're afraid, but you are perfectly safe. I would never hurt you. I'm going to show you something else now. And I don't want to scare you. You saw the secret door in the pantry- a wall of shelves that was a door? Now, I'm going to show you another one." He led her back through the passageway to the bookcase at the foot of the stairs. "This one leads to the room for the wood furnace. We'll need to start it to keep the heat up in the house. I built the wood burner room a good distance from the wine cellar because heat and wine don't mix." Mary Frances nodded her understanding, and Matt reached under another shelf to release another secret lock. The bookcase moved, revealing another doorway. Matt led her inside.

Mary Frances looked around at a gray, concrete room. Even the ceiling was concrete. In the middle of the room was a large, metal box with a door. Eight big ducts came out of the top of the box and rose to the ceiling then disappeared through openings in the concrete above. "Here it is! It's just a wood burner that I've put inside a big plenum. And I've rigged thermoelectric fans in the ductwork. A thermoelectric fan doesn't need outside electricity. If one part is above 85 degrees and the other is below 85, it will make its own electricity. It's cool here in the basement and hot inside the plenum. The fans drive the hot air to the cabin above! It works pretty well, and it doesn't put any drag on the battery bank. Because the regular furnace is propane, we could run it off the battery bank. But what if the propane runs out? I like to have back-ups for the back-ups." Mary Frances smiled at him, enjoying his excitement in explaining his heating device.
Why was I uncomfortable coming down here? she asked herself. *I'm too paranoid, I guess.*

"Over here is my firewood chute," he said, indicating the square hole in the wall. "Instead of carrying firewood through the house, I just throw it down the chute from the workshop."

"Matt, I don't know what to say," she said. "I've never seen anything like this. What a surprise all this is down here!"

Walking back to the wine cellar, Matt returned with the two chairs, "Here, sit down," he said. "This will take a couple of minutes, so we can sit while I get this thing going." He opened the door of the plenum, then opened the door to the woodburner inside. Kneeling, he lit the paper and kindling inside and adjusted the air flow as it caught fire. "Very impressive, Mary Frances! You and pinochle."

"I don't know about that," she said with a sigh. "I hope

we didn't make Frederic angry."

Matt smiled. "I have to ask," he said. "Were you pretending you didn't remember how to play pinochle? Asking for a cheat sheet... then, asking about the nines?"

"No, of course not!" Mary Frances said. "I hadn't played in a few years."

"How did you learn to play like that?" asked Matt. "You said you weren't very good."

"I learned from my aunt and uncle. They were incredible card players. Compared to them, I'm not very good. My aunt and uncle had several friends who would get together and play frequently. Frederic's confidence caused me to believe they were that good, too."

"Yes, but how did you do it? Why didn't you bid the first hand?" he asked. "Tell me the strategy."

Mary Frances smiled and said, "Well, most people try to win the bid *just* to name trump. But when they do that, they're also telling the other players what they're holding. I didn't bid the first time to find out if our opponents understood that. They didn't. I had a decent hand and didn't want them to know." Matt nodded.

Mary Frances continued, "Paying careful attention to the meld and watching the play go around the table a couple of times, I had a pretty good idea of what cards were where. Also, I fed counters to you and didn't give up any more than necessary. Counting trump is the key to taking the last trick. I don't think anyone knew I was doing that."

Matt studied her and smiled. Leaning forward, he put more firewood into the firebox, shut the door and adjusted the air. "Does that work with people, too? Give me an example."

Mary Frances thought for a moment. "Well, it's kind of like Mrs. Joiner in the cafeteria. Some people don't like her, but I do. I think it's because I understand her. You see, she gives everyone her cafeteria speech and how we're to behave both at work and in our private lives. She gave Dagny *the speech* on Wednesday. It goes like this. 'You work on the first floor. Everyone else on floors two through six are higher than you, and you must always remember that. You're not to talk to them or be friendly with them. If you do, you'll get yourself in trouble like those girls who got pregnant.' Matt's eyebrows raised slightly as he listened. "Some of the girls in the cafeteria don't like Mrs. Joiner because of these speeches, but I think I understand," she continued. "I suspect that sometime way back, Mrs. Joiner had her heart broken by a man who was above her, status wise. It affected her whole life, and so she believes she's looking out for us by warning us. I look beyond what she says and ask myself why she says it. In playing cards, I observe and analyze. I ask myself why the other players bid and play the way they do."

"Using your pinochle theory, what can you tell me about me?" Matt asked.

"You're very complicated, Mr. Archer. I'm not sure," answered Mary Frances, carefully.

"You don't have to be sure, just an observation. I'm curious," he insisted.

"Well, I find it odd that there are no archery trophies in your house," she commented. "Maybe I just haven't seen them because they're all displayed in.... say, your bathroom?" she smiled. "But I don't think so... I'm not sure what that means."

"So, you know about that?" he asked in surprise.

"Another girl in the cafeteria told me about your archery accomplishments," Mary Frances answered.

"And how do you know about the girls getting pregnant?" he questioned her further.

"After you rescued me and we were driving, you and Frederic were talking about Brian Eastman. That's when I realized you worked at Veritas and that you were on the sixth floor. I was afraid because I'd heard the stories about the man who's gotten all those girls pregnant. It occurred to me it might be you since I hadn't been told the man's name. So, I pretended to text my mother that I was alright, but I actually texted a coworker who knows everything about everyone. I asked if his name was Matt. But it wasn't you, fortunately. She texted right back that his name was Hanson and that Matt was Matt Archer. If you had been Hanson, I would have jumped out of the car at a stop sign and run to a house. She also told me other things about you, including your impressive archery skills."

Silence hung in the air, and Mary Frances saw a troubled look on Matt's face. Conscious of the awkwardness, she said, "I'm sorry, Mr. Archer. I wasn't trying to be nosy. I guess Mrs. Joiner just has us all paranoid about men from the sixth floor."

"Mary Frances, you're amazing. No need to apologize. You did the right thing. I didn't realize so many people had heard about Hanson. You know more about this than I do. How many girls?"

"Four, but I don't know that for a fact. It's gossip," Mary Frances said. "It could be an exaggeration."

"No wonder you were hesitant to come with me," he said. "I am ashamed that our employees have such a low opinion of the men on the sixth floor."

"It's not all the men. It's just the one. People think very highly of Mr. Borland. They like Mr. Eastman, and I've not heard anything bad about you or anyone else. It's just the one."

"Nonetheless, I apologize... The fire's going strong now," Matt said, pointing to the glass window in the woodburner. "If you look up in the plenum, you can see the fans turning, pushing warm air through the ductwork. Let's go upstairs now. I'll come back down in a few hours and load some more wood." The two returned to the pantry, closing the secret doors behind them.

"It's about time to start getting things together for dinner," said Mary Frances as they exited the pantry. She gathered ingredients on the island and considered what kind of salad would pair well with lamb chops. She was working on the cherry/disaronno sauce when Sophia joined her in the kitchen.

"Can I help?" Sophia asked.

"Sure," Mary Frances answered. "You can stir this over a very low heat." Mary Frances adjusted the small burner on the range and placed the sauce pan over the low flame. "What a stove!" she said. "These ranges are manufactured one at a time in France."

"They are beautiful," agreed Sophia as she took the wooden spoon and started slowly stirring. "Did you like the workshop and the wine cellar?"

"He's amazing, isn't he!" said Mary Frances. "It seems he can make anything he puts his mind to."

"You know, he likes you," said Sophia. "Very few people have ever seen the wine cellar, much less what's beyond. You should feel very privileged."

"Oh. Have you seen the wine cellar, too?" asked Mary Frances.

"Yes," answered Sophia.

"I was a little scared when I saw the secret door open and could see down the stairs," she explained. "For a second, I thought it was a dungeon. Like a torture chamber or something."

"So that's what Matt meant!" said Sophia.

"Did he tell you?" asked Mary Frances.

"Yes, he said you seemed afraid, but he didn't know why," said Sophia.

"It's stupid, Sophia, but when I saw those stairs going down in the dark, the *Fifty Shades of Gray* book popped in my head. I've never even read it, but some of my coworkers have. They said the man had a secret torture room where he'd tie up women and whip them," Mary Frances said. "Don't tell him. I'm embarrassed I thought such a thing. And now, I've blurted it out!"

"I won't tell," Sophia laughed. "I can assure you Matthew doesn't have a secret torture room. He has his secrets, but they're not anything like that," Sophia said, stirring the sauce. "But did you catch what I said? Matt really likes you."

"Yes. I like him, too. I am so grateful that he... all of you... rescued me," Mary Frances said.

"I don't think you understand, Mary Frances," said Sophia. "He likes you, and that doesn't happen. He showed you things he's never shown another woman. The way he studies you- he's analyzing you. That may not seem like a compliment, but it is."

Sophia's words tumbled around in Mary Frances' head as they worked on in silence. *I like him, too... very much. But Sophia is the one who doesn't understand. There's no way someone like Matt would ever be interested in me. And if he was, if he did want to take me on a date, I would have to decline. Why is life like this? It's so unfair. Besides, Sophia is mistaken. Matt is surrounded by smart, beautiful women every day. He could have his pick. He's very kind to me, but there's no way it's any more than that. Sophia is wrong.*

Mary Frances continued preparing dinner while Sophia set the dining room table.

Matt went about lighting candles in the great room, dining room and then in the kitchen. "We have electricity, but using candlelight instead of electric light will make the batteries last longer... plus, it's more romantic," Matt said.

Did he say 'romantic'? Mary Frances asked herself. *No, he didn't mean it like that. Sophia has it all wrong.*

When it was time for dinner, everyone gathered around the dining room table. Mary Frances explained how she had made the cherry sauce with all the various ingredients. The group listened intently and then dove in. Dinner was an overwhelming success. "Mary Frances, these are the best lamb chops I've ever had," said Matt. Everyone felt the same way.

"This cherry sauce is incredible," said Fredèric. "And you work in the cafeteria at Veritas? Unbelievable!" Mary Frances glowed, receiving high praise for her culinary accomplishments. Sophia watched Mary Frances as Matt praised her. She could tell that she particularly enjoyed Matt's compliments.

"I'll help Mary Frances do the dishes while you two boys check on the fire downstairs and get some more wood in for the fireplace. Then let's meet in the great room and have an after-dinner drink. Matt, do you have any 43?" asked Sophia.

"I do!" said Matt. "Great choice!"

The men went about the firewood detail as the women cleared and washed the dishes. "Have you tried 43?" asked Sophia.

"Yes, a few times," said Mary Frances. "It's very good. Supposedly, it's an ancient Roman recipe."

A short time later, the four friends were in the great room seated around a roaring fire while Matt poured everyone a cordial of Licor 43. "I'd like to propose a toast to our guest, Mary Frances," said Matt, raising his glass. "To Mary Frances, chef extraordinaire and pinochle hustler!" Everyone laughed spontaneously, then raised a glass.

"And to Matt, our host," said Sophia. "We don't know for sure, but probably thousands of people are without power right now and getting cold. Matt, we appreciate you and your cabin and how comfortable we are, eating like kings and sleeping warmly."

"It's my pleasure," Matt said. "Why don't we turn on TV and see how people are faring?" he said, picking up the remote. At the push of a button, the TV raised up out of a cabinet to the side of the fireplace. The news was grim. A half million people in Tennessee were without power, and emergency services were overwhelmed. Ambulances were trying to navigate the slick roads to get the sick to hospitals while National Guard trucks worked to get people without heat to warming centers. When the news report switched to national news, they saw that it wasn't just Nashville, but a band of ice hundreds of miles wide that included St. Louis, Memphis, Louisville, Cincinnati, and on to Pittsburg. In total, millions of people were suffering. The death toll across the country was already over one hundred. Also disturbing was a report that several buildings were on fire in St. Louis. Apparently set by arsonists, the firefighters were struggling to fight the fires as they contended with slick roads and freezing hoses.

Sitting together in silence after the news report, Mary Frances said, "Gosh, I feel guilty. We're so comfortable here. I had no idea how dire this situation is. This is serious!" For a second, tears started to well up in her eyes. She was glad there was only candlelight and firelight illuminating the room. She blinked her eyes and looked up at the ceiling as Matt watched her. He turned off the TV.

For the next few minutes, no one spoke. Instead, they listened to the fire crackle and sipped the 43. Finally, Frederic broke the silence. "Matt, are you investigating any new economic/cultural correlations at Veritas?"

Slowly, Matt took another sip of his 43 and quietly answered, "We're always looking for more indicators for the Endex, Frederic." Mary Frances was puzzled as she looked at Matt, then Frederic and finally Sophia. *What does that mean?* she wondered. *Matt understands. Sophia seems to, but I don't.*

"It's been going on for several decades actually, the rise in crime and particularly crime driven by mental illness as opposed to financial motivation," Matt said. "But what we've been trying to get a grip on is systemic risk. It's so complicated, yet basic."

"What is systemic risk?" asked Mary Frances. "I'm a little lost in this conversation. Weren't we talking about the blizzard and how people are suffering?"

Everyone was quiet for a minute as Mary Frances tried to make sense of it all. "Mary Frances, we are talking about the blizzard, but we're talking about our world in general, too," Matt answered. "You understand that with the blizzard comes risk. We just heard that over one hundred people have died. Directly or indirectly, those deaths have occurred because of the blizzard. But lots of things can increase risk. What Fredèric was getting at is, why would people set buildings on fire in St. Louis? It doesn't make sense, does it? And particularly when we're struggling with a blizzard. The question is not only why would people do this, but is the occurrence increasing, decreasing, or staying the same? As terrible as it is, we understand why a fanatic flies a jet airplane into the World Trade Center in New York. It's a fanatical, religious motivation. But why would a man haul an arsenal of weapons up to his hotel room in Las Vegas and kill all those people? We don't know. Authorities are still trying to figure it out. Then all the school shootings. No logical reason. Fredèric was wondering if we have any idea why this is happening. He's wondering because it's increasing."

"OK," said Mary Frances. "But what is systemic risk?"

"Oh, yes, systemic risk," Matt said. "Maybe I can explain it with a bicycle analogy. First, let's consider a child's tricycle. Very simple. No gears, direct drive. No brakes. The child simply stops pedaling to stop the tricycle. Then, let's consider a very high-end bicycle. I saw a bicycle a few weeks ago in a shop in Memphis that cost $15,000. It had things on it I'd never heard of. Hydraulic brakes, and would you believe it, an automatic transmission. It had a rechargeable battery to operate a motor that changed gears. That was one expensive and complicated bike. Now, Mary Frances, which is better- the trike or the fancy bicycle?"

"That's very hard to say because there are several ways to look at it," she answered.

"That's correct," Matt said. "Let me ask the question in a different way. Which bike is more likely to break down?"

"The fancy one," answered Mary Frances.

"That's right," said Matt. "But does that make sense? The

tricycle probably cost $40 or $50 versus the high-end bicycle's $15,000 price tag. Shouldn't the more expensive one be more reliable?"

"You would think," said Mary Frances, "but it's so much more complicated. There are more things to go wrong."

"Correct," said Matt. "And by the way, there are very few bicycle mechanics in the state of Tennessee who can fix that bike. Now, why in the world would someone pay $15,000 for something that's going to break?"

"Probably because it's very fast, easier to pedal maybe," answered Mary Frances.

"That's right. The benefits," he said. "We are all willing to pay to receive benefits even if those benefits come with problems. Systemic risk is the risk that the fancy bicycle will break down due to its complexity. More systems equal more complexity equal a greater chance of failure. So, take that thought and look for other things like that in your life. Do you have a credit card, Mary Frances?"

"Yes, of course. Everyone does," she answered, cautiously.

"How many times in the past year did you receive notification that your card had been cancelled due to a security breach, and a week later you got a new one in the mail?"

"Twice," she said.

"You had to go to the trouble of changing the credit card number on all the automatic payments you have in place. Not to mention that your identity could have been stolen. That would be problematic at the least and very costly at the worst. But you put up with it anyway and can't wait to get the new credit card in the mail. The whole credit card/ banking system becomes more complex every day. Consumers love the benefits, but the whole system comes with ever-increasing risk. That's systemic risk."

"Yes, I understand that now. You're right," she said. "But does that have something to do with your job? Why do you study this?"

"We are warm and comfortable tonight," Matt said. "But we've just seen that millions are not. Why is that?"

"Because of the blizzard?" Mary Frances asked. Her voice

was serious, yet unsure.

"We're in the blizzard, too," said Matt. All eyes were on Mary Frances. Matt thought, *She is so deductive in cards, but I don't think she's ever considered this. That's not surprising. Most haven't.*

"Don't upset her, Matt," said Sophia, standing up from the sofa and yawning. "We've had enough of this kind of talk for tonight. Anyway, I'm sleepy. Come, Fredèric, let's go to bed. Thank you, Mary Frances for a wonderful dinner. I'm going to accept your offer of help for dinner tomorrow night."

"You're welcome. I'm glad you liked the lamb chops," said Mary Frances.

"Good night, guys," said Matt as he rose from his chair. "See you in the morning." Matt walked to the fire and arranged the coals with the poker before adding more firewood. As the wood caught fire, the flames danced. The only sound was the crackling from the fire.

"Are you sleepy, too?" asked Matt. It was just he and Mary Frances alone in the great room.

"Only a little," she said, not wanting the evening to end. *What am I doing? I should just go on to bed.*

Taking a seat, Matt sat next to Mary Frances on the leather sofa.

"I'm sorry if I upset you," Matt said. "Sophia was concerned that I did."

"Oh, you didn't," she said. "I'm just trying to understand it all."

"Would you like to continue talking about it or wait for another time?" Matt asked.

"I've never considered things like this before," she said. "If you're not too sleepy, can you explain it again?"

"OK. We are warm and comfortable tonight while others aren't because this cabin is not part of the system," Matt said. "The cabin is part of the system when the system works, but is independent of it when it doesn't. I don't have to have *their* electricity. I make my own. Another concern is food. People depend on the supermarket for food; but if the shelves are bare, I can provide my own."

"It's scary to think about it, isn't it?" Mary Frances said, trying to take it all in. "Life has become so complicated that something could cause it to all malfunction."

"Yes, but that doesn't mean it will. It could, but no one can exactly predict the future," Matt said. "I don't want you to worry about it. This will be over in a few days. The snow will melt, and life will go back to normal."

Mary Frances watched the fire, reflecting on the conversation. It was bitterly cold outside, and now she was even more aware of how easy it could be to freeze to death on such a night. She recalled Matt's concern over her getting too cold after she'd slid off the road. *He helped me up when I fell on that snowy hill,* she thought. *He's been taking care of me from the beginning.* Turning her eyes from the fire, Matt was looking at her.

Feeling drawn to each other, Matt put one arm on the sofa back and reached out with his other hand and touched hers. Slowly, Mary Frances moved to him as she rested her head on his shoulder. He pulled her closer. She shivered, not from cold but from his touch. Mary Frances closed her eyes, savoring the moment. Melting into his embrace, she laid her head on his chest as Matt slowly reclined on the sofa. As she listened to the beat of his heart, Matt reached down beside the sofa and brought up a blanket, spreading it over them. The fire crackled as they both drifted off to sleep.

Chapter 5
Friday

Mary Frances dreamed she was back in Charlotte. It was her home city, but there wasn't anything she recognized. As she walked down a sidewalk, she came to the edge of town and was then walking in the country. It started to get colder. She had a foreboding that something was following her. She started to run, but her feet were too heavy. Behind her were angry, gray clouds dumping mountains of snow. She was trying to get away, but the snow was getting closer. Then the snow was falling on her, and she felt like she was being buried alive. Crying for help, she felt a warm hand on her face and heard a voice. It was calling her name.

"Mary Frances, wake up," the voice said. "You're having a bad dream. You're OK."

Matt was brushing the hair from her face as she opened her eyes, only half awake. The glowing coals in the fireplace came into focus, and she discovered Matt's face was just inches from hers. Mary Frances was on her side, her back against the sofa and her front against Matt. Realizing she had fallen asleep in his arms, she tried to get up. "Oh, my goodness! This is inappropriate."

"It's OK," he said as she climbed over him and got to her feet.

"I'm so sorry," she said. "I didn't mean to fall asleep."

"Mary Frances," he said, standing up. "You didn't do anything wrong. Don't be upset."

"I'm sorry," she said again and ran off to her bedroom, closing the door behind her. She sat on the edge of the bed conflicted. *What have I done? What was I thinking? But I wanted him to hold me. How can I face him tomorrow? Mary Frances, you must stop this.* She changed into her pajamas and crawled under the covers. Mary Frances eventually went back to sleep but not without having that same conversation with herself a dozen times.

When morning came, Mary Frances showered and dressed in the clothes she had worn to work on Wednesday. She peaked out into the great room to see who was up. Although no one was in sight, she noticed that the fire was going strong. Mary Frances decided to take refuge in the kitchen where she found Sophia. "Good morning, Sophia," she said, quietly.

"Good morning to you," said Sophia, opening a package of bagels. "How do toasted bagels and cream cheese sound?"

"That sounds great," said Mary Frances. "I'll make the coffee."

"Did you sleep well?" asked Sophia. "Did you and Matt talk long after we went to bed?"

"Uh, not too long," she answered. "Is Matt up yet?"

"Yes, he's downstairs feeding the wood burner," Sophia said. "Amazing how well it heats the cabin, don't you think? It's warm all the way back in the bathrooms. Are your bathroom and bedroom warm?"

"Yes, toasty," Mary Frances answered.

Just then Matt emerged from the pantry, "Good morning, ladies. I hope you slept well. Mary Frances, I was just looking at the batteries, and they're down to 13.1 volts. Can you help me charge them up after breakfast?"

"Of course," Mary Frances answered, thinking, *He doesn't need my help.* She looked away, still embarrassed from the previous night.

"I've got to get that lazy husband of mine out of bed," said Sophia. "I'll be right back." She left the two of them alone in the kitchen.

Mary Frances looked at Matt with wide eyes that said,

Are you upset with me? Matt smiled and whispered, "It's alright." Then speaking in a normal voice, he said, "Would you like to mill some flour today? We could when we fire up the boiler after breakfast. Didn't you mention you like to make bread... or did I dream that?"

"Yes, I'd like that. Technically, I'm a pastry chef, so that would be fun," Mary Frances answered, deciding that everything was OK with Matt. "What kind of wheat do you have?"

"I have Hard Winter Red and Durum," Matt said.

"You have Durum?!" Mary Frances asked, smiling with surprise. "How much do you have?"

"Lots. I don't know how much, but I'm absolutely sure there's enough for your bread and pastries," Matt responded as Sophia walked back in the kitchen.

"How about three cups of the Durum and three of Hard Winter Red? Do you have that much?" Mary Frances asked.

Sophia laughed and said, "Mary Frances, I am sure he has at least that much." Matt smiled at Sophia. Mary Frances seemed satisfied with the answer and began looking through the refrigerator.

"May I use these raspberries, Matt?" she asked.

"Of course," he said. "Use anything you want. Are we having them for breakfast?"

"No, we're having bagels and cream cheese," explained Mary Frances. "Sophia might want to use the raspberries for dinner tonight."

Just then Fredèric stumbled into the kitchen, rubbing his eyes. "You can go back to bed after breakfast, Fredèric," Matt kidded his friend.

"Quit encouraging him, Matt," said Sophia as everyone sat around the island for a quick breakfast.

"Well, if you'd leave me alone at night and let me sleep, maybe I wouldn't be so tired," Fredèric said. Sophia's eyes flashed, and he knew he was in trouble.

Laughing, Matt said, "Mary Frances, let's you and I go down and see about getting the flour to mill. Grab your coffee and bagel."

Mary Frances took her breakfast and followed Matt to the

pantry. Once downstairs and into the wood burner room, Matt closed the door. "Oh boy, Sophia was mad," he said, laughing. "Fredèric shouldn't have said that. He really embarrassed her." Mary Frances smiled and thought, *I assumed he meant that she was stealing the covers, but now I think he was referring to something else. No wonder Sophia was embarrassed. Thank goodness Matt didn't say anything about me!*

"Matt... about last night," Mary Frances said as Matt opened the door to the wood burner and threw in three more logs. "I just want to apologize again. I shouldn't have fallen asleep there."

"Mary Frances," he said, closing the wood burner door. "I told you there's nothing to apologize for. You did nothing wrong. I'm not mad at you. We were just talking about some things that are potentially scary, and I think it frightened you. It was late, and you just went to sleep."

"Thank you," she said. "It won't happen again."

"Well, that's unfortunate. I was hoping it would," he said, smiling at her. She looked down at the floor embarrassed at his comment. "Are you OK? Sometimes I think I make you nervous," observed Matt.

"Well... yes, kind of," she said. "But the truth is, I'm having a wonderful time. I've talked to my roommate, Dagny, several times. She's a bit aggravated at me because I'm here, warm and comfortable, like I'm on vacation at a resort while she's sleeping on a sofa and cold."

"Is this the same girl that kicked our CEO out of the cafeteria?" he asked.

"Yes, same girl," Mary Frances laughed.

"And she's your roommate?" he asked.

"Almost," said Mary Frances. "She's moving in with me as soon as this blizzard is over. I have a two-bedroom apartment, and we could share expenses. I've only known her one day, but I like her."

"OK, Mary Frances Foster," said Matt. "Let's see about your flour. Do you remember there's a secret door in the pantry and one in the book case?" Mary Frances nodded. "Well, there's another one. In fact, there's always another one." Mary Frances looked at him, questioningly. "I'm going to show you something now. I don't want to upset you, and no, it's not a torture chamber."

Mary Frances followed him to a rack with various cleaning supplies, some old, paint cans, and newspapers all the while thinking, *Did Sophia tell him...? And I was embarrassed about falling asleep last night!* Matt reached up to a hole in the concrete wall, pushing an unseen button. The rack moved back and disappeared into a dark doorway. *Another room,* thought Mary Frances.

Mary Frances slowly walked in, not sure what she was seeing. "What is this place?" she asked. In the center of the sizeable room were warehouse racks like the ones used in the Veritas cafeteria full of food. Canned goods, dehydrated food, and freeze dried food. Stacked four high and covering 25 feet of wall were white, sealed pails, each one labeled with a date and either *wheat, rice*, or *beans*. On the opposite wall was a rack holding black rifles with green, military ammunition boxes stacked underneath. "Matt, what is this? Why do you have all this?" she asked, a bit shocked.

"Do you remember what we were talking about last night?" he asked. "How there is risk in the systems we are all so dependent on?"

"Yes, I remember," she answered, quietly.

"This allows us independence from those systems, if need be," he said.

"Do Fredèric and Sophia know this is here?" Mary Frances asked.

"Yes, they do," he answered. "In fact, they have a similar place on their farm back in Switzerland." He let her take it all in before explaining further.

"Mary Frances, there are a lot of people who are concerned about the future," he continued. "You might be surprised how many people have rooms like this and you don't realize it."

"Matt, why did you show me this?" Mary Frances asked.

"I'm not sure. My intuition told me to. I felt that I should," he said. "I will ask you not to tell anyone else about this. Can you promise me that?" She nodded her head. "Good. Now, let's get some wheat, and then we can talk more while we're firing the boiler and charging the batteries." They went to the wall lined with white, sealed pails, and Matt took one down from the stack. It was labeled *Durum*.

Mary Frances looked at all the pails and asked, "How much is in each bucket?"

"Roughly 40 pounds," he answered.

"No wonder Sophia was laughing when I asked if you had six cups!" Mary Frances said. "Matt, there's enough food here to last for years!"

"Depending on the number of people, yes there is."

"What is that back in the corner?" she asked, looking down one of the aisles at a machine coming out of the concrete floor."

"That's water," he said. "It's a well. If there was ever a problem, it wouldn't take but a few days for the water towers to run empty and then there would be no water when you turned on the tap. This cabin has its own well. It's electric, and as we're going to do in a minute, we make our own electricity." Matt opened the white pail and started scooping out three cups of durum wheat. Then he did the same with some Hard Winter Red. "Will six cups be enough?" he asked. "You can have more if you want."

"Six will be fine," Mary Frances responded.

"So, have I scared you again?" Matt asked as he replaced the lid on the pail and snapped it in place to seal the O-ring.

"I don't know, Matt. I don't know what to think," she answered. "Are you really worried that something will happen that will make all this necessary?"

"Let's go upstairs and get the boiler going, and we'll talk about it," he said as they went back through the two secret doors and up the stairs to the pantry. Mary Frances then followed him to the workshop. Matt opened the firebox door on the boiler and lit the fire that was already built. "I always keep the fires built so that if I need to get it going quickly, I'm not wasting time splitting kindling." Next, he walked over to the woodpile, opened a trap door in the floor and threw 25 pieces of firewood down the chute to the woodburner room. Taking a couple of folding chairs from the corner, he placed them in front of the boiler. "Let's sit here, so we can watch the gauges and enjoy the warmth at the same time."

Mary Frances studied all the gauges and valves coming from the boiler. *Is this for real? And what does all this cost? And why is he showing this to me? He said I might be surprised at how many people have preparations like this. Really? I do like him, but is this normal? Everything else about him seems normal.*

"Mary Frances, I hope you don't think I'm crazy," he said. "I don't want to scare you. Let me try to explain. First, everything you're seeing is preparation for the possibility that we could experience a problem, a problem that could disrupt the systems the world depends on. Second, I'm not saying there will be a problem because I don't know. No one can predict the future. Third, it's my belief we are more likely to have a problem than in years past."

"Matt, how do you afford all this?" she asked. "I'm sure you make more money than I do, but all this is really expensive. I'm taking in Dagny as a roommate to share expenses so I can start saving to someday buy a house. And Matt... all the guns back in the storage room... those are assault rifles, aren't they?"

"I'm pretty sure I make more money than you do, but I did get a jump sharp financially when my uncle passed away 10 years ago. He had no children, and he left his estate to me. He, too, was concerned about the future. We had talked about it when I was a teenager. There was a letter that was included in his trust, advising me to prepare. Yes, this is a very nice place for someone 33 years old, and what's underground makes it even more expensive. So, between my salary and my inheritance from my uncle, that's how I've paid for it.

"Now, let's discuss the rifles. Yes, they are what some people call assault rifles, but I don't like to call them that. They aren't for assaulting; they're for defending. Part of the system society depends on is law enforcement. If law enforcement ever disappeared, we have to be prepared to defend ourselves."

"But the police won't just disappear," Mary Frances said. "That doesn't make sense."

Matt leaned forward and opened the firebox door on the boiler. He moved the burning firewood inside with a poker and put in three more pieces of wood. "I don't literally mean they disappear," he said. "But they could disappear from their jobs. Mary Frances, how many policemen does it take to keep you in line, to keep you from robbing banks, dealing drugs and murdering people?"

Mary Frances chuckled and said, "Well, none, of course, because I don't do those things. There's nothing to stop with me or others like me."

"That's the reason we have relatively few policemen," Matt explained. "There are three kinds of people out there. Fortunately, the majority are good people who don't need any encouragement to behave in a civil and moral fashion. But then there are those who would break the law if they thought they could get away with it. And there are the ones who are going to cause mayhem, no matter what. So, you see, the police are a deterrent to crime. The fear of getting caught and going to prison keeps those people in check.

"Now consider this. What if the power is out, there's no water, and people are hungry? Everybody, even decent, law-abiding people will be looking for food and water. Are there enough police to stop them from breaking in houses or from taking food and water by force?" Mary Frances pondered the question and slowly nodded her head in understanding. "Let's say it's time for a policeman to go to work, but he's afraid to leave his family because he feels he needs to stay home to protect them; the police effectively will *disappear*. With no police, the situation deteriorates because people start to understand there is no consequence for breaking the law. There would be no one to protect you but yourself. You must rely on yourself."

Having taken it all in, Mary Frances said, "So, all that food has been stockpiled because the grocery stores would empty out quickly, and truck drivers would become too afraid to deliver more food." Matt nodded his head as she continued. "And if the people at the waterworks don't go to work to run the water department, we would be without water. And medicine... people couldn't get their prescriptions refilled."

"It can be overwhelming if you think about it too much," Matt said. "Hopefully, we live our lives and nothing like this happens. It's important to not miss out on today because of worrying about tomorrow." They sat in silence for a moment as Mary Frances continued processing the discussion. Matt wondered how she was taking it. He was encouraged by her calm demeanor.

"We're almost up to pressure, so I'm going to turn on the steam engine and charge the batteries. Now, we watch the pressure gauge and from time to time pump more water into the boiler. That reroutes the used steam into the condenser and back to this tank. We use the hand pump to move water back into the boiler when it gets too low. Look at this sight glass on the side of the boiler. The water should not get below this line." The engine came to life as Matt turned on the steam. The alternator began generating electricity. "The battery bank is down to 12.9 volts, so we'll charge until we get it up to the mid-14s. Mary Frances just watched and thought, *People wouldn't believe this. I hardly do. But seeing is believing!*

"May I change the subject for a minute?" asked Matt as he applied a drop of oil on the crosshead of the steam engine.

"Yes, of course," said Mary Frances. "Let's talk about something else for a while."

"OK," Matt said. "Mary Frances, are you seeing anyone? Do you have a boyfriend?"

"Me? No, of course not," she answered, laughing nervously. *And I was expecting a less intense topic of conversation,* she thought.

"That's good!" he said. "Because when the blizzard is over and life is back to normal, I'm going to ask you out on a date."

Mary Frances was at a loss for words. *What am I going to do? Nothing, Mary Frances. When the snow melts, you'll go get your car, and get your life back to normal. It will be like this never happened.* "Oh, Matt, you can't ask me on a date," she said.

"Of course I can, and I will," he responded. "I've got to tell you something. I haven't had this much fun in ages. I really enjoy you. Your personality. You're smart and genuine. And being pretty doesn't hurt either," he smiled.

"Stop that," she said, blushing. "I'm not smart, and I'm certainly not pretty. Besides... we both work at Veritas, and my boss has forbidden such as that. I'm on the first floor; you're on the sixth."

"You must be in denial because you're very smart and

very pretty, 'Miss I have a Master's degree and don't tell anyone.' And as far as Mrs. Joiner is concerned, I outrank her. There's no policy against me asking you out on a date. I showed you all this so you'll know what you're getting into if we started dating. There aren't any other secrets like ex-wives and children."

Mary Frances closed her eyes and listened to the *chuck, chuck, chuck* of the steam engine, trying to decide what to say or do. *Sophia is right. He does like me. He has shown me a private side of his life. I do want to go out with him. But it will never work.*

After a few moments of silence, Matt asked, "Have I upset you? Some people might consider me to be paranoid, but I consider myself just better prepared than most." Mary Frances remained quiet. "Unless you don't feel the same, but I think you do," he added.

"Matt, I do like you," she said at last. "I don't find myself attracted to very many men. I don't dislike them; I just don't let myself think about them like that." Her mind raced as she debated how much to divulge. "I have had the best time here with you. I would never have believed being snowed in could be like this. I almost wish the snow would never melt." *Why did I say that? I've not been completely honest, but I just want this last day or two with him. It's perfect.*

"Is something wrong, Mary Frances?" he asked, sensing she was troubled.

"Matt, why would you want to date me? There are so many attractive women where we work. Some are absolutely beautiful. You could have your pick," she said.

"And what makes you think you're not one of those beautiful women?" he asked as she rolled her eyes. "Yes, there are lots of pretty women at Veritas, but they're so plastic. I've dated some of the them, and one time is all it takes. They're fake. They like me because of my position. They have no interest in me. And they will do *anything* to keep my attention."

Matt stood up and moved the pump handle to put more water in the boiler, then opened the firebox door to check the fire. "I need to stay here and watch the boiler, but I'd like more coffee. Would you mind going to the kitchen? Maybe you'd like some, too."

"Yes, good idea," Mary Frances said, glad to have a break.

"Be thinking about how you want the flour- fine, medium or coarse," said Matt. "I'll set the grind on the mill, so we're ready when the batteries are finished." Mary Frances picked up the coffee cups. As she headed for the kitchen, she could feel his eyes on her.

Calling back, she asked, "Can I have two cups milled fine, and four cups medium? Just blend the two types of wheat."

"You can," he smiled.

Mary Frances almost ran out of the workshop, leaving the door ajar. *Oh, my God! He makes me nervous, the way he looks at me. And, how crazy is this- I'm supposed to be struggling to keep warm in a blizzard. Instead, I wish I could freeze time and stay here with Matt forever.*

Mary Frances returned to the workshop with two coffees, having had a chance to regain her composure. Matt thanked her and asked, "Was something said about raspberry tarts this morning?"

"Yes," said Mary Frances. "The fine flour is for the tarts. The medium is for the bread."

Once the batteries were charged, Matt shut off the steam; the engine stopped. Then, he switched the belt from the alternator to the mill. Mary Frances poured two cups of wheat into the mill hopper as Matt turned on the steam and very quickly they had two cups of fine flour. Stopping the steam again, he changed the grind to medium, then turned the steam back on while Mary Frances poured; they quickly had four cups of medium flour.

"I love this," Mary Frances said, excitedly. "Flour this fresh will make some wonderful raspberry tarts for dinner this evening." Matt listened and smiled, enjoying her delight in such a simple thing as flour. "Matt, I just thought of something. Your stove is gas, but isn't the oven electric? Won't that use a lot of electricity from the batteries?"

Matt laughed and said, "Don't tell me again that you're not smart. Yes, it would use a lot of electricity, but the Chateau has two ovens. The one on the left is electric, but the one on the right is gas. Just use the one on the right, and you'll be fine. And if that doesn't work, there's a wood-fired oven out back.

I'd just need to shovel the snow off it first."

"You have a wood-fired oven?" Mary Frances marveled. "I love bread from a wood oven, of course pizza, too. But no, the oven in the house will do. I'll just have to suffer and use the La Cornue," Mary Frances teased, pretending to roll her eyes and shake her head. Matt laughed.

"You'll have to come back when the snow has melted. We can make pizzas in the wood oven," Matt suggested.

"I would like that very much," she said. *What am I doing? I'm leading him on. I'm acting like I want him to ask me on a date. I'll have to refuse. Maybe he'll forget about me when the blizzard is over. But he's so much fun to be with. And Dagny is right. He is handsome.*

"OK, the flour is ready. I'm going to bleed off the steam and shut down the boiler. Later today, I want to call the wrecker service about getting your car back on the road," Matt said, watching her as she left for the kitchen. He was still trying to understand her reluctance to answer his question from their earlier conversation.

Mary Frances found Sophia busy in the kitchen as it was close to lunchtime. "It looks like Matt did have enough flour after all," she said, teasing Mary Frances as she placed the bowls of flour on the island.

Mary Frances smiled and said, "My goodness, yes. Now I see what you meant. Matt said you have extra supplies like that in your home in Switzerland."

"We do," she answered. "We have a small farm up in the mountains. Switzerland has always been very prepared for emergencies. I guess it's because we're so small. There are only a few ways into our country because of the mountains. We can dynamite those passes and completely cut our country off from the world. Back home, every man from age 18-50 is in the army. They all have an FN FAL rifle and 1,000 rounds of ammunition at home. That's normal for us. Almost everyone keeps extra food at home, too. Some more than others. Frederic and I have two cows and six goats on our farm, so we make our own cheese. Does this seem strange to you, Mary Frances?"

"Yes, kind of," she said. "I grew up in the city. I've never considered what would happen if there was no food or electricity. And the guns scare me. I don't like guns."

"I know," said Sophia, softly. "But there are evil people in the world. From almost the very beginning, evil people have been killing others. Remember Cain murdering Abel in the Bible? Evil has been with us since then. If you are unable to defend yourself, you will perish. Because we have been fortunate enough to always live in peace, we may forget that evil exists, but it's always there. We don't have guns to harm people but to defend from evil."

"Matt was in the army, wasn't he?" asked Mary Frances and Sophia nodded. "So, he's used guns?"

Sophia nodded. "Does that frighten you?" she asked.

"Yes," Mary Frances said. "The guns do, but Matt doesn't."

"He's a good man," Sophia assured her. "Fredèric and I know him quite well. You can trust him."

Mary Frances went to her bedroom and closed the door. Picking up her phone, she sat on the bed and called her mother in Charlotte. She halfway didn't expect her mother to answer.

"Hello."

"Hello, Mom. It's Mary Frances."

"Oh, hi. I saw you called a few days back. I meant to return the call. How are you? Did you get any snow in Nashville?"

"Yes, Mom. We got a lot of snow and ice."

"Really. You didn't lose electricity, did you?"

"We did, but we got it back quickly. How are things in Charlotte?"

"We got a little snow, not much. I hate to cut it short, but George is waiting on me. We're going to the movies. We'll talk soon."

"OK. Bye, Mom."

Mary Frances sat on the bed, holding the phone. As always, her mother was distant. Mary Frances had cringed at the mention of George's name. Shaking it off, she dialed another number.

"Dagny! It's Mary Frances. How are you? Do you have electricity?"

"Mary Frances! No, we've lost electricity! It's really cold in here! We're all wearing so many layers of clothes we can hardly move. How 'bout you?"

"Yes, we have power. Ours went out, too, but Mr. Archer has a backup system, so we're fine."

"Are you lucky or what!? We're running out of food fast, and I think it will be gone by tomorrow. Hopefully, by Saturday or Sunday, we can get out to a grocery store and buy some supplies. Oh! And, Mary Frances, we have another crisis. We're almost out of toilet paper! I don't know what we're going to do."

"We're OK on food. We have enough. When this is over and you can make it to my apartment, you're welcome to move in."

"Thank you, thank you, thank you. I want to take a nice, hot shower so badly. The water heater here is electric, so no hot water. Don't tell me, Mr. Archer has lots of hot water, too. I'm envious, really envious! I'm not going to take food or heat or hot water for granted again. Or toilet paper!"

"We can talk about all this when you get moved in. I'm sure we'll both have lots of stories to tell."

"But everything's alright with you, Mary Frances? Mr. Archer is still treating you OK?"

"Yes, I'm fine Dagny. I'll see you in a few days."

"If I don't answer my phone, it's because it's dead. There's no way to charge it. But I can charge it when I start my car. I'll see you soon, Mary Frances. Bye!"

The conversation with her friend left Mary Frances feeling almost guilty. She glanced over at the white cord that was charging her phone. Through the window, there was ice coating the trees and snow drifts as far as she could see. Walking into the bathroom, she opened the cabinet under the sink and found stacks of toilet paper. *I've taken all this for granted,* she thought. *There's no concern for food here, but Dagny is almost out. Millions are suffering, cold and hungry.* Then, reflecting on the past few days, she felt blessed.

It's because of Matt, she decided. *He found me and brought me here. And to think I didn't want to go with him at first. And he likes me. He thinks I'm fun. Nobody thinks I'm fun. Well, that will change when he finds out how boring I am. But he's never going to find out because very soon the snow will melt. I'll be gone, and he'll never give me a second thought. There will be no date. He's not going to bring me back to make pizza in the wood oven. This will all seem like a dream.* Mary Frances left her bedroom to return to the kitchen. The fire crackled as she walked through the great room that was toasty and warm.

"We just hit 0 degrees, or 32 degrees as you Yanks say," said Fredèric. "It's starting to melt outside."

"Looks like a good day for a hike. Are you interested, Mary Frances?" asked Matt as he walked to the French doors and surveyed the snow.

Before she could answer, Fredèric interrupted. "Sophia, I'm going to call the airline and see about getting our flight back home rescheduled for Sunday," he said. "There's no telling how backed up the airports are from all this."

Why did Matt ask me to go on a hike? Mary Frances wondered. *Does he want to be alone with me? Or is he only being polite?*

Matt glanced back toward the island where Fredèric and the women were eating their sandwiches. "Mary Frances, let's call a wrecker service and find out how backed up they are," said Matt. "With the melting, maybe the main highways are starting to look better. I'll see if we can schedule them for Sunday. If it all works out, we can take Fredèric and Sophia to the airport and then meet the wrecker at your car. How does that sound?"

He's taking care of me again, she thought. "Thank you," she said. "Do you think my car will start?"

"I'm optimistic," Matt said. "You didn't crash into anything. You just gently slid down the hill, slowly spinning. It was a soft landing. I think your car may be OK."

"I hope so," she said. "That was a wild ride because I couldn't stop or steer. I couldn't tell what was happening; it was the strangest feeling."

"It could have been much worse," said Sophia. "But... Oh, wait! You got stuck here with us for three days!" The guys laughed.

"It's been wonderful," said Mary Frances. "You have all been so gracious. I felt guilty as I was talking to my friend, Dagny. She's in an apartment with three other girls. They have no electricity. Their food is almost gone. And they're running low on toilet paper. It made me think about what Matt and Frederic were explaining last night. None of that had occurred to me before. Dagny will be OK because in a day or two she can get out and buy supplies, but this was only a little blizzard. It's only been a few days. And to think, what would happen if a problem lasted longer?"

As everyone finished lunch, Matt asked, "Can I interest anyone in a cappuccino?" All were in favor. Matt filled the La Pavoni espresso machine with water, and Mary Frances got out the cups and milk. Sophia and Frederic went to the great room, and Frederic added more wood to the fire.

"Thanks for helping, Mary Frances," Matt said.

"It's not work. I like to help you," she said. *How could I not like this? Cappuccinos in front of the fireplace, snow outside, a handsome man... and those blue eyes!*

"Mary Frances?" Matt said. She suddenly realized he was talking to her. "Mary Frances, Earth to Mary Frances." She smiled and nodded. "Fill up this frothing pitcher to this mark," he instructed. They quickly made four cappuccinos. As Matt was adding the frothed milk to the last one, he said, "I've tried and tried, but I just can't do the espresso art- you know, the leaves and hearts. I've watched baristas do it, but I just can't seem to get the hang of it."

Mary Frances laughed and said, "Finally, something you can't do!" Matt smiled. Each carried two cappuccinos into the great room where Frederic and Sophia were waiting.

After sipping coffee for a minute, Frederic said, "So, you don't have any thoughts as to why it's happening, Matthew?"

Mary Frances sat back and watched Matt, curious to hear his response. "No, only theories," he began. "Some of Thomas Jefferson's writings are interesting. When he was stationed in France after the revolution, he made some observations I find intriguing. Paris, at the time, was one of the largest cities in the world. Compared to the urban areas Jefferson had seen in our country, it was huge. He noticed a difference in people. Of course, Jefferson was a big agrarian. He believed that the country life is not only the best life, but the one we were created to live. I've no idea if he had an influence on them, but it's interesting to see people like Thoreau espousing the same thing a few decades later. Anyway, Jefferson thought the Parisians were weak. Not only decadent, but helpless. He worried about how our country would be when most of the people lived in cities. He worried that we would become weak, too. I think it was one of the factors that caused him to pursue the Louisiana Purchase. More land meant more frontier... more opportunities for us to live close to the land instead of in cities."

"Do you think that's true... that living in a city weakens people?" asked Sophia.

"Perhaps," said Matt. "There's a lady at Veritas whose family has lived in a house with a fireplace for 10 years and never built a fire. They don't know how. Is that because they live in a city, or because they have a furnace to keep them warm? Perhaps it's all the same thing. The more things we don't do for ourselves, the more dependent we become. They have a fireplace to keep warm if the power goes out, but not the ability to use it. It's one thing to not build a fire, but it's another to not build the fire because you don't know how."

"Last night you mentioned the school shootings. Would that have anything to do with not knowing how to build a fire? I know that sounds odd, but is there a connection?" asked Sophia.

"Some might say that not being able to build a fire means that the individual has lost touch with his world. He's lost," Matt said. "The land, the trees, the firewood, the fire- those were all normal parts of our world just a few years ago. But for the children of today, the world is not real. It's video games, movies, social media. People don't even have to go to a store any more to shop. They certainly don't grow or kill their own food. They find a mate by reading a profile on a dating site."

"Or you could always pull one out of a car in a snowbank," said Fredèric.

"Fredèric, stay on the subject," said Sophia as she gave

him a stern look. Fredèric smiled, proud of his own cleverness.

Mary Frances tried to steer the conversation by asking, "And as people lose touch with the creation, do they lose touch with the Creator?"

"Yes, I think so," Matt responded. "To me, it's all connected. It's not that living in a city removes the connection to God. But living in a world that increasingly rejects God, you lose God. Without God, everything is meaningless, and a world without meaning is a frightening prospect. Evil creeps into the world. It drives people insane and causes them to do horrific things." The group became very quiet in their thoughts.

"I told you she was smart," Matt said.

Just then Fredèric's cell phone rang. After taking the call, he said, "OK, we're good to go for Sunday. We need to be to the Nashville airport by 10:00 am. Can you take us, Matt?"

"I think that can be arranged," Matt said. "Mary Frances, I'm going to call the wrecker service and see if we can get an appointment for one in the afternoon. We can deliver the Steiners to the airport, eat lunch, and then get your car out. I'm not sure if there will be many restaurants open by Sunday. We'll see."

Matt got up, threw another log on the fire and stepped away from the group as he called the wrecker service. Finished with the conversation, he returned and reported, "Sunday it is, airport at 10:00, wrecker at 1:00. The wrecker guy was relieved that we didn't need want him today. The snow plows have one lane open on the interstates. He said most of the roads are still impassable, but it's melting. People have been airlifted out of stalled cars and put in high school gymnasiums. The 101st out of Fort Campbell has been helping with that, using their helicopters to rescue stranded people. They've been delivering pallets of MRE's with Chinooks."

"Let's turn on TV and see what the news is saying," said Sophia.

"I hope things are looking up," Matt said as he picked up the remote and turned on the TV. Switching to a local station, they watched a reporter in a helicopter flying over Nashville. The snow was so deep that in places it was impossible to tell where the streets were. Cars were bumps under a white blanket of snow. Mary Frances thought about one of those bumps being her car. Her mind ran through the past few days. *Veritas, Mrs. Joiner, Dagny telling Mr. Borland to leave the cafeteria... that seems so long ago. Will these four days be a distant memory when this is over?*

The news wasn't all bad. When the report was finished, everyone felt more positive. The snow was melting and people were being helped. Matt turned off the television and said, "I'm starting to get a bad case of cabin fever. I'd like to take Mary Frances for a short walk out in the snow. "Sophia, would you mind loaning her your snow suit and boots?" Matt asked. "Your gear may be a little big, but it should work for a short walk."

"Of course," said Sophia. "It'll work. Mary Frances, what do you think?"

"Sure," she answered. "But we're making bread and raspberry tarts for dinner tonight. Could I make the bread dough first so it could be rising while we take our walk?"

"Good idea," answered Sophia. "It's kind of lucky Fredèric and I lost at pinochle. It gives me the opportunity to hone my cooking skills with you, Mary Frances. Your lamb chops were amazing!"

"I'm glad to help," said Mary Frances, "and I am so sorry about the pinochle game."

"Don't apologize," said Matt. "If you're good, it's not bragging; it's just a fact!" They all laughed as Mary Frances blushed at his praise.

Soon enough the dough was done, two batches. One batch, for the raspberry tarts, was wrapped and waiting in the refrigerator. The second batch, for the whole-wheat bread, was rising on the island.

Sophia outfitted Mary Frances in her snow suit to wear over the sweat pants and hoodie. Matt met them in the kitchen, already suited up in camouflaged coveralls and the same parka he'd been wearing when he pulled Mary Frances out of the snow bank. "She has on three pairs of socks so my boots aren't so big," said Sophia.

"We won't be gone long," Matt said to the Steiners as he and Mary Frances stepped out onto the back deck. "Let's walk around to the front of the cabin and up the drive," Matt said, helping Mary Frances manage the three steps of the deck. "I'd like to see what the road looks like. How are those boots doing?"

"I wish I'd had them the day of the blizzard," Mary Frances said. "They're very nice. Warm and dry. My feet aren't cold at all."

They carefully trudged through the deep snow. "If we were going very far, I'd use snow shoes," Matt said. "But they're kind of hard to walk in, making it easy to trip." Noticing she was having trouble keeping up, Matt slowed down and offered a hand to steady her. "Let's walk up the drive to the road and see if anyone's been down it. I don't expect it to be plowed."

The one-lane drive wound through the woods. Mary Frances remembered that when they had first arrived, she'd hardly been able to see a thing. "It's so pretty, the snow," she said. "And so quiet. All I hear is the sound of our boots crunching in the snow." She liked holding his hand even though it was through two pairs of gloves.

Reaching the end of the driveway, Matt said, "Well, it looks like only one or two cars have been down my road. Even with melting, there will still be lots of snow on Sunday. But it'll be no problem for the Range Rover."

"I really like your SUV," Mary Frances said. "I'd never ridden in one of those before."

"Thank you," Matt said. "Range Rovers can do things most other vehicles can't. Sand, mud, fording rivers, just to name a few. And range. It can travel over 600 miles on one tank. The ability to go great distances without refueling could be important someday."

Turning around, the two headed back to the cabin. As they trekked through the heavy snow, Mary Frances thought, *I'm liking this way too much. I must keep control of my emotions. He said he's going to ask me on a date, but I doubt it. When he doesn't, I can't be disappointed. I'd have to turn him down anyway.*

"Are you frozen?" Matt asked, reaching the steps to the deck.

"No, I'm actually warm from the exercise," she answered. "That was a workout."

"Let's get back inside so you can work some magic on those raspberry tarts," he said. Before entering the kitchen, they stomped their boots on the deck to knock off the snow. Once inside, they began removing boots. Matt noticed Mary Frances was having trouble with hers. "Sit down here, and I'll help you," Matt said, pulling out a chair for Mary Frances. She sat down and extended a boot. When he tugged at the boot, it didn't give but pulled her forward in the chair. "It's stuck," he said.

Matt went down on one knee and rested her leg on his other knee. Then taking the calf of her leg in his left hand and pulling on the boot with the right, he freed the boot. *Oh, my*, she thought, *Who knew this could be so much fun? He's very strong, but gentle. I'd walk ten miles in the snow just to have him help me with my boots again.* Matt winked at her as he placed her foot back on the floor. Then he removed the other boot. But before releasing her foot, he tickled it. Mary Frances squealed and jerked her foot away while Matt laughed.

"That's just a test to make sure you don't have frostbite," he laughed.

Mary Frances found herself trying to suppress a smile. *He is just so charming! What am I going to do? I'm going to get back to my life and away from him. Oh! I don't want the snow to melt.*

"What's going on here?" said Sophia, appearing in the kitchen to find Matt kneeling at Mary Frances' feet.

"Just helping with her boots," Matt answered, smiling and winking again at Mary Frances. "OK, break's over, Mary Frances Foster. Time to get back to work!" Mary Frances took off the snow suit while Matt went to his bedroom to change his clothes.

"Can I watch as you do the tarts and the bread?" asked Sophia.

"Certainly," said Mary Frances. "You can help me, and then I'll help you with dinner. Have you decided on this evening's menu?"

"I've checked the fridge. What do you think of steak, baked potato, and asparagus with hollandaise sauce?" asked Sophia. "I know Matt and Frederic would like that."

"That sounds great!" said Mary Frances. "You can't go

wrong with that menu."

"Any ideas of what we could do to make it a little different?" asked Sophia.

"One suggestion would be searing the steaks, then finishing them in the oven," explained Mary Frances. "You could finish them with tarragon butter. I believe we have the ingredients. Have you tried that before?"

"No, but it sounds wonderful!" said Sophia. "Don't tell the men what we're doing. Fredèric was bragging on your lamb chops with the cherry sauce. I want to surprise him with the filet."

"Of course. Your secret is safe with me," whispered Mary Frances. "I need to work on the bread and tarts now. Then, I'll show you how to make tarragon butter. We only have one gas oven because of the power outage, so I want to get the bread and tarts done before you need the oven for the filets." Sophia smiled, nodding her head, and the two women started to work.

Back in the great room, Fredèric and Matt sat by the fire. "How was your hike?" asked Fredèric. "What did the road look like?"

"Tracks from maybe two cars. There will be plenty of snow to push through on Sunday, but by then maybe some of the highways will be plowed," Matt said.

"This has been fun," said Fredèric. "I'm almost glad we had to rescue your friend. It's been fun for Sophia to have another woman here. I've enjoyed her as well, not to mention her cooking."

"She's interesting," said Matt quietly, so the two in the kitchen couldn't overhear them. "She is such a refreshing change from what I've been used to lately. Did I tell you what happened about three months ago?" Fredèric shook his head. "Well, it was after five o'clock. I was working late, compiling the GDP numbers for Europe for the meeting the next morning. This girl from accounting walked into my office. I didn't know who she was. I just knew she wasn't from my department. Anyway, she said nothing, closed my door behind her and walked right up to my desk. She was wearing a maroon dress that wrapped around and tied on the side. Without saying a word, she pulled the bow, and the dress unwrapped and fell off. There she stood in black bra and panties."

"Oh, my God, Matt," said Fredèric. "What did you do?"

"Well, Fredèric, I laid her down on my desk, and ...." Matt said as Fredèric leaned forward, hanging on every word. Matt waited a second to build the suspense, then laughed. "I'm kidding, Fredèric. I told her to put her dress back on. I mean, she was beautiful, but to think she would do that. I felt sorry for her."

"God, things are complicated today," said Fredèric.

"Definitely," Matt said. "And with men getting in trouble for sexual harassment... You never hear about what some of the women do. It's true some men take advantage of their positions. Veritas has a guy on the sixth floor who's problematic. More investigation is needed, but I strongly suspect we're going to terminate him. But honest to God, Fredèric, that's what she did."

"Now, back to your story, Matt," Fredèric said. "You left off with a naked woman in your office. Then what happened?"

"She stood there for a few moments just looking at me, waiting. She was kind of like a deer in the headlights. I never reacted," said Matt. "Then, she picked up her dress and put it back on. As she got to the door to leave she said, 'Please, don't tell anyone.' And I haven't, until now. You live on the other side of the world."

"Wow," said Fredèric. "I've had girls hit on me in a bar or at a Christmas party but nothing that brazen."

"But, my point is this," said Matt. "Last night, Mary Frances went to sleep on my shoulder, right here on the sofa. When she woke up, she was distressed. It was as if she'd done something terrible. She was really embarrassed."

"I see what you mean," said Fredèric. "What a contrast!"

Matt got up from the leather sofa, threw a log on the fire and opened the liquor cabinet. "How about something to drink?" offered Matt. "I've got some Woodford Reserve here... official bourbon of the Kentucky Derby. Would you like some?" Fredèric replied in the affirmative, and the two men relaxed by the fire, enjoying the bourbon as they talked about the world.

Chapter 6
Tarragon

"Wow, I've never had a New York strip this good," said Fredèric. "How did you do this?" Sophia smiled and glanced over at Mary Frances.

"It's just a new recipe I decided to try," Sophia said. "It's finished in tarragon butter in the oven after I seared it on a cast iron skillet."

"Tarragon butter?" said Fredèric, looking at his wife skeptically. Then he moved his attention to Mary Frances who quickly looked down at her filet and started cutting another piece. Matt smiled, watching the exchange.

"You'd better write down that secret recipe for tarragon butter before you forget it, Sophia," teased Matt. The men strongly suspected the tarragon butter was a Mary Frances creation but praised Sophia's filets just the same.

"I can't wait for dessert," said Sophia, trying to get the conversation off tarragon butter. "Mary Frances' tarts are as light as a feather. And how about a movie tonight? Everything works, so we could find a movie on Netflix or Amazon Prime. We could look on the Dish menu, too. What kind of movies do you like, Mary Frances?"

"I don't like scary movies or movies with a lot of violence," she answered.

"That eliminates about 90% of them," laughed Fredèric.

"I'm sure we can find something," said Matt. "We'll let you two girls pick the movie."

"I don't know if that's a good idea!" said Fredèric.

Sophia's dinner was a complete success, and Mary Frances' raspberry tarts were the grand finale. The girls cleaned up the kitchen while the men carried more firewood to the great room and refilled the woodburner in the basement. When the men came back upstairs, Mary Frances and Sophia had relocated to the great room, searching for movies on Dish. "We've found a movie! It starts in 10 minutes!" said Sophia.

"What is it?" asked Fredèric.

"*Dirty Dancing*!" said Sophia.

"Oh, no. Not *Dirty Dancing*!" exclaimed Fredèric. "Matt, it's your house. You can veto the movie decision."

"True, but I like that movie, and I haven't seen it in a long time. Besides, we have some real talent in the kitchen, and we want to keep them happy," said Matt. "Ten minutes is just enough time to make some popcorn. Mary Frances, come help me." Fredèric knew he'd lost. Mary Frances went to the kitchen with Matt, leaving Sophia smiling in the big, leather chair.

Just as the movie was starting, Matt and Mary Frances came around the corner with two bowls of popcorn. Matt handed his bowl to Sophia and then sat down next to Mary Frances on the sofa.

"I love to watch them dance," Mary Frances whispered to Matt.

"You remember Baby's name is Frances, don't you?" Matt said. "Do you like to dance?"

"No, I don't know how," she answered.

"Does that mean you can't dance like you can't play pinochle?" kidded Fredèric.

"Well, I can't dance like they do," smiled Mary Frances. "Patrick Swayze is such a good teacher."

"He is," Matt whispered to her. "I like it when he's trying to teach her how to follow. So, do you know how to follow?"

Mary Frances caught herself scooting closer. Her internal dialogue resumed its tug-of-war. *You shouldn't do this. It's magical to feel him next to me. Why are you letting this happen?* "My turn to put another log on the fire," Mary Frances said.

When she returned to the sofa, Matt whispered, "Are you cold?"

"A little," she said. Matt reached down to the side of the sofa and found a blanket that he spread over them. Then, he put his arm on the back of the leather sofa as she snuggled closer. *I don't want to go back on Sunday. If only time could stop. Is he just being nice to me, or does he really like me? Maybe he will ask me on a date; I could be honest and tell him. Oh, but that would end everything.*

The four watched the movie and enjoyed the fire in the cozy, cabin ambience. And for Mary Frances, it did seem like time had frozen. Outside, the world was cold and silent. Millions of people struggled to keep warm while waiting for electricity to be restored. But inside, the refuge of the cabin was snug and intimate. The movie ended with the dance at Kellerman's, and Frances finally got the courage to do the lift. Sophia applauded and Mary Frances quietly wiped away tears.

"Great movie," said Matt. "Good choice." Fredèric rolled his eyes.

"Well, I've had enough fun for this evening. It's time to head to bed," Fredèric said with a yawn. He stood and stretched.

"Yes, that was fun!" Sophia agreed then gave her husband a big hug. "Oh, Fredèric! Let's take lessons and learn to dance like that," she added enthusiastically.

Fredèric glared at Matt over her shoulder while silently mouthing the words, "See what you've done!" It took all the control Matt had to not laugh out loud.

"Goodnight, you two," Sophia said. As the Steiners left the room, Sophia continued, "Fredèric, we can start those lessons as soon as we get back to Switzerland." Matt knew better than to laugh. He and Mary Frances looked at each other and grinned.

Matt and Mary Frances were alone again. The great room was suddenly quiet. There was a faint smell of wood smoke from the fireplace. Mary Frances became lost in her thoughts as she watched the fire dance. He liked the way her hair shined in the firelight.

"Have you ever wondered what happened to Johnny and Baby?" Matt asked.

"Dagny and I were talking about something like that on Wednesday," Mary Frances answered. "People seem to divide themselves into groups. Johnny thinks he's not as good as Frances when he really is. And Mrs. Joiner in the cafeteria sees the world that way also. We're on the first floor, and they're on the sixth floor." Silence hung in the air as the two watched the fire. "For Johnny and Baby, for that short time in the summer, none of those rules existed. But when they left Kellerman's, the real world was waiting for them. And those divisions still exist."

"Those divisions only exist if we buy into them," Matt said, watching Mary Frances' eyes. "Johnny's belief that he was inferior made him inferior. All he had to do was reject the premise that he was inferior. But that's easier said than done sometimes." Matt got up and walked to the fireplace. He poked the logs and put two more pieces of firewood on the red coals.

"So, are you enjoying being snowed in? Are you glad you slid off the road, or can you not wait for Sunday?" Matt asked.

"Oh, Matt," she sighed. "It's like the movie. I've had the time of my life. I will never, ever forget these four days."

Matt walked back to the sofa and sat beside her. He reached out and gently placed his hand on her face. As he looked into her eyes, she knew. *Oh, my God! He's going to kiss me. Oh, I want him to kiss me, but... I mustn't.* Matt pulled Mary Frances to him. Electricity shot through her as their lips finally met. Hesitating for only a moment, she surrendered. Wrapping her arms around him, she felt transported to another dimension. The kiss was gentle at first, becoming more passionate as he kissed her again and again. She felt secure as his chest pressed against her. The touch of his tongue on her lips caused Mary Frances to shiver. *This isn't right*, she thought. *It's not being fair to him. But, I'm falling in love.*

"Mary Frances?" Matt asked, holding her carefully and brushing the hair from her face. "You're shaking."

"Umm.... I know," she responded. "I can't help it."

"Was that too fast?" he asked.

"No, ... Yes," she said. "It was wonderful. I've never

experienced a kiss like that. It's just...." Mary Frances broke into tears and sobbed against Matt's chest as he held her. Finally, able to speak, she said, "I'd like to go to bed now."

"Would you like to sleep here again... on the sofa with me?" he asked, carefully.

I want to be close to him. This is such a struggle. Seeing the tenderness in his eyes, she wondered if he had any idea of what she was feeling. She nodded her head, then wrapped her arms around him. As they reclined on the sofa, Matt threw the blanket over them and kissed her on the forehead. "If you wake up in the night," he said, "don't jump up and run to your bedroom. OK?"

"OK," she whispered softly. *What will I do when I have to go home? I love him.*

Chapter 7
Saturday

Saturday morning dawned clear and bright as the sunshine reflected off the snow. Looking out every window of the cabin, icicles hung from the gutters and sparkled like diamonds as they dripped and melted. Mary Frances woke up in Matt's arms to find Matt already awake. "Good morning, sleepy head," he said. "How'd you sleep?"

"I've never slept so well," Mary Frances answered. "I kept my promise. I'm still here."

"You did," Matt responded. "I slept very well, too. Whenever you're ready, let's make some coffee and see about breakfast."

"This is wonderful," said Mary Frances, "but we should get up before your other house guests find us here." The two lingered a few moments longer, enjoying each other's touch.

After breakfast, Matt went to the workshop and checked if power had been restored. It hadn't. He fired the boiler and ran the steam engine for several hours, recharging the battery bank. Once Sophia and Mary Frances tidied up the breakfast dishes, Mary Frances brought Matt another cup of coffee. Conversation turned to Veritas, family and God. The topics allowed them to explore each other's minds and begin discovering a compatibility. Matt was still somewhat puzzled by certain aspects of her. Shortly before lunch, as Matt and Mary Frances were sitting in lawn chairs monitoring the steam engine, Frederic arrived in the workshop.

Immediately, they sensed something was wrong.

"Matt, we turned on the news to see the weather. There's been a mall shooting in California and a bomb has gone off in Rome by the Vatican," Fredèric said, breathing hard like he'd run from the great room. Matt and Mary Frances quickly returned with him to the TV in the great room to listen to the report. As always, the news was vague at first. An unidentified person in Los Angeles had walked into a mall and started shooting. The death toll was 22 thus far with another 40 injured. In Rome, a delivery truck arriving in the Vatican had exploded by the Papal Palace, the residence of the Pope. There was no official word if the Pope had been injured. The news video from Rome showed dozens of ambulances, many police and pure chaos in St. Peter's Square.

"Oh, my God," said Sophia. "Not another one, and now the Vatican."

"What are you thinking, Matt?" asked Fredèric.

"The next 72 hours is critical," he responded. "We believe the frequency is important. Each incident is crucial, but society will hold together if there's enough time between incidents. When incidents start coming so fast that people become too afraid to continue performing their jobs is when everything starts to change."

"What do you mean, *everything starts to change*?" asked Mary Frances, looking up at Matt.

"People have become accustomed to shootings and terrorist attacks," Matt said. "No one likes it, but the fact is we're getting used to them. Because we're used to them, life goes on. We all go to work the next day and the world continues to function.

"Do you remember that after 9/11 the New York Stock Exchange was closed for a week? That's because everyone was so shook up that we were afraid the financial markets might crash simply from emotion. Do you know that restaurant revenue declined 50% for a month after the attack? People were either too afraid to leave the house or were so emotionally distraught that they didn't want to eat. But today, the markets, whether it's the stock market or the local restaurant, aren't affected by a shooting or a bomb. We've gotten used to it. But if they started happening every day, multiple times a day, across the country and the world, we think people would react. React by not going to work because of fear."

The four watched the TV in silence. Finally, Fredèric asked, "Matt, you're still running the *vacation index*?"

"Yes," Matt said, glancing at Mary Frances to see how she was handling it all.

"Any variation?" asked Fredèric.

"No, still within the normal range," Matt responded.

"If it moves out of normal, shoot me an email that goes something like, *Thinking about taking a vacation to Antarctica*," Fredèric said. Mary Frances was overwhelmed with the news report and the conversation that made very little sense to her. In frustration, she left the group and went to her bedroom, closing the door behind her.

"Maybe I'd better go check on her," Sophia offered.

"No, let me. I should," said Matt, leaving Sophia and Fredèric to monitor the news.

Matt knocked on Mary Frances' door. "Mary Frances, may I come in?"

Mary Frances, sitting on the edge of her bed, said, "Yes, of course."

Matt entered the bedroom and quietly closed the door behind him. "Are you OK?" he asked, concerned.

"Yes, I'm just confused," she said. "So often I don't know what you're talking about. And I hate to always be asking, *What does that mean?*"

"I'm sorry," Matt said. "That's rude of us. We shouldn't do that. May I explain it to you, the vacation index?"

"Please. That doesn't even make sense. What is it?" she said.

"It'll take a bit to explain, so kick off your shoes and make yourself comfortable," he said. Mary Frances did just that, scooting up on the bed and placing a pillow behind her back.

Matt paced in front of the bed in deep thought, considering what and how much to say. "Mary Frances, you've seen that my house is a little different than most. I've shown you things that I've not shown most people. You recognize there is a distinct possibility of problems in the future. We've talked about that." Mary Frances nodded her head. "Fredèric and I are not the only people who are aware of this. Many people have prepared for a *disruption of services.* Many people have bought places in the country, perhaps a small cabin with a wood burning stove and space for a garden. Others may have bought 3,000 acres in Montana and built an armored compound. Quite a few have homes in New Zealand, believing that island nation would be a safe haven if everything collapsed. These are real examples of people who have prepared for such an event. But how does anyone know how bad, *bad* must be before going to that safe place? How do you know when to get on a plane and fly to New Zealand or head to your place in the country? Part of what we do in the research department at Veritas is economic and financial research. Then there's another type of research for some of our clients, the clients who have prepared. We try to predict if collapse is imminent." Matt paused to assess Mary Frances' understanding and well-being.

"These examples, are they real people you know?" she asked.

"Yes, they are," Matt answered. "And there are thousands like them. Is this interesting? Shall I continue?" he asked.

"Yes, please," Mary Frances responded. "And tell me about the vacation index."

"One of the tools in our analysis is the vacation index. There's no way to determine what everyone is thinking, but there is a clever way to discover what CEO's are thinking. You've heard of the Standard and Poor's 500? That's the 500 biggest companies in the United States. The 500 individuals who are the CEO's of those companies are very wealthy. While we don't know about all of them, we do know that many of them are concerned about the future and have prepared for a collapse. When those CEO's, who have made preparations, decide to leave, then we will conclude they believe crisis is imminent. These people won't post on Facebook, *The World as We Know It Is About to End.* They will simply and quietly go on vacation. They will recognize they could be mistaken. They will hope they *are* mistaken. And if so, they can easily return from a relaxing and restful vacation. But if they're right, they are already out of the city and to their safe place where they will wait it out."

"But what if they've gone on a real vacation?" Mary Frances asked.

"We have 500 information collectors, one on the executive floor of each of the companies, who tell us when the boss is on vacation. The average for S&P 500 CEO's on vacation at any point in time is 12%, which can vary between 8% and 20%. But it's never been over 20%. If the world situation is looking questionable and we see the vacation index over 20%, we will start to get concerned because it means that universe of 500 intelligent and knowledgeable people is concerned, too."

"Then... the information collectors are like spies?" asked Mary Frances.

"You could say so," Matt said. "We don't disclose any specifics to anyone. We don't care which ones are on vacation. The only thing we care about is the percentage on vacation. And yes, we pay the collectors for the information. Some of the 500 are our clients, and they find this information interesting, too, especially when they're part of the data."

"My life used to be pretty simple," sighed Mary Frances. "I'd go to work. I'd pay my bills every month. Go to church on Sunday.... Then in less than a week, there's a blizzard, I have a roommate, I meet you and I'm afraid the world is going to end!"

"It's easy to say *don't worry about it*, but please, don't worry about it," Matt said, walking over to the side of the bed and sitting down next to Mary Frances. "The future always seems scary because it's unknown. A collapse may never happen, or it may happen 500 years from now. I'm almost sorry I've told you all this. I don't want you to be worried. And I'm concerned that by sharing all this with you, you may turn me down when I ask you out on a date."

Mary Frances looked down and closed her eyes.

"I can't go out with you, Matt."

Is this the right thing to say? Of course, he'll want a reason.

"Mary Frances, I am going to ask you out," Matt said. "You can say *no*. I'm a little confused because I'm almost 100% sure you like me and would like to go out with me. You're not married. You don't have a boyfriend."

Mary Frances gave Matt a nervous look. Matt smiled. "So unless you look me in the eye and say *I do not want to go out with you*, I'm going to ask you out," he said. Mary Frances put her face in her hands and said nothing. Matt reached out and put his hands on hers, leaned forward and kissed the top of her head. Then, without another word, he walked out of her bedroom.

The afternoon and evening passed in a solemn mood. The TV stayed on as they followed the developments from the mall shooting and the Vatican. Mary Frances came out of her bedroom around dinner time and helped Sophia with the meal. Mary Frances found some chicken breasts in the refrigerator and enough potatoes to mash. Sophia noticed her new friend's downcast demeanor and tried to talk to her about it, but Mary Frances wouldn't discuss it. After dinner, Mary Frances went to her room and closed the door. Even though the day wasn't a strenuous one, the news was; everyone was tired. Frederic and Sophia had a long day ahead of them, so they turned in early.

Matt had turned off the TV and was sitting on the sofa watching the fire when the door to Mary Frances' bedroom opened, and she walked out.

She sat next to Matt, looking down at her hands. When she looked up, she said, "I'm sorry. Please don't be upset. It's not you. It's me." Matt reached over and took her hand. "Can I have this last night?" she asked. "I have to remember all this. This has to last me forever."

"What do you mean? Do you want to sleep here on the sofa like we have before?" he asked. Mary Frances nodded her head. Matt pulled her to him, and she wrapped her arms around him. He laid back and adjusted the pillow behind his head while she rested her head on his chest. Matt threw a blanket over them.

Should I explain it to him? she thought. *This is such happiness. I don't want to ruin it.* Matt held her and wondered as to why she was so conflicted. The cabin was silent as it always was at night. Just far enough away from the traffic of the city, there was no sound of road noise or of airplanes overhead. The only sound being the crackling of the fire, the two soon fell asleep.

Chapter 8
The Thaw

Sunday morning arrived too soon in the cabin. Mary Frances lingered a few moments in that place between sleep and consciousness. She savored Matt's warmth and the rising and falling of his chest as he breathed. The steady rhythm of his heart held feelings of security and love. Slowly, she eased away from Matt's embrace, taking care not to disturb him.

In the kitchen, Mary Frances prepared a breakfast of scrambled eggs and sausage complimented with horseradish. Returning to the great room, she knelt by the sofa and momentarily watched Matt sleep before whispering in his ear, "Are you hungry? Breakfast is ready." Matt opened his eyes and smiled. "Stay right here," she whispered. "I'll bring it to you."

In no time, she was back with breakfast, placing it on the coffee table. As Matt rubbed the sleep from his eyes and put his feet on the floor, she went to work on the fire, moving the coals together and putting on more firewood.

The morning passed quickly as the group prepared to return to the lives they knew before the blizzard. Mary Frances returned the borrowed clothing to Sophia then began cleaning up the kitchen. She also took time to wander through the great room and into her bedroom, taking in every detail. She needed to remember.... forever. Fredèric and Sophia packed and rolled their suitcases to the garage ready to load in the Range Rover.

Matt checked the electricity and discovered service had been restored during the night. He switched the house back to grid mode. Across Middle Tennessee, power was being restored and people were starting to feel warm again for the first time in days.

When it was time to leave for the airport, Fredèric and Sophia said their goodbyes. "If you're ever in Switzerland, come see us," Sophia told Mary Frances as she hugged her. In a whisper, Sophia added, "I hope things work out for you and Matt. You make a nice couple." Mary Frances smiled. Once everyone was in the Range Rover, the garage door opened, and the diesel engine came to life. Slowly and without a slip, the heavy SUV backed out into the snow, then proceeded down the drive and through the woods.

The road was still completely covered in snow, but it was packed down from some traffic that had ventured out. A short distance from Matt's drive, a red sedan was off in the ditch and mostly covered with snow. The interstate highway was better, though hundreds of abandoned, snow-covered cars littered the side of the road. Semi-trucks and trailers, some overturned, added to the frozen disarray between Franklin and Nashville. Every mile or two someone could be seen shoveling the snow off a vehicle or trying to get one started. The sparse traffic was slow but steady, and soon the Steiners were delivered to the Nashville airport to begin their journey back to their lives in Switzerland.

"Mary Frances, did you think to call The Grove to see if power has been restored at your place?" Matt asked as she moved to the front seat.

"I'll do that now," she answered. Having made the call, she was happy to learn power was back on as of 4:00 a.m. *This is so nice riding here next to him,* she thought.

"You're being unusually quiet," Matt said. "Is something bothering you?"

"I'm fine," Mary Frances answered softly.

"Would you like some bar-b-que for lunch? Martin's on Belmont?" he asked.

"I've not been to that one, but I've heard of it," she answered. "Yes, I would like that."

"Well, then it's a date," Matt said, glancing at her as he

drove. "And you said you wouldn't go out with me. You've just agreed to go for bar-b-que at Martin's. Sounds like a date to me!"

"No, it's not," she protested. "You're just taking me to my car, so it's not a date."

"I not so sure," he said. "Maybe I'd better check with Mrs. Joiner to get her opinion. She seems to be the authority on the subject at Veritas."

"Please, don't do that," Mary Frances pleaded. "I'm probably in enough trouble already."

"I don't see what's wrong with us going out for lunch, considering I've already slept with you three times!" Matt said, with a big grin on his face.

"We did not!" she said, protesting.

"We did," he repeated. "I remember it very clearly."

"But sleeping together, not *sleeping together,*" Mary Frances said.

"Well," Matt said, shaking his head, kidding with her, "it sounds the same to me. Can we consult Mrs. Joiner?"

"Please, Matt," she cried, starting to get upset.

"I'm just playing you," he said. "I'm not going to tell anyone what happened or didn't happen. It's no one's business but ours. I'm just trying to get you talking and maybe not so sad." Mary Frances looked at him like she was going to burst into tears.

Martin's Bar-B-Que was packed as Matt searched for a place to park. It was the first day businesses had started to open after the blizzard. The restaurant was full of hungry people, many of whom were getting their first hot meal in days. Customers passed the time viewing the country music and bar-b-que memorabilia on the brick wall as they waited to place orders. When Matt and Mary Frances got to the cash register to pay, Matt started to pay for both, but Mary Frances wanted to pay for hers. "Mary Frances, I'm going to pay for your lunch," he said. "It's not a date. It doesn't mean anything. I just want to, so put your billfold away." Mary Frances gave in and put her billfold back in her purse. The pulled pork sandwiches were excellent as always.

"Mary Frances," Matt said, as they lingered at the table after lunch, "There's something we should talk about; you're really confusing me. You're happy and seem like you're having a great time. Then you're sad, and I think you're going to cry. You hold on to me all night like you're afraid I'm going to escape. Then you say you can't go out with me."

"I'm sorry," she said, looking away.

"I'm not giving up on you, although maybe I should," Matt said. "I truly enjoyed being snowed in with you. Partly because it was a four-day weekend. Partly because we were warm and ate well, but mostly because of you. I'm glad you slid off the road, and I found you."

Mary Frances turned back to Matt. "I'm glad you did, too. This has been the best four days of my life. I know I'm confusing. I just never expected to meet someone like you. I never imagined someone like you existed."

"But you're still going to turn me down when I ask you out on a date?" he asked.

"Yes," she said. "It's not fair to you."

The two left the restaurant and drove south in silence to where Mary Frances' snow covered car was still at the bottom of the hill. Matt reached across the center console and took her hand. Mary Frances placed her other hand on his, caressing it. Moments later, the wrecker pulled up. Mary Frances handed her keys to Matt as he got out of the Range Rover to speak with the wrecker operator. Soon, the cable was spooling off the winch, and the operator was pulling it down the hill to the Toyota. The wrecker pulled the car up the hill and onto the shoulder with no difficulty. Matt brushed snow off the windshield and started the car. Luckily, there was no damage to Mary Frances' car, as Matt had predicted. The wrecker driver secured the cable and pulled away, off to his next assignment.

"Matt, I didn't pay him," said Mary Frances as the wrecker drove away.

"I did," Matt said. "It's all taken care of."

Mary Frances shook her head and said, "Why do you do that? Thank you."

"Because I like to," he said. "You're welcome. Now, just because I got your car out of the ditch doesn't make this a date. Just so we're clear," he said, trying to get her to laugh.

"Thank you for everything," she said, blinking back tears.

"For the wrecker, and lunch, for the last four days, for rescuing me. I will never forget this." Then she got in her car and drove off, tears streaming down her face. Matt was left standing on the side of the road, wondering what had happened.

Mary Frances made her way through Brentwood in a daze, wiping the tears from her eyes. When she was about a mile from home, the phone rang through the Bluetooth in her car. Mary Frances recognized the name on the caller ID.

"Hello, Dagny."

"How's it going? Have you got your car out yet?"

"Yes, I'm driving right now. I'll be home shortly."

"Does your offer still stand? Can I move in today? Please say yes."

"Absolutely. Aren't you going to ask if the electricity is on?"

"Great! Who cares. Any place is better than here. I'm going to load my car right now. I found The Grove in my navigation program. I'll be there soon. I want to hear everything. Bye!"

Mary Frances pulled up to The Grove entrance and put her pass code into the gate computer. The gate slowly swung open, and she drove in as the gate closed behind. It was a surprise to find the roads of the complex already cleared of snow. *Maybe it's good that Dagny is moving in today,* she thought. *I feel so alone now. I miss him already. Maybe he'll not bother me. Except it wouldn't be bothering me. I wish I could get back in my car and drive to his cabin.*

Mary Frances opened the door to her apartment and for some reason felt surprised that everything was just as she'd left it Wednesday morning when she went to work. Everything was the same at her apartment, but she certainly wasn't.

Chapter 9

Dagny

"Mary Frances, it's Dagny. Can you buzz me through?"

"Sure, the code is 8945."

"Wow, so much security! This is a fancy place!"

"I'm in 912. Just follow the road. It winds around. I'm the ninth building, first floor. You'll see my Toyota."

"Be right there, roommate!"

Mary Frances hardly had time to change into something more comfortable when her doorbell rang. It was Dagny at the front door with four suitcases. "Come on in, Dagny. We're letting all the cold air inside," Mary Frances said and suddenly remembered when Matt had said that to Frederic. "Let me help," she said, rolling in a big suitcase.

"Mary Frances," cried Dagny, hugging her. "You have no idea what this means to me. What a nice place! This is luxurious compared to where I was."

"Come down the hall; I'll show you your bedroom," said Mary Frances.

"Oh, my!" said Dagny. "This is so nice. And here's my bathroom. My very own bathroom!" Mary Frances continued the tour, and Dagny continued to carry on about the apartment.

"You get unpacked," said Mary Frances. "We'll need to go down to the office tomorrow and get a sticker for your car.

We have to let them know you're subleasing from me."

"OK, I'll be quick. Then, I must hear all about the past four days," Dagny said. "There's nothing to tell from my long weekend. Four girls, one bathroom, no electricity, no food- well, almost no food. It was like those survival shows on TV." Dagny quickly unpacked her suitcases, hanging up clothes and arranging folded clothes in the chest of drawers.

"Mary Frances, I'm going to take a quick shower now.... or maybe a long shower. My very own shower! Such luxury!"

After the shower, Dagny found Mary Frances in the living room. Dagny was chattering away while still drying her hair with a towel. Finally, she noticed that Mary Frances wasn't listening. "Hey, roomie, are you alright?"

Mary Frances was trying not to cry. "No, Dagny, I'm not alright."

"What's wrong?" asked Dagny, sitting down next to her on the sofa. "Tell me. What's going on?"

"Dagny, I haven't known you very long," said Mary Frances, "but I feel I can trust you. I need to talk to somebody. I don't know what to do."

"You can talk to me," Dagny said. "I can be a good listener."

Mary Frances looked at Dagny, blinking back tears. "Dagny, the last four days have been the best four days of my life. It was magical. And now it's over."

"What happened?" asked Dagny. "Why was it so wonderful? Do you mean because it was a nice house, and you had a real bed with your own bathroom?"

"Yes, all that is true, but it was because of Matt. He's wonderful, Dagny," Mary Frances said, working to regain her composure.

"Tell me about him," said Dagny, reaching out and patting Mary Frances' hand.

"Where do I start? He's not at all what I expected from a vice president on the sixth floor," she said. "I was disoriented after my car slid off the road. I couldn't see a thing but snow, and then there he was. I've never thought I needed a man. I've always known I would have to take care of myself, but there he was- digging me out of the snow. I was cold, and he was so worried about me. He was concerned I'd get hypothermia. I've just never had anyone worry about me. And, yes, his house, his cabin, is amazing. Warm and cozy. It feels so safe."

"Tell me about Matt," coaxed Dagny.

"I guess I expected him to be obnoxious and full of himself, but he wasn't at all," Mary Frances explained. "He's very smart, which is no surprise. He was also very kind to me, and I didn't expect that.

"There was another couple, friends of his from Switzerland. They challenged Matt and me to a game of pinochle. As it turns out, I'm a better pinochle player than they expected. We beat them. But the best part was how Matt enjoyed watching me play. Of course, I cooked for everyone. Matt was good to help with that. He has a fabulous kitchen. We discussed all kinds of subjects, including his work and how it all connects to the world. He's interesting."

"But what did you do all weekend... play pinochle?" asked Dagny.

"Heavens, no!" said Mary Frances. "We took hikes. We talked. We put firewood in the wood burner to keep warm. We talked. We watched a movie. We talked and laughed a lot. And we ran the steam engine to recharge the battery bank."

"Did you say,' We ran the steam engine'?" asked Dagny. "You can run a steam engine?"

"It does sound strange," Mary Frances laughed, "but yes, *now* I know how to run a steam engine."

"Hmmm.... That's different. So, does he like you? Do you think he might ask you on a date?" asked Dagny. "How about Mrs. Joiner?"

"If he asks me, I will turn him down," said Mary Frances.

"Stop! I don't get this. Have I missed something? You told me you've just had the best four days of your life. You were just telling me about this great guy," Dagny said, shaking her head. "Why would you *not* want to go out with him? You're afraid of Mrs. Joiner, aren't you?"

"No, it has nothing to do with Mrs. Joiner," said Mary Frances. "It's just not fair to Matt."

"Elaborate, Mary Frances!" demanded Dagny.

Mary Frances wanted to trust her new friend but wasn't quite there yet. Trying to change the subject, she said, "Dagny, you know people are going to think we're sisters."

"Yes, probably," answered Dagny. "But we're talking about you and Matthew Archer right now. So, as your sister, I want to know what's going on!"

"Well, I'm not sure how it happened. It was Thursday night. The Steiners had gone to bed. Matt and I were in the great room on the leather sofa. There was only the light from the fireplace. I didn't mean for it to happen. I wanted him to hold me. I ended up in his arms, and then, I guess I went to sleep. I didn't mean to fall asleep, but I did. Then, I did it again Friday night and then again Saturday night. It was heaven, Dagny. Just the thought of lying next to him, his arms around me, the fire in the fireplace. I could hear his heart beat."

"Mary Frances!" said Dagny. "When you say you slept with him three times, do you mean slept with him or *slept with him*?"

"Dagny!" scolded Mary Frances. "No, I mean I went to sleep with him. That doesn't mean what you're implying."

"Well, you need to be careful how you tell the story because a lot of people may take that to mean the later. Still, that's something! I've got to know; did you ask him the next two nights? How does that happen, Mary Frances? Excuse me, Mr. Archer, I'd just like to cuddle up with you again on your sofa and spend the night. Is that OK with you?"

"No, of course not," sighed Mary Frances. "The Steiners would go to bed, and we would continue talking. I liked being alone with him. I wanted to feel his touch, so I scooted close to him... and we'd go to sleep. It just happened."

"Is there anything else?" asked Dagny.

"He kissed me," Mary Frances admitted.

"I knew it!" squealed Dagny. "Was it good?"

"Yes, Dagny," sighed Mary Frances. "It was the best kiss I've ever had."

"But, he didn't try to get you into his bed?" asked Dagny.

"No, he didn't," Mary Frances said. "He was very respectful. Very cautious, like he didn't want to scare me."

"OK, OK, but I still don't understand," said Dagny. "Do you hear yourself? This smart, handsome man rescues you in a blizzard. Oh, and did I say rich? He must make a lot of money. So, you're snowed in with him and have the best four days of your life. Explain to me why you don't want to go out with him!"

"Dagny, if I tell you, will you swear not to tell anyone?" asked Mary Frances.

"Of course," answered Dagny, looking at her friend very seriously.

"Dagny, two months after I graduated from college – I was 22 – I got sick. At first I thought it was the flu. I went to the doctor. I had cancer, Dagny." Mary Frances sat quietly letting Dagny absorb what she'd just said. "There are many ways to treat cancer. It all depends on the type and the stage. For me, it was chemotherapy. I went through seven rounds of chemotherapy. There's good news and bad news. The good news is that the success rate is high and so far, I am still in remission. It's been six years, and if I make it to seven without a recurrence, then I'm in the clear; I'm probably cured permanently. The bad news, is that the chemotherapy means I can't get pregnant. I can't have children, Dagny. Children are important to men. I can't fulfill that. So, if I dated Matt and we got serious, I would have to tell him. Then, he'd break up with me."

"But you don't know that," said Dagny, looking at her friend with compassion.

"No, but I know most men want children," Mary Frances said. "Marriage is hard enough without waiting for the day my husband gets mad and leaves because I can't give him children. It is simply better for me not to date, not marry and live by myself." Dagny moved over next to Mary Frances and hugged her.

"It sounds like Matt Archer likes you, Mary Frances," Dagny said. "What will you do if he does ask you out on a date?"

"I'm going to do my best to hide from him," she said. "He didn't ask for my phone number, but he's very resourceful. He can find it. I'm not going to answer my phone if I don't recognize the number."

"Am I the only one who's aware you spent the blizzard

at Matt Archer's house?" asked Dagny.

"Yes, though I texted Jane to ask a question. I don't think you've met her. I had to know the name of the VP on the sixth floor who has gotten all those girls pregnant. When I first discovered Matt worked at Veritas, I needed to know if he was *that* man. I told Jane I was just curious, but I couldn't tell if she believed me."

"Mary Frances, don't be surprised if Matt shows up in our cafeteria looking for you," warned Dagny.

"I hope not," said Mary Frances. "I hope he gets so busy with his work that he forgets all about me."

"You don't really mean that," said Dagny. "I understand your situation, but I don't believe you'd be unhappy if he came looking for you." Mary Frances gave a sad smile as Dagny continued. "Be honest with Matt. Is it fair to not let him decide?"

Chapter 10
Veritas

The warm front that arrived Sunday night did wonders melting the snow. Traffic was flowing better than Mary Frances anticipated as she drove her new roommate to work. The two made their way into the building and changed into their white uniforms right on time to start another week. Just as they reached the cafeteria dining room, Mary Frances heard her name being called.

"Mary Frances, Mary Frances!" called Jane, running to catch up. "So why all the interest in Lynn Hanson and Matt Archer? What's going on?"

"No reason, Jane," said Mary Frances as she quickly walked across the cafeteria dining room with Dagny following. "I was thinking about the situation on the sixth floor, and it's not right to paint all those men with the same brush. It was bothering me. I just couldn't figure out which one was which. Have you met Dagny? This is Dagny Bennett, and today is only her second day. She just moved to Nashville." Mary Frances was desperate to change the topic from Matt Archer.

"Nice to meet you, Dagny," said Jane. "How did you two fair in the blizzard?"

"Have you heard? We're roommates. I've moved in with

Mary Frances at the Grove," said Dagny while Mary Frances listened, a bit nervously. "We lost power but did OK. We didn't get too cold, and we had food to eat. Didn't we, Mary Frances?" Mary Frances smiled and nodded just as Mrs. Klein walked into the kitchen.

"OK, girls and boys, listen up," Mrs. Klein called in a loud voice so everyone could hear. "Gather around. I hope y'all had a pleasant four-day weekend although many of you didn't have electricity. I'm glad y'all made it back. You know what to do. Jane, give the produce an extra look. Some of it may have to be thrown out since it's been in the fridge too long. Mary Frances, get started on food prep, and keep Dagny with you. Teach her what to do. I'm going to check on our delivery status since we received nothing on Thursday and Friday. Maybe we can still keep the menu for today. Margaret, you may have to rethink dessert since we may not have the ingredients, but let me see when our Thursday truck will be arriving.

"Mrs. Klein, there's the bell for the loading dock," said Jim. "Hopefully, it's Thursday's truck. I'll go check."

"Great, keep me posted, Jim," said Mrs. Klein. "Now, let's get started, everyone!"

Mary Frances showed Dagny how to bring up the meal plan on the computer. Together, they perused the printout, and then Mary Frances started instructing her in how to locate all the ingredients to begin preparation. "No one is likely to ask about the blizzard now," said Dagny, "because everyone is too busy working. By tomorrow, it will all be forgotten."

"Thanks for covering for me with Jane," said Mary Frances.

Dagny smiled as she carried a #10 can of tomatoes to the prep table. "No problem, roommate. We've got to look out for each other!" The morning passed in a whirlwind of activity as all the various components of Monday's lunch were prepared. Mary Frances and Dagny were out in the cafeteria, preparing the serving line when Jane came running up.

"Mary Frances, Dagny!" she whispered loudly, motioning for them to lean in closer. It was obvious from her expression that she had news. "All hell has broken loose on the sixth floor! There were behind-closed-door meetings this morning. You'll never guess what happened!"

"No idea, Jane. What happened?" asked Mary Frances as she and Dagny listened closely.

"They fired him!" said Jane. "He's cleaning out his desk as we speak!"

"Who? Who got fired?" asked Dagny.

"Lynn Hanson!" said Jane, looking left and right to see if anyone else was within earshot. "Don't tell anyone!" she whispered as she went back to the kitchen to tell the others.

"Oh, my God! They fired him," said Dagny as she and Mary Frances continued to work. "That's *the* guy on the sixth floor, right?"

"Yes, that's him," said Mary Frances. *Oh, my! Did I have anything to do with this?* she wondered. "Dagny, I confessed to Matt that I had been asking the name of the guy on the sixth floor with the bad reputation. Also, I told him about the four girls. He seemed somewhat aware of the rumors but was surprised that there were four different girls. Matt seemed upset that this was going on and people were believing that everyone on the sixth floor was like that. Did Matt fire him?" Mary Frances wondered aloud.

"Matt's not his boss, is he?" asked Dagny. "Does he have the authority to do that?"

"Dagny, Matt owns 5% of Veritas. Mr. Borland owns 51%. Mr. Eastman owns 15%, I believe. And there are several investors who don't work here. Matt may have told Mr. Borland, and now... Lynn Hanson is gone. I may have caused this."

"And what if you did?" asked Dagny as she moved stainless steel sections into position on the serving line. "It sounds to me like Mr. Lynn 'Casanova' Hanson got what he deserved."

"Yes. I suppose I'm just afraid of causing trouble. If this is true, that he's fired, I hope he doesn't find out I mentioned it to Matt," said Mary Frances.

The two continued working, and soon the lunch crowd started filing through. Mary Frances kept an eye out, ready to disappear into the kitchen if Matt came in. But as one o'clock appeared on the digital clock on the wall, he was nowhere to be seen. Shortly thereafter, Mr. Borland, Mr. Eastman and Mrs.

Martin came through the serving line and took a table in the far corner of the cafeteria. By then, the dining room was clearing out. As Mary Frances and Dagny started taking down the serving line, Mary Frances saw Mr. Borland motioning to her. "Dagny, Mr. Borland wants to talk to me," said Mary Frances. "I'll be right back." *What is going on, and why do they want to talk to me?*

As Mary Frances walked up to their table, the CEO said, "Mary Frances, sit down, please. Do you remember Patricia Martin from HR? And I believe you know Mr. Eastman, our chief economist." Mary Frances nodded and sat down, scared to death. "You will be hearing, if you haven't already, that Lynn Hanson has been terminated. He has already left the building and will not be returning."

"We were aware of the rumors," said Mrs. Martin, "but didn't realize the full extent of the problem until we learned there were four separate incidents. That information has been investigated and found to be true. Things like this are very complicated because sometimes there are women who claim to have been harassed when they weren't. Then, there are other times when legitimate victims don't come forward. Mr. Hanson was *definitely* a problem."

"Hanson wasn't bothering you, was he?" asked the economist.

"No, sir," replied Mary Frances. "I wasn't even sure of his name. I just knew there was a vice president on the sixth floor who .... well..."

"She thought Matt was Hanson," said the CEO to the others. "Matt was pretty miffed to learn that employees in the rest of the building believed what they did about the sixth floor. I was, too. We are not going to be the morality police. It's not our place to interfere in the private lives of our employees. But we must have a workplace where everyone can be comfortable and be treated with respect. So, I just wanted to tell you personally, Mary Frances, that Lynn Hanson is no longer at Veritas Strategies. Also, I wanted to assure you that your name was not mentioned in the interaction with Hanson. We maintained your privacy and anonymity. I want to thank you for bringing our attention to this matter. We knew he was problematic but didn't realize how problematic. So, thank you."

Everyone at the table stood and thanked Mary Frances, shaking her hand. Out of the corner of her eye, she saw Mrs. Joiner talking to Dagny and looking in her direction.

As the three executives left the cafeteria, Mr. Borland turned back to speak privately with Mary Frances. "So, did you do OK during the blizzard?" he asked. Mary Frances was speechless, unsure as how to respond. "It's OK," Mr. Borland said. "Your secret's safe with me. Matt told me. I'm glad he was there when you went off the road." Mary Frances stood silently in front of the CEO, wondering exactly what Matt had told him. "Hey, could you do something for Matt's group? They've been covered up all day. They haven't had time to eat. Could you put together six lunches and take them up to the sixth floor? The team is working in the small conference room, not the big one."

"Yes, sir. I'll do it right away," replied Mary Frances.

"I'll take care of Mrs. Joiner. Don't you worry about her," he said. "I saw her watching us. There's no doubt she's dying to know why we were talking to you." Mr. Borland walked off toward Mrs. Joiner's office but turned for a second and called to Mary Frances. "Get Dagny to help take lunch up to Matt and his crew," he said with a smile.

Mary Frances hurried back to Dagny and said, "Dagny, we need to make six lunches and take them up to the sixth floor."

"Wow! Really?" said Dagny as she sat down a stack of dishes. "What did Mr. Borland want? Mrs. Joiner was grilling me, but I had no idea."

"It was about Lynn Hanson," said Mary Frances. "They checked into his behavior, and he *has* been fired."

"Was it because of what you told Matt?" asked Dagny. Mary Frances nodded her head. "Well, I'm impressed they fired him," Dagny added. The two quickly made up six lunches with drinks, utensils and napkins.

Mrs. Joiner approached, pushing a stainless steel cart on rollers. "Here, use this to transport the food upstairs. Mary Frances, Mr. Borland was very complimentary of you, Dagny and the cafeteria in general. He told me to keep a watch out in the future for anyone like Lynn Hanson. You know, of course, that he was fired as he should have been. Behavior like that will not be tolerated. We have a unique position here in the cafeteria to watch out for things like that. If you see anyone misbehaving, you must let me know. It will be taken care of."

"Will do, Mrs. Joiner," said Dagny as she and Mary Frances left the cafeteria. Dagny gave Mary Frances a sly smile while Mary Frances suppressed a grin, a sisterly connection growing between them. They pushed the cart out into the hallway and to the elevators.

Chapter 11
The Sixth Floor

When the elevator doors closed, Mary Frances and Dagny burst out laughing. "Mr. Borland may be creating a Gestapo with Mrs. Joiner as the head Nazi!" Dagny giggled.

"Oh, I think he knows exactly what he's doing. He has her number; he's just making her feel important," said Mary Frances.

"Mary Frances, have you ever been up to the sixth floor?" asked Dagny.

Shaking her head and smiling, Mary Frances said, "All day I've been trying to figure out how to hide from Matt, and now I have to go find him. The crazy part is that I can't wait to see him."

Dagny smiled at her friend and asked, "Do you think Matt told Mr. Borland about you and the blizzard?"

"Yes, I'm certain he did, but I don't know how much," answered Mary Frances. "I didn't get the impression Matt gave him details because Mr. Borland didn't act like there was anything else to it."

Dagny watched the numbers of the floors change as the elevator rose to the sixth floor. *I wonder why Mr. Borland asked Mary Frances to take the lunches up to the sixth floor? He could have just told Mrs. Joiner. I bet that man has a reason for almost everything he does.*

"Here we go," said Dagny as the elevator door opened, and she pushed the cart out into the hallway. The two were immediately struck with the difference in the top floor. The hardwood floors and the dark crown molding were a stark contrast to the institutional look of the rest of the building. "Wow, I thought this was a nice building," whispered Dagny, "but this sixth floor is something else!"

As they approached a young woman impeccably dressed in a brown suit with contrasting light, beige heels, Mary Frances said, "Excuse me, we have lunch for Mr. Archer and the Research Department. Could you direct us to the small conference room?"

"Sure," she responded, pointing down the hall. "You're headed in the right direction. It's that way and to the right. My, how nice! The Research Department must have some pull to get lunch delivered like this!"

"Thank you," said Mary Frances, and they continued down the hall to the conference room. Upon reaching the door, Mary France could feel her heart beating faster as she knocked.

The door was opened by a good-looking, young man. The top button of his dress shirt was undone, and his tie was loosened. His sleeves were rolled up, and his light, brown hair was a bit disheveled. "Hi," he said, looking first at Dagny and Mary Frances and then the food. "What do we have here?"

"We're from the cafeteria," said Mary Frances. "Mr. Borland asked us to bring lunch."

"Fantastic! I'm starved," he said, holding the door open for them to enter. "Hey, Matt! Check this out. Borland sent us lunch!" The other five turned from the conference table that was covered in graphs, charts, and laptops.

"Mary Frances!" said Matt, standing up from his seat at the head of the conference table. "Zander, this is Mary Frances," he said, introducing the man who had opened the door. "And you must be Dagny," Matt said. "Everyone, this is Mary Frances Foster and Dagny Bennet from the cafeteria. Ladies, this is Zander, Joe, Steven, Frank and Elizabeth."

As Mary Frances greeted everyone she thought, *No one here has ever heard my name, except Zander who keeps smiling at me.*

"Thanks for doing this. We haven't had time to eat lunch, and we're starved," Matt said. Mary Frances and Dagny started setting the plates of food on the table as everyone made space by moving computers and papers.

The smell of grilled salmon with dill sauce, baked potato, broccoli, and freshly baked bread filled the conference room as Mary Frances and Dagny uncovered the plates. "I hope everyone likes salmon," said Mary Frances.

"Smells wonderful," said Steven as the rest nodded in agreement.

"Are you *the* Dagny that kicked the CEO out of the cafeteria?" Zander asked as Dagny placed his lunch in front of him.

Closing her eyes and nodding her head, she replied, "Yes, I'll admit that was me, but I didn't know who he was. And I didn't really kick him out. I just told him he would need to come back when we officially opened."

"No, it was great!" Zander said, grinning at Dagny. "Everyone thought it was funny, including the CEO. We all know about it because he was telling the story."

"Well, I wish someone else in this great big building would do something stupid, so everyone would forget about what I did," Dagny replied, trying to hide her embarrassment.

"We'll leave the cart for dishes and utensils when you're finished. Later this afternoon, we'll come back and get it," Mary Frances told Matt as she and Dagny walked to the door. Matt rose and followed them into the hall.

"Mary Frances, I'd planned to come down to the cafeteria for lunch today, but we've been covered up," Matt said. "I didn't want you to think I'd forgotten about you." Dagny caught Mary Frances smiling at Matt. "Lots of things are happening, the least of which is the Lynn Hanson deal."

"Yes, we've heard," said Mary Frances. "Mr. Borland, Mr. Eastman, and Mrs. Martin from HR came down to talk to me about it. It did make me nervous."

"It's all good," Matt said. "Getting rid of him is a win for everyone but Lynn Hanson. He was a huge liability, not to mention the chaos and turmoil he was causing. He deserves worse. Someone should kick his ass."

Mary Frances was taken aback at Matt's words while Dagny responded, "Mr. Archer, I like the way you think." Matt smiled.

"I'll see you later, Mary Frances," Matt said. "Hey, what's your number?" he asked, retrieving a cell phone from his pocket. "I'll need it to call you, won't I." Mary Frances recited her phone number while Matt entered it in his phone.

The two girls from the first floor waved to Matt as the elevator doors closed. "Oh, my God, Mary Frances," said Dagny. "He's gorgeous. And to think, you slept with him three nights!"

"Don't say that, Dagny," chided Mary Frances. "I did not *sleep* with him! I've already explained that!"

"He's going to call you. I can tell. And you are going to say *yes* when he asks you out! Because if you don't .... he can ask *me* out. I'll go out with him if you won't!"

Mary Frances looked at her roommate, trying to suppress a grin. "I should say no, but I doubt I can. I'll just have to explain everything soon, so he can dump me. Then I can try to forget about Matthew Archer. But, it would be wonderful to go out on a real date with him."

"Ya think?" asked Dagny. "What kind of magic spell did you cast on him? I need to know your secret. Does it have something to do with steam engines?"

"Speaking of men, it appeared to me that the man who answered the door... *Zander*?... was paying a lot of attention to you," said Mary Frances, as the elevator doors opened.

"Really?" asked Dagny, hopefully. "I wondered, but I wasn't sure. He's cute. Who is he?"

Mary Frances shrugged her shoulders and said, "It appears he's in the Research Department and works with Matt."

"Well, find out more about him from Matt .... Mr. Archer. Ha! You get to call him Matt, and I have to call him Mr. Archer. Don't let Mrs. Joiner hear you calling him Matt," cautioned Dagny. "And what's the deal with the Research Department? Don't they study economic stuff? What's so important that they can't even eat lunch? Not that I minded taking them lunch. Find out more about Zander."

Mary Frances and Dagny returned to the cafeteria and

resumed work. Dagny's question as to what could be so important that the Research Department didn't break for lunch nagged at Mary Frances. She remembered just a few days before when Matt had explained the unusual work in his department. *Are things getting worse?* She couldn't help but wonder.

Chapter 12
Research

"Good work everyone. That just about wraps it up for today," Matt said to the five analysts from Research. They'd just given their reports and were finishing their grilled salmon, another working lunch. "We'll meet again Wednesday. I want the early earnings projections, particularly for manufacturing, Steven. And I especially want to know about autos. Elizabeth, let's hear about retail and the Christmas projections. Joe, the normal on Europe, and I'm very curious about high-end watch sales for this year. Plus, I'd like a year-to-year for the past ten. Frank, we'll need the projection on Consumer Discretionary for the US. We're finished; see you Wednesday.... Zander, stay for a minute."

Everyone gathered papers and laptops to exit the conference room. After the room had cleared, Zander said, "Matt, she's pretty!"

"Well, of course. Did you not believe me?" Matt answered, grinning ear to ear.

"Yes, but she is," Zander said. "She seems quiet."

"Yes, but don't think she's not smart," said Matt. "She's surprising."

"What do you know about her side-kick, Dagny Bennett?" asked Zander.

"Nothing really. Just the story about her running Borland

out of the cafeteria," said Matt. "She's new. She's just moved in with Mary Frances. Why the interest?"

"She's a little firecracker," Zander said. "I kind of like her. Might ask her out."

"Good luck, buddy," said Matt. "I still can't get over Mary Frances thinking I was Lynn Hanson. She was going to jump out of the car! I'm glad he's gone."

"Do you think we've heard the last of him?" asked Zander.

"I hope so," said Matt. "Now, back to business. I'm almost ready for my meeting tomorrow with Borland and Eastman. Looks like the TP Index is steady, and the M0/M3 ratio is normal. The Vacation Index is at 16%, but with the holidays, that's expected. I know violence is up, arson, rioting, but it doesn't look like any of that has spilled over into the economy. It's the BDI that has me concerned. Ever since '08, I'm paranoid over the Baltic Dry Index. So, see if you can figure out why it's dipped. Call our contacts at the ports and see if something has changed. Have some ships just entered service after being on the hard for two years? Why is the BDI off? Something seasonal I don't understand? I need the information first thing tomorrow morning."

"You got it boss," said Zander taking a folder from his brief case.

"What's that!?" asked Matt.

"I'm just making some notes on what you need," said Zander. "I don't want to forget anything."

"No, the folder. It says *Endex,*" Matt observed.

"Yeah, that's what I call it," said Zander. "Y'all never actually gave *the* index a name, so I did. It needed one to differentiate it from all the other indices we use."

"Huh, that's pretty clever," said Matt, "but don't leave it lying around. If the public saw that word and found out what this index attempts to do, all hell would break lose."

"I understand," said Zander as he returned the folder to his brief case and left the conference room.

Zander stopped in front of the elevators to catch a ride down one floor to his office. When the elevator door opened, there was Mary Frances. "Hey, Mary Frances!" said Zander. "Twice in the same day!"

"I'm back to get the lunch cart," said Mary Frances. "Has everyone gone from the conference room?"

"Everyone except Matt," replied Zander. "If you hurry you can catch him. Hey, your buddy, Dagny... How's she doing? She's new, right?"

"Yes. This is only her second day, but she's doing fine," replied Mary Frances, suspecting Zander couldn't care less about Dagny's work performance and was really wanting to find out more about her. "She's my roommate, but I just met her last week. She seems very nice. I like her."

"Well, thanks again for the great lunch. It was much appreciated!" he said as Mary Frances stepped out of the elevator, and he stepped in.

"Bye," said Mary Frances, giving a little wave as the doors closed. Mary Frances smiled to herself as she walked down the hallway. *I'm right! He likes Dagny.* When Mary Frances arrived at the conference room, the door was open.

"Hello?" she said, peeking around the corner to see if anyone was there.

"Mary Frances!" said Matt, looking up from his laptop. "Come in."

"I don't want to bother you," she said. "I just came for the cart."

"Come over here. Sit down," Matt said, smiling at his former houseguest.

"I have to get back to the cafeteria," she said. "There's a lot of work to do."

"You're not going to get fired," he said, pulling out a chair and motioning for her to sit. "I won't let them," he smiled. Reluctantly, Mary Frances sat down.

Matt was seated at the head of the conference table, angled toward her. Mary Frances glanced around the room nervously, taking in the oil paintings on the wall and the heavy, mahogany table that must have literally weighed a ton. Then her attention shifted to Matt. His dark, blue eyes and brown hair brought back memories of the blizzard and lying against his chest in front of the fireplace.

"Are you OK?" he asked, wishing he could read her mind.

"Yes, just nervous," she said.

"You know, I got used to you during the blizzard," he said. "I'm sort of in Mary Frances withdrawal." Mary Frances looked at him, then closed her eyes not sure of how to respond. "So, since you're here, I want to ask you out for Saturday night. Shostakovich, Symphony No. 10 at the Nashville Symphony. I'll pick you up at your apartment at 5:30. We'll go to Moto for dinner. Then to the symphony at 8:00."

"Matt, I need to explain something," she said, leaning back in her chair and placing her face in her hands. Then, moving her hands down almost like she was praying, Mary Frances looked up to the ceiling then back at Matt. Knowing she was very serious, Matt didn't say a word. He settled back in his chair to listen.

"I've said I can't go out with you. I want to explain why." Taking a deep breath and swallowing, she continued. "It's not that I don't want to. I want to very much. It's something about me. Six years ago, I was sick. It was cancer," she said. "It required chemotherapy. I was very fortunate because the treatment worked. The doctors say I'm cured permanently. But what I've been avoiding telling you... is I can't have children. The chemotherapy did that. It cured me, but I can't have children." Mary Frances blinked back tears as she watched Matt for any reaction. "Men want children, so that's why I don't date. I'm telling you this, so you'll understand."

Matt sat quietly, taking it all in. Mary Frances said no more and waited for his reply. Still fighting tears, she looked away determined not to cry in front of him. "Well, Mary Frances, I'm going to have to think about this," he finally answered.

"Of course," she said, starting to get up. "I understand completely."

"OK, I've thought about it," he continued. "5:30 Saturday evening. Wear a nice dress. I'm wearing a suit. Most guys don't wear a tux to the Nashville Symphony. So, your dress doesn't have to be a long, evening gown. Have you been to Moto in the Gulch?"

Mary Frances was in shock as she listened to his voice repeat the details of a Saturday night date. "So, you still want to go out with me?" she asked. "You didn't think about it very long. I assumed you meant a longer time."

"Yes. I still want to go out with you Saturday night, Mary Frances Foster," he said. "You really had me going there. I'd wondered what you were referring to when you said there was some reason you couldn't. I was imagining all sorts of things."

"But... " Mary Frances started, hardly able to believe it.

"Mary Frances, maybe you didn't notice, but I really enjoyed the blizzard. When I woke up this morning, I missed you."

"Matt, you haven't told anyone about us... sleeping together. Like Zander?" Mary Frances asked.

"Of course not," he replied. "I told him you got snowed in with us. You know, about your car and all. You haven't told anyone, have you?"

"Dagny. And I said we slept together three nights. I made it very clear to her that it was just sleeping, but she keeps kidding me about it. She thinks it's so funny," said Mary Frances. "I shouldn't have given Dagny such details."

"That is kind of funny," laughed Matt. "I can hardly blame her for kidding you about it. It's just too easy. Just as long as she doesn't tell anyone else. I don't want to become the new Lynn Hanson around here!"

"No, she won't tell anyone," said Mary Frances. "I've only known her a short time, but she's already a good friend. She's the reason I told you about my situation. She convinced me I should."

Matt reached over and took her hands in his as he said, "She sounds like a very good friend. I'm glad you listened to her. So, we're good for Saturday night?"

Mary Frances nodded her head and smiled, amazed that there was the possibly of a future with the man who'd rescued her in the snowstorm.

Chapter 13
Shostakovich

"Aren't you glad you listened to me?" said Dagny. "Am I a great roommate, or what!" Mary Frances had waited until the drive home to share the news. The privacy of the car was the first and best opportunity to tell Dagny about her conversation with Matt.

"Yes, I'm glad I told him, and he still wants to go out with me," said Mary Frances. "My fear is he didn't consider it long enough. He only thought about it for three seconds. I'm worried that it won't be OK later on. But, it might be... he's so different. I don't completely understand him."

"Time out!" said Dagny, making a T sign with her hands. "Will you be still? Listen to yourself! Don't be borrowing trouble. Here's what you should be focusing on– Saturday night. Nothing but that! Are you happy that Matt Archer– extremely handsome Matt Archer, the VP of *Somethingorother* at Veritas Strategies, is taking you to dinner at some fancy restaurant and then the symphony?"

Without taking her eyes off the road, Mary Frances nodded and smiled in agreement.

"Good! Then that's what you're going to think about and nothing else," Dagny continued. "Like, what dress are you going to wear? How are you going to do your hair? What about your nails? You want to look hot... but not too hot." Mary Frances continued to smile as she drove to the apartment while her friend carried on and on. "He's definitely into you since you've been asked out on a real date, even after you've slept with him three times."

"Dagny!" cried Mary Frances, her face changing from happy to aggravated.

"I can't help it!" cried Dagny as she laughed so hard tears came to her eyes. "I won't tell anyone, but it's just too good to let go. Catching her breath, Dagny said, "I'll make a deal with you. You stop telling people that I ran the CEO out of the cafeteria, and I'll lay off the *sleeping with Matt* thing."

Mary Frances gave her new friend a quick glance and said, "Promise?"

"Pinky promise!" responded Dagny as she held out her pinky finger. They both laughed.

"I happen to have some other news," said Mary Frances, raising her eyebrows and acting like she probably wasn't going to tell what it was.

"What? What news? Tell me!" demanded Dagny.

Mary Frances smiled and surrendered without a fight. "Zander... who opened the conference room door... I think he's interested in you."

"Are you kidding me? Really?" Dagny asked, suddenly more serious. "What gives you that idea?"

"When I went back for the lunch cart this afternoon," replied Mary Frances, "I ran into him. He was asking lots of questions about you."

"Oh, man! I should have volunteered to go get that cart," said Dagny. "If we ever do that again, I get to go back for the lunch cart. I kind of sensed that while I was talking to him. But I decided it was just me. Gee, I like him, too. Mary Frances, this is most definitely the best job I've ever had. And you're the best roommate!"

The rest of the week passed uneventfully until Matt and Zander ate in the first-floor cafeteria on Thursday. They lingered a little too long by the serving tables talking to Mary Frances and Dagny. Jane noticed. At her first opportunity, Jane approached the women. Looking to her left and right as if she was doing something clandestine, she whispered, "Mary Frances, do you know him, Matt Archer? You were asking about him last week. Remember the text you sent me during the blizzard?"

"Well, yes, kind of," answered Mary Frances, thinking quickly. "Monday, the CEO had us prepare some lunches for the Research Department. They had been too busy to eat, so we helped out. Mr. Archer and his associate were just thanking us."

"His *associate* is Zander Fromm. He's an analyst in the Research Department. Matt Archer is his boss," informed Jane in an authoritative tone.

"You know everyone!" said Dagny, complimenting Jane. "Gosh, your talents are wasted here in the cafeteria. You should be in HR." Jane nodded in agreement. "So, Mr. Fromm... is that German?"

"No," scolded Jane. Mary Frances watched with amusement. "Maybe his parents or grandparents, but he's from Louisville, Kentucky. UK grad, economics, US Army, played basketball in high school but not good enough to make the UK team. Single. Dated Teresa Drew in accounting last year. He likes to run. He's done some races, 10K's or whatever you call them."

"You definitely belong in HR," Dagny continued. "You're so smart." Jane ate up the compliments as Mary Frances bit her tongue, trying not to laugh as her friend skillfully wrangled information out of the cafeteria busy body.

When Jane finally left, Mary Frances tried to look serious. "You are so bad!" she whispered to Dagny. Dagny smiled and winked at Mary Frances as they continued working.

At last it was Saturday. Mary Frances spent most of the day preparing for her date with Matt Archer. She had considered buying a dress but already had a new one hanging in her closet. When she had first moved to Nashville, she had been wandering around Nordstrom at Green Hills when she saw it. She'd tried it on and had fallen in love. It was an excessive and impulsive purchase, but she did it anyway. Now six months later she felt that maybe the move to Nashville, the new job and the new dress were all for a reason.

After a morning manicure and pedicure, she stopped by

the Nordstrom shoe department. She found a pair of Ted Baker London Skalett pumps in black with contrasting, gray soles which would be perfect for the gray, lace, midi dress. Visualizing the outfit together, she thought, *Sexy. But not too sexy as Dagny would say. I have a black clutch. Not too much jewelry. My simple, silver bangle and silver loop earrings. I hope French nails were a good choice.*

Mary Frances purchased the shoes but continued obsessing. *I've never spent this much on a pair of shoes. They weren't as expensive as the Gucci's or the Christian Louboutin's, but they were expensive! With Dagny splitting the monthly rent, I have a little more wiggle room in my budget. I should start saving money. But these shoes are so pretty! I hope Matt likes my outfit. Why am I so worried about this? He seemed to like me in Sophia's sweat suit, so surely he'll be pleased tonight.*

Mary Frances was ready by five o'clock, thirty minutes early. "Mary Frances, you look beautiful," said Dagny when Mary Frances entered the living room modeling the outfit. "He's going to fall in love with you, if he hasn't already. And your hair is amazing!" Mary Frances' long, dark hair curved around the back of her neck, falling in a cascade of curls over her left shoulder.

"Are you sure?" asked Mary Frances. "Does everything look right?"

"Perfect," her friend replied. "Just remember to stand up straight, shoulders back, and deep breaths. That'll give you a little extra *personality*!"

Mary Frances smiled and shook her head as Dagny laughed.

Mary Frances' phone rang at exactly 5:30. It was Matt requesting she open the gate for him. She gave him the code and in a few minutes, he was at the door. "Wow! You are beautiful!" he said, checking Mary Frances out from head to toe. Mary Frances glowed from Matt's compliments as they walked to the vehicle.

"Have you been to Moto? I chose it because I thought with your culinary background you would enjoy it," Matt said as they drove through Nashville toward the Gulch.

"No, I haven't," responded Mary Frances, "but I've heard wonderful things about it."

"I enjoy the sommelier and the wine pairings he comes up with. Some of them are just spectacular!" he said.

"Thank you for this evening, Matt," she said.

"You shouldn't thank me until I take you home," he laughed. "Our date may be a complete bust. You never know."

"I'm sure that won't happen. Moto is incredible, and then the Symphony. I also want to thank you for asking me out and being very patient," she said, trying to explain. "And for saving me in the blizzard." Matt didn't respond with words but reached across the console and took her hand.

"So, you must like the color blue," she commented, trying to steer the subject to something more comfortable.

"Yes, how did you know?" he asked.

"Just a guess. Blue La Cornue, blue Range Rover," she said.

"You're very observant," he said. "You should have been an analyst."

"What does CFA mean?" asked Mary Frances. "I've seen those letters after your name sometimes."

"Certified Financial Analyst," Matt answered.

"Can you tell me more about what you do?" Mary Frances asked. "You told me some during the blizzard, but I still don't completely get it. It's very interesting."

"I'm glad you don't completely get it," he laughed, "because I don't either. It's a strange profession. Hmm, what is something else we do? Well, we look for black swans."

"Black swans?" she said. "You don't work with birds."

"It's a metaphor," Matt explained. "You see, prior to 1697, all the swans that people had seen were white. Then, a Dutch explorer found black swans in Australia. The point is that no one knew to be looking for black swans because no one had seen them before. Who knows, maybe there are purple swans somewhere. So, an example of a black swan might be the internet. If we could go back 50 years ago, no one could have imagined the internet, but here it is today. Because the future is unknown, we can only think about it in today's terms. But the future won't be like we imagine because of the black swan effect."

"I never thought about it like that," Mary Frances said.

"And we always must be aware of how we behave because of this," said Matt. "Here's an example. September 11, 2001. The attacks of that day were all executed with large, commercial airliners. So, we react to that by going overboard on airport and airline security. Try taking a pair of fingernail clippers on a plane. Our human tendency is to believe that the next attack will be exactly like the first one, another attack using a jet. Meanwhile, municipal water systems are incredibly vulnerable as are power plants. Chances are, the next one won't be an attack using a jet. It will be something else. It's predictable that it will be something no one has thought of- no one except the terrorist."

"Your world is so different than mine," said Mary Frances. "I don't like to think about things like that."

"I don't want you to," said Matt. "I want you to think about what you're going to have for dinner and what you're going to hear at the symphony. I want you to enjoy tonight. I'm sorry about getting so paranoid. But you asked, and that's something we do... look for black swans."

The evening went wonderfully. Mary Frances thoroughly enjoyed the food and the wine at Moto, being uniquely able to discern spices and ingredients in the various courses that Matt couldn't. Every bite was culinary bliss for her, and Matt enjoyed her delight in it.

At the symphony, Mary Frances was once again delighted. Walking in on Matt's arm in her new dress and new shoes made her feel like royalty. Holding onto his arm, she thought, *His suit fits him perfectly, and the fabric feels so fine. It must be Italian.* Making their way to their seats, Mary Frances was awed by the huge chandeliers illuminating the concert hall. The ornate woodwork and the red, upholstered seats were stunning. The experience was overwhelming!

The Shostakovich Symphony was moving in the near perfect acoustics of the symphony hall. At intermission, Matt whisked his date away to the Founders Hall where they were plied with wine and miniature pastries. Matt had excused himself for a moment when Mary Frances heard a familiar voice.

"Mary Frances? Is that you?" the voice said. She turned around to see Mr. and Mrs. Borland standing behind her.

"Mr. Borland!" she said. "How nice to see you!"

"Our paths just keep crossing this week," he said. "Let me introduce my wife, Marsha. Marsha, this is Mary Frances Foster. She works with us at Veritas. Mary Frances, are you here by yourself?" he asked. His question was answered as Matt came walking back in.

"Jim, Marsha, I see you've found Mary Frances," said Matt.

"Yes, we have," said the CEO. "And may I say, Mary Frances, you look stunning tonight."

"Slightly different than the cafeteria uniform," Matt commented.

"Yes, I should say so," said the CEO.

"Are you enjoying the symphony?" asked Mrs. Borland.

"Yes, I am, thank you," said Mary Frances. "Matt took me to Moto, and the symphony, and now the Founders Hall. Everything has been wonderful."

"Your friend Dagny isn't here, is she?" asked Mr. Borland.

"No, we left her at home," said Matt.

"She's Mary Frances' friend and roommate; they work together," the CEO explained to his wife. "She's the one who kicked me out of the cafeteria last week. Remember, I was telling you?"

"Oh, yes," said Mrs. Borland. "You tell your friend that she has my permission to kick him out of the kitchen anytime she wants. I do it all the time. He just gets underfoot." They all laughed and visited until it was time to return for the rest of the Shostakovich symphony.

When the symphony ended, the concert hall erupted into almost deafening applause. Fifty years later, Mary Frances would still remember that night, her first real date with Matt. When Matt took her to her apartment at the Grove, he walked her to the door, and kissed her goodnight. It was the second time he'd kissed her. As Mary Frances lay in bed that night and drifted off to sleep, she took that kiss with her into her dreams.

Chapter 14
Matt

As Mary Frances and Dagny settled into the routine of being roommates and co-workers, their relationships with Matt and Zander developed also. Matt Archer continued giving Mary Frances his attention and taking her out on dates. Dagny Bennett was overjoyed the evening Zander Fromm called to ask her out. Working together on the *Endex*, Matt's and Zander's work relationship grew into friendship. The world seemed to settle down and become a bit more peaceful as Christmas approached.

One evening as Matt was taking Mary Frances home from a movie he asked, "Mary Frances, what are you doing for Christmas? Will you be going home to Charlotte?"

"No, I'll be staying here in Nashville," she said.

"I expected you'd be going home to see your parents," Matt said as he pulled up in front of Mary Frances' apartment. Mary Frances looked down at her hands. "Is something wrong?" he asked.

"I probably need to tell you something," she said. Matt pushed the button on the dash, turning off the diesel engine and sat back in the leather seat.

"This is kind of complicated," she said. "It's about why I don't go home very much. You see, my father is really my step-father. My dad passed away when I was a sophomore in high school. About a year later, my mom remarried .... George. I never did like him, but I guess my mom does."

Matt stayed quiet and listened as she continued. "Anyway, my mom works at Macy's. One night she had to work late, actually all night, to count inventory." Mary Frances stopped. Still looking down at her hands, she took a deep breath and exhaled.

"I was asleep in my room when I felt his hands on me. George. For a second, it seemed like a bad dream; but then I was awake, and it was no dream. I screamed and started hitting him. Fortunately, he's not any bigger than I am. I jumped out of bed with him after me and made it to the bathroom. I got the door shut and locked. I'm faster than he is. He tried to get me to come out, but I wouldn't. At first he talked nice, but then he got mean. He told me I'd better not say a word to my mom. He started calling me terrible names and threatening me. I didn't say anything; I just held my breath as I could see the doorknob turn as he tried to force his way inside. I was afraid he might kick the door in, but he didn't. Eventually, he got tired and gave up. But before he did, he said one last thing through the door... really quiet. He said I wasn't normal and that I was frigid."

Matt remained calm but was raging inside as he reached over and took her hands. "I'm so sorry," he said.

"I didn't come out of the bathroom until morning. I slept on the floor. I laid a bunch of towels on the floor because the tile was so cold. Then, the next morning when I saw my mom, I told her." Mary Frances sniffed, taking her hand from Matt to wipe her eyes. "My mother didn't believe me. George told her I had been acting crazy, and he was *worried* about me. She didn't believe me, Matt. My own mother! She wanted me to see a counselor. So, that was the day everything changed. My mother chose George instead of me. I try my best to not be angry, but how does a mother do that to her child? I have no doubt I'm right. I know what he did.

"After school that day, I went to Home Depot and bought a lock. A friend helped me install it on my bedroom door. From then on, that door was bolted every night. No one ever talked about it again, but there it was... always the elephant in the room.

This may sound odd; but more than what George did, it's my mom not believing me that hurts the most. I decided the best option for me was to finish my education and move to Nashville to start over."

Matt opened the center console and got a tissue for Mary Frances. "Looking back, I was lucky," she said. "It could have been much worse. It's just that I lost my father and then my mother. There's one other thing," she said, looking up at Matt. "You have been so patient. I can't imagine what you must think about me. Every time we kiss, I get nervous and we stop. I didn't even know what that word meant when he called me that. I had to look up *frigid* to see what it meant. What if I am? I keep hearing him say those words through the bathroom door."

"Mary Frances, you're not," Matt said. "He said that to hurt you and to make you doubt yourself. It was cruel."

"Yes," she said, "but I don't really know. And I keep wondering if I am... if something is wrong with me. I needed to explain it to you. That's why I sometimes act like I do."

"Mary Frances, I'm sure that's not the case. Time will take care of it," Matt said. "Try not to worry.'"

"I hope so," she said. "But, I'm afraid you'll become tired of me getting nervous. And I'm afraid of disappointing you."

"Mary Frances, I love you," Matt said. The words made Mary Frances' heart almost stop. "I know you're a little nervous. But I'm patient- most things not so much- but with you, I am. It's easy. I don't get aggravated with you. I don't get mad at you. And it's not possible for me to be disappointed in you.

"Have you noticed how well we get along?" Matt asked. "You're the other part of me. I don't have to be anyone other than who I am. I love you, and nothing will change that."

"Oh, Matt!" Mary Frances said, filled with emotion. The relief of finally telling him everything and his response were overwhelming. "I love you, too!" she exclaimed as she threw her arms around Matt. It was a moment she had never imagined possible.

As the moment passed, Matt smiled and said, "This all started because of Christmas. I was going to invite you to my house. Do you remember me telling you about the wood-fired oven?" he asked. Mary Frances nodded.

"How about pizza for Christmas?" he asked.

"That would be wonderful," she answered. "But could I bring someone with me?" Matt was caught off guard. "Dagny's parents are going to California for Christmas because her sister lives there. So, we had planned to celebrate Christmas at our apartment, but I'd rather go to your cabin. Could I bring Dagny?"

"Sure, the more the merrier! And I'm not sure what Zander is doing, but if he doesn't have plans, should I invite him?" Matt asked.

"Yes, invite him, too," Mary Frances said as she gave Matt another kiss.

Once inside the apartment, Mary Frances went directly to Dagny's room where she found her roommate sound asleep. "Dagny, wake up!" she said, leaning over and gently shaking her friend.

"What is it? What's wrong?" asked Dagny, rubbing her eyes trying to wake up.

"Dagny, he told me!" Mary Frances said. "He told me he loved me!"

"That's great," said Dagny, yawning. "Did you wake me up to thank me?"

"No... But yes, thank you for convincing me to say yes when he asked me out," she said. "Dagny, he loves me. I suspected he did, but I wasn't sure. I didn't believe anything like this could happen to me. It's like we were made for each other. He's wonderful. I am so in love with him!" Mary Frances sat on the bed with her friend, in the dark, the only light coming in from the hallway. She felt even happier, having shared her excitement.

"You know what's next, don't you?" asked Dagny, stretching her arms as she continued to wake up.

"No, what do you mean?" asked Mary Frances.

"He might propose," said Dagny. "He might ask to marry you."

"Oh, Dagny, that's not going to happen," she said. "That would be way too much to hope for."

"Well, we need to have a talk about this, just like the

talk we had on the dating thing," said Dagny. "If he asks you to marry him, you say, *Yes*. Now, let's practice. *Mary Frances, will you marry me?*"

Mary Frances giggled. "Yes!" she said.

"Very good. We'll practice that a few times every day until you get it down perfectly," said Dagny as the two girls laughed.

"But I have more news," said Mary Frances. "I'm going to Matt's for Christmas, and you're invited, too."

"That sounds like fun," said Dagny. "I'd like to see his house. And with my family gone to California to see my sister, that would be great."

"I also asked Matt to invite Zander if he isn't going to Louisville to see his parents," added Mary Frances.

"With news like that, you can wake me up anytime," said Dagny. "Seriously, I want Zander to go home if he can; but if not, a romantic Christmas in a log cabin with that fireplace I've heard about at least a million times sounds perfect!"

Chapter 15
Christmas

Between work and too many Christmas get-togethers, December was hectic. There were parties at Veritas, another at the Grove, shopping to be done, gifts to be wrapped and travel plans to be determined. Zander's parents decided to visit his brother for the holidays. Since Zander was going to be alone, Matt included him for Christmas at the cabin. Matt prepared the outdoor oven for pizzas and bought a bottle of port just in case Mary Frances asked for some.

"Are you going to get Matt a Christmas present?" asked Dagny one evening at the apartment.

"Yes, but what do you get a man who has a La Cornue range, matching Range Rover, and a steam engine?" answered Mary Frances. *Not to mention tons of all kinds of supplies and guns in the basement*, she thought. "I actually already have his gift, Dagny. I hope he likes it," she said. "It's an LP of the Shostakovich Symphony Matt took me to on our first date. I hope he doesn't have it already. There's a record player in his great room, and I think he likes to listen to music on the old records. Are you going to get Zander a gift?"

"Yes, I'm making him cookies," said Dagny. "He has the most amazing metabolism. He eats like a horse and never gains an ounce. If I ate like he does, I'd weigh 300 pounds!"

"Not fair!" said Mary Frances. "Don't you hate people like that!"

On Christmas morning, a Friday, Mary Frances and Dagny shared a light, holiday breakfast and then got ready to drive to Matt's. "I checked the weather," said Mary Frances. "After what happened with that blizzard, I pay more attention than I used to. There is a slight chance of snow. There's not supposed to be any accumulation, but I'm wearing my boots, just in case. I won't be running around in the snow in ballet flats ever again!" The drive to Matt's was easy as there was almost no traffic. Soon, they were on a country road and then turned up a single lane drive into the woods.

"This is where you spent the blizzard?" asked Dagny as they wound through the trees. Mary Frances nodded.

"This is so cool," Dagny said as they approached the house. "What a beautiful cabin! This just occurred to me, Mary Frances. If you two got married, you would be living here!"

"Dagny, stop saying that," scolded Mary Frances.

"Can I still be your roommate when you're living here?" asked Dagny, teasing her friend.

"Dagny, don't talk like that. I'm afraid you'll forget and say something in front of Matt," said Mary Frances as she put her Toyota in park and turned off the engine. The front door opened as Matt and Zander came out to greet the girls.

"Did I see some snow?" said Matt, winking at Mary Frances as he opened the car door for her. "Look at those boots! You're ready this time, aren't you!"

"Yes," Mary Frances answered, smiling at Matt and remembering the moment he had opened the door when he'd rescued her in the blizzard. "I learned my lesson."

"Merry Christmas, Mary Frances Foster," Matt said, giving her a kiss as she got out of the car.

"Merry Christmas, Matthew Archer," she responded as she admired his sweater and jeans. "Let's get inside by the fire," she said, remembering the fireplace and being with him.

"Do you think they know we're here?" Zander whispered to Dagny as they followed behind. Matt had his arm around Mary Frances as they laughed about something. Dagny smiled and shrugged her shoulders.

Once inside, Matt closed the massive wooden door behind them. As Dagny gazed around the room at all the logs and beams, she could hardly take it all in. "Wow, this is like something out of a magazine," she said. "This is magnificent." Then her eyes caught sight of the huge, stone fireplace across the great room. Looking at Mary Frances, she exclaimed, "And what a fireplace!"

"Come in!" said Matt. "Merry Christmas, and welcome to my cabin. Let's all sit by the fire, and I'll get us something to drink. Coffee? Eggnog? Port?" Dagny and Mary Frances then saw the Christmas tree, probably 10 feet tall, standing on the side of the great room near the door to Mary Frances' bedroom. The tree was covered in tiny, white lights and gold ornaments.

"Eggnog sounds wonderful!" said Dagny. Gazing around at the log and stone interior of the great room, she was enveloped in its warmth and security.

"You two sit by the fire, and I'll help Matt," said Mary Frances.

"Coffee for me," said Zander. Mary Frances nodded and disappeared around the corner of the stone wall into the kitchen. As soon as she was in the kitchen, Matt was waiting and took her in his arms.

"That wasn't a very good kiss I gave you outside," he whispered as he kissed her again. "You're so cute in your snow boots!"

"I love you," she said. "This is the best Christmas ever! There is no place I'd rather be than here with you."

The four friends spent the day together, eating, drinking, and exchanging gifts. Matt loved the LP of the symphony. Mary Frances was pleased he didn't have the Shostakovich Symphony No. 10. He immediately put it on the turntable and beautiful, background music filled the room. Dagny gave Zander the chocolate chip cookies she'd made for him, and he started sampling them immediately.

"Those look delicious," said Matt. "Let me try one."

"Heck, no! Your girlfriend's the chef," said Zander. "Have her make you some. I'm not sharing!" Dagny was pleased and proud. Everyone laughed while Zander guarded his box of cookies.

"I won't share my cookies, but I have a gift for all of us," Zander said, pulling something from his pocket. "Four tickets to the Grand Ole Opry."

"Son of a bacon bit!" said Dagny. "I've always wanted to go!"

"I've never been either," said Mary Frances, excitedly.

"Thanks, Zander," said Matt.

When Dagny opened her gift from Zander, she found a pair of fleece-lined house slippers and a pair of heavy, wool socks. "It's because you're always complaining your feet are cold," he said. Mary Frances agreed.

Finally, Matt gave Mary Frances her gift. When she opened the small box and saw the gold bracelet, she was stunned. "It's so beautiful, Matt," she stammered. "I've not seen one like it before." She studied the design of gold, spiral links.

"The design is from ancient Greece," he said.

"I love it. Thank you," she said, taking the bracelet out of the box. As Matt slipped it on her wrist, she asked, "Does the design have a meaning?"

"Back in the days of ancient Greece, the port cities were busy, prosperous places," Matt explained. "But the interior of the country was agricultural. It was quiet and peaceful. That area was called Arcadia. The design is from Arcadia."

Mary Frances touched the bracelet, admiring it on her wrist. Curious about Matt's elucidation, she made a mental note, *I must look this up and read about Arcadia.*

"Arcadia," said Zander. "A place of peace. Sounds wonderful." The four relaxed by the fire, listening to the music... lost in their thoughts.

"I'm going out to the patio to light the oven," said Matt. "It'll take about an hour to get up to temperature. Mary Frances, come go with me. I'll show you how to get a wood oven started. Then, we'll come back, and I'll help you with the pizza dough." The two put on coats and went out the kitchen door onto the back deck. Once the fire was going in the oven, they returned to the kitchen to work on the pizzas. The sound of music in the great room had been replaced by the television.

Zander came around the corner into the kitchen and said,

"Matt, you need to see this. It's all over my social media, so I turned on the TV."

Dagny was standing in front of the television as the others joined her. The four watched in silence. Another bomb had been detonated inside the Vatican, killing an unknown number of people. The news cameras showed the chaos of police, ambulances and panicking people. Next, the news anchor switched to Westminster in London where a similar scene was occurring. Finally, the scene moved to Beijing where thousands of protestors were marching towards a column of Chinese tanks in Tiananmen Square. Before their eyes, the friends, who had been enjoying a peaceful Christmas together, watched as the tanks opened fire on the protestors, mowing them down.

"Oh, my God in heaven," Dagny cried. "What is going on?"

Zander's stony guise was mirrored by Matt. The demeanor of the men did not go unnoticed by Mary Frances. "Turn it off," Matt said, realizing the news would cast a cloud over Christmas.

"How can this happen on Christmas!" said Dagny.

"Zander, why don't you and Dagny throw some more firewood on the fire," said Matt. "Mary Frances, you need to check on the dough to see how it's rising." Everyone silently complied and went about their duties as Matt opened his laptop and began bringing up various charts and graphs.

After a while, Mary Frances came in the great room and said, "Matt, should I go out and check the fire and see the temperature in the oven?" Matt continued focusing on the laptop screen but finally responded.

"Yes, good idea," he said, closing the laptop and standing. "I'll go with you."

"Is everything alright?" she asked. "This is bad, isn't it? Will it affect your index?" Matt looked at her in silence. "This is serious," she said, answering her own questions.

Matt put an arm around her and turned her toward the kitchen. "Let's go check on the oven," he said.

The events in the news cast a cloud over Christmas. Mary Frances had planned the Christmas pizza baking to be a fun activity as each one of them would build their own pizza, adding the toppings they liked. Then, the pizzas would be taken outside to the oven and Matt would bake them. At 900 degrees, it would only take a short time to produce a perfect pizza.

Mary Frances put all the various toppings from pineapple to pepperoni in bowls on the island and rolled out the dough into four circles, one for each of them. When everything was ready, Matt went back to the great room where he found Zander and Dagny on the sofa, talking quietly. "Pizza time!" he said. "Come on in."

All were gathered in the kitchen when Mary Frances said, "I've rolled out a crust for each of us. Build your pizza the way you like. Matt will be outside tending the oven. Just take it to him, and he'll bake it. The oven is very hot, so it will only take about two minutes per pizza. Matt, if you'll fix yours before you go outside, I'll bring it with mine."

"Before we start," Matt said, "let's say a prayer. We mustn't forget the real reason for Christmas." Everyone nodded in agreement and bowed their heads. "Heavenly Father, on this Christmas Day, we thank You for the gift of Your son, Jesus. We thank You for the blessings of this year and ask Your blessing and guidance in the year ahead. Please be with and comfort those who are suffering in today's attacks, and we pray that the violence stops. Thank You for these friends who have joined me today to celebrate the birth of Your son. We pray these things in His name. Amen."

The pizzas were made quickly and taken to Matt who was waiting outside. Mary Frances was right in that it only took a couple of minutes at 900 degrees. Because the winter air was almost freezing, it felt good to stand by the open door of the oven as the heat spilled out. Soon, everyone was inside gathered around the roaring fire in the great room, enjoying the pizza and drinks including spiced cider, Christmas sangria and ale.

As they were finishing the meal, Matt said, "I want to thank you all for coming today and spending Christmas with me. It would have been lonely without your company."

"Thanks for inviting me," said Dagny. "This is such a great place to celebrate Christmas. We just need about two feet of snow!"

"No, no, not another blizzard," said Matt. "Once a year is plenty!"

"Yes, but I've heard all about it from Mary Frances. It's not fair!" teased Dagny. "While I was freezing, starving and contending with three other women, she was here in this five-star ski lodge. Nice and warm, fireplace and all, flannel sheets, and hot water! Not to mention, her very own bathroom!" They all laughed at her dramatic accounting of the blizzard.

"Well, if it looks like we're going to have another one, you're welcome to come over, Dagny," said Matt.

"How about me?" asked Zander.

"Yes. You too, Zander," said Matt, laughing.

"But really, thank you," said Dagny. "I would have been alone, too. My parents flew to California to be with my sister and her family. They have two kids. I love my niece and nephew, but my parents are just crazy about their grandchildren. I don't blame them, but sometimes it's like I don't exist."

"That's interesting," said Zander. "My brother lives in San Francisco, and my parents are always going there to see my two nephews. My brother and I are very different. We get along, but not really. He's very liberal, and I'm the opposite. It's kind of the same with my parents. We get along, but we don't see eye to eye on lots of things. It was the Army and Afghanistan. They don't understand me. We're just different."

"I'm an only child. I don't get along very well with my mother and stepfather," said Mary Frances. "Even though our situations are different, I can relate."

"Matt, how about you?" asked Zander. "Where is your family?"

Matt smiled a sadly and answered, "I'm from right here in Nashville, Brentwood actually. Like Mary Frances, I'm an only child. My parents both died in a car accident when I was in college in Knoxville at UT. Drunk driver. They were coming back from a movie."

"I'm so sorry," said Dagny. "I had no idea."

Mary Frances looked at Matt, feeling his sorrow. "So, even if you don't get along with your family," he said. "It's still better than not having them.

"I guess we all have some things in common," said Zander. "It can be hard to talk about, but thank you all for sharing. It makes me feel a little better somehow."

"Zander, I get it, that people don't understand you... because of Afghanistan," said Matt. "What was your MOS?" Mary Frances and Dagny looked at Matt, unsure as to the meaning of the acronym, and then at Zander to see if he understood."

"Eleven Bravo," Zander answered. "I was a SAW gunner." The two women were still confused and looked back at Matt.

"Really! A SAW gunner," responded Matt with an expression that indicated surprise and interest. Mary Frances, who was learning to read Matt, could see the wheels turning in his head. She wondered why.

"That's right, boss," said Zander. "Brass to the grass." The two men laughed.

Matt and Mary Frances picked up the dishes and took them to the kitchen while Zander threw another log on the fire. In the kitchen, Mary Frances whispered to Matt, "What is a SAW?"

Matt answered, "That stands for Squad Automatic Weapon. Every infantry platoon has one."

"Is that important? I could tell that interested you," she said. "And what's with brass and grass?"

"Maybe," Matt smiled. "It's just interesting that Zander has experience with that weapon. The SAW is belt fed, so he was referring to how you load the weapon correctly."

Mary Frances thought, *He's answered my question but not completely. Why is this important?* Matt pulled her close to him and whispered in her ear, "Everyone will be going home after a while. I want you to stay. Zander can take Dagny home."

"I shouldn't," answered Mary Frances.

"You've never been in my bedroom," Matt said. "I think there's something there you'd like."

"Matt, I don't think I'm ready yet," said Mary Frances.

"What in the world are you talking about?" Matt answered with a sly grin. "I was talking about the fireplace. I know you like fireplaces, and there's one in my bedroom. Not to mention, my bed is more comfortable than the sofa."

Mary Frances gave Matt a stern look and said, "You think

you're so clever." Then, she smiled. "What will Zander and Dagny say?"

"Not a thing," he said. "In fact, they might want to be alone themselves." Mary Frances remembered the blizzard and how it felt to sleep next to him. She watched his blue eyes as he waited for her answer.

"OK, but sleeping means *sleeping*," she said, as Matt kissed her again.

When it came time to leave later in the afternoon, Matt said, "Zander, would you take Dagny home for Mary Frances? She's going to stay awhile, so it would be great if you'd give Dagny a ride back to the apartment." Zander quickly agreed.

Back in the kitchen, Dagny asked Mary Frances, "When are you coming home? I know what's going on here."

"I'm not sure when I'll be home, Dagny," Mary Frances answered. "Maybe this evening. Or I might stay all night since tomorrow is Saturday. And it is just *sleeping*."

"Don't worry about me," said Dagny. "I'll be fine, all alone, no one to talk to, all by myself."

Mary Frances smiled at her friend and said, "If you're trying to make me feel sorry for you, it's not working."

"OK, I'll see you when I see you," said Dagny.

Matt and Mary Francis stood on the sidewalk and waved as Dagny and Zander drove away. As they walked back in, Matt said, "You were here for four days during the blizzard, and I don't recall you were ever in my bedroom. I want to show you the fireplace."

Matt's bedroom was like the others in the cabin with the wooden plank floors, log walls and beams overhead. The difference was the stone fireplace positioned beside the queen-sized bed. "Shall I light it?" Matt offered.

Mary Frances smiled at him and said, "OK. You know I have a thing for fireplaces. I just love them, especially stone ones."

"I do, too," he said. "And they have to be wood burning. I realize the ashes and firewood are more work, but they're still better than the gas ones." Mary Frances leaned back against the bed and watched him as he kneeled and struck a match. The fire was already prepared and caught very quickly. Soon, the fire was blazing, igniting the firewood he had placed over the kindling.

"Gosh, it's beautiful," Mary Frances said. "A fireplace in the bedroom. What a wonderful idea!" She could smell the faint scent of smoke, and it reminded her of a campfire.

"Now, I'm not trying to seduce you," Matt said. "Well, maybe just a little. But if you stay, we could sleep here tonight." Mary Frances studied him as he talked. She was torn. "There is something just magical about sleeping by the fire," he continued. "Yes, it's nice in the great room, but here, it's even better. You can hear the fire crackle and watch the flames from the fireplace dance on the ceiling."

Mary Frances imagined lying in bed with Matt, the firelight dancing around them. She thought, *I want him to make love to me, but this will change everything. What if he's disappointed?* "Matt, I don't have any pajamas," she said, coming up with an excuse.

Matt walked over to the chest of drawers that he opened and produced a package wrapped in red with a green bow. "Merry Christmas," he said, handing the gift to Mary Frances.

"Another present!" she said, touching her bracelet. "The bracelet is so nice. You shouldn't have gotten me something else."

"Open it," he said.

Mary Frances untied the bow and gently pulled open the red wrapping paper. She broke into a big smile and started laughing. "Well, aren't you always thinking ahead!" she said, holding up a pair of women's flannel pajamas. "And of course, my size exactly. You realize you're making it very hard for me to say no."

The remainder of the afternoon slipped by with laughter and the perfection of simply being alone together. When evening came, Matt went in the bedroom and returned to the great room, wearing pajama bottoms and carrying Mary Frances' Christmas present. Thinking about how much she wanted to be with him every minute of every day, she took the gift from his hands. Mary Frances went in the bathroom and returned a few minutes later, wearing her new pajamas.

"How sexy!" Matt said.

"They are not," she responded, "but they are warm, and I like them a lot. Thank you!" Matt grinned and, taking her in his arms, kissed her. Turning off the lights, he took her hand to lead her to his bedroom. The only light in the cabin was from the fireplaces.

Together, they walked to the master bedroom, and by the fireplace side of the bed, he pulled down the covers. Then Matt put her in bed, carefully covering her. Tending the fire, he added two more logs. Mary Frances admired the muscles in his arms as he worked on the fire. *This is dangerously wonderful,* she thought. *He is so big and strong... If I say no, will he listen?... But I don't want to say no.*

Lying on her side and watching the fire, she felt Matt climb into bed. He snuggled up behind her, wrapping an arm around her. Kissing her ear and then her neck, his hand moved up and caressed her. Mary Frances turned to him and said, "Matt, this will change everything."

"Yes, it will. I love you, Mary Frances," Matt said. "I think I understand your hesitance. I'm going to love you forever. Nothing can change that. Nothing."

Mary Frances wrapped her arms around him, and they held each other in a long embrace of reassurance. When Matt's lips touched hers, she was swept away. This was the moment she'd never dreamed possible. "I love you, Matt," she whispered.

Matt's kisses moved down her neck to her breasts as he unbuttoned her pajamas. Delicious electricity coursed through her body as she passionately returned Matt's kisses. He pulled her pajama bottoms down to her knees as she brought up her feet to help him, taking them off. Mary Frances felt herself in an emotional kaleidoscope of kisses and caresses as she felt his body against hers.

Matt threw the covers back and was kneeling between her legs. He grasped her by the ankles and pulled her toward him. *Oh, my God!* she thought in breathless anticipation.

Lowering himself onto her, he whispered, "I love you, Mary Frances."

"I love you, too," she said as he pressed against her. Small, sensual sounds escaped her lips as the firelight reflected all around him on the ceiling above. In sweet surrender, she felt him push deep inside her. Moving faster, he covered her in kisses, finally climaxing inside her. With his weight on her and his arms around her pinning her to the bed, she felt completely owned and cherished by him.

When Matt raised himself up a bit, he kissed her gently on the lips. Slowly, he pulled out, then bent down and kissed her belly button. He rolled over beside her, pleasantly spent. Matt lay with his eyes closed as his breathing slowed, and Mary Frances watched him.

Matt opened his eyes and turned to her and said, "Come over here." She placed her head on his chest and wrapped her arm around him as he encircled her in his arms.

"Matt, was it OK?" she asked.

"Hmmm, it was wonderful," he said, becoming drowsy. "Shhh, don't talk now. Just lie here, and let me cherish you," he whispered. "You're beautiful."

Matt pulled the covers over them as the fire cast its glow around the room. He held her, feeling the warmth of their bodies together. As his fingers and toes tingled, he slipped into that paradise of afterglow.

I love him so much, she thought as she listened to the beat of his heart. *Don't ever leave me, Matt Archer... for I would absolutely die.*

A while later, after both had dozed in and out of sleep, Matt got up and went to the fireplace. Mary Frances watched him rearrange the fire and put on another log. *Is he mine?* she wondered. *I am most definitely his. He completely owns me. I want him to feel the same.* Mary Francis never took her eyes off him, admiring his body and unruly hair.

"Are you OK, sweetheart?" he asked, looking into her eyes.

"Yes, I think so," she said. "But I'm most concerned with how you are. Was I satisfying? I think you enjoyed me, but I'm not for sure. I want to please you, so you must show me what you like."

"Mary Frances," he said with a sigh. "You don't understand me yet. Yes, I enjoyed you very much. And yes, I will teach you how to please me. But I don't love you for sex. I love you for you. If you would have said no, I would have still loved you. Granted,

I would have gotten somewhat frustrated, but I would still love you."

"Matt, one month ago, I believed I would never have a boyfriend," she said, pulling the covers up to her chin. "Then, the blizzard and you. I'm forever changed. You own my heart. I belong to you completely. I have never felt like this in my life."

"I love you, Mary Frances Foster," he said, brushing her hair to the side and studying the features of her face. "It will all be fine. I think you're worried about our future. So, to allay those fears, I want to first ask you out tomorrow night to dinner and a movie. You stay here tonight, and I'll take you home in the morning. Then, I'll pick you up at 5:30 for dinner. Also, Jim Borland's birthday is coming up in mid-January, and Marsha Borland is throwing him a surprise party. I've been invited with strict instructions from Marsha that you are to be my date." Matt watched her to see if she was understanding.

"How did you know what I was thinking?" she said, putting her hand over her mouth.

"I'm not going to leave you," he said. "I will always love you."

"But you remember that I can't have children?" she asked.

"Shhh," he said, putting his finger on her lips. "I want you to stop worrying about things. I just want you to be happy."

Mary Frances shook her head and smiled, "Right now, the bathroom would make me happy."

"It's right there," Matt said, pointing to the bathroom door.

"Yes, but I'm naked," she said. "The only thing I have on is my bracelet."

"Have you forgotten what we just did?" he asked.

"No, of course not," she said, seriously.

"OK. I'll close my eyes," he said, "but when you come back, I want you naked."

"Matt!" she exclaimed. Then with a big smile, Mary Frances said, "OK, but close your eyes." Jumping out of bed, she ran to the bathroom and was back under the covers in record time.

"You didn't look, did you?" she asked.

"Of course, I did," he laughed. "You don't want me to lie do you?"

"Matt!" she exclaimed. "What am I to do with you?"

"I'll think of something," he said, smiling. "But, Mary Frances, I do want to talk about something that's serious." Mary Frances was a bit puzzled. "You know about our work at Veritas." She nodded her head in understanding. "If, God forbid, anything ever did happen, and I'm not saying it will... But if it did, you must come with me. You have to let me take care of you."

"Yes, Matt," she said, nodding her head in agreement. "I will be right here with you. I will help you. Whatever you tell me to do, I will do it."

Matt nodded his head and smiled, "Thank you, I don't know what the future holds exactly, but I want you with me. There's just one other thing..." Mary Frances continued to listen carefully. "We wouldn't be coming *here*," he added.

"Why not?" she asked. "Your house is so perfect, plus you have so many supplies."

"Yes, but the population density is too high," he explained, quietly. "We would need to disappear to a place where no one could find us."

"Where?" Mary Frances asked. "Where could that be?"

Matt touched her bracelet and said, "Arcadia."

Chapter 16
Mrs. Joiner

Mary Frances and Matt rang in the new year at a party downtown that ended with fireworks over the Cumberland River. Little did anyone know, more fireworks were coming. Mary Frances was amazed how her life had changed so quickly and how happy she was. Dagny and Zander continued to get better acquainted. Spending more time together, they discovered their personalities complimented one another, and the two became inseparable. Life at Veritas continued.

"Dagny, have you made any new year's resolutions?" asked Mary Frances on the drive to work.

"Those things just set me up for failure," answered Dagny. "So, I resolve not to make resolutions. How about you, Mary Frances?"

Mary Frances laughed at her friend's outlook on life. "Matt told me we've made a joint resolution to get in better shape," she said.

"Yeah, I need to do that, too, so if Mrs. Joiner ever finds out about us and our boyfriends, I can run. And I don't have to outrun Mrs. Joiner," said Dagny. "I just have to outrun you!"

"Very funny, Dagny," replied Mary Frances as they laughed together. "We've run into several people from Veritas when we've been out on a date. In fact, that happened two nights ago at the

New Year's party. Maybe she'll never find out. But if she does, I'm prepared to stand up to her." The two navigated the Nashville traffic, finally arriving at Veritas.

As they got out of Mary Frances' Toyota and started across the parking lot, someone called, "Hey, Dagny!" Two women who had also arrived for work were hurrying to catch up.

"Sandra, Ginny! Good to see you both!" said Dagny. "Mary Frances, have you met Sandra and Ginny? The three of us started on the same day. Sandra is Compliance and Ginny is Operations. How are you both doing?"

"We're fine, just freezing!" said Ginny, buttoning up her coat. "Did you have a nice Christmas?"

"Yes, we did," said Dagny. "Mary Frances and I are roommates now. We both work in the cafeteria, so it's perfect for us to car pool."

"So do we," said Sandra. "Ginny and I live close to each other in Mt. Juliet, so we car pool, too."

"Are you liking Veritas and your new job?" asked Ginny.

"Yes, I do," said Dagny. "How was Christmas?"

"Great," said Sandra. "Our boys are little, and they love the decorations, Santa and the presents."

"We had a good Christmas," said Ginny, "except my husband bought a puppy for the boys. He's just a baby..."

"Your husband or the dog?" interrupted Dagny as they all laughed.

"True in both cases, but I was referring to the dog. He already weighs 65 pounds, and he's wrecking my house! All he wants to do is play and chew. He's already chewed up two pairs of shoes and one purse. I'm at my wit's end." The women were laughing at Ginny's Christmas tale of the new dog as they entered the building and went their separate ways.

After changing into cafeteria uniforms, Mary Frances and Dagny were headed to what was expected to be a typical day at work. "Very shortly, you'll be getting the uniforms with your name embroidered on the pocket," said Mary Frances. They were almost to the kitchen when Mrs. Joiner appeared, blocking the way.

With her hands on her hips and feet placed apart, she

said, "Miss Foster. My office. Now."

This is it! Dagny thought. *Here it comes. Someone has told her. Is she going to fire Mary Frances? Can she do that? How about me? Am I next?* Dagny swallowed hard and continued around Mrs. Joiner, feeling like she was abandoning her friend.

"Sit!" ordered Mrs. Joiner, pointing to the chair in front of her desk. Mrs. Joiner walked around and took her seat facing Mary Frances. "I am appalled and greatly disappointed! I have it on good authority that you were out on a date with Matthew Archer." Mary Frances was silent, showing no emotion. "Did you not hear me when I said that there will be no fraternizing with men at Veritas? Much less a man from the sixth floor! Of all my employees, you are the last one I would have dreamed to do this. I should terminate you this minute. However, you are an excellent employee, so I am prepared to give you another chance. You are to have no further contact with Mr. Archer. Is that understood?"

Mary Frances took a deep breath and exhaled, carefully considering her next words. "Mrs. Joiner, I love my job at Veritas. You're a good boss, and I like you very much. But I can't do that." Mrs. Joiner's eyebrows furled together as anger boiled up inside of her. "I can't because I love Matthew Archer. Mrs. Joiner, there is no rule at Veritas that prohibits employees from dating. With all due respect, you can't make up your own rules. Not to undermine your authority, but I doubt you can fire me for something that isn't a violation of a company policy."

"What planet are you living on, young lady?" said Mrs. Joiner, her face turning red with anger. "Were you not paying attention to what happened with the Lynn Hanson debacle? When Mr. Archer tires of you, he will drop you like a hot potato, and then I'll have an emotional, pregnant employee in my cafeteria to contend with."

"Mrs. Joiner," Mary Frances said, softly. "There are men like that; I do understand. But not all of them are like that. I don't know what the future holds, but I can't imagine Mr. Archer is one of those men. I believe he loves me. Please, stay out of this."

"If that's the way you want it, then that's the way it will be," said Mrs. Joiner. "I will write up your termination, indicating lack of performance here in the cafeteria and your failure to remediate. You will sign it and then leave."

"Mrs. Joiner," Mary Frances pleaded. "Please don't do this to yourself. That's not legal. Mrs. Joiner, I took Labor Law in college. There is not a problem with my work performance, and we both know it. Therefore, I will not sign a document that says there is. I don't want you to get yourself in trouble, Mrs. Joiner. You can't win. You know who Mr. Archer is. Do you actually believe he's going to allow you to terminate me based on some trumped up lack of job performance when it's really because I'm his girlfriend? How about Mrs. Martin in HR? She would come unglued if she found out you were doing this. Then, there's our CEO. Mrs. Borland is preparing a surprise birthday party for him next week. She has given Mr. Archer strict instructions that he is to bring me. Do you want to explain my termination to her?"

Mrs. Joiner sat behind her desk, trembling, "That's a lie. You don't know Mrs. Borland. You've never even met her."

Mary Frances sighed and said, "No, Mrs. Joiner, it's not a lie. Everything I have said is true. I do know Mrs. Borland. Matt took me to the Nashville Symphony on our first date. We met the Borland's in the Founders Hall during intermission. Now, Matt has instructions from Mrs. Borland to bring me to Mr. Borland's surprise party."

Mrs. Joiner's lower lip began to tremble as she broke into tears. "I just want to protect you girls. I don't want anything bad to happen to you like it did with ..."

Then she buried her head in her arms, sobbing on her desk.

Mary Frances kneeled by Mrs. Joiner, patting her back while she cried. "Don't cry, Mrs. Joiner. Everything will be alright. I won't say a word to anyone about our conversation today. No one will know." Slowly, Mrs. Joiner regained her composure and raised her head. Recognizing the kindness that she was being shown, Mrs. Joiner thanked Mary Frances and gave her a hug.

"There's just one more thing, Mrs. Joiner," added Mary Frances, "so you won't be surprised." Mrs. Joiner got a tissue from her desk and wiped her eyes as Mary Frances continued.

"Dagny Bennett is dating Zander Fromm. He's in the

Research Department with Mr. Archer. I just wanted to tell you." Mrs. Joiner nodded her head, wiped her eyes and smiled. Mary Frances quietly left the office, closing the door behind her.

"What happened?" asked Dagny, carrying a large pan of asparagus. Mary Frances had just returned from Mrs. Joiner's office.

"It all worked out," Mary Frances answered. "She understands now, and it will all be fine. Don't worry about Zander, either. I took care of it." Dagny didn't say a word as she wondered how her friend had done it. But she could tell that Mary Frances wasn't going to give any details.

Later that morning, Mary Frances felt her iPhone vibrate. It was a text from Matt.

Hey MFF, how's your morning? Wanted to let you know that I'm eating up here today. Got some honchos in from Merrill, so Jean Claude is doing lunch.

My morning is going great. Nothing unusual. I want to hear all about what JC does for lunch.

Will do. BTW do you like to hike?

Hike? As in walk in the woods?

Yep

I've never done it. I'm a city girl. I did go on one hike with you. Does that count?

Sure! Wanna take another one?

OK.

After work, I'll take you to REI. It's close. I'll get you some good hiking boots. This weekend let's go to Radnor and hike around the lake. It's only 1.35 miles. That's a nice short hike to get you started.

OK. Meet you on the parking lot. See you then.

See you then.

As Mary Frances and Dagny were setting up the serving trays in the cafeteria, Mary Frances said, "Matt wants me to learn how to hike. I guess I'll like it. I've never done anything like that. He wants to buy me hiking boots."

"Hiking is fun," said Dagny. "We hiked all the time when I lived in Sparta. There are waterfalls all around there. It's lots of fun. You'll like it."

"But how about animals and snakes?" Mary Frances asked.

"You are a city girl, aren't you," laughed Dagny. "There are no snakes in the winter. People are the only snakes you need to worry about. Matt will take care of you. So, is hiking part of your new year's resolution?"

"Must be. He texted me an invitation to go on a hike. He's taking me shopping for boots after work," Mary Frances said. "Can you drive my car home?"

"Sure thing," said Dagny. "Sounds like I'll be eating alone again. I'm concerned. I think my roommate has a boyfriend. Sometimes she just goes MIA on me, and I have no idea where she's gotten off to."

Mary Frances winked at Dagny, and they both laughed.

Chapter 17
Changes

Jim Borland sat at his desk reviewing a report when the chief economist joined him with his copy and a cup of coffee. The CEO's office was modern chic, steel and ironwood with abstract paintings. The wall of windows behind his desk afforded a view of Brentwood, a combination of office buildings and trees that in February were still a month away from leafing out. "What do you think, Brian?" Jim asked. "Have you studied the report?"

"Yes," the economist said as he sat down and made himself comfortable. "The trend continues. Violent protest continues to escalate along with non-violent." The door opened, and Matt Archer stepped in, carrying his laptop and several reports.

"Sorry, I'm late," Matt said as he took a seat next to the chief economist.

"No problem," said the CEO. "Let's go over this month's report, Matt. Tell us what you see."

"As I say in the conclusion, both violent and non-violent protests continue a slow escalation along with incidents of police brutality and alleged police brutality as tensions continue to rise between the population and the police, primarily in the demographic of lower socio-economic. But the escalation is slow enough that it's not affecting economic participation or the behavioral patterns of the majority. Translated, the population is getting used to school shootings, protests, and clashes with the police. If this happens slowly enough, giving the people time for it to become normal, they will continue their lives without change. People will continue to buy things and go to work every day. The risk, of course, lies in the possibility that it escalates faster than the people can digest. If they ever become scared enough to not leave their homes, then they'll not go to work. If enough don't go to work, then the economy loses traction, and we can slip into recession, depression, or at worst... complete collapse. On a positive note, this hasn't happened. As Brian knows, even better than I, the GDP is growing nicely. Inflation isn't bad, and employment is improving. International indicators are favorable, too, with Europe finally experiencing some growth, and the emerging markets reporting strength.

"Any idea why the Baltic Dry has slipped?" asked the economist.

"Yes, there were several ships that had been in dry dock for repair," answered Matt. "These came back on line at year end. This increased the supply, thus dropping the BDI. Cosco will be putting several ships in the yard for repair next month, and the index will return to where it was in December. It's just an anomaly as ships enter and leave service for repair." The CEO and chief economist nodded their heads as they continued to study the report.

"Hmmm, it's changing, but so far there's no affect," said the CEO. "*Your* index has moved into the 90's while the economy does well. What's your opinion, Brian?"

"Well, it'll go until it doesn't," the chief economist said. "We tend to look for cause and effect. We see these problems and expect the economy to be affected, but we must remember there are thousands of forces driving the economy. While we focus on a handful, we can't ignore the others. The United States has the cheapest energy on the planet. That's true regardless of how many shootings there are. The economy prospers. Washington has relaxed regulations. Again, true regardless of how many questionable police shootings there are.

"That's why we have this meeting every month. We hold

steady and watch Matt's index," continued Brian Eastman. "My concern is that the predictive sociological numbers of your index have never been higher. Houston, we have a problem. It's just a question of how that problem is resolved. Relatively gently, with minimal economic disruption, or with a lot of pain."

"So, are we in agreement that we maintain a *Hold* for this month?" asked the CEO. Matt and Brian nodded. "OK then. Matt, how often do you update your index?"

"If we're in *Buy* territory, monthly. *Hold* territory, then it's weekly. If we ever move to *Sell*, which would be anything greater than 100, then daily," Matt answered.

"Matt, your work on this is invaluable, on so many levels," said the CEO. "We appreciate you very much. If you ever feel the need to increase the frequency or budget on your index, just say so."

"I will," Matt said.

"I don't want to be paranoid. I'm an optimistic person, but this continues to worry me," said the CEO. "Brian and I have shared with you before about our own preparations. We have recently added another five years' food supply and an additional 100,000 rounds of ammunition. I remember that you also have made certain preparations. You have the same information we have. You provide that information. We will tell you what we're going to do, if anything, and when. Of course, we rely on your strictest confidence. I pray that all of this will have been for naught."

"My sentiments exactly," said Matt. "And your situation has been and will continue to be held to the highest level of secrecy."

"One last thing," said the chief economist. "Ellen Gentry, the Fed Governor out of Atlanta, called me today." At those words, both the CEO and Matt turned to the chief economist. "Perhaps you may recall," he said, "Ellen has been a fan of mine for some time. She was one of my biggest supporters when I testified before Congress back in '07 and '08 on the mark-to-market accounting law. She has gotten hold of our research and wants to know more. The Federal Reserve is every bit as concerned about the situation as we are."

"How did she get her hands on our research?" asked Matt.

"Across the backyard fence," said Brian. "One of our clients who subscribes to it happens to be her neighbor. He saw her out in the backyard and suggested she might like to read it. Then, he handed it to her over the fence." The CEO smiled and shook his head." When she saw Veritas Strategies on the report, she called me. Here's the deal. She wants to come visit us. Matt, she wants you to explain the index. She also wants to bring her two closest friends, the Fed Governors from Boston and Chicago."

"Interesting," said the CEO.

"She wants to come next week," said Brian. "Can you be ready by then, Matt?"

"Yes, of course," said Matt, already planning the best way to present his index to the visitors.

"They want it very low key," said Brian. "No one is to find out they're here. We'll meet on the sixth floor. Jean Claude can prepare lunch. They come in, and they leave. Fed Governors aren't widely known, so no one will notice. Employees will assume them to be from UBS or Merrill. You know, we never named the index. Should we do that before the meeting?"

"Zander Fromm in my department calls it the Endex, with an E," said Matt with a chuckle.

"I like it," said the chief economist. "But let's just use that internally. When referring to it outside the company, let's stay with the Index with an I. There's no need to scare folks."

"I agree," said the CEO. "OK, we're set. Sounds like a plan. Brian, call your friend and confirm the date and time. Matt, you get to work. We'll have a short meeting the day before to make sure we have all our ducks in a row." As they were leaving the meeting, the CEO said, "Hey Brian, do you know why God created meteorologists?"

"No," replied Brian, knowing the answer was coming.

"To make economists look good!" laughed the CEO.

Chapter 18
Dagny

Hey, Dagny!

Hey, Zander!

Do u like hockey?

Yes, I luuuuuuvvvv the Preds!

I snagged two tickets for the game tonight.

Can I go pleeeeeease?

Wanna grab a bite before?

Yes. When??

Now. I'll meet you by your car in 5.

"Mary Frances, can you drive my car home?" asked Dagny as she changed out of her uniform as quickly as possible. "Zander is taking me to a Predators game tonight, and he's picking me up in about three minutes!"

"Sure," said Mary Frances. "Just leave me your keys. What's a Predator?"

"Hockey, Mary Frances. They're Nashville's professional hockey team," Dagny explained while thinking, *My roommate must have been living under a rock all her life.* "See ya!"

"Have fun!" Mary Frances called after her friend who was running out the door.

In the parking lot, employees were leaving for the day as Dagny looked for Zander. As he came up behind her, he tapped her on the shoulder. "There you are," she said. "So, how did you get Predators tickets?"

"Matt got them from a company that shall remain unnamed. They use our ETF's," he explained as they got in Zander's car. "Matt's not really into sports. He'd rather hike or target shoot. He called and asked if I could use them."

"Sweet!" said Dagny. "Isn't that interesting! Mary Frances didn't even know who the Predators were, and Matt doesn't want free tickets to a game. He gives the tickets to you, and now I get to go to a Preds game!"

"Matt really likes her. They make a pretty good pair," said Zander as they pulled out of the parking lot.

"For sure, she's absolutely crazy about him," said Dagny. "What is it about her that he likes so much?"

"I have the inside scoop," answered Zander. Dagny couldn't wait to hear. "Matt told me. He said she's pretty but doesn't think she is, and she's smart but doesn't flaunt it. Matt is smart and appreciates a smart woman, but not one who's arrogant. He's always commenting about how kind she is. I've worked with him for two years now, and I can tell he really likes her. He's never talked like this about anyone else."

"Matt's right," said Dagny. "She's very kind. And she's very smart, but she doesn't let on like she is. She's a great roommate and my best friend. Have you noticed that we kind of look alike?"

"A little," he smiled. "You could pass for sisters."

"Yes. Of course, I'm the prettier one!" Dagny laughed. "And I like hockey, unlike Mary Frances, so I'm more fun. Right, Zander?"

Zander kept his eyes on the road and smiled.

When Dagny returned from the game that night, Mary Frances was on the sofa in her pajamas, eating popcorn and watching Netflix. "Hey, roommate!" said Dagny as she closed the door behind her and locked it. "Is there enough popcorn for me?" she asked.

With her mouth full of popcorn, Mary Frances nodded and held up the bowl for Dagny to see.

"OK, don't eat it all. I'll be right back," said Dagny. Quickly changing into pajamas, she returned to the living room and plopped down next to the popcorn bowl and Mary Frances.

The episode ended a few minutes later, and Mary Frances turned off the TV with the remote. "How did we do?" asked Mary Frances, trying to talk sports.

"How did we do?" asked Dagny.

"The Predators. The Nashville Predators, Dagny. Did we win?" asked Mary Frances.

"Oh, yes, the Predators!" said Dagny. "I just wasn't expecting you to ask that. Yes, we won. You follow hockey, Mary Frances?"

"Not particularly," Mary Frances answered, "but everyone else seems to, so I'm trying to be a good Nashvillian." The two girls laughed and ate popcorn together. "So, how is Zander? Did you two have a good time at the game?"

"We did," said Dagny. "Did you know that Matt gave us the tickets? That was very nice of him, but I don't think he's a big hockey fan. And I have it on good authority that his girlfriend isn't either." Mary Frances smiled as she popped another piece of popcorn in her mouth.

"You guys have been going out quite a bit, Dagny," said Mary Frances. "What do you think of him?"

"Mary Frances, he's great. I really like him. I keep expecting he'll stop asking me out, but he doesn't," said Dagny.

"Why would he stop asking you out?" asked Mary Frances. "I think Zander likes you. And you get along great. You're always laughing together."

"You're right," said Dagny. "You wouldn't know it at first, but he's funny. He's always making me laugh."

"He's sweet on you," said Mary Frances. "The day I went up to the sixth floor to get the cart, I knew it."

"But, Mary Frances," Dagny sighed.

"What? What's wrong?" asked Mary Frances.

"I'm just afraid he's out of my league," said Dagny. Mary

Frances looked at her friend with surprise. "No, I am," Dagny continued. "I've never had such a smart boyfriend. He's not my boyfriend. I should say I've never dated anyone so smart."

"Dagny, you're smart! Why do you think you're not?" asked Mary Frances.

"You don't get it, Mary Frances," said Dagny, hunting for another piece of popcorn among the unpopped kernels. "You're from Charlotte. You have a bachelor's and a master's degree! I'm just a regular girl from Sparta, Tennessee."

"Having college degrees doesn't mean someone is smart," said Mary Frances. "I've known some PhD's who didn't have enough sense to come in out of the rain, but we called them *Doctor*."

"Yes, but Zander not only has the degrees. He's smart," said Dagny. "My big worry is that he thinks I'm something I'm not."

"What am I missing here, Dagny?" asked Mary Frances. "Zander is very impressive and doing very well in his career. He's handsome. And he seems to like you, a lot."

"Mary Frances, you're my best friend," Dagny explained. "If you haven't noticed, I look up to you. I wish I was more like you."

"Dagny, you're my best friend, too," said Mary Frances. "I'm flattered that you wish you were more like me, but I don't understand why or how. Truthfully, I sort of envy you. You're braver than I am. And you're funny. I wish I were funnier. Sometimes I'll think of something funny, but I'm afraid to say it for fear it won't come out right."

"Oh, Mary Frances," said Dagny, starting to tear up. "You're so good. I'm not that good. I don't think you've ever done anything bad. Well, I have. And I'm afraid Zander might find out."

Mary Frances set the popcorn bowl on the coffee table and put her arms around her friend as she cried. "Oh, Dagny, I've never seen you cry. I'm the one who's supposed to cry around here. You're the strong one who never cries." Mary Frances held her as she sobbed.

"I'm such an idiot," said Dagny. "Why am I so stupid?"

"Dagny, what do you mean?" asked Mary Frances letting

go of her friend and just holding her hands. "And where do you get that I've never done anything wrong? Of course, I have."

"Right, like what have you done wrong?" asked Dagny.

"Well," said Mary Frances, thinking about the question. "In high school, several of us from my Algebra 2 class left the school football game at halftime and TPed our teacher's house! He never found out who did it. I worried we'd be discovered, but we never were."

Dagny looked at her friend and rolled her eyes. "You are so bad, Mary Frances!" she said, sarcastically. "Is that the best you can do? Have you ever been drunk? Have you ever smoked pot?"

"Well, once I was at a slumber party at Emily Stanton's house. Emily raided her father's bar and found a bottle of whiskey. I drank some, but I didn't get drunk. Truthfully, I don't understand why people like it. But, I know all about wine because of pairing. A good wine paired correctly can make a great meal even better; although, I'm careful not to overdo. I don't want to get drunk. I'm afraid of what I might do. And, no, I've never done drugs."

"Well, roommate," said Dagny, nodding her head. "I have. There was a time back in Sparta, well.... I was wild. Let's just say that Emily Stanton probably would not have invited me to her sleepover." Starting to cry again, Dagny said, "I am so ashamed and mad at myself. You probably hate me now. I hate me. Your parents would never have allowed you to be friends with me. What if Zander ever found out about how I was? You're right, he's impressive... more impressive than I deserve."

"Dagny, listen to me," said Mary Frances. "The things you did... and you don't need to go into detail... but the things you did, are you sorry you did them?"

"Oh, yes. I'd do anything if I could go back and change it," Dagny cried.

"Good, that's important," said Mary Frances. "And have you talked to God about this? Have you told Him you're sorry?"

"Yes, a thousand times," said Dagny between sniffs.

"Then God has forgiven you, and it's as if it never happened. It is forgiven and forgotten," Mary Frances reminded her.

"Yes, I understand that, and I believe it... but Zander,"

cried Dagny. "He wouldn't want me if he knew. I'm afraid Mary Frances. You could take Matt to your high school reunion and not have a worry in the world. I could never take Zander to something like that for fear of what someone might say to him."

"Oh," said Mary Frances, softly. "But, nobody's perfect. It's time to forgive yourself. You have a great thing going with Zander, and you don't want to mess that up. And I wouldn't want to see that happen either... Dagny, I have a confession to make."

"You do," sniffed Dagny.

"Yes," continued Mary Frances. "Christmas Day after you and Zander left, I slept with Matt. And I don't mean sleeping."

"I know," said Dagny. "I could tell."

"You could tell?" Mary Frances asked with surprise.

"Of course. It's not difficult. The way you acted. The way you walked. The way he looks at you," said Dagny. "And if I'm not mistaken, it was your first time."

"Oh, my goodness," said Mary Frances. "Do you think others can tell? The way I walk... how is it different? I had no idea."

"No, most people don't pay close enough attention, but I could tell," said Dagny. "And, I'm right, aren't I?" Mary Frances nodded her head. "But it's OK, Mary Frances. He loves you. Just watch the man. He adores you. He's going to marry you."

"Oh, Dagny, stop it," said Mary Frances. "Now you're going to make me cry. I can't even imagine that he would want to marry me. I shouldn't have let him make love to me, but I wanted to. I didn't want to stop him. Maybe you've forgotten, Dagny, but I can't have children. So, you feel out of your league? How about me? Every time Matt calls or wants to go out with me or wants to make love to me, I'm just amazed. He doesn't seem to be aware of my flaws."

"But, Mary Frances, you are so kind," said Dagny. "That's what he sees. He only sees your goodness. And he adores you. I still say he's going to marry you."

"Perhaps that's how Zander is, too," said Mary Frances. "My grandfather told me once that we should look at people, not based on the things they'd done in their life, but rather on what they would do if they had the chance to do it all over again. Maybe Zander understands you better than you give him credit. Maybe he understands you better than you understand yourself. If you love him Dagny, just love him. Be kind to him, and let him love you back.

Chapter 19
Senderismo

The dark blue Range Rover moved down the winding country road through the hills of Tennessee, disappearing from time to time into pine forest only to emerge again into open country. The SUV was headed east toward the Caney Fork River. The winter earth was still asleep and spring was yet a month away as Matt and Mary Frances made their way to a trailhead that would lead to a waterfall.

"That was very nice of you to give Zander the hockey tickets," Mary Frances commented. "Dagny was so excited to get to go."

Matt smiled, pleased that the Preds tickets had been so appreciated. "Hockey can be interesting to watch. It's just that I'd rather do something myself than watch someone else do it. You know, something like taking a hike to a waterfall with a pretty girl."

Mary Frances was delighted over the compliment. She had been worried that as her relationship with Matt became more serious, he would grow tired of her, but it hadn't happened. Each weekend was a new experience as Matt took her to different places that were as eclectic as the symphony to hear Tchaikovsky or Tractor Supply to get some cored wire for Matt's mig welder. "Matt, can I ask you a question? It's about hiking."

"Sure, what do you want to know? Hiking in Spanish is *Senderismo*. *Sendero* means trail, so *Senderismo* means the act of using trails, thus hiking. Just some trivia in case you're ever a contestant on Jeopardy," Matt said, grinning.

"You think you're so clever," she said. "And you are. But my question isn't of a linguistic nature." Matt enjoyed the way they could tease each other.

"It's just...well, I can't help feeling there's more to this hiking than just hiking. I enjoyed our hike around Radnor Lake two weeks ago, and I'm excited to hike to this waterfall. Sometimes I've noticed you watching me... not that I don't like that. But it's how you watch me, like you're analyzing or evaluating something. And when we finished the Radnor Lake hike, you had me remove my boots and socks to inspect my feet! Of course, you may look at my feet any time you wish," she said with a smile. "It just seemed odd."

Matt sighed as he steered the SUV around a curve. "It is odd. I'm sorry. I should explain. There is a reason for what you're describing." Mary Frances kept her eyes on him. "Do you remember Christmas Day when I said that if things ever got bad that we wouldn't be at my cabin?"

"Yes, I remember everything about that day," she said as Matt reached over and squeezed her hand.

"Then, you'll recall the part about Arcadia. Arcadia is not close. It's a drive of several hours and then a 25-mile hike. I am pleased that so far you're enjoying hiking. Or perhaps you're just humoring me. But what you don't realize is you're in training. I should have told you. We're breaking in your boots. We're building you up to 25 miles. The care of your feet is very important. It's important that your feet are dry. It's important that you don't get blisters. So, I made you take off your boots and socks at Radnor because I was seeing how your feet did on that short hike. Today's hike is one and a half miles to the waterfall and the same back, a total of three miles. So, you can see what we're doing, gradually increasing the distance. I should have explained it. I apologize."

"Oh, my! A 25-mile hike!" Mary Frances exclaimed. "Now all the attention to my feet makes sense. You're taking care of me like in the blizzard. Thank you."

Matt nodded and was silent for the next mile. "I don't want anything to ever happen to you," he said. "I love you. When we're apart, even a short time, I miss you."

"I understand. I'm the same way," Mary Frances said. "I want to be with you all the time. I love you so much that sometimes I want to tell everyone."

"There's so much I can't control, but I can buy you good boots and help you break them in," Matt said.

"You're wonderful and full of surprises," Mary Frances said, recognizing that Matt was always thinking ahead. "Do you think things are getting worse? I can't tell. There have been so many school shootings that they all blur together for me. I see that much."

"That's a great question," he answered. "Yes, it's getting worse when it comes to things like shootings, but the economy is actually doing well. Therefore, we continue to monitor it. The Endex has recently been noticed by some important people, and they'll be coming to Veritas next week to learn more. That should be interesting."

"Will you be speaking?" Mary Frances asked.

"I will," he answered, glancing over at her.

"Matt, I am so proud of you," she said. "I still can't believe I have a boyfriend, and then to have a boyfriend who is so smart." The SUV pulled into the small, gravel parking area at the trailhead. One other car was already there. Matt took a small rucksack out of the back of the SUV before locking the vehicle.

"Matt, do you have your pistol?" she whispered, and he nodded. "The first time you hugged me, I felt it. It made me uneasy, but now I'm more used to it."

"I almost always carry," he said. "What's the point of owning a pistol if I don't have it with me?" Checking for their cell phones, the two started down the trail. "I've tried to time this to be at the waterfall at lunch time," he said. "See the cloud cover. I've got rain ponchos if it rains. There's a rock overhang at the waterfall. We can have lunch there and take shelter if it's raining."

"This doesn't scare you at all, does it?" she asked, following him down the trail into a gorge strewn with boulders.

"No, it doesn't," he smiled, looking back at her and helping her over a small boulder. "You're not afraid, are you?"

"No, not with you beside me, but I would never do this by myself," she answered. The two walked on in silence for a while. Matt would spot wildlife like a red-tailed hawk or a deer. Then, he'd put a finger to his lips and point out what he'd seen. Mary Frances' face would light up when she saw it, too.

"Look at these," he whispered, pointing out some small, brown mushrooms growing on a log. "I wouldn't eat this kind; I'm sure they're poisonous. It's too early for morels. Too cold. But, if we're lucky, we might find some oyster mushrooms, and we could sauté them for lunch."

"Really? So, you can tell the edible ones from the poisonous ones?" she asked.

"Not all of them, but some of them," he answered, quietly. Then, somewhere ahead Matt heard muffled voices. Touching a finger to his ear and pointing ahead, he whispered. "Hikers, let's see how quiet we can be."

Matt and Mary Frances walked on up the trail as the voices became louder. When the hikers, two guys and two girls, came around a corner in the trail and came face to face with Matt, a girl screamed. "Y'all scared me to death!" she cried. The other three laughed at their friend.

"Sorry about that," Matt said. "We assumed you heard us. We heard you."

"How could you hear them, Brooke, when you're forever talking?" asked one of the young men.

"How far to the falls?" Matt asked. "Are we about halfway?"

"That's right, about halfway," the other man answered. "Hope the rain holds off for you. The falls are going strong after all the rain we've had."

"Thanks, have a good one," said Matt as the two groups continued in opposite directions. A way down the trail, Matt said quietly to Mary Frances, "Remember that. We heard them a long way off, but they never heard us. If you ever must move in the woods without being detected, noise discipline is very important. No talking. If you must talk, whisper or use hand signals." Then,

Mary Frances watched Matt do something very odd. He jumped about a foot into the air. "Did you notice anything?" he asked.

"No... except you jumped," she said puzzled. "Why did you do that?"

"Did you hear anything?" he asked as he jumped again.

"No! It was silent," she said.

"There are several items in my rucksack that could rattle. Metal against metal can be heard a very long distance. It's important to pack so that doesn't happen. Everything must be strapped down. Magazines must be wrapped with electrical tape so they won't rattle. Always jump before setting out to be sure nothing makes noise."

"Matt, why would we take magazines on a hike?" Mary Frances asked.

"Not the kind you read," he explained. "Magazines hold cartridges. I like three 30-round magazines here," he said, patting his right hip, "and three 30-round magazines here," he said, patting the other. "With one in, that's 210 rounds. Some like them here," he said patting his stomach with both hands, one on the right and the other on the left, but I don't because when you hit the dirt they are very uncomfortable. I like them more to the side." Mary Frances listened, not completely understanding what he was talking about. "I'm sorry. That's too much information. I guess you're learning that I do that, go into too much detail. Magazines hold bullets. They can rattle around and make noise. So, you do things to make them quieter." Mary Frances nodded, understanding the concept.

The two headed down the trail again. From time to time, there was a light sprinkling of rain but nothing to break out the ponchos. After the trail came down to the foot of a cliff, they followed along its base. Walking along the trail, rocks towered on their right. Matt stopped and pointed into the woods.

"What is it? What do you see?" Mary Frances asked.

"Lunch," he replied as he headed out into the forest. Mary Frances followed. Kneeling by a fallen oak, Matt pointed to a bunch of white mushrooms. "These are oyster mushrooms. See how they don't have a stem? The fins support the cap. If you put them on a piece of paper for 30 minutes or so, you should see lavender spores. That's called making a spore print. It's part of the identification process." Matt pulled out a knife and carefully cut the mushrooms off the tree. "There's way more than we can eat for lunch. We'll cook up what we need for now and take the rest home. I can dehydrate some for you. They're great on pizza or spaghetti." Mary Frances watched him and thought, *If we were lost, we would be OK. Matt knows where to find food. He's just as comfortable here as he is in his office at Veritas.*

A short distance later, they heard the roar of the waterfall. They heard it before they saw it. When they came around the corner of the cliffs and Mary Frances saw it for the first time, she said, "Matt, it's beautiful."

"Actually, it's a waterfall over a cave," he said. "Let's go check it out!" They quickly made their way up the trail and were soon standing in the cave, looking through a curtain of water at forest beyond. "Someone has built a fire here before," Matt said, pointing to a circle of blackened stones. "Let's gather some firewood, and I'll get a fire going." Matt dropped his rucksack. Together, they gathered small twigs and then larger, downed wood and brought it all to the cave. Mary Frances watched Matt as he got on his knees and very quickly had the fire started. Then, he spotted a large log off to the side of the cave and rolled it to the fire. "This will make a good place to sit," he said. "Ladies first," he said, offering half of the log to Mary Frances and then sitting next to her. Carefully adding larger twigs and branches, their campfire was soon established.

Warming their hands by the fire, the rain set in. Under the cover of the rock overhang, it was completely dry. "Matt, this is so cozy. It's hard to describe, but it's like during the blizzard. Being dry and warm is so simple, but so comforting."

"And don't forget food. Are you hungry?" Matt asked, and she nodded. "You're always cooking for me," he continued, "and with good reason. You're only about 400% better at cooking than I am. But today, I'm cooking." Starting to unpack the rucksack, he said, "First, I want to get a nice bed of coals, so while we're waiting we'll have a glass of Malbec. It should pair nicely with the filets."

"Oh, Matt! This is amazing," she said as he opened the

bottle of wine and poured into two, red, Solo cups. Soon, he had a potato wrapped in aluminum foil lying in the coals baking and two, small filets grilling on the fire. But the best part was when he produced a tiny bottle of olive oil and poured it into a small frying pan and sautéed the mushrooms they had just found. "Matt, this may be the finest meal I've ever had!" Mary Frances said, excitedly.

"Hardly!" he said. "I would vote for lamb chops in cherry sauce. Do you remember making that for us when we were snowed in?"

"Of course, I remember," she said. "But, I'm supposed to be competent in the kitchen. That's what I went to school for, but you! You're good at so many things." They ate while enjoying the rain and the waterfall. When they finished, Matt produced a small tea pot and made them both a jasmine tea.

"This is so comforting," Mary Frances said, holding the mug between her hands. "Why is this, Matt? People work so hard for bigger houses and fancier cars and more money." She snuggled up against him as they sat on the log in front of the fire. "But if you're warm, if there's a fire in the fireplace, if you have food to eat and if there is love- nothing else matters. I wouldn't trade this moment with you for any amount of money." Matt put his arm around her and held her close. "Matt, when we hike back and return to Nashville, can we go to your cabin? Can we have a fire in the fireplace and just sit together on the couch? Maybe you can make me a cappuccino. I'll help. You can cover me up with one of those wonderful blankets, the white ones with the stripes. When it's dark, let's build a fire in the bedroom fireplace. I want to be under the covers and watch the fire and feel you next to me.

The rain slacked off a short time later, and they hiked out. During the ride home, Mary Frances reflected on her day with Matt. *Trust... I have no doubts. The more I learn about Matthew Archer, the more I am certain we are meant to be together. I even trust him with my life*. Shortly before arriving at Matt's cabin, snowflakes began to fall. "Oh, Matt, look!" Mary Frances said. "It's snowing. Let's get snowed in again. There's nothing better than being snowed in with you."

Chapter 20
The Fed

It wasn't just another day at Veritas. It was the day Ellen Gentry and two other Federal Reserve Governors were meeting with Veritas Strategies to learn more about the Endex. All preparations had been made to pick them up at the airport and shuttle them to the Brentwood office. Their identity had not been announced, and it was being treated as just another visit from a client. Jim Borland, the CEO, was seated at his desk drinking a cup of coffee and reading *The Wall Street Journal* when Elaine, his assistant, appeared at his door. "Mr. Borland, we have a problem," she said.

"What's wrong, Elaine?" he asked, putting down the paper.

"It's Jean Claude, Mr. Borland," she said with despair. "He's in the hospital."

"In the hospital? What's happened?" the CEO asked.

"His wife just called. He started having stomach pains last night and ended up in the emergency room with appendicitis. Jean Claude's in surgery right now at Vanderbilt." Just as Elaine finished, Brian Eastman and Matt Archer walked in.

"Are we ready for this today?" asked Brian.

"Not quite," said the CEO. "Elaine has just informed us that Jean Claude is in surgery having his appendix removed as we speak."

"What should we do?" asked Elaine. "We can't take our guests to the cafeteria because someone might recognize them. We could bring food up here I suppose. We can't order out for pizza; it's the Federal Reserve! What a time to have our chef get sick!"

"Hmmm," said Brian. "We didn't plan for this."

"I have a solution," said Matt.

"What?" said Elaine as the other two men turned to hear his idea.

"Mary Frances Foster in the cafeteria. Pull her out of the cafeteria, and bring her up here."

"Mary Frances, the girl in the cafeteria?" asked Brian. "Are you serious?"

"Yes, I am," said Matt. "Hardly anyone knows it, but she's a chef, and I can personally attest to her culinary expertise." The phone started ringing outside at Elaine's desk, and she hurried out to answer it. A minute later, she came running back in.

"Mr. Borland, it's Ellen Gentry. She said not to bother you, but she's asking if she can bring another guest."

"Did she say who?" he asked.

"The Vice Chairman of the Federal Reserve," she answered, intently.

"You've got to be kidding. He's the new one. The President just appointed him," said the CEO. After the new development sank in, he continued. "Actually, I'd like to meet him. Sure, tell her to bring him. We can always run down to McDonald's and feed them hamburgers and fries," the CEO kidded. Elaine ran out of the office to deliver the message.

"OK, Matt, you're certain Miss Foster is up to this? You're not biased, are you?" Borland asked.

"I am biased, but she is very talented," Matt responded, honestly. "You won't be disappointed."

"Elaine, call Mrs. Joiner in food services and tell her to send Mary Frances Foster to my office right now," decided the CEO.

The meeting continued on the sixth floor while in the cafeteria everyone was hard at work. Mrs. Joiner emerged from her office and marched through the kitchen looking for Mary

Frances. When she found her, Mary Frances sensed something was different. "Is something wrong, Mrs. Joiner?" Mary Frances asked. Dagny and Jane were within earshot, and their ears automatically perked up to hear what was about to happen.

"You have been called to Mr. Borland's office, Mary Frances," she said. The look on her face said, *What have you done? What kind of trouble have you gotten yourself into? This cannot be good.*

"Yes, ma'am," Mary Frances answered as she turned to a sink and washed her hands before walking quickly through the cafeteria and out to the hallway that led to the elevators. Her eyes met Dagny's as she walked past, and Dagny could tell she had no idea what was happening. Mary Frances waited in front of the elevator as it came down to the first floor, feeling that it was taking forever. As she emerged from the elevator and headed down the sixth floor hallway, Elaine approached her. "Mary Frances?" she asked as Mary Frances nodded. "Come right in; they're waiting for you."

"They?" she asked, while thinking, *How many of them are there?* "Have I done something wrong?" she questioned.

"Heavens, no!" said Elaine. "We're hoping you're the solution."

"Mary Frances, come in," said Jim Borland as Elaine showed her in. The whole situation had Mary Frances completely intimidated until she saw Matt smiling at her as she entered. Between his smile and Elaine's comment, she felt a little more at ease though not completely. "Mary Frances, we have an unusual situation this morning," the CEO said. "It seems that our executive chef, Jean Claude, is in surgery having his appendix removed." He paused for a moment to let Mary Frances absorb the news. "The problem is that we have the Vice Chair and three Governors of the Federal Reserve here today. Our plan was to feed them since they've flown all the way to Nashville to meet with us. With Jean Claude in the hospital, that has become complicated. Ordinarily, we would just take them out to a restaurant, but this isn't an official trip. The Fed Governors must stay low key. Someone might recognize them, and that could cause all sorts of speculation as to what they were doing here in Nashville. Matt has suggested you. He says you're a very talented chef and that you could step in for Jean Claude today."

"I'd like to talk to Mr. Archer, if that's OK?" she answered.

"Of course," said the CEO, motioning to the VP of Research. "Matt."

Matt and Mary Frances stepped out into the hall and closed the door. "Matt, should I do this? Do you think I can?" she asked.

"Of course, you can do this," said Matt, gently placing his hand on her shoulder. "You are very talented, and we really need you."

Mary Frances smiled and bit her lower lip. "OK, I will do my best. If I mess up and I get fired, it's your fault." Matt winked at her and opened the door to reenter the CEO's office.

"Yes, I'll do it," she answered. "I'm honored to have the opportunity."

The CEO smiled. "Anything you want. Just tell us what you need," said the CEO. "Lunch for 10 people. Jean Claude has one assistant, but you can have more help if you need it."

"Do you have any suggestion as to what I should prepare?" she asked.

"Lamb chops with cherry sauce," said Matt, "exactly like you prepared for the Steiners and me."

"Fredéric Steiner?" asked Brian Eastman. "You've cooked for Fredéric Steiner? When did that happen?"

"Brian, you weren't left out on purpose," laughed Matt. "Do you remember the blizzard back in December? Fredéric was here in Nashville. He wanted to stop by and visit you, but the snow storm happened. He and Sophia were staying with me. It was just after I'd picked them up at the airport when we came across Mary Frances, stranded because her car had slid off the road. She stayed with us for the duration of the storm." A look of illumination appeared on Brian's face. Mary Frances blushed as it dawned on the Chief Economist how the VP of Research had met Mary Frances.

"So, you'll get to sample her cooking today, Brian," Jim Borland said with a chuckle. "This sounds great to me. Mary

Frances, I'll leave the details up to you. Do you need any help?"

"Could I have Dagny Bennett?" asked Mary Frances. "I'm sure we will need ingredients from the store. I could send her with a list, and then she could help me when she returned."

"Sure. Elaine, call Mrs. Joiner and have her send up Dagny Bennett," said the CEO. "Mrs. Joiner is going to get upset if I keep stealing her people like this," he laughed, finding it quite funny.

Elaine led the way to the executive dining room. *This is so nice!* Mary Frances thought. *Real china, linen napkins, and sterling silver utensils.* Mary Frances met Jean Claude's assistant, Julie, and together they started planning what they hoped would be a great lunch for the visitors from the Federal Reserve.

When Mrs. Joiner told Dagny Bennett to report to the CEO, everyone around her in the kitchen stared. *They think I'm getting fired. I probably am,* Dagny told herself. *Has Mary Frances already been canned, and I'm next? Resigned to her fate,* Dagny walked out of the cafeteria and to the elevators. *Dang! I just got the uniforms with my name on them,* she thought as she pushed the up arrow. She was utterly confused as Elaine, the CEO's executive assistant, met her at the elevator and escorted her to the sixth-floor kitchen. There she found Mary Frances and Julie working on the menu.

"Dagny," said Mary Frances, "we're sending you to the supermarket to get these ingredients," she said, handing Dagny a list. "Get back as fast as you can, but don't get a speeding ticket." Dagny was dumbfounded. For once, she had nothing to say. "We're not fired, Dagny," Mary Frances said. "The executive chef is in the hospital, and we have to fill in for him. I'll explain it all later. Here's a Veritas P-Card to pay for it. Hurry back!"

When the four VIPs arrived, Elaine was in the lobby to welcome and direct them to the sixth floor where Brian Eastman and Jim Borland were waiting. "Come in!" said the CEO as Elaine arrived at his office with the guests.

"Ellen, great to see you!" said the chief economist, walking to Ellen Gentry and giving her a hug. "How's my favorite Fed Governor?"

"Brian, so good to see you," she said. "And thank you

for letting us stop by on our way to Washington on such short notice. We appreciate it very much."

"It's our pleasure," said the chief economist. "This is Jim Borland, CEO of Veritas Strategies," he said, introducing his boss to the Fed Governor.

"It is so nice to meet you," she said, shaking the CEO's hand.

"And this is Steven Plinnon, Fed Governor-New York, Mark Sutton- Fed Governor-Chicago and Vice Chairman of the Federal Reserve, Richard McCaslin," Ellen said, introducing each of her companions.

"I'm pleased to meet you," said the CEO, shaking hands with all of them. "We are honored that you've decided to visit. Thank you for your interest in our research that I understand you obtained across your backyard fence," the CEO said with a smile.

"I'm afraid that's the truth," Ellen Gentry said. "We spend millions on research, and then your neighbor hands you a report that's better than anything we've seen."

"We're glad you think so," said Brian Eastman. "Shall we move to the conference room and delve into it a little deeper?"

"We're eager to hear more," said the Chicago Fed Governor. "It's quite concerning what's happening in the country, and we're trying to understand it."

The group moved out of the CEO's office and to the conference room. The conference room was glass-walled on two sides, with a huge, mahogany table in the center. After everyone was seated, Elaine and an administrative assistant brought in coffee and water.

Just as the group had settled in, Matt Archer arrived. He was dressed in a perfectly tailored, navy blue, Zegna suit which set off his eyes. A blue, Zegna tie with gold, diagonal stripes lay against a starched, white shirt. Black Ferragamo shoes and belt completed the uniform that he wore effortlessly. Matt had carefully selected every detail, and the group before him understood the message. Some would have found it hard to believe he was as comfortable welding or splitting firewood as he was in the boardroom.

"Ah, here's Matt," said the CEO. "Everyone, this is Matt Archer, our VP of Research. Matt is the architect of the Index you're here to learn about today. I believe it's best to let him explain what we're doing, and then you can ask questions." The CEO introduced the room to Matt and stepped away to let Matt take the stage.

"Thanks, Jim," Matt said. "I'd like to approach today's presentation in three parts. First, how we came up with the concept. Second, how our Index works. Third, what are we seeing now. Because there are time constraints as you have a plane to catch later this afternoon, I'll ask you to hold questions until the end.

"I will start by saying we came up with the original idea for our Index after reading the work by Arkansas State and Ohio State on the Arab Spring. I've supplied the link in your report if you'd like to read it. This work was groundbreaking in that they were able to accurately predict the Arab Spring phenomenon that spread across the Arab world by studying changes in various sociological as well as economic components of those countries. The two professors tracked riots, protests and terrorist attacks. They tracked the participation rate of the youth cohort. And they followed communication trends. What they predicted was the point at which a country reached the critical level of destabilization where revolution could occur.

"We, at Veritas Strategies, took that concept and applied it to our country but with a different twist. We're not looking for a revolution, specifically, but rather a destabilization that could lead to societal breakdown. We realized the need for such research when we discovered that a common topic with investment clients and their financial advisors is the possibility of a societal breakdown, wherein basic services no longer functioned-electricity, water, medical, police. We discovered that at least one fourth of clients consider preparedness for this possibility as part of their financial plan. Food storage, ammunition stores, and in many cases, a remote survival location represent major investments for this group. For some, it may simply be extra food stored in the basement. For others, it may be purchasing several thousand acres in a remote location and building a fortified compound. We began this project to supply our clients with a tool that could help them determine how the country was trending and when it may be appropriate to activate a survival plan.

"We are both fearful of the frailty of our economy and society and optimistic at how incredibly resilient the economy and the American people are. We all remember the fall of 2008 as the economy teetered on collapse; we all held our breath wondering how far it would fall before stabilization.

"To understand and predict, our Index has two basic components, economic and societal. The economic side isn't anything new... GDP expansion or recession, unemployment, work participation, inflation/deflation, and the usual leading indicators. We weight and score them, arriving at a number for that half of the Index.

"The societal side is a little different. We look at a variety of things all of which are detailed in your report. We search Reuters News every day for 50 key words that lead us to incidents of instability, protest, strike and terrorism. We rank incidents as violent or non-violent. We use Reuters News because, while it isn't perfect and does contain bias, it is less biased than the others. We look at violent crime, mass shootings, stabbings, acid attacks, and vehicular attacks. We look at data relative to males in the youth cohort. Young men who are engaged: working, forming families and participating in society are far less likely to become a destabilizing force.

"Finally, we have several unique sub-indices that would be more indicative of destabilization further into the cycle. One is the vacation index, wherein we track the vacations of the CEO's of the S&P 500. We have determined it is common for 12% of this cohort to be on vacation at any point in time. It has gone as low as 8% and has never been greater than 20%. This is a very wealthy and very prepared group of people. We hypothesize that in a severe destabilization event many CEO's would "go on vacation" meaning that they would be moving their families to a personal, prepared point of safety and survival. Any vacation number above 20% would cause us to believe that this highly informed group believes that destabilization is imminent. We have people in all S&P 500 companies reporting.

"Another of the sub-indices is the TP index, TP as in toilet paper. Almost all toilet paper in the US is manufactured by five companies. Toilet paper is one of those things people take for granted; although, it is very essential. If the general population were to believe that destabilization and the disruption of services were imminent, we would expect runs on grocery stores to stock up on and hoard toilet paper. Because toilet paper is so bulky, stores can't store much of it and trucks can't haul much of it, making it difficult to restock quickly. We have people in each of the five companies who report toilet paper sales weekly. A toilet paper shortage would also panic the population causing more hoarding of other commodities. We predict this will happen because it already has. In 1973, when host of 'The Tonight Show,' Johnny Carson, commented on a toilet paper shortage as a joke, it actually caused one. A real toilet paper shortage would be much worse.

"Another consideration to factor in is systemic risk. Probability of collapse goes up every day because our world becomes more complex every day. The more complex, the greater the systemic risk. We all have experienced the frustration of computer programs that don't work as they should. We are all aware of data breaches and the havoc done by hackers, both individual and from other governments like Russia and China. While we don't have a way to measure it, increasing systemic risk coupled with societal problems would make a collapse more probable.

"So, what does our Index show us now? Thus far, there isn't correlation between societal and economic factors. While we are seeing, and have been seeing an increase in acts of violence, police brutality, public brutality against police, and both violent and non-violent protests, that hasn't affected the economy. The economy, as you are aware, is expanding and doing quite well across the sectors. Why is this when we have all these steadily increasing societal problems like school shootings? It's because the population has had time to adjust. While no one likes it, it has become a fact of life. Schools are adapting, adding security and locking doors. While it often doesn't make the national news, there is an increasing number of shootings that are being thwarted or minimized by individual citizens with concealed carry licenses. All of this has happened slowly enough for people to adjust. Therefore, we monitor the speed of change as well as the change. We believe that destabilization and severe, societal upheaval will occur when acts of violence become so frequent and widespread that individuals make the decision to not go to work. This is particularly damaging for essential services. If policemen decide to not go and work their shifts, believing they should stay home to protect their own families, then crime would skyrocket. If medical workers stayed home, the hospitals would collapse. If firefighters stayed home, arsonists would become active. A sector that you at the Fed are most interested in, of course, is banking. What if banks couldn't open because no one showed up for work? Transfers wouldn't happen. The economy would grind to a halt. What if the New York Stock Exchange couldn't open because no one was there when the bell rang? The financial ripple effect would be devastating.

"Our Index is currently at 91, having risen six points in the past 12 months. It has never been this high since inception nor has it been this high in back testing. We view 100 as extremely serious, with anything greater than 110 as critical. Remember that the score of 91 is with good economic numbers. If we saw the societal numbers going up and then started to see it affect the economy, we would be very concerned. If we saw a 110, for example, and the vacation index shot to 80%, and there was a toilet paper shortage... well, we would be very concerned for the future," Matt concluded.

"Thank you, Matt," said Brian as the four from the Federal Reserve looked at their reports. "Are there any questions?"

"Yes," said the Vice Chairman of the Fed. "Matt, how do you account for the violence data? There's so much of it. How do you make it meaningful?"

"We use a time series regression with a negative binomial model," Matt answered. The Vice Chairman nodded as he continued to study the report.

"Is your model static, or does it evolve?" asked Steven Plinnon, the New York Governor.

"Always evolving," answered Matt. "We're always searching

for meaningful input. One thing we're trying to get our heads around is the work integration of the youth cohort and how it relates to stability. I'm sure you're aware of the problem in China with a shortage of young women due to several decades of the one child policy. This has a destabilizing effect on that country, increased crime, mental issues and lowered productivity. While we don't have that, we do have a participation deficit in our millennial population, particularly in males. While young women are going to college in increasing numbers, there are fewer young men going to college than 10 years ago. Marriage is also in decline, and the reproduction rates for millennials is considerably less than previous generations. In trying to understand this, we've run word searches on the 50 top songs each year for the past 50 years, relative to love. Not surprisingly, if you think about it, there has been a steady decline in the number of songs about love. Particularly in the past 20 years, love songs have plummeted. If music reflects the culture that generates it, then this is disturbing and could explain the millennial tendency to not date, to not form relationships with the opposite sex, not marry and not reproduce. These can be contributors to destabilization in an economic/societal crisis."

"Gentlemen, I'm impressed," said Ellen Gentry. "I would seriously like us to consider receiving this research on a regular basis as another insight as we direct policy." The other three from the Federal Reserve nodded in agreement.

"Done," said Richard McCaslin, the Vice Chair of the Fed.

"It would also be great to get weekly M0 and M3 numbers instead of waiting for the monthly, public numbers," said Matt, "to track cash."

"We will check into that for you," said Richard. "Let us know if there's anything else we have that could help you."

"Thanks, Matt," said Jim Borland. "If there are no further questions, let's all move to the dining room and have some lunch." Everyone agreed and continued to talk among themselves as they walked down the hallway to the dining room, the CEO talking to the Fed Vice Chair, Ellen Gentry visiting with Brian Eastman, and the other two Governors bombarding Matt with more questions.

"Here they come, Mary Frances," said Dagny as she peaked

around the corner of the executive dining room and saw the group headed their way.

"We're ready. I can't believe we got it all done in time, but we did. I hope they like it," said Mary Frances. As the group came through the door into the dining room, they were welcomed with a myriad of smells and a beautifully set table.

"That smells delicious," said Ellen, and the others agreed. "What are we having?"

"Lamb chops," said Matt, "with a cherry sauce that's to die for."

The group took their seats, and Dagny and Julie served as Mary Frances described the dish being placed before them. "The sauce is cherries marinated in port and cherry jam with cardamom and mint," she explained.

"Oh, my! This is heaven," said Ellen Gentry after savoring the first bite. "Miss... Mary Frances," she asked, reading the blue letters of the name embroidered on her white coat, "Are you the executive chef here at Veritas?"

"No, ma'am. I'm...well," she stopped, not sure how to explain as all eyes had turned to her.

"We had a bit of a crisis this morning," explained Jim Borland. "Our executive chef is in the hospital. He had an emergency appendectomy early this morning. We thought about ordering out for pizza, but instead we brought Mary Frances up from the cafeteria to cook for us today."

"You work in the cafeteria?" asked the New York Governor. "You should be a chef in a restaurant in New York City."

"Thank you; you're very kind," Mary Frances said. "I'm pleased you like it."

"Well, this has been a great visit," said the Vice Chair. "Jim and Brian, thank you for inviting us. Ellen, thank you for including me. Matt, very impressive. Thank you and we look forward to working with you. And finally, what a lunch! Thank you, Mary Frances."

Mary Frances smiled. She felt relief that lunch had been well received. She liked the warm feeling of being part of the Veritas team. From all outward appearances, she was calm; but inside, she was exuberant. What pride she felt in knowing the meeting had gone well and hearing the praise given to Matt, her Matt!

When the group from the Fed left to make their way back to the airport, the CEO called the group to his office. Mary Frances was shocked to find herself included. "What can I say," he began. "This could not have gone any better. Brian, thank you for your work and this connection to the Federal Reserve. Matt, excellent, just excellent, thank you. And then after a great meeting was the spectacular lunch! Mary Frances, the lamb chops were the icing on the cake! I apologize for questioning your culinary ability. I, too, can't believe you're working in the cafeteria with these talents. Thank you, everyone."

When they filed out to return to work, Matt stopped Mary Frances in the hallway. "You're amazing," he said.

"You are, too!" she exclaimed.

"We should celebrate," Matt said. "Let's invite Dagny and Zander. They were part of this, too. Dagny helped you in the kitchen, and Zander is a big part of the research."

"Saturday night. I'm thinking Prime 108 in Union Station," Matt said. Mary Frances nodded her approval, admiring her man in the blue suit. Giving a silent prayer of thanks, her heart was full.

Chapter 21
1911

The first payday of April fell shortly after the visit from the Federal Reserve. Mary Frances would never forget seeing that paystub. The $5,000 bonus and a personal thank you note from the CEO were very unexpected surprises. She had never been happier, and life with Matt got better with each passing day. Dagny and Zander continued dating, and the relationship between them grew stronger. Connections deepened as the four friends spent more time together. Veritas posted record first quarter earnings. The economy kept expanding, and the markets kept pace. At least once a week, the news reported another shooting or bombing but as had been happening more and more, everyone noticed less and less. The news was like that, not seeming real, until an event became personal.

"Where are you?" Dagny called into the storeroom.

"I'm back here, making out an order," Mary Frances called back.

Dagny followed the voice and found Mary Frances with a clipboard, counting inventory and inputting numbers on an iPad. "There you are," Dagny said. "Everything's cleaned up and put away from lunch. Should I start on some prep for tomorrow?"

"Sure thing, Dagny. You can start on......" The ear-splitting sound of the fire alarm stopped Mary Frances in mid-sentence.

"What is that?" Dagny yelled, covering her ears.

Mary Frances shrugged her shoulders and motioned for Dagny to follow. The two left the storeroom and ran through the kitchen to the cafeteria where the rest of the cafeteria crew was gathered.

In the sixth-floor conference room, Jim Borland was conducting a meeting with all the department heads. The elevator doors opened, and Lynn Hanson emerged. No one had seen him as he entered the building and got on the elevator. Calmly, he walked toward the conference room. Everyone on the sixth floor was engrossed in work, concentrating on computer screens, busy on the telephone and absorbed in reports. Lynn Hanson moved stealthily, looking left and right while taking care to remain undetected. *Today is the day*, he thought. *I'll show them.*

The CEO was reviewing a report from the VP of operations on the first quarter of the year when Lynn Hanson appeared in the conference room. Sitting behind the CEO and taking notes was his assistant, Elaine. Lynn Hanson grabbed Elaine, jerking her to her feet. She screamed as her papers fell to the floor. With his arm around her, he pinned her arms against her body. Then, he pressed the muzzle of the .45 caliber 1911 Colt pistol against her head.

"Yeah, I've got you sons of bitches all together here in the same place!" Lynn Hanson shouted, spewing the words with rage. "Nobody move, or I'm blowing this bitch's head off."

Everyone in the conference room was stunned. Disbelief was followed by apprehension and fear as reality set in. Hanson jerked Elaine around so she was exactly in front of him, using her as a human shield. She screamed again. Her coworkers focused on the massive, steel pistol at her temple. Somehow, the rest of the building remained unaware of what was transpiring on the top floor. Also unnoticed was Matt Archer's right hand. He slowly reached down, slipping it into his computer case on the floor.

"Lynn, think about what you're doing!" said the CEO.

"Shut up, old man, or I'll shoot you first!" screamed Hanson. "You're next, Patricia Martin, Head of HR!" Matt's fingers silently unsnapped the hardware on the computer case. Slowly, he lifted the heavy, leather flap.

"So, you all thought you'd get rid of me, didn't you? Fuck you! I was tired of this chicken shit place anyway. But you've crossed the line, Patricia Martin. I can't get a job anywhere because when they call here you tell them about me." Everyone sat perfectly still, focused completely on Lynn Hanson. *Elaine, don't move,* Matt thought. *That's good, Elaine, be calm. Don't move.* His hand carefully moved down into the computer case as his fingers wrapped around the grip of another .45 caliber 1911 pistol, a Kimber.

"And what business is it of yours?" he growled. "All those bitches wanted it. They asked for it. It's not my fault if they got knocked up!" Matt slowly brought the pistol out of the leather computer case, his index finger on the side of the trigger guard and his thumb slowly pressing the safety down to fire.

"Lynn," said Matt, calmly.

"Shut up, Archer!" Hanson screamed. "Fuck you!"

"Lynn, put the gun down, now," Matt said, firmly.

"And I said, 'Fuck you,' Archer! Do you want to die, too?" screamed Hanson.

"I'm going to ask you one more time," said Matt, unflinchingly. "I will not ask again. Put the gun down."

"Hey, asshole! Are you blind? *I've* got the gun. *I've* got all the power now, not you, assholes," Hanson yelled. "I'm going to kill Jim Borland and Patricia Martin today, and there's nothing stopping me!"

Even though the room was full of witnesses, most weren't exactly sure what happened next. Matt Archer rose to his feet. Some remembered a red dot in the center of Lynn Hanson's forehead just before a deafening roar as the .45 went off in the enclosed room. Elaine screamed as Lynn Hanson went limp and collapsed, dead before he hit the floor. The wall behind him was splattered red with blood and brains. All eyes were riveted on the wall as everyone sat frozen in place.

Calmly, Matt Archer removed the magazine and laid it on the conference room table. Jim Borland took a sobbing Elaine in his arms. Matt ejected the round in the chamber, locked the slide open and placed the bullet and pistol on the table next to the magazine. Next, he took out his cell phone and dialed 911.

"We need police and ambulance at Veritas Securities, 1270 Maryland Pike, Brentwood," Matt said, his voice sure and steady. "My name is Matthew Archer. I feared for my life and the lives of my coworkers. He was going to kill us. We are on the sixth floor. Please, hurry." Matt hung up and calmly sat down. Just then, the alarm sounded as someone activated the security system.

"Lockdown!" yelled Mrs. Joiner, closing and locking the door to the cafeteria. "Active shooter in the building!"

"Mrs. Joiner!" shouted Mary Frances, "How do you know?"

"That alarm means *Active Shooter* in the building!" she shouted back. "We are to lock everyone in and wait for the police."

"Any idea where or who or what's going on?" shouted Jane.

"No!" Mrs. Joiner yelled. "No clue! No one comes in or leaves!" Mary Frances and Dagny immediately sat down together and covered their ears as the alarm was deafening. Mary Frances' mind went to Matt. Was he safe? Dagny's mind was on Zander. What neither of them knew was that by then, it was all over. But it would be 20 minutes before the police gave the all clear, signaling locked doors to be opened, allowing employees to emerge from lockdown.

When, at last, the alarm ceased, there was an abrupt silence. Then the occupants of the cafeteria heard shouting. They moved to the doors that Mrs. Joiner had locked and peered through the small wire-reinforced glass windows into the hallway. "We're on lockdown until the police direct us to come out," said Mrs. Joiner. "Nobody is leaving." A six-man swat team ran past the windows.

"What is happening?" Dagny whispered to Mary Frances. "I'm scared for Zander and Matt." Mary Frances nodded, blinking back tears.

Finally, a policeman came to the cafeteria doors and instructed Mrs. Joiner to open them. The cafeteria staff cautiously moved into the hall and followed him to the lobby. Through the lobby windows, they saw police everywhere. As police came in and out the front doors, Mary Frances could hear helicopters overhead. Employees were scurrying down the stairs instead of taking the elevators to evacuate the building. As they passed, Mary Frances and Dagny caught bits and pieces of conversations.

"I don't know... I heard it was on the sixth floor... Yes, shots were fired... EMT's went up the elevators... Someone has been shot... I heard it was Lynn Hanson who came back in the building... I heard it was Matt Archer." Mary Frances' knees buckled at Matt's name. Dagny steadied her as Mary Frances' heart almost stopped. Then, between the fear and panic, an upsurge of energy came into her. Mary Frances ran for the stairs with Dagny following close behind.

Up the stairs, up all six flights, the two women ran as Mary Frances prayed, *Please, don't let it be Matt! This is all my fault. I cannot live without him. Please, don't take him from me.* Reaching the sixth floor, Mary Frances burst through the door into the hallway, through a group of people and on toward Matt's office. Zander Fromm turned to see Dagny and Mary Frances running toward him. He grabbed Mary Frances as she tried to run past.

"Please, please, is it Matt? Where's Matt?" Mary Frances cried, trying to break away from Zander. Dagny swallowed hard, feeling great relief at the sight of Zander. She silently thanked God as she tried to help her boyfriend control Mary Frances.

"Mary Frances!" Zander said as the others in the hall watched. "Matt's fine. He's not hurt."

"Where is he? Someone downstairs said that Matt Archer was shot!" she cried.

"No, that's not correct," Zander said as he and Dagny tried to console their friend. "Matt shot Lynn Hanson. Lynn Hanson came in with a gun and was going to kill the CEO, Patricia Martin, and Elaine, I think, but I wasn't there. I don't have the details, but Matt is OK."

"I have to see him!" cried Mary Frances. "I won't believe it until I see him!

With his arm still around her, Zander guided Mary Frances through the crowd of Veritas employees gathered along the hallway outside the conference room. "The police don't want us beyond this point, but there he is," Zander said, pointing through the glass wall of the conference room. Matt was standing, talking to three policemen. On the opposite end of the conference room, two EMTs were working on the floor.

"Oh, my God, Zander," said Dagny. "The wall. Look at the wall in the conference room!" Mary Frances gasped as her eyes focused on the blood-stained wall behind the EMTs. Zander and Dagny stood on either side of Mary Frances to support her and stop her if she started running again. But she stood silently, her eyes locked on Matt.

After he had finished with the police, Matt exited the conference room and immediately spotted Mary Frances. As he walked straight for her, she broke away from Zander and Dagny and ran to him. As they embraced, Mary Frances buried her face in Matt's chest, overcome with emotion. "I'm fine. I'm not hurt," Matt said, caressing her hair while he let her cry. "Everything's OK now."

Finally calming down a bit, Mary Frances felt the overwhelming need to look at Matt. She pulled from their embrace just enough to see his face and stared intently into his eyes. She found reassurance as she touched his face, then his chest, then his arms, convincing herself he was indeed uninjured.

"I was so afraid when I heard your name," Mary Frances confessed when her breathing began to return to normal.

Matt continued to hold and comfort Mary Frances. "I know," he said. "I know you were afraid."

The CEO, who had also been giving his statement to the police, approached Matt and Mary Frances. He put his hand on her shoulder, feeling helpless to do anything more to console her. Mary Frances wiped her eyes and turned, still holding onto Matt's arm.

"Matt," Jim Borland said, "we owe you our lives. I'm certain Patricia and I would be dead right now, and probably others as well, if it hadn't been for you. Thank you."

"What happened?" asked Mary Frances, regaining her composure. "Is Lynn Hanson in there... in the conference room?"

Matt didn't answer, but the CEO did. "Mary Frances, I'm sure you recall that Lynn Hanson was terminated in December. He apparently was having trouble finding new employment and blamed us. He came in today with a gun."

"And you shot him?" Mary Frances asked, looking to Matt in disbelief. Matt nodded. "But how? He had a gun."

Before Matt had a chance to answer, the CEO explained,"It was so fast I didn't know what was happening at first. Hanson held Elaine hostage with a gun to her head. It looked like it was over for her. Then, Hanson said he was going to kill me and Patricia Martin, too. Thankfully, Matt is a good shot... an excellent shot. There's no doubt Matt saved us."

An attorney from the firm's legal department joined the group. "I've just gotten off the phone with the state's attorney," he reported. "I've explained what transpired. He's assured me no charges will be filed against Matt. It was self-defense."

"Thanks," said the CEO. "Should there be a wrongful death suit from Hanson's family, we will pay for all of it, Matt."

"I wouldn't worry about that," said the attorney. "No judge would hear it. When someone walks into a building full of people saying he's going to start shooting, all bets are off."

The CEO thanked Matt again and then moved to join another group who had also been in the conference room. The EMTs came through the crowd, pushing a gurney with a black body bag that had been zipped up. Everyone quickly stepped back to allow plenty of room because no one wanted to come in contact with the body bag.

Matt and Zander stepped away from the crowd, leaving Mary Frances in Dagny's care. Once they were out of earshot, Zander said, "Good job, boss! That was some fine shooting."

"Thank you," Matt said, quietly. "I never wanted to have to do that again. I never thought I'd have to."

"Damn! Weren't you afraid for the hostage?" Zander asked. "He had the gun to her head. If I had been in your shoes, I'd have been afraid he'd squeeze the trigger just from reflex."

Matt glanced around, making sure they were still out of earshot. "1911, Zander. He had a 1911. Single action and the hammer wasn't cocked. Maybe Hanson didn't understand 1911s are single action. I wondered why it wasn't cocked. He was so worked up it's possible he'd forgotten to chamber a round. I kept watching his thumb. If he'd gone for the hammer, I'd have dropped him sooner. I wanted to give him a chance to put the gun down. Because it was single action, I knew it wouldn't go off even if he squeezed the trigger when I shot him. I knew I had time to make the shot before Hanson could cock the hammer. My biggest worry was that Elaine wouldn't hold still."

"Hmmm... single action. I hadn't considered that," said Zander.

"I'm sure no one else in the room did either," said Matt. "I'd like to know if he had a round in the chamber, but then again I don't want to know. It doesn't matter; Hanson said he was going to kill people. I tried to get him to lay the pistol down. I wish he would have."

When the CEO rejoined Zander and Matt, Mary Frances and Dagny did as well. Mary Frances stayed very close to Matt, reaching up and touching his arm from time to time, continuing to assure herself he was unharmed.

"I want you all to go home now," said the CEO. "Veritas is closing down early; we will remain closed tomorrow, so everyone can rest and begin to recover. Since tomorrow is Friday, that will give everyone a three-day weekend. Matt, are you OK to drive?" Matt nodded silently.

Zander followed Dagny home to stay with her. Mary Frances insisted on going home with Matt. It was as if she was afraid to let him out of her sight. She cooked for him and stayed by his side for the next three days. Throughout the weekend, all four of them considered the frailty of life and experienced a new appreciation for one another. Each and every day was precious.

Chapter 22
Aftermath

The following Monday wasn't a typical one at Veritas Strategies. Instead of the normal discussion of activities during a long weekend, the employees all needed to discuss what had transpired the previous Thursday. Matt was bombarded by coworkers the moment he walked in the door as people greeted him, expressing gratitude for his level-headed action and bravery. It continued in the elevator as he rode to the sixth floor. Elaine made a beeline for him as he was entering his office. "Matt, you saved my life," she said. "I was going to die. I'm so glad you were there. Thank you. And my family thanks you."

One by one, co-workers who had been in the conference room that day made it a point to find Matt and convey their sincere appreciation. Shortly before noon, there was a knock at his door. It was the woman who had paid him a visit the previous year, the one whose name he still didn't know. "Come in," Matt said, recognizing her as the woman who'd taken off her dress in his office.

"I just wanted to stop and say thank you for what you did last week," she said. "There is no telling how many people he might have killed if you hadn't intervened. I also wanted to apologize for my behavior a while back. I shouldn't have done that."

Matt nodded and smiled, not knowing exactly how to respond. "I'm just glad we were able to stop Hanson before he hurt anyone," he said. "About the other thing... you're a very attractive woman. You don't need to do that."

The woman nodded her head. "My friends tell me you're dating someone from the cafeteria?" she asked.

"That's right," said Matt.

"Is she pretty?" she asked, still trying to understand his rejection.

"Yes, she is," he answered.

"Well, she's a lucky girl," she said. "I'll be going now. I'm sorry."

Down on the first floor, cafeteria conversations were a little different. "Have you heard Mary Frances is dating Matt Archer? How long have they been going out? How in the world did those two meet?"

"I knew it!" said Jane, cornering Mary Frances in the kitchen. "I knew the moment you texted, asking about Matt Archer. So, come on. Let's have the details."

"Jane, I'm just kind of private. That's why I never talked about it," said Mary Frances.

"Yes, but how did you meet?" asked Jane as others started gathering around to hear.

"He rescued me during the blizzard," she said. "I was driving home from work when a semi ran me off the road, and I slid down a hill. Matt... Mr. Archer happened to be behind me. He stopped and helped."

"You're kidding me!" said Jane.

"Some people have all the luck, don't they!" said Dagny, overhearing the question and answer session. Mary Frances gave her a stern look.

"So, then what happened?" asked Jane. All eyes were on Mary Frances.

"My car was stuck. It was snowing hard, too hard to get me home and then for him to make it back home safely. So, he took me with him." Everyone's eyes widened as they glanced around at each other. "No, it wasn't like that," said Mary Frances. "There were other people present all the time. He was very kind."

"Yeah, right!" said Jane. "Well, just how many days were you *stranded* with Mr. Archer?"

Dagny stepped forward, raising both her hands, and said, "Hold it! I don't like what you're implying. Look, I'm her roommate. I knew all about this because I was talking to her on the phone the whole time. Mary Frances had her concerns at first, but he was a complete gentleman. And by the way, while I was freezing and sleeping on a couch, Mary Frances had her own bedroom and bathroom with hot water! Now, I better not hear any of you spreading any stories about Mary Frances or her boyfriend. Got it?" Heads nodded in agreement.

"What's going on here?" asked Mrs. Klein as she walked up on the group. "If a bomb went off, it'd get all of you!"

"We're only talking to Mary Frances," said Jane. "It was her boyfriend who took out Lynn Hanson." Mary Frances cringed, hearing the words *took out.*

"Yes, I've heard," said Mrs. Klein. "Without a doubt, Mr. Archer saved many lives here at Veritas, and we're all more than appreciative. But at 12:00 noon, hundreds of hungry employees will come through those doors, so let's get a move on." Quickly, the cafeteria crew resumed the meal prep.

The questioning continued at lunch. Chicken wasn't the only thing being grilled that day as curious people spoke to Mary Frances as they moved through the lunch line. "Mary Frances, are you dating Matt Archer? Mary Frances, is it true that Matt Archer is your boyfriend? Mary Frances, what's he like? He's not violent, is he? Mary Frances, does he have a brother?"

By the end of the day, Mary Frances was worn out from all the attention. "I hope everyone gets this out of their systems so tomorrow can be back to normal," she said as Dagny drove them home. "In all my life, never have so many people wanted to talk to me. If this is what it's like to be a celebrity, I want no part of it."

That evening, the women relaxed over a quiet dinner that was a stark contrast to the workplace drama. But Dagny couldn't let it go. "How annoying is that Jane!" she said. "She's as bad as a gnat in your nose!"

"Yes," laughed Mary Frances, "and I'll bet she's been that

way since birth, bless her heart. Surely, soon, it'll be somebody else's turn for the spotlight."

When Matt called that evening, he and Mary Frances had a long discussion about their unusual Monday. Mary Frances filled Matt in on every detail, and Matt did the same, omitting the detail of the woman who stopped by to thank him and apologize.

Chapter 23
Ninety-Six

"Good job. We'll meet again next week," said Matt, dismissing the research department from the small conference room. "Zander, stay just a minute," he said, as everyone else filed out and returned to their offices.

Things were slowly normalizing after the Lynn Hanson incident. The glass walls of the main conference room had been covered in paper, blocking the view from the outside. Inside, the workers removed everything, table, chairs, art and carpet. The walls were torn out and the sheetrock was replaced. When all was finished, the room was completely new, an attempt to make those present on that terrible day feel as if they were in a different place.

"Sit down, Zander. I want to talk to you about something," Matt said as he closed his laptop and put papers back in folders.

"Is everything alright?" Zander asked, sensing a different mood from Matt.

"Everything's fine," Matt said, leaning back in his chair and stretching. "I want to talk to you about our Endex."

"What part of it, Matt?" Zander asked.

Matt exhaled. "Zander, we've worked together almost three years now. You understand the Endex because you helped build it, and you compile it every month. You understand it's purpose- to attempt to predict, for lack of a better word, societal collapse." Zander nodded his head. "I don't talk about this openly with others in the department. None of them understand the true purpose of their work because their focus is on an individual component. But you see it all, and you understand the implications. You saw the number this morning, 96. I know you're aware that's up from 91 the first quarter. You understand the trend."

Zander nodded again not quite sure where his boss was headed. "We said we would issue an alert to our clients if the Endex hit 100, but I'm almost afraid to do so because we could be accused of inciting panic. I will be meeting with Borland and Eastman tomorrow to discuss this. Do we shut down the Endex or continue to operate it privately and not tell anyone? Do we have a responsibility to let people know? And how do we know it will even work? We're trying to predict something that's never happened before. Then, there are our friends at the Federal Reserve. We must continue because of their interest. What do you think, Zander?"

"The Endex scares me," he answered. "I hope it's wrong. It forces me to think about what I would do if things got bad."

"How are you and Dagny getting on?" Matt asked. Zander was surprised that Matt had changed the subject.

"Great. Really, well," said Zander. "I've been waiting for her to change. You know how that goes. The girl you see at first isn't the real girl, not her real personality. So many are putting on an act at first. Maybe guys do that, too. Anyway, Dagny hasn't changed. When it comes to her, what you see is what you get. I like her, and I'm pretty sure she likes me. It's surprising how well we get along; even though we're very different, it seems to work."

Matt nodded his head and then asked, "Have you ever thought about her relative to the Endex?" With that, Matt sat back in the leather, conference room chair, his hands together with his index fingers raised to his lips and studied Zander's reaction.

Zander's eyes narrowed, and, with a slight smile, he realized that Matt hadn't changed the subject at all. "Are you asking if my plans would include Dagny?"

"That's exactly what I mean," Matt responded.

"Yes, I've thought about it," Zander said. "Our prediction is that 90% won't survive. I want to be in the 10% that do, and I want Dagny with me."

"Do you have a plan?" asked Matt.

"Kind of, but not really," Zander answered. "We'd have to get out of the city. It's suicide to be around millions of desperate people fighting over dwindling resources. But resources are needed. We must be able to eat and stay warm. I'd feel most secure heading out into the woods as far as I could get, away from people. But shelter, food and water are necessities. Camping out long term is tough. It's likely we'd end up freezing, sick and dead. Who knows how long it would take the world to stabilize."

There was a long silence before Matt spoke. "Zander, we started the Endex because there are so many clients who have worried about this, and they want guidance. Some of these people have even made extensive preparations for this possibility. What if I told you some might be seeking other like-minded people to join them?"

"Do you know someone like this, or are you speaking hypothetically?" asked Zander.

"No, not hypothetically," Matt answered. "I know someone specifically."

"Can you say who?" asked Zander.

"I'm talking about me, Zander," Matt said.

Zander took a deep breath and exhaled. He had hoped that was where Matt was heading but wasn't sure. As they'd worked on the Endex together, Zander had often wondered if Matt had a personal plan. "Are you asking if I would... if Dagny and I would join you if things got bad?"

"Yes," Matt said, still watching Zander's every nuance of facial expression and body language.

"Yes, I would. And I think Dagny would, but we've never talked about this," Zander said. "Do you have a plan, Matt? Where would we go?"

"Zander, I know exactly where we'd go. I've been working on it for years. You're exactly right in what you said earlier. It could get very ugly, very fast. The best way to survive would be to get away from people and be completely self-sufficient while we wait for things to stabilize however long that might be. I own 100 acres that is surrounded by a national forest. It is many miles from any civilization. That's where we'd go."

"Is there a road to it?" asked Zander.

"No road," Matt answered. "It's some distance from here. I won't say where because you don't have a need to know. No one knows where it is. First, we would drive, and then we'd hike. There is no road to it and no trail. It is as remote as you can get. It took me years to find it."

"How about food and shelter?" asked Zander.

"I built a cabin, and it's well-stocked with just about everything you can think of to make it on our own. There's a 20-acre lake stocked with fish, spring fed. The rest is woods. Plenty of deer. I've fenced in an acre for the garden."

"How in the world did you do that? There's no road? How did you get all that in there?" Zander asked.

"Chinooks," Matt said. "I have a buddy who owns a Chinook helicopter business. Most of his work is lifting big, air-conditioning units up on top of buildings when a crane won't reach, but he can be hired for anything. He'll even airlift in a crew of Mexican construction workers to build a lake and a cabin, if asked. That's what I did. The construction workers never knew where they were. We sat up tents and camped while we built."

"No shit!" said Zander. "When did you find the time to do all this?"

"Vacations," said Matt.

"So that's why you never talk about where you go on vacation. We always assumed you went to Cancun or Hilton Head to play golf."

"I don't play golf, Zander," said Matt.

"And you were building all this out in the woods somewhere," Zander said, still amazed. "This is unbelievable!"

"I've told you this, Zander, because I believe we would work well together. We work well together here. You are strong and healthy, and you have the right mindset. You're a good worker. You're not lazy. You were also infantry. I would feel much better having someone with me who can handle a bad situation."

"Matt, you've blown me away with all this," Zander said. "There's no other answer but yes. Yes, I would be honored to be a part of your plan."

"I have been watching Dagny," said Matt. "She's a hard worker, and I like her, too. Mary Frances and she have become best friends. Sometimes, it's almost like they're sisters. Mary Frances knows about my plan in only the most general terms. But she does know there is a place for us to go if things get bad. I'm sure she would be very pleased to have another woman along. I'm not ready to tell either one of them because I don't want to scare them. We could be wrong; things could go the other way and improve. The Endex number could fall, but I want to be ready."

"Thanks, Matt," Zander said as they stood up and the two men shook hands. "I've been concerned about this and didn't know what to do. I've been thinking about buying an AR-15. I should probably go ahead and do that."

"You can if you want, but it's not necessary," said Matt. "You still remember how to run a SAW, don't you?"

Zanders mouth fell open in shock. "Matt, are you saying you have a SAW? Are you shitting me? Is that why you mentioned that at Christmas? You were interested in that I'd been a SAW gunner."

Matt winked at his friend and said, "We'll talk more. For now, I just want you to think about this conversation. When we talk again, I want to hear any questions or concerns you have. I've tried to think of everything, but there're probably things I've overlooked. You may come up with something I haven't." Zander nodded. "Also, OPSEC. You say nothing about this to anyone, including Dagny. It's not time yet. We will but not yet."

"Yes, sir. Understood, sir," said Zander, easily falling into the slight change in role of Matt as his boss to Matt as his commanding officer. The two men walked out of the conference room and back to their offices, the rest of the company having no idea of what had just transpired.

The following day, Matt and Brian met with the CEO in his office. "How are you doing, Matt?" asked Jim Borland, referring to the aftermath of the Lynn Hanson incident. "Is there anything you need? After what you did, please tell us if we can do anything for you."

"Thanks, but I'm doing OK," he answered. Matt had been concerned that he might have dreams about it. After returning from Afghanistan, he was very tense and had trouble sleeping that first year. He'd had dreams about Afghanistan and, for a time, had been afraid to go to sleep for fear of having another nightmare. He'd also had to watch himself because he could get angry very quickly, but he controlled it. Over time, the dreams subsided. He never told anyone.

"What I want to talk about is our Endex," said Matt. "It isn't OK."

"Yes, I saw the 96," said Brian.

"My concern," said Matt, "is that the Endex has steadily been rising for two years. When we started, 100 seemed very far away, but now at 96, we're close. We decided, if you recall, that at 100 we would issue a warning to our clients who receive our research report. My concern is that I don't want to start a panic. The last thing we need is to turn on the news and hear that Veritas Strategies predicts the end of the world as we know it."

"I agree, Matt," said Brian. "I've wondered if we should have ever started this Endex, but we have. Not to mention that our friends over at the Federal Reserve have so much interest in it now."

"Do we have to make a big deal out of 100 or 110 or 120?" asked the CEO. "We decided that those numbers were significant, but we never told anyone else. If it goes to over 100, we just report it. We know what it means, but we probably shouldn't elaborate on it."

"Correct, because we don't know at what point things would fall apart," said Brian. "It may have to get to 200 or 300 before we experience collapse."

"I like that," said Matt. "We'll continue to run the Endex and monitor it. If it goes over 100, we will just report the number. I'll show you the research piece before we release it, for your approval."

"That sounds good, Matt," said Jim.

"Brian and I would like to ask you another question of a more personal nature," continued the CEO. "We're sure you are concerned over what you're seeing on the Endex, the increase in violence, shootings and riots. We would like to ask if you've given any thought to what you might do if things get bad. You'll remember that Brian and I go hunting out in Montana every year. We own a 3,000-acre ranch there, and while it is a great place to hunt, that's not the primary reason we own it. We've built a compound there. That's where we and our families will go if things get bad. You've told us that you have made plans of your own, but you are welcome to join us. You'd be a great addition. Of course, Mary Frances is included in that invitation, if you'd like that and if she's agreeable."

"Jim, Brian, I'm honored by the invitation and that you feel we would be assets," said Matt. "I must decline however. I, too, have been preparing for several years now, so I have a place. Of course, Mary Frances will go with me."

The CEO and the chief economist smiled and nodded, understanding Matt's situation. "Conditions are getting very serious, very quickly," said Jim. "I've been thinking about this more and more. Matt, let us know the second anything substantial changes with the Endex."

"Will do, and yes, it is getting serious," Matt said. "When we created the Endex, we decided to increase the frequency of calculation to weekly if it rose to 100 or greater. By all indications, it's time to do so. The three then agreed to meet again in another week.

Chapter 24
Ninety-Nine

Memorial Day passed, and so did another week. The research department had calculated the Endex, and it was at 99. When Matt met with the CEO and the chief economist, he explained, "OK, we're up another three points. You'll notice that the societal data held steady and even dropped a little. What's causing the move to 99 is we're starting to see slippage in the economic data. GDP is leveling out. We were expecting 2.5% growth, and it now looks more like 1.75%. Unemployment kicked up a little. That was unexpected. Notice the Baltic Dry. After working through the ship anomaly, it looks like it's slipped unexpectedly. So, it's the economic side that's pushed it to 99. We're just one point below 100. We'll continue to monitor it weekly. Speaking of which, I'm leaving on vacation Monday. I'll just be gone a week."

When Matt got back to his office, he called Zander. "Can you come up when you have a chance?" he asked. Zander showed up at his door five minutes later. "Zander, I want you to take a few minutes to fill this out," said Matt.

"What is this?" Zander asked, looking at the form.

"Just some information I need," said Matt.

"But why do you need my shoe size and what size jeans I wear?" asked Zander, rather confused. "Food and drug allergies?"

"Trust me. You'll thank me later," said Matt. "I'm going on vacation next week. You'll still be able to get me on the cell phone if you need me."

Next, Matt walked down six flights of stairs to the cafeteria where he found Mary Frances making lasagna in the kitchen. "Mary Frances, I want to take you out tonight. Did Dagny drive today?"

"Yes, she did," answered Mary Frances, wondering why Matt had come down to the kitchen in the middle of the morning. Matt's appearance in the cafeteria did not go unnoticed. "What's going on, Matt?" Mary Frances whispered. Matt noticed Jane watching them out of the corner of her eye.

"If you'll come a little closer, Jane, you'll be able to hear better," said Matt. "That way you'll have the story straight when you retell it." Jane scampered away, embarrassed over getting caught eavesdropping while Mary Frances did her best to not laugh out loud.

After work, Matt was waiting for Mary Frances when she came out the front door of Veritas. At least 50 people saw her get in the Range Rover. "It's funny, but this would have made me nervous a few months ago," she said. "And now, it seems that absolutely everyone at this company knows I'm your girlfriend!" Mary Frances expected him to smile, but he didn't. "Matt, what's wrong?" she asked.

"We need to talk. You've been cooking all day, so let me take you out to eat. There's a little place over on Nolensville Pike that has the best pupusas. Have you had pupusas?"

"No, I haven't. Matt is everything OK?" she asked as her stomach started to churn. *Is he going to break up with me?* she wondered.

"No. There's a problem," he said, "and I need to talk to you about it."

It's because I can't have children. He's changed his mind, she thought.

"Mary Frances, what's wrong?" Matt asked, glancing over at her as he drove. She was silent. "I want to talk to you about the Endex," he said.

Mary Frances closed her eyes and breathed deeply, thinking, *What an idiot I am!* "I can't remember exactly how much I've explained, but it's at 99," he said. "Maybe I'm so close to it that I can't see it objectively, but things are getting worse."

"Matt, what should we do?" she said, reaching over to

touch his arm. Mary Frances was greatly relieved that he was talking about the economy and not breaking up with her. *But wait a minute, losing my boyfriend versus the world falling apart? I don't want either to happen!*

"I want to talk to you about Dagny and Zander," he said. "When I built Arcadia, it was just me. I considered asking others to go with me if that ever became necessary, but it was just me at first. Then I met you, and I realized I would want you with me. It's getting much closer, Mary Frances. This could really happen. I've been thinking, and I want your honest opinion. How would you feel about asking Zander and Dagny to join us? There would be so much work to do, and having four people improves the division of labor. Also, Zander was infantry. If there ever was a problem, that would be very beneficial."

Mary Frances nodded and said, "Matt, that had occurred to me already. I like the idea. Dagny and I get along fine working together and as roommates. She's like the sister I never had. And I like Zander. The two of them are good together."

They parked in front of the restaurant. As they were crossing the parking lot, Mary Frances said, "Matt, tell me about Arcadia. I know you have this all worked out. You've thought about this far more than I ever could, but is there room for Dagny and Zander? You've not told me what's there."

Matt opened the door for Mary Frances as they entered the restaurant. Everyone stopped talking, turned and looked at them. They were the only Anglos in the place; everyone else was Latino. Taking a booth, the waitress approached them with a cautious look on her face as if she was thinking, *They must be in the wrong place.* She placed the menus on the table and asked, "Can I get you something to drink?"

"Dos micheladas y cuatro pupusas, por fa. No necisitamos los menus. Porque esta tan triste aqui? No hay musica? Me gusta salsa o merengue, por favor," Matt said. "O cumbia, si te gusta." Mary Frances watched and listened as Matt and the waitress conversed.

The waitress broke into a big smile as she said, "Por supuesto, señor!"

The two couples at the next table smiled at the waitress

and then to each other as everyone in the restaurant returned to their food and conversation. Almost immediately, merengue started to play as the waitress pushed buttons on a music system by the cash register.

Matt smiled at Mary Frances, stood and held out his left hand to her. "What?" she asked, perplexed.

"Let's dance. Do you like merengue?" he asked.

"Matt, I don't know what that is, and this is a restaurant," she whispered.

"It doesn't matter. No one cares. They'll probably start dancing, too," he said.

"I don't know how," she said, starting to be embarrassed. "I've never heard this song!"

"The song is 'Suavemente' by Elvis Crespo," Matt said, smiling, "and nobody knows us anyway. The worst that can happen is they tell us to stop or throw us out. Then, you'd get to tell Dagny how we were thrown out of a bar. That would be a great story!"

Matt waited, still holding out his left hand. Mary Frances stood and reluctantly took it. He led her to the open area by the cash register. Taking her right hand in his left and placing her left hand on his shoulder, he showed her the basic steps. Very quickly, Mary Frances was dancing. Once again, the other customers turned and watched. Then, two waitresses started dancing together, and then the two couples at the neighboring table got up and joined in. "See, I told you," Matt said, laughing. "Isn't this fun!"

Mary Frances just laughed, shaking her head and thinking, *This is another side of Matt I've not seen before.*

After the song ended, everyone applauded; Matt and Mary Frances were suddenly everyone's best friends. Mary Frances was a little embarrassed by all the attention. They walked back to their table where two micheladas were waiting for them. "What are these, Matt?" asked Mary Frances.

"A michelada is kind of like a Bloody Mary made with beer," he said. "I love it when I can teach *you* something about food and drink that you don't already know! Next will be the pupusas!" Mary Frances took a sip.

"This is good," she said. "You're going to have to teach me how to do that... merengue... at home, so I don't embarrass myself the next time you drag me to a restaurant and start dancing! That was fun!"

"OK, it's a deal," he said. "And there're a couple of other things I need to teach you," he said, winking at her.

"Matt!" she whispered, unsure if she found it annoying or funny. Matt laughed as she shook her head and rolled her eyes.

"Now, then. Where were we?" he asked, taking a sip of the michelada. "I believe you were asking about Arcadia."

"Yes, what kind of place is it?" she asked. "I'm very curious."

"Mary Frances, several years ago I bought 100 acres of land. It's very remote. In fact, this land is completely enclosed in a national forest. National forests are huge with hundreds of thousands of acres, sometimes millions. There are no roads to my land, no towns, and no people for miles. There's a 20-acre lake in the middle of the property. It's almost completely wooded as is the national forest around it," he explained.

"But where would we live?" she asked.

"I built a cabin," he said.

"Oh, Matt, another cabin!" she said. "You know how I am about cabins. They're my favorite kind of house. Does it have a stone fireplace?"

Matt smiled and answered, "Yes, there's one in the bedroom. In the main room, there's a Jodel wood burner. It has a big, glass window in the front to view the fire. The wood burner is more practical for heating, but the fireplace in the bedroom is just because I wanted one. It's not as luxurious as my cabin in Tennessee. It's more rustic, but I've tried to make it as comfortable as possible. There's a spring on the hill above the cabin, so it has plumbing and running water. There are inside bathrooms. There's not constant hot water, but because I built a wood-fired water heater, we can have hot water for baths and washing when it's fired up."

"It sounds wonderful," she said, intrigued. "Tell me about the kitchen."

"It has a wood-fired stove, stone countertops and a big, copper sink," he explained. "Outside, in a kitchen pavilion, is another stove and wood-fired oven. That's for use in the summer to keep the heat out of the cabin."

"And this is in the woods on a lake?" she asked.

"Yes, and the lake is stocked. It's full of fish," he said.

"But how are the bedrooms? Is there room for Zander and Dagny?" she asked, just as the waitress arrived with two plates of pupusas. They thanked her, and she thanked them for dancing and invited them to dance some more.

"There are two bedrooms and also a bunk room with four more beds," he said.

"I bet there's a battery system with a steam engine, too," Mary Frances said.

"Yes, and solar and a turbine that's powered off the spring. So, we have three ways to make electricity for the batteries," he said.

"Matt, I've told you this before," she said, "but I'm going to say it again. Being snowed in with you for four days was the best thing that has ever happened to me. I love being with you. I can't think of anything better than being with you in a cabin somewhere. This all seems surreal. I understand most people aren't seeing what's happening in the world. They see it, but they don't get it. I don't want the world to fall apart. But if it does, being with you, hidden away somewhere in the woods in a cabin sounds wonderful. Just perfect."

The waitress came back to check on them and brought the ticket. "Perfect means that nothing else could be better, Mary Frances," Matt said. "Do you mean there isn't anything else in the world that would make you happier?"

"No, not really," she said. "Being with you brings me more happiness than I ever imagined."

"Well, I *almost* agree with you. I've never been so happy as I've been with you," he said, "but there is one thing that would make it perfect." Mary Frances looked at him, wondering what that could be.

"What would make it perfect for me is having you as my wife," he said. "Mary Frances, will you marry me?"

Mary Frances was stunned. Hearing the words sent her into a state of complete shock. *Did I hear that right?* she thought.

Oh, my God! I'm sure that's what he said. But, I'm never supposed to get married; no one is supposed to ever want to marry me. Tell him, tell him yes. But she was unable to speak.

"Mary Frances?" asked Matt. "Did you hear me?"

"Yes," she answered. "I can't believe what I heard. Are you sure?"

Matt reached across the table and took her hands, "Yes, I'm positive. I've been trying to think of a more romantic way of asking you, but everything is happening so fast. I've been carrying this around in my pocket for a week, waiting for the right moment. This probably isn't the most romantic place in the world, but I don't want to wait any longer." With that, Matt reached in his pocket and brought out a small, black, velvet box. He opened it and placed it before her.

"Yes, I will marry you!" she said. No amount of blinking could hold back the tears, and Mary Frances started crying uncontrollably. Their waitress couldn't help but notice as did everyone else in the restaurant.

Mary Frances almost choked with emotion as she saw the diamond engagement ring sparkling against the black velvet. *Oh, Matt, it's beautiful!* she thought. *Am I really going to get married? I am. Matthew Archer wants to marry me. Me!*

Matt took the ring out of the box and gently put it on Mary Frances' ring finger. The next thing Mary Frances knew, the whole restaurant erupted into applause. She looked around, smiling and wiping her eyes with a napkin. Then everyone gathered around their booth to congratulate them and see the ring. The happiness was contagious.

On the drive home, Matt said, "Mary Frances, sometimes I'm not very good with words. I'm always thinking about things I want to tell you when we're apart; but when we're together, I can't find the words. I just want to tell you that you have an effect on me I've never experienced before. You make me want to be better. Maybe because you always think the best of me, and I want to live up to your expectation. I'm not sure exactly, but you make me a better man." Mary Frances held his hand as he drove. Kissing his hand and holding it against her cheek, Matt could feel her tears.

"Mary Frances, I'm going to be gone for a week," he continued, carefully. "I'm leaving tomorrow. This isn't for publication, but I'm taking another load of supplies to Arcadia."

"Matt, can I go with you?" she asked and then added, "But how will you do that? Didn't you say there are no roads?"

"Helicopter. I have a buddy who owns a big, twin-rotor helicopter. That's how I've gotten everything into the property. I palletize the load, then have them deliver it and me to the cabin. Five days later, they extract me. That gives me five days to get everything stored and to make sure everything is in good shape at the cabin. Then, it's back to the airport, back to my SUV and I drive home." He paused for a minute. "No, it's best you stay here. I'd like to take you, but you should stay. I want you to plan the wedding. We need to talk about it, but if things keep deteriorating like they have been, then we mustn't wait too long."

"I don't want to wait very long either," Mary Frances said.

"I have lots of supplies at the cabin, but I don't have a pastor to perform a wedding ceremony," Matt said, smiling at his fiancée. Mary Frances smiled back, still overcome with emotion. "Mary Frances, a quick question. It's a little unusual, but I need to find out. You and Dagny look to be about the same size. Do you know her sizes? Shoe size, bra size, is she the same as you?"

"Matthew Archer!" said Mary Frances. "Why in the world would you ask about things like that?"

"Clothes, Mary Frances," said Matt. "If we have relocate to Arcadia, it could be for years. There won't be any stores to buy a new pair of shoes. I've already bought everything for you- jeans, shoes, boots, socks, coats, underwear. But since we're including Zander and Dagny, I need to buy more. This will probably be the last load of supplies to be airlifted in. I've tried to think of everything, but I've probably forgotten something. I'll be picking up all the meds such as antibiotics tomorrow morning. Oh, find out if Dagny takes any prescription medications."

"Matt, I'm sorry," Mary Frances said. "I never thought of any of that. Our clothes will wear out. Yes, Dagny is my size in everything. I'm an inch taller, but that's the only difference. Matthew Archer, how do you know my shoe size and my bra size?" Matt just winked at her and ignored her question. Mary Frances figured he must have checked when she'd been in the bathroom. "Matt, could this happen soon?"

"I hope not," he said. "But I want to be ready if we do have to leave suddenly. Mary Frances, what about your mother? How do you feel about leaving her?"

"It worries me because I love her," she said. "But I left her, or rather she left me years ago. We'll invite her to the wedding, but I will not invite George. My mother won't come. She's already chosen George. I'd like Mr. Borland to give me away. Do you think it's alright if I ask him?"

"Yes, just ask. I'm sure he will," said Matt.

"And Matt, let's not have a big, expensive wedding. I don't need a dozen brides' maids. Maybe Dagny will be my maid-of-honor. I want to be married in your church and then have a small reception; wedding cake and punch is enough. Then, we can go home to your cabin. Mary Frances started to get emotional again as she considered her life and how it was changing. "Matt, are you sure it's OK that I can't have children? It's a lot for you to give up."

"Yes, I'm sure," he said. "Mary Frances, I never thought I'd get married either. Not for the same reason, but because I never found anyone that I wanted to marry. Then, you appeared. Mary Frances, I truly believe you are a gift from God, sent directly to me in a snowstorm. As much as I try to predict, I have no idea what the future holds. I do know that God will guide us and help us, and I know I want to be with you." Mary Frances closed her eyes and pressed his hand against her face as Matt drove them back to the Grove. She thanked God for completely changing her life and for the man sitting next to her.

Chapter 25
Plans

As Matt pulled up in front of Mary Frances' apartment, she said, "There's Zander's car! He must be visiting Dagny. I can't wait to tell them!" They parked and hurried up the sidewalk. Mary Frances unlocked the door to find Dagny and Zander sitting on the couch, glued to the television.

As they entered, Zander said, "Have you heard about this? Are you aware of what's happening?" Mary Frances and Matt closed the door and quickly sat with their friends. "There were three attacks," Zander explained. "All at baseball games- Boston, Cincinnati and Denver. Matt, these weren't single gunmen. There were several at each location. They were waiting outside the gates when the games ended and started shooting." The four friends watched the frantic updates which bounced back and forth from city to city. The reports were confusing. No one understood what was happening or why, but it was evident that the death toll was over a thousand. Cincinnati alone already had 351 confirmed fatalities.

"Have the gunmen been killed?" Matt asked.

"No," answered Zander. "From what I can tell, they all escaped. This was very well executed."

"My intentions were to leave tomorrow for a week, but now...," Matt's voice trailed off. "Zander, mute the TV for a second." Zander pushed the button as they all turned to Matt. "This is as good a time as any to have this conversation. We're all here together. I need to determine if everyone is in agreement. As you all are aware, I own a place that I hope to be safe in the event of a total collapse. If I decide that we need to go there, Mary Frances has told me she wants to go with me. In fact, there's more news; she's also agreed to marry me." As Zander and Dagny processed what they'd just heard, Mary Frances smiled and held up her left hand.

"You said *yes*!" said Dagny. "All that training worked!" she said, laughing and hugging her friend.

"Training?" asked Matt.

"You know how she is," laughed Dagny. "I had her practice how to say *yes*, if you asked. I couldn't let her say *no*."

"Well, I'm glad you had the foresight to train her," said Matt, laughing, too. Zander patted his buddy on the back and congratulated the couple.

"Mary Frances, you know about the work Zander and I do with the Endex," Matt said, changing the subject. "Dagny, do you understand what we do?"

"Just a little," said Dagny, becoming serious.

"The bottom line is we monitor the country and the world," Matt said. "Zander and I are afraid the world may be heading to a point of instability that could result in societal collapse. Because our modern world is so dependent on its systems, we fear that would result in a tremendous loss of life. I've prepared a place I call Arcadia. I believe it would be a safe place to wait out the collapse. Mary Frances is going with me. There is room. Would you two like to come with us?"

"What do you mean... societal collapse?" asked Dagny.

"That means a condition where basic services like police, medical, food and water distribution no longer function. The expected consequence is no law and order. People turn to violence to get what they need. We predict that electricity would no longer work, potable water would not flow and the supermarkets would be empty. There would be complete chaos, resulting in a massive reduction in the population."

"Matt's right," Zander said to Dagny in affirmation. "This has been coming for some time. It won't be safe here, if this happens. Dagny, we need to do this. Will you come with me?"

Trying to comprehend it all, Dagny studied the faces of her three friends. She glanced at the muted TV showing the carnage in Cincinnati. Her thoughts then turned to her parents, her sister and her family in California. Then turning to Zander, she hugged him. "Yes, I'll go with you," she answered.

"Now, I have one more question, Dagny," said Zander, holding her hand. "Before we leave, will you marry me?" Matt grinned slyly as Mary Frances put her hands to her mouth in shock.

"Yes, I will," Dagny squealed in delight and kissed her fiancée.

"I'm sorry I don't have a ring yet," said Zander. "I will have one for you soon."

Mary Frances removed the red, elastic hair tie from her ponytail. "Here, Zander," she said, offering it to him. "You can use this for now."

Zander smiled and took the hair tie from her. Taking Dagny's hand, he began twisting the elastic band around her ring finger. "Now, all the guys will know you're taken," he said with a laugh.

"I love it," Dagny laughed as Zander finished adjusting the red elastic. "And it's just my size!

"Well, congratulations you two! I happen to know a jeweler...," Matt said as everyone laughed, happy to share the special moment together. Things are moving so fast. I planned to be gone for a week... more preparations. Now, I'll wait a day or two to see if this calms down. I'm almost afraid to leave. Since the rate of malfunction is increasing, we need to be ready to leave at any moment."

"Where are we going?" asked Dagny.

"Arcadia," said Mary Frances. "It's safe, and it's far from people. Only Matt knows where it is. We can survive there. Think back to the blizzard, Dagny. Do you remember how hard it was for you and how comfortable it was for me? Remember how cold you were and how jealous you were because I was warm. You were so close to running out of toilet paper and food! Now, imagine how bad it would have gotten if the blizzard had lasted just another week. In a way, that's what Matt is talking about. That's how it will be.... and worse. Arcadia is where we can be safe and warm and have food to eat. Arcadia is where we survive until the world heals."

"Listen to me closely, everyone," said Matt. "Mary Frances is correct. The blizzard was a great example of how it could be. Only the blizzard will seem like a picnic in comparison. We are very pleased that you two are joining us, but I want to warn you to not tell anyone. We can talk about it in private between the four of us. When you have questions, just ask me. But don't breathe a word of it to anyone outside this circle. Is that understood?" The friends nodded in agreement. "I hope there's time to get the last load of supplies to Arcadia," Matt continued. "If there isn't, we'll still be OK, but I'd like to get in one last load."

"Matt, we might be there a long time? Like years?" asked Dagny as Matt nodded. "What about feminine supplies? You know, once a month."

Matt nodded. Mary Frances' eyes got bigger as she thought, *I never considered that!* "Taken care of," Matt said. "Supplies for many years are already in place."

"How about medicine?" asked Dagny. "What if someone gets hurt?"

"I have substantial medical supplies on site," said Matt, "and I'm picking up antibiotics tomorrow. I didn't want to buy them too soon because of expiration dates."

Dagny nodded her approval, and Mary Frances silently thought about how her fiancée had thought about things she hadn't.

"You girls need get to work on wedding plans," Matt said. "If you'd like, we could get married together at the same ceremony. It's just an idea." Mary Frances and Dagny smiled at the suggestion.

Elated, the brides-to-be simultaneously exclaimed, "A double wedding!"

Chapter 26
One Fourteen

Mary Frances and Dagny were now harboring the secret Matt and Zander had long guarded. The men had been working on the Endex for years; having information others did not had become normal to them. But for Mary Frances and Dagny, it was new. When co-workers expressed excitement over the upcoming double wedding, it was a strange feeling for the women who knew more was going on in the world than their wedding. Their timetable had been moved up... because of the Endex.

Dagny had been afraid of Mrs. Joiner's reaction to the news of their engagements, but Mary Frances assured Dagny that she would accept it. "I have no idea what may have happened to Mrs. Joiner in the past; but because Matt and Zander want to marry us, I think she will be pleased." Mary Frances was right. When the girls shared the news, Mrs. Joiner was moved to tears and gave them big hugs.

The news of the attacks on the baseball games brought more cries for assault weapon bans and the repeal of the Second Amendment. The total casualties came to 1,019 dead and 2,027 wounded. Matt closely watched the news for the next two days to see if more attacks came. They didn't. But baseball game, restaurant, and movie theatre traffic dropped in half in response to the shootings as people became worried about safety in public places.

Three days after the attacks, Matt told Mary Frances good-bye and left for Arcadia. While life continued normally at Veritas for Mary Frances, Dagny and Zander, Matt stepped into another world. He drove to another city where he met his friend who owned the helicopter business. In an adjacent warehouse were cases of all types of supplies, along with over 100 Amazon packages Matt had sent to the helicopter company. His friend had carried them into the warehouse where they accumulated awaiting Matt's arrival. He spent a day unpacking and repacking the contents and then palletizing them for transport to Arcadia.

The next morning, Matt lifted off with the supplies aboard the big, twin- rotor helicopter. An hour and 15 minutes later, they landed in a remote location where three pallets were rolled off in a small, open area between a log cabin and a small lake. Matt waved as the helicopter took off. The pilot had instructions to return in four days to pick up Matt. The helicopter quickly disappeared from sight as the landing zone was surrounded by forest, but Matt could hear the thump-thump-thump of the rotors for another minute. Then, there was silence.

Standing by the lake, Matt turned to gaze at the cabin. It was the key to their survival. The finality of the situation was weighing on him. With previous trips, he had never worried if something was forgotten because he could always bring it the next time. This was the last trip, and he knew it. The years of work at Arcadia were now about to be put to the test.

Closing his eyes, Matt became aware of a light breeze that carried a faint scent of pine trees. The singing birds reminded him he wasn't alone. Then, he bowed his head. *Heavenly Father, thank You for getting me this far. Everything I have is from You. I'm afraid there are hard times ahead. Please give me the strength and wisdom to get us through this. Amen.*

The next three hours were spent carrying supplies into the cabin. It was smaller than his cabin back in Tennessee but plenty big for four. He walked through the cabin, wondering what Mary Frances' reaction would be. Matt smiled because she would like the stone fireplace. As he walked through the kitchen, he wondered if she'd like it considering what an accomplished chef she was but then decided she would. The house had three bedrooms and three bathrooms that were probably an unnecessary luxury, but Matt realized little creature comforts would make an extended stay easier. A built-in bookcase was loaded with books. Matt reached under one of the shelves to release a latch. One of the sections swung out, revealing a stairway that led down to the basement.

Matt checked his watch before he began the job of carrying the new supplies downstairs. Realizing Mary Frances was probably on her lunch break, he walked over to a desk where he plugged in his phone before he called.

"Hey, Mary Frances."

"Matt! Did you make it?"

"Yes, I'm here, and everything went as planned. Is everything good in Nashvegas?"

"Yes, we're all fine. The cell phone signal is better than I expected."

"I have a booster antenna that I plug into. I hear you loud and clear."

"I hear you fine, too. So, what are you doing? Did you have time to eat lunch?"

"I've been carrying supplies inside because it looks like it's going to rain. I'll get some lunch as soon as we hang up.

"Is everything OK at the cabin?"

"Yes, everything looks good. I'll check all the systems, but I'm sure they're fine. It's warm today, so I probably won't bother to fire up the water heater. I'll just take a cold shower tonight. Did I mention there's an outdoor shower to use in the summer? I'll use all the plumbing while I'm here just to make sure it's working."

"Matt, I don't want us to have to go. I just want to stay in Nashville and have a normal life with you. I do want to see Arcadia sometime, like for a vacation. Maybe everything will calm down and get better."

"I understand, Mary Frances. Arcadia would be a good vacation spot. I can't wait for you to see it. It's all forest, and it's surrounded by mountains. The lake is clear and full of fish.

I'll teach you how to fish!"

"I hate to end our call, Matt, but it's almost time for me to get back to work. Can we talk again tonight?"

"Of course, I'll call you. You get back to work now before Mrs. Joiner fires you!"

"Matt, be very careful. I don't want anything to happen to you. I love you."

"I love you, Mary Frances."

Walking back to the cafeteria, Mary Frances reflected on how her life had changed since moving to Nashville. *First, this wonderful job!* she thought. *Then, Dagny. Then, the blizzard and Matt.* She looked down at her engagement ring, admiring it. It wasn't a good idea to wear it in the kitchen, but she couldn't bear to take it off. She was so proud of the ring, wanting everyone to see it! *He loves me and wants to marry me. And we will be married soon.* She worried about Matt flying in the helicopter and being alone at Arcadia. Then, for some reason, she remembered that Matt had been in Afghanistan. *Thank goodness, I didn't know him them. I wouldn't have been able to bear the worry of him being hurt or worse.* Calculating when he had been in Afghanistan, she realized it was the same time she had been in the hospital and breathed a prayer. *Thank you, God, for taking care of us both.*

"Hey, break's over!" said Dagny, snapping Mary Frances out of her thoughts. "Do you think we can pull everything together for the wedding in two weeks? That weekend works for my family."

"I think so," said Mary Frances. "Matt doesn't have any family, and my mother won't come because of George. Zander's family is in Louisville. Can they make it that weekend?"

"I'll ask Zander after work today," said Dagny. "If we get the green light, we can get married in two weeks."

"Dagny, we need wedding gowns," said Mary Frances. "I admit I said I wanted a simple wedding, and I do. But I've always dreamed of a beautiful, white wedding dress. I never believed I'd get to wear one. That's why it's important to me. Would you like to go shopping Saturday?"

"Sounds good! Let's go!" said Dagny. "But, hold it... If I'm your maid of honor, and you're my maid of honor, but we're getting married at the same time, then how are we going to do that?"

"Now, let's not make this complicated," said Mary Frances. "We both want a beautiful, simple wedding. Of course, we can be maids of honor and brides at the same time."

"I don't know," said Dagny, making a face. "Are we going to get the rings confused? What if Zander gets Matt's ring? And when I'm holding your flowers and you're holding mine, then we're both still holding flowers."

"You're not making any sense. This will work, Dagny. Trust me. It's just like a regular wedding," said Mary Frances.

"Well, if you're sure. I'll take your word for it," said Dagny, shrugging her shoulders as they returned to the kitchen.

When Matt returned from delivering supplies to Arcadia, he drove straight to Veritas. He arrived just a few minutes before 5:00 p.m. and surprised Mary Frances as she, Dagny and Zander were walking out to their vehicles. Mary Frances ran to him as he got out of the Range Rover. She hugged him like he'd been gone a year instead of a week. As the four of them were talking she would touch his arm or his shoulder from time to time, subconsciously making sure he was really there.

"Hey, it's Friday, guys! No work tomorrow!" said Matt, smiling at Mary Frances. "Let's go out for dinner. My treat. I'd like to give y'all a report on Arcadia. And I'd like to catch up on everything here."

"Sounds good, Matt," said Zander. "We need to talk about the Endex. I've finished calculating it for last week. It's at 114."

"I knew it would be over 100," said Matt, seriously. The look on his face said *I was hoping I was wrong.*

"Dagny, you girls can go home and change," said Zander. "Then, we'll all meet at the Grove and go from there." Everyone agreed except Mary Frances. "I've missed you so much," she said to Matt. "I know it would be extra driving but could you take me home to grab some clothes? Then we could go to your cabin to get ready. I know that's silly, but I don't like being separated from you."

"Sure, we can do that," said Matt. "We can still meet up at the Grove at say... 7:00? Does that give everyone enough time?"

"Better make it 7:30," said Dagny. "Mary Frances can take a long time to get ready!" Mary Frances stuck her tongue out at her friend as they all laughed.

"Casual," said Matt. "Nothing fancy!" And they all jumped in their cars to begin the weekend.

It turned out that Dagny's suggestion of 7:30 instead of 7:00 was a good one. When Matt and Mary Frances arrived at the cabin after stopping for her clothes, Matt said, "Would you like to shower alone, or would you prefer the more ecologically sound choice of showering with a friend?"

Mary Frances was caught off guard for a second and couldn't respond, but then quickly recovered and came back with, "I care deeply about the planet and would prefer the latter." Matt led her into the bedroom and quickly started unbuttoning her top while simultaneously kicking off his shoes.

As he pulled off his shirt and then his pants, he continued to undress Mary Frances as she said, "I believe you missed me, Mr. Archer. I can tell you're very glad to see me!" Mary Frances squealed as he pushed her down on the bed. Their lovemaking was intense as Matt thrust into her. Then, he turned her over. "Matt, what are you doing?" she asked as she felt him push deep into her. But her hesitation of the new position quickly subsided as she exploded in orgasm.

Lying next to each other afterward, with Mary Frances in his arms, Matt asked, "Was I too hard on you? Too rough?"

"Matt, that was intense," she said, still breathing a little faster than normal. "It did hurt a little." She laid with her head on his chest, holding him tightly. "But I liked it," she whispered. "And I'm very sure I had an orgasm. I'm still shaking. That's never happened before, as I'm sure you've noticed."

"You most certainly did have an orgasm," Matt said, stroking her hair. "So, I can say with complete certainty that you are not frigid."

"I guess I'm not," she agreed, thinking again about how different her life had become.

They made it back to The Grove right on time. "I'm glad Dagny suggested 7:30," said Mary Frances as they parked. "We needed the extra 30 minutes, but it wasn't my fault!"

"It certainly was your fault," said Matt, "and I'll tell them so if they ask!"

"Matt, you wouldn't dare!" Mary Frances said.

"It's entirely your fault," he said. "You've been spoiling me, and I've become accustomed to it. A week is too long for me to go without you."

"I love you so much, Matt," she said. *He loves me. He's going to marry me. And he wants me, all the time.*

"Have y'all been to Plaza Mariachi?" Matt asked as they piled in the Range Rover. "It's down Nolensville Pike. It's like a Mexican town inside a building. There are shops and restaurants. There's also a band tonight." None of the others had been there. All agreed they were up for something new.

"Tell us about Arcadia," said Zander. "Did everything go as planned with the supplies?"

"It did. No problems," said Matt. "Everything was fine at the cabin, and everything worked."

"Matt, Zander has me walking miles every day in my new boots," said Dagny. "Is that really necessary? If we must go, can't we just ride in a helicopter like you do?"

"That's good that you're breaking in your boots," answered Matt as they wound through the city traffic. "The reason we need to walk in, is so we'll have a vehicle when it's time to return. If we flew out of the airport where the helicopter is, that's where our SUV would be. Also, it probably wouldn't be there when we decided we could go home. I have a place to hide this vehicle that's walking distance to Arcadia. Some folks might consider 25 miles through the woods to be a little far, but it's doable."

"Matt, I think you've planned for just about everything," said Zander.

"I hope so, but probably I've forgotten something," said Matt. "Someday when we all realize what I've forgotten, we'll have a good laugh. I just hope it isn't something important."

"Matt, I think I told you the Endex came in at 114. That's a new record. We can go over the numbers Monday," said Zander. "All the economic numbers slipped a little. And the societal numbers were up. It only takes turning on the TV to see that violence is up. Vacations were up 2 points."

The four parked at the restaurant and walked in. Plaza Mariachi was packed as they walked down the street of Mexican shops toward the food court area. "The numbers would be worse," Zander continued, "but the stock market keeps going up."

The four could hear the band playing as they continued walking. Then Matt said, "I know that as the GDP continues to slip, we'll see the debt to GDP ratio climb. It could very easily climb to default levels, especially if Congress does what they always do and starts spending money to stabilize the slide. If borrowing goes up, so does the debt. If GDP goes down enough, we're looking at possible default on the national debt. Also, most our national debt is in T-bills. Those turn over in a year or less. As the treasury-buying market starts to doubt the treasury's ability to pay, it will demand higher interest. Those higher interest rates will start to manifest immediately as the T-bill debt rolls over. The Treasury will be wishing they'd locked that in longer term, but they didn't. Higher interest rates, higher debt service, quicker default." Mary Frances and Dagny listened quietly as Matt and Zander discussed the situation, not completely understanding the implications, but fully understanding that it wasn't good. "So, if you're sitting on a bunch of dollars and you're afraid there could be a devaluation and default, what do you do, Zander?" asked Matt.

"Get rid of the dollars before they become worthless," said Zander. "I'd get rid of anything that was US Treasury linked like cash, CD's, Treasury bonds, bills, or notes. I'd buy gold, silver, real estate and stocks."

"Yeah. Me, too," said Matt, thinking it through. "I wouldn't really care if any of those sectors were historically overvalued. I'd buy them anyway just to get rid of the cash. Could that be driving the stock market? Are people starting to worry about a default so they're moving cash to the stock market?"

"Disintermediation," said Zander as Matt nodded his head.

"Can you boys stop talking about all that stuff?" pleaded Dagny. "My head is starting to hurt."

"Matt, this place is so noisy," said Mary Frances. "The band is so loud we can't hold a conversation." Every table was taken in the food court; a band was playing on the stage and people were dancing.

"Yeah, we can go somewhere else," said Matt as he grabbed Mary Frances' hand. "Just one dance and then we'll go somewhere else."

"Not again, Matt!" Mary Frances cried as he pulled her onto the packed dance floor. "Is this merengue like at the other place?"

"Nope, this is bachata," said Matt. "Just follow my lead." Dagny and Zander watched.

"You're doing great!" said Matt as he turned his fiancé.

"I don't think so," said Mary Frances. Matt pulled her against him and they turned together while Matt laughed. When the song ended, Matt led Mary Frances back to Zander and Dagny.

"There's a little Peruvian restaurant just across the parking lot," said Matt. "Let's try that. I'm fairly certain it will be quieter there."

"You guys are good!" said Zander. "I didn't know y'all knew how to dance."

"Oh yeah, Mary Frances has been dancing for years," said Matt. "She makes me look good." Mary Frances shook her head and smiled. Dagny laughed at her friend as the four crossed the parking lot to the restaurant.

"Have any of you had chupé?" asked Matt as they entered the restaurant. "I recommend it. It's very good." The restaurant was about half full and much quieter, although there was a music video playing on a big screen TV.

"Well, I'm very concerned about that money stuff y'all were talking about," joked Dagny after the waitress took their drink order. "I've got $93.24 in my checking account as of right now, and I'd be ruined if I lost that!" Everyone laughed as they perused the menu.

"I was feeling a little guilty about the money I will be spending on my wedding dress," said Mary Frances, "but if I understand what you're saying, maybe that's OK. Are you saying our money could become worthless?"

The waitress came back and took the order for dinner. Matt gave Mary Frances a look of *I'll answer that as soon as she takes our order.* When the waitress left, Matt continued, "If the treasury can't borrow enough to support the deficit spending because the market no longer trusts their ability to pay, then the U.S. will have no choice but to print money. The Fed will buy back bonds, thus reducing the debt, with printed money. That will result in inflation. Prices on just about everything will go through the roof. The next step will be devaluing the currency. Now, the largest bill is the $100 bill. They'll start printing $1,000 and $10,000 bills. The last step will be the introduction of the new dollar, a new currency to replace the existing one. Then comes conversion, except the conversion rate would probably be something like $100,000 to $1. So, if you had $100,000 in your checking account Dagny, you'd get $1 of the new dollar. Wealth in cash would be wiped out. Of course, $100,000 worth of debt would become $1 in the new currency. So, you wouldn't want to own any Treasury bonds, notes, bills, cash or savings accounts or checking accounts. That whole process would be chaotic and catastrophic for most. How bad would depend on how society holds together. Lots of countries have gone through this. The U.S. hasn't, so most Americans don't understand how it works. Our biggest concern is how we'd hold up if this was combined with the electrical grid going down, cyber-attacks and general lawlessness in the population. It could get incredibly bad. That's the reason for Arcadia."

"Wow, Matt, you really know how to liven up a party!" joked Dagny as Mary Frances closed her eyes and shook her head at the comment.

"I'm sorry," Matt said. "I'm bad about that. Somebody asks a question, and I give a long complex answer. Let's change the subject to something more enjoyable. How are the wedding plans shaping up?"

"It looks like we can get married two weeks from tomorrow," said Mary Frances, watching Matt to see his reaction. "Zander's family can come then and so can Dagny's. We checked with your pastor, Matt, and the church is available. Dagny and I are shopping tomorrow for wedding dresses. We need to see about the wedding cake and punch for the reception, but we're making progress. We're trying to keep it very simple, and we're trying to not spend too much money. Instead of sending invitations, we're calling people to invite them. That's better due to such short notice."

"Well, you gals have been busy while I've been gone," said Matt. "I'd like to propose a toast." They held their drinks high as Matt said, "Here's to the four of us. May we have a bright future as we navigate the difficult times ahead."

The friends laughed and talked over dinner. Mary Frances felt Matt's leg under the table as he moved it next to hers. She was watching a YouTube on the big TV when she said, "Look at that video." The group turned to see five girls wearing sequined outfits somewhat reminiscent of a baton twirler's. They were singing in Spanish and dancing.

"That's Aqua Bella," said Matt.

"Aqua Bella? Beautiful water?" asked Zander.

"Yep, Peruvian restaurant, Peruvian music," answered Matt.

"Do you know what they're saying, Matt?" asked Mary Frances.

"I bet there's not a person in Perú who doesn't know this song. It's called *Pasito Tun Tun*."

"They sure are talented," said Zander.

Dagny smacked his arm and said, "I know what you're looking at!"

"What did the girl in the middle just say, Matt?" asked Mary Frances.

"That's Marina, and she said, 'Solo hay una'... There's only one," Matt answered. "She's talking about the group... There's only one Aqua Bella."

"You know her name?" asked Dagny. "No, you don't. Twenty dollars says you don't."

"I do," said Matt. "Are you sure you want to make that bet, Dagny?"

"Don't do it, Dagny," said Mary Frances. "Matt is a walking database of trivia." But Dagny wouldn't back down and was shaking Matt's hand as the waitress delivered the bill.

"Excuse me," Matt said to the waitress. "We have a little bet going on that you may be able to help us with. Are you Peruvian?" The waitress nodded, wondering what it was all about. "So the group singing on the video, Aqua Bella," Matt continued. "I'm going to name each of them and I want you to tell my friends here if I'm correct." The waitress smiled and nodded. "The three in the middle are Alhely, Marina and Maricarmen. The two on the outside are Cynthia and Nancy."

"Yes, you're correct!" said the waitress.

"Dang it," said Dagny, hitting the table with her palm. "Sorry, Zander. Now, I won't be wearing a veil at our wedding."

"Oh, Dagny! I tried to tell you," laughed Mary Francis as Dagny got out her billfold.

"Put your money away, Dagny," said Matt.

"No, a bet is a bet, and I lost," said Dagny.

"Here's the $20," said Zander, shaking his head. "I've got you covered, Dagny. Perhaps we should discuss financial matters before we get married."

"Well, let's add it to our waitress' tip," Matt said when everyone stopped laughing.

The four talked and finished their drinks. When the music video changed to another song, Matt said. "Mary Frances, listen to this last song. It's a duet. That's Maricarmen Marín, the same Maricarmen from the previous video."

"She's pretty," said Mary Frances, "and she has a pretty voice. What are they saying?"

"This song is *Hasta el Fin del Mundo*," said Matt. "Until the End of the World. They're saying that they will love each other forever." The four listened to the music, contemplating love and that, perhaps, the title wasn't metaphorical. The song ended and the group was quiet as they walked to the Range Rover.

"Thanks for bringing us here, Matt," said Mary Frances as they got in. "The food is very good. I'm just surprised that there aren't more people here on a Friday night."

"It's starting to happen all over the country," Matt said. "People are more cautious about going out in public after the attacks at the baseball games." When dinner was finished, the couples returned to The Grove.

"Mary Frances, are we going to see the baker tomorrow about the wedding cake?" asked Dagny as they stood outside the apartment. Mary Frances nodded. "We could look at wedding dresses and shoes afterwards. I already know what kind of shoes I want."

"Yes, to the baker and dress shopping," said Mary Frances. "But you can't possible know what shoes you want until you find the dress."

"I do," responded Dagny. "It won't matter."

"If you say so. Let's go around 10:00," suggested Mary Frances. Matt whispered something in Mary Frances' ear. She smiled and nodded.

As Zander and Dagny started inside, Mary Frances caught her roommate, "Dagny, I'm going back to the cabin with Matt, but he'll bring me back tomorrow around 9:30. By the way, he's insisting on paying for the cake."

Dagny smiled and said, "I think Zander is going to spend the night here with me, so that works out fine." Everyone said goodnight as Matt and Mary Frances returned to the Range Rover.

Mary Frances held Matt's right hand as he drove south through the darkness. "Matt, do you ever think about the future, like seasons or Christmas?"

Matt glanced at her with a puzzled expression. "Before my illness, life seemed to have an infinite number of summers and birthdays and Christmases. Then when I got sick, I started wondering if I'd see another birthday. In time, I got better; I felt like there were an infinite number of birthdays again. But now, watching everything happening in the world and experiencing the Lynn Hanson incident, I find myself having those feelings again. Do you ever think like that?"

"I do. I understand exactly what you mean," Matt said. "When I was in Afghanistan, I thought like that a lot. When you see death and realize you could be next, then you start to think like that. Every time I turn on TV and see what's happening, I start to get that feeling like when I was in the army."

"Why is this happening to us?" asked Mary Frances. "Why now?"

"Why not?" answered Matt. "History is full of calamity. Wars, plagues, economic catastrophes, all sorts of disasters. I keep hoping this will turn around, but, honestly, I don't think it will. Fortunately, we're well-prepared. If the worst happens, we will be so much better off than most."

"We will be," she said, squeezing his hand.

Chapter 27
2 (Wedding)

The double wedding was only a few days away. Mary Frances and Dagny felt much excitement as the big day approached. Weddings are typically stressful with all the planning and logistics, all the food and drink, guests coming from great distances, the music and the flowers all adding to the complexity. But the simplicity of this wedding almost removed any stress, allowing the brides to enjoy the moment.

"You know Matt is always talking about systemic risk," Mary Frances told Dagny, "but our wedding is so simple that I think we may have reduced the risk of having problems." The women laughed.

Zander's parents were coming from Louisville, Kentucky, and his brother and his family from California. Dagny's parents were coming from Sparta, Tennessee, along with her sister and her family. Mary Frances had called her mother about her engagement and upcoming wedding. She'd invited her mother but made it clear that George wasn't invited. In the end, her mother had declined as Mary Frances had expected. Keeping with tradition, Mr. Bennett, Dagny's father, was going to give her away. Mary Frances was planning on asking Mr. Borland to walk her down the aisle.

Mary Frances called Elaine, the CEO's administrative

assistant, Monday morning from the phone in the kitchen.

"Hello, Mr. Borland's office."

"Hello, Elaine. This is Mary Frances Foster, in the cafeteria."

"Yes, Mary Frances. What can I do for you?"

"Would it be possible for me to speak with Mr. Borland? I'm sure he's very busy, but I'd like to speak with him in person."

"I'm sure he'd be glad to talk to you, Mary Frances. When is your lunch?"

"My lunch is 1:00 – 1:45."

"I tell you what, if you could come up here at 1:30 today, I'll get you in."

"Today? Wow, that's fast! Yes, that would be great!"

"Mary Frances, you helped us out when the Federal Reserve people were here. Not to mention who your future husband is."

"Thank you, Elaine. I'll be there at 1:30."

Mary Frances walked back to where she was preparing pasta in the kitchen and thought, *I still can't get used to this. Elaine is acting like I'm someone important. I'm the same person I always have been. Being privileged is such an unusual feeling for me.*

Mary Frances arrived at Elaine's desk at exactly 1:30. Elaine showed her into the CEO's office, and he arrived a few minutes later.

"Mary Frances, so good to see you," Mr. Borland said, shaking her hand between both of his as she stood to greet him. "How are the wedding plans coming?"

"They're coming along quite nicely," she answered. "In fact, that's why I asked to see you today." The CEO smiled and leaned forward, giving her his undivided attention. "Mr. Borland, I'd like to ask if you would walk me down the aisle at the wedding. You see, my father passed away when I was in high school. I'd be honored if you would."

"I'm the one who's honored," said the CEO. "Of course, I'll do it. You and Matt are very important to me. You may not know how much."

"Thank you, Mr. Borland," she said. "I really do appreciate it."

"Mary Frances, may I give you some advice?" he asked.

"Of course," she said, wondering what he was about to

say.

"Mary Frances, things are changing rapidly," he said, watching her eyes for understanding. "None of us can know the future, but we are entering uncharted territory. If things continue as they are, life will become very hard for all of us." Mary Frances nodded. "Only the strong will survive. Only warriors will survive. You, Mary Frances, are marrying a warrior. You saw that side of Matt during the Lynn Hanson incident. Of course, that scared you. Matt is a good man; but, have no doubt, he will destroy anybody or anything he perceives to be a threat. Understand, it means your chances of survival are greatly increased because of who your husband is. Zander Fromm is the same kind of man. Don't get mad at Matt or Zander if either seems moody or angry. Don't get upset if they seem hard. Don't be surprised by nightmares. And finally, in the days ahead, if Matt and Zander tell you to do something, do not question them. Do it immediately. You should explain this to Dagny also."

Mary Frances nodded in agreement and said, "Thank you for those words. Dagny and I will remember them.

"I understand what you're referring to when you speak about the future being uncertain, although not as well as Matt does. I have complete trust in Matt. Because of him, I am certain that we will be OK. But when I think about everyone else, it's so distressing. Will you and Mrs. Borland be alright? Will Mr. and Mrs. Eastman be alright?"

Mr. Borland smiled and nodded. "Yes, Mary Frances, we will be fine. You may not be aware, but there are many people who have prepared for something like this. I know there is a special place Matt has prepared. I haven't been told the location because I don't have a need to know. We, too, have such a place. If it becomes necessary, that's where we will go. Brian and I will go on vacation. We'll take our families, including our wives, children and grandchildren. We just won't come back. You and Matt will go on vacation with Zander and Dagny, too. We may never see each other again, but, hopefully and with enough time, we will. Someday, we will return here and start over. We may or may not start Veritas up again. It will all depend on what the country needs to rebuild. There may not be a need for investment products at first. Perhaps food, basic transportation, and electricity will be more pressing. But we will rebuild. Enough of this, back to the wedding. I would be honored to walk you down the aisle. You just tell me where and when. I'll be there."

Mary Frances hugged the CEO as she left his office. Almost in tears, she thought about the future and her friends at Veritas. She pictured her mother back in Charlotte. There was no way George could take care of her if things got bad. She stopped short, considering what that would mean. Mary Frances had chosen Matt. She shuddered to think about what it would be like if there was no electricity, food or water for the millions of people in cities across the country. As she got in the elevator to return to the cafeteria, Mary Frances prayed that God would spare the world from such a disaster.

Two weeks later, the wedding day arrived with perfect, blue skies that contrasted with the white, puffy clouds and white steeple of the Brentwood Baptist Church. The brides were dressed and adding the final touches. Having chosen matching veils, the brides clipped them into the back of each other's hair. Mrs. Bennett stuck her head in the door and said, "Ten minutes, girls!"

"You do have Matt's ring?" asked Mary Frances as she double checked to make sure she had Zander's ring. Dagny nodded. "I will hold your flowers while you and Zander say your vows. Then, you will hold my flowers while Matt and I say ours." Both nodded in agreement. They continued to review every detail of the ceremony until Mary Frances said, "I'm just not going to worry about it anymore. If we've forgotten anything, we'll just have to make do. I'm just going to focus on Matt."

"Mary Frances, I can't believe all this has happened," said Dagny. "Heck, I'm just a regular girl from Sparta, Tennessee. Do you remember when Zander first asked about me? I didn't believe he could be interested in me. And now, we're getting married! It's amazing how well we get along. We're very much alike. I love him so much."

"I remember, Dagny," said Mary Frances. "I can't believe this either. It's like a fairy tale. Your Zander and my Matt... aren't we lucky! I know God gave me the idea to move to Nashville and take the job at Veritas. And God sent the blizzard so Matt would find me... so I'd find him."

Classical piano music greeted the wedding guests as they arrived and were seated in the church sanctuary. For what was to be a small wedding, there were easily over 150 people in attendance. The ceremony was to be traditional and simple, yet elegant. But the fact that it was a double wedding left the ceremony somewhat less traditional and simple.

As the prelude came to its close, Matt and Zander took their places at the altar. Impeccably dressed in black tuxedos, white shirts and black bow ties, the grooms eagerly awaited the entrances of their brides. A gerbera daisy boutonniere was pinned to the lapel of each man's tuxedo.

"Are you sure you won't trade boutonnieres with me?" Zander whispered to Matt.

"No, Zander. Dagny was very specific. Mine is the white one. Yours is the pink one," Matt responded, trying not to laugh.

Then, the traditional processional began. The doors to the vestibule opened, and Dagny appeared on the arm of her father. She was radiant. Zander's bride wore a long, white, tulle and lace, fit and flare gown with a court length train. It had cap sleeves and an illusion neckline over a sweetheart bodice. In Dagny's hand was a bouquet of pink gerbera daisies. Dagny beamed as her eyes met co-workers from Veritas and friends and family from Sparta. As Mr. Bennett walked his daughter down the aisle to Zander, glimpses of her shoes appeared beneath the scalloped hem of the dress. On her feet, Dagny wore bright, pink Converse All Star sneakers. Zander, full of love for Dagny, watched his bride coming toward him and finally understood why he was wearing a pink daisy on his lapel.

Once Dagny and Mr. Bennett were in place at the altar, the processional began again. Mary Frances stepped into the doorway on the arm of Mr. Borland. Matt's bride was glowing. Mary Frances wore a long, white, sleeveless, A line gown with sweep train. The illusion neckline and bodice were both covered in lace applique. Layers of tulle fell gracefully from the fitted waist. Ballet flats made of white lace occasionally peaked out from under the layers of tulle. She carried a bouquet of white gerbera daisies sprinkled with small coral roses. Mary Frances could hardly hold back the tears as Mr. Borland walked her down the aisle to Matt, passing everyone who had come to celebrate their marriage. *She's beautiful and she's mine,* thought Matt as he watched her.

The pastor began by turning to Dagny and asking, "Who gives this woman to be given in marriage?"

"Her mother and I," said Mr. Bennett.

Then the pastor turned to Mary Frances and Matt, asking the same question.

"We do!" responded Dagny, Zander, Matt, Mr. Bennett and Mr. Borland in unison. Chuckles filled the auditorium.

The ceremony was short and traditional. Mary Frances and Dagny had talked about what kind of wedding vows they wanted and easily agreed on the old, original ones from medieval England. Dagny and Zander went first with Mary Frances holding Dagny's flowers. Matt also acted as Zander's best man; so, when it came time for Dagny's wedding ring, he handed it to Zander. Mary Frances gave Zander's ring to Dagny at the appointed time.

Then, it was Matt's and Mary Frances' turn. Mary Frances was so overcome with emotion that at times it was difficult for her to speak. Composing herself, she repeated her vows while looking lovingly into Matt's eyes. *I, Mary Frances Foster, take thee, Matthew Archer, to be my wedded husband; to have and to hold from this day forward, for better for worse, for richer for poorer, in sickness and in health, to love, cherish, and to obey, till death us do part, according to God's holy ordinance and thereto I give thee my troth.*

Matt's vows were just like Mary Frances' but with two exceptions. His vows did not include *to obey* after the promise of to love and cherish. At the end, he continued as he placed the ring on her finger, *With this Ring, I thee wed, With my body I thee worship and with all my worldly goods I thee endow. In the name of the Father, and of the Son and of the Holy Ghost. Amen.*

The couples said their *I do's*, the pastor pronounced them man and wife and gave permission for the grooms to kiss their brides. The audience burst into applause as the pastor presented the four for the first time as married couples.

Soon, the ceremony was over, and it was on to the reception. The wedding party stood outside the sanctuary and greeted their guests as they moved to the fellowship hall. At the front of the hall were two, beautiful, white wedding cakes of equal height. The Archers' cake was made of four, round layers of vanilla cake, covered in white buttercream icing. White daisies and coral roses spiraled around the layers. The Fromms' cake was four, square layers of carrot cake with white buttercream icing. Pink daisies adorned the layers. Dagny and Zander were the first to cut their wedding cake, both holding a sterling silver knife while Mary Frances, Matt and the guests looked on.

When it was Mary Frances' and Matt's turn, Dagny loudly whispered, "Oh, no! Stop! We used your knife! I knew we'd mix something up! We do have the right wedding rings, don't we? I hope I didn't marry the wrong groom!" The guests all started laughing at Dagny's outburst.

Mary Frances looked at the engraved cake knife she was holding and saw *Dagny and Zander* engraved on the blade. She smiled and looked at Matt and then said to Dagny, "It's OK, Dagny. We'll trade knives and start again. It's easy to wipe off the icing. Here's *your* knife." After the second cake was cut, it was served along with punch while the brides and grooms visited with friends and family.

When Matt and Mary Frances finally had a private moment, Matt whispered in her ear, "How does Mary Frances *Archer* sound to you?"

Mary Frances smiled at her new husband and, leaning over to him, answered, "It sounds perfect."

"Are you still sure about the honeymoon?" he asked.

"Absolutely! There is no place I'd rather go than your cabin," she said quietly. "It's where I first got to know you. It's where we first made love. If I could be there with you for the rest of my life, I'd be happy."

"Yeah, but Zander and Dagny are going to the Smoky Mountains," Matt said.

"Yes, to a cabin in Tennessee," Mary Frances said. "Oh, gosh, and where are we going? To a cabin in Tennessee!"

"But I want you to have a honeymoon," said Matt.

"I'm serious, Matt. There's no place I'd rather go than your cabin," Mary Frances explained. "I tell you what, someday in the future you can take me somewhere. How would that be?" All around them, guests were talking and laughing, eating cake and drinking punch. Matt enjoyed watching it all while wondering if the future would allow for such traditions to continue.

"Mary Frances, if the world keeps going the way it is, I won't be able to take you anywhere for 20 or 30 years," Matt said.

"I know," Mary Frances smiled and nodded. "So, let's make a date for 40 years from today. You're going to take me on a honeymoon trip in 40 years!" she said. Matt laughed and shook his head.

"Matt, I'm really very simple. I don't need presents or fancy clothes. You don't have to take me to expensive restaurants to make me happy. This, right here, today... you've made me the happiest woman in the world. I can't believe that I'm Mrs. Matthew Archer."

Dagny and Zander made their way across the room to Matt and Mary Frances. While the girls talked, Zander motioned Matt over to the side. "You probably haven't seen the news," said Zander.

"No, I've been kind of busy the past hour or so," answered Matt with a chuckle. "What's going on?"

"The reports are still coming in," said Zander, "but it looks like the water systems of several cities have been poisoned. New York, San Francisco, Minneapolis, and Louisville. I'm glad my family is here and not back home in Louisville."

"It doesn't let up, does it?" said Matt. "Has anyone taken responsibility?"

"No, not yet, but we're talking about big casualties on this one, Matt," said Zander. "We'll know in 48 hours, but it could be over 250,000 dead."

"Don't say anything to the girls," said Matt. "Let them enjoy their day. We don't want to spoil it. This news will freak out the population who are already afraid to go to a ballgame. Now, they'll be afraid to drink the water. As soon as you return from your honeymoon, we'll talk. We may be getting very close, Zander. If the Chinese or the Russians launch a cyber-attack that takes down the grid or the banking system, the world may not hold together."

Soon, the reception was winding down, and it was time for the couples to leave. Outside the church, the newlyweds' vehicles had been filled with multicolored balloons. Matt helped Mary Frances into the Range Rover, carefully ensuring all her dress was inside before closing the door. Zander did the same with Dagny; then, the men walked around to the driver's side of each car while waving to their friends. The two vehicles pulled away, down the church drive and onto the street. Zander and Dagny made their way across town to Interstate 40 headed for the Great Smoky Mountains. Matt and Mary Frances had a much shorter drive.

Arriving home, Matt parked in front of the cabin instead of pulling around the side to the garage. Helping her out of the SUV, they walked together to the front door. Unlocking it, Matt opened the door; then, he picked up Mary Frances and carried her across the threshold into the house. Matt pushed the door closed with his foot and carried her through the cabin to their bedroom. "I'd light the fire in the fireplace, but it's 95 degrees out there," Matt said.

"I love you," Mary Frances said. "I am going to love you and cherish you and obey you, just like the vows said. I want you to tell me if I do anything that upsets you so that nothing ever comes between us. I want to make you happy."

"Mary Frances, you have never done anything that makes me angry," said Matt. "I want to make you happy, too. I just worry that our lives may be different than what we have planned. But I promise you, I'll do my best to make you happy and comfortable. Comfortable may sound like a strange word, but you remember the blizzard?" Mary Frances smiled and nodded. "Having a roof over your head, being warm when it's freezing outside, having food to eat and water to drink, not to mention hot water to take a bath. Have you seen those shows on TV where a couple is looking for a house and the wife sees the kitchen and declares it *unacceptable*. I shudder to think how such a woman would react if she didn't have any kitchen or even a house. I don't know what the future holds, but I promise to take care of you to the best of my ability."

"Matt, whatever our life is like, it will be wonderful because it's with you," said Mary Frances.

Matt kissed his wife and hugged her while she savored the feeling of his arms around her. "Matt, the best thing is that I get to stay here every night. I no longer have to sleep alone. I will feel you next to me every night for the rest of my life."

Matt looked at his wife and touched her cheek. "Would you like me to help you out of this dress?" he asked.

"I know what you want to do," said Mary Frances, giggling as Matt unzipped the back of her wedding gown. He kissed her neck as her wedding gown fell to the floor. She lay back on the bed as Matt tore off his tuxedo that ended up in a pile on the floor next to her dress. "I do want a fire when it's cold outside. Every night," she said. Matt growled an unintelligible *uhhuh* as his kisses moved down to her stomach.

I'm the luckiest girl in the world, she thought. *Matthew Archer is my husband. We're in our home. He's making love to me, and all is right with the world.*

Chapter 28
Unintended Consequences

For Matt and Mary Frances, it was an idyllic honeymoon at the cabin. In the Great Smoky Mountains, Zander and Dagny also enjoyed their secluded cabin. The men didn't talk about the problems in the country and the world. They found that if it wasn't brought up, their brides weren't aware of what was happening. Neither mentioned the poisoning of the water systems so as not to rob their wives of any happiness. Mary Frances and Dagny were very content and secure in the world of their husbands and new lives together.

Matt and Zander stayed in contact via text messages. Discretely monitoring the unfolding events on his cell phone, Matt learned there were threats of war coming out of North Korea and Tehran. At the first opportunity, he had called a friend who lived on the Tennessee River in Kentucky to ask if there had been any unusual traffic on the river. As feared, the friend told him that 50 barges loaded with military vehicles and armor had passed his house, heading south the day before. The 101st Airborne Division at Fort Campbell, Kentucky was moving equipment south to Mobile Bay to be loaded on ships. The army was preparing for something.

Across the country, people were starting to feel the strain. Not realizing the cause at first, emergency rooms across the country started dealing with an influx of panic attacks. People believed they were having heart attacks only to find their symptoms were due to worry and stress from recent events. When the hospitals reported this to the CDC in Atlanta, the experts made the connection and reported it to Washington where the government did nothing because there was nothing they could do.

Next came a spike in suicides that brought on another wave of suicides, and then another- each greater than the one before. Funeral homes across the country were having trouble handling all the funerals. Many had to be delayed due to a lack of caskets. All of this brought on another unanticipated problem. A combination of deaths from baseball game shootings, water system poisoning, suicides and related health issues had created thousands of orphans. Family services departments of all the states were overwhelmed with homeless children. With the water poisoning in Louisville and the baseball shooting in Cincinnati, the Kentucky Department of Health and Family Services was particularly inundated with orphans.

The day Zander and Dagny returned to work from their honeymoon, Zander received a call at his office.

"Hello, Zander."

"Mom, is that you? Is everything alright?"

"We're fine, Zander. Did you have a nice trip?"

"Yes, we did, Mom. We're back in Nashville and back at work. What's up?"

"Zander, this is a lot to ask, especially since you've just gotten back from your honeymoon, but do you think you could take off Friday and come here to Louisville?"

"Well, I probably could. Matt is my boss, and I'm sure he'd say OK. What's going on?"

"This world is just going crazy, Zander. I don't know how bad it has to get before it gets better. Do you remember your second cousin, Kurt? And his wife, Karen?"

"Yes, barely. I haven't seen him in years. We never really knew each other even though we lived in the same city."

"Well, Kurt and Karen have a little boy, Sam. He's 10

years old, going into fifth grade."

"Yes."

"Kurt and Karen drank the water when the water department was sabotaged. They were buried last week. Sam didn't drink any of the contaminated water, so he's OK. But he's an orphan now."

"Good God! What was the death toll in Louisville? Thank God y'all didn't drink any tap water that day."

"Yes, we were lucky. The death toll is 29,000 and rising. They're still finding people dead in their homes."

"So, where's the boy?"

"Kentucky Health and Family Services have him. Sam and over a thousand other orphans. They say there hasn't been anything like this since the Spanish influenza epidemic in 1918."

"Didn't Karen have a sister? Will the boy go with his aunt?"

"Yes, she had a sister. But she and her husband were killed at the baseball game in Cincinnati. We are the boys only relatives. This is a lot to ask. It's also very sudden. I don't know how Dagny would feel, but would you consider taking him?"

"But Mom, we just got married!"

"Yes, Zander, I get it. Your dad and I would take him, but I think we're too old. Your brother has his hands full with his family. I'm asking because this orphan problem is happening across the country. There are thousands and thousands of them. To make it even worse, it seems that adoptions have suddenly stopped. Everyone is so afraid of the future that they're not willing to adopt a child. We understand there are plans to take an abandoned military base and turn it into a huge orphanage. It almost sounds like a concentration camp for children."

"I don't know, Mom."

"Could you, please, come home on Friday, and we could go visit him?"

At five o'clock, Dagny and Mary Frances walked out of the Veritas building. No longer carpooling, the women looked for their husbands' vehicles. This was the first time they hadn't car pooled. "Mary Frances, is this not amazing!" exclaimed Dagny.

"We ride to work with our husbands now and ride home with them!"

"Yes," said Mary Frances. "Do you think this will start to feel normal after a while? I still can't believe it!"

"But, I'm going to miss riding with you, roommate," said Dagny.

"Me, too," said Mary Frances. "We haven't even had time to talk about your honeymoon."

"And I want to hear about yours, too!" said Dagny. "Since you already live in a cabin in the woods, you're on a perpetual honeymoon!" Mary Frances smiled at her friend and thought, *I'm going to miss Dagny.* Soon, Mary Frances spotted Matt and met him at the Range Rover. As they drove off, she saw Dagny greeting Zander with a hug in the parking lot.

"This is so cool, riding home from work with you," Dagny said to Zander. "How was your day? Did you research and analyze anything interesting today?"

"My day was OK," said Zander. "Was everything good in the cafeteria?"

"Busy. I hardly got to talk to Mary Frances," said Dagny. "I'm looking forward to some girlfriend time with her."

"My mother called today," Zander said, seriously.

"Is everything alright?" asked Dagny.

"Well, not really," Zander said. "I'm glad you're sitting down. You're not going to believe this." Dagny looked at Zander, sensing how solemn he was. "I have... *had* a second cousin named Kurt. He and his wife Karen drank the water in Louisville last week. They died." Dagny's eyes widened, but she remained silent and waited for her husband to continue. "They had a son, Sam. He's 10 years old, fifth grade. He didn't get the bad water. But now he's an orphan. There's no family, except me... us. He's in some kind of holding facility in Louisville with hundreds of other orphans. My mother wants me to go to Louisville and meet him. She's hoping we'll adopt him." There was silence as Zander let Dagny consider the situation.

"Zander, I think you should go," Dagny said.

"Really?" said Zander.

"Yes, and I leave it up to you. If you decide we should

adopt him, then we will," Dagny said.

"Are you serious, Dagny?" asked Zander.

"Yes. I promised to love, cherish and obey you," Dagny said. "This is a very serious position you're in. You don't need me giving you grief. If you decide that we should adopt the boy, I promise to do my best to be a good mother to him."

"Dagny, I'm stunned," said Zander. "I didn't know how you'd react. I have no idea what I'll find when I get there, but I'm going to Louisville on Friday. You're amazing."

"I'm not really," said Dagny, "God has blessed me so much. And maybe He needs us to help this poor boy. So, I leave it up to you. You have my total support, no matter what you decide."

Zander explained the situation the next day to Matt and asked for Friday off. "Unintended consequences," said Matt. "There are always unintended consequences. I never thought about orphans. Of course, there will be orphans- lots of them."

"But Matt, does this affect Arcadia? If I decide to adopt him and if we have to go, can we bring him? Is there room? Is there enough food?"

"Yes. It will make it harder getting there," Matt said, "because it's a 25-mile hike. It's not easy. He's a fifth grader. Some fifth graders are small and weak, while others may be 100 pounds and strong. Either way, we'll make it. There are enough resources. I've overdone everything, mostly because I have no idea how long we'll need to survive on our own. But after a few years, we should be able to produce all our own food. Yes, we can handle another mouth to feed. Hopefully, he's strong and healthy.

"Thanks, Matt," said Zander. "I'll keep you up to speed on everything."

"I assume you've talked to Dagny about this?" asked Matt.

"Yes, and she's leaving it all up to me. She will support my decision," Zander said.

"That's commendable. I'm impressed, Zander. You just might have yourself a fine wife there," Matt said with a grin. "I'm not going to mention this to Mary Frances yet. She gets kind of emotional when it comes to the subject of children. I'll tell her if you decide to bring him home with you."

Friday morning, Zander was up early and on the road to Louisville. He made it to his parents' house by 11:00 a.m. As he sat down in the living room, his mother said, "Zander, we want to prepare you for what you're about to see." Zander was puzzled. "The state is housing all these orphans in an old National Guard Armory," she explained.

"It would take 10 armories to house them in decent conditions," Zander's father continued. "The children are packed in like sardines. The kitchen isn't adequate to feed them, and the bathrooms..." Zander's father paused, and his mother interjected.

"The bathrooms are horrible. The smell is awful," she said. "The state is in charge of this, but the situation is deplorable."

"How many kids are in this armory?" Zander asked.

"Hard to say, Son," answered his father, "but I'd guess at least 600. They're everywhere. The lucky ones are on cots. Most of them are sleeping on the concrete. The problem is they keep getting more children."

"The social worker told us that no one wants to adopt them because everyone is so shook up over what's going on," said Mrs. Fromm. "Adopting a child is a big deal, a huge responsibility. The future is so unsure that no one wants another child to take care of."

"Well, let's go," said Zander. "I want to see this for myself."

Even with his parents' warning, Zander wasn't prepared for what he witnessed. Zander Fromm had been in the army in Afghanistan, so he was familiar with seeing bad things. The situation in the Louisville armory was worse than bad; it was appalling. The Fromms parked in the lot outside the building and entered through the front doors. A social worker met them, expecting their visit as Zander's mother had called for an appointment. The four of them passed through the heavy, steel doors of the gymnasium and into a scene from a concentration camp movie. Hopeful eyes turned toward the massive, steel doors. Every square inch of floor was covered with cots or blankets. There was barely enough room in the aisles to sidestep. Many children had not bathed in over a week. The sound of crying children echoed throughout the gymnasium. A second later, Zander and his parents were hit with the nauseating smell of sewer from the bathrooms.

"I apologize for the stench," said the social worker. "We're trying to get it fixed, but we're having trouble. Actually, the problem is the facilities weren't designed for this number of people. The plumbing can't handle it. Regardless of the reason, it's terrible. There's another major problem. People aren't coming to work. Whether it's getting a plumber in to deal with this or our own employees, we're experiencing lots of people just not showing up for work." Zander listened closely, remembering Matt's prediction.

"We've divided the boys from the girls with the centerline on the basketball court; girls on the left and boys on the right. If you look along the line, you'll see a boy in a blue shirt, sitting on his cot. That's Sam," the social worker explained. Through the sea of children, Zander picked out his cousin, a ten-year-old boy with unruly, blond hair. Zander imagined it had been a long time since he'd had a bath or put a comb to his hair.

"There is another problem we didn't discuss when we spoke on the phone, Mrs. Fromm," said the social worker. The Fromms turned to her anticipating what the problem might be. "Do you see the little girl Sam is talking to?" she asked. Zander moved to the left to get a better view. Sam was sitting on his cot talking to a little girl directly across from him. The cots were so close that Sam's knees touched her cot, the centerline hardly visible.

"Her name is Hannah," explained the social worker. "She has no siblings. No other family. Her mother drank the water. She hasn't spoken since her arrival. We can't talk her out of wearing that dirty, hot sweater. For some reason, Hannah has attached herself to Sam. She follows him everywhere. She gets anxious when he has to leave her even for a minute to go to the bathroom. You can see he's talking to her, and she's listening. She seems to like that. She finds comfort in his presence."

"She's from Louisville, too?" asked Zander. "How old is she?"

"Yes, she's from Louisville," the social worker answered.

"She's eight; she will be a third grader."

"What are you getting at?" Zander's father asked the social worker.

"I'm saying that we don't know what will happen to her if we separate them. She's very attached. Since you're considering taking Sam, is there any possibility you could take Hannah, too?"

Zander surveyed the mass of children packed in the gym. His heart told him to help them all, but he couldn't. Instantly, an idea came into his head. "How much does Hannah weigh?" he asked.

The social worker gave Zander a strange glance then looked in the manila folder she was carrying under her arm. "53 pounds. Her file indicates 53 pounds. She's a skinny little thing. She may weigh even less now. None of the children are eating like they should. It's probably the smell. Let me bring the children over so you can meet them."

Zander and his parents watched as the social worker maneuvered through the rows of cots to retrieve Sam and Hannah. "Why did you ask how much she weighs, Zander?" asked Mrs. Fromm.

"It occurred to me that Matt and Mary Frances might be willing to take Hannah. Matt will ask me that very question," Zander said. To Zander's parents, the explanation didn't answer the question. But they didn't press him.

Soon. the social worker returned followed by Sam, who in turn was followed by Hannah. Sam appeared to be strong and determined. At 100 pounds, he wasn't tiny like the little girl who stood by his side. Blue eyes and unruly blond hair with a dirty and very wrinkled shirt and jeans summed up his appearance.

Hannah was a full head shorter than Sam. Her dark, brown hair hadn't been touched by a brush or shampoo in two weeks. She had brown eyes and a light complexion that included a streak of dirt on her left cheek. She was dressed in jeans and what used to be a white t-shirt. A dirty, purple sweater three sizes too big completed her ensemble.

"Sam, these folks are your family. This is Mr. and Mrs. Fromm and their son, Zander," the social worker explained.

"Hello," said Sam.

"Hello, Sam," said Zander's mother. "We are so sorry about your parents. Your mother, Karen, was my cousin." Sam nodded, expressionless. "

"And this is Hannah," said the social worker. "Hannah is very quiet."

"She doesn't talk," said Sam. "I take care of her." Hannah stood by his side, motionless and without expression.

"How do you take care of her, sweetheart?" asked Zander's mother, moving closer and brushing some hair out of Sam's eyes. He tolerated the attention.

"I take care of her when we go through the food line. The bigger kids were stealing her food. She stays with me, and they leave her alone," Sam said with a tone of determination in his voice. Mrs. Fromm moved over to Hannah and, dropping to her knees, hugged the little girl. It was all Zander's mother could do to not break into tears.

"Excuse me a minute," said Zander. "I need to make a phone call." With that Zander walked out of the gym and outside to the front steps and fresh air. Pausing a moment to gather his thoughts, he called Matt.

"Hey, Zander."

"Hello, Matt."

"How's it going in Louisville?"

"It's terrible, Matt. You wouldn't believe it. I'm at an old National Guard Armory that's been turned into a holding facility for orphans. There are hundreds of kids here. The children are dirty. The sewer is backed up. The stench is horrible."

"Oh, my God! Why aren't they taking better care of them?"

"It's the government, Matt. Why would we expect anything different? Remember the arena in New Orleans during Katrina? It's like that."

"Have you found your cousin?"

"Yes, I just met him. He's tougher than I expected. He can hold his own with the other kids. Matt, they're fighting over food. There's a little girl he protects. He doesn't let the bigger kids take her food."

"Good Lord, Zander. This is hard to believe. This is going on, and we've heard nothing about it."

"It's not surprising. The Department of Health and Family Services has never had a problem like this before. There probably isn't funding for it. The Governor should declare a state of emergency. I'm taking my cousin. I can't leave him here in this hell hole. This place is like survival of the fittest. But Matt, I have a question. I'm afraid the little girl will die without Sam. When I saw her, I thought of you and Mary Frances. Would you want to take her?"

"How much does she weigh?"

"I know you're wondering if you can carry her 25 miles. According to the records, she weighs 53 pounds. She even resembles Mary Frances. Dark brown hair, brown eyes and light complexion."

"How would we do it? Would Mary Frances and I need to come to Louisville?"

"I'm not sure. I'll ask, but I get the impression that the normal rules and regulations governing adoption are set aside due to the sheer volume of orphans."

"OK, we'll take her. Just let me know what we need to do."

"Aren't you going to ask Mary Frances?"

"There's no need. I know what she'd say. Don't tell Dagny about the little girl. Let's keep this between us for the time being. Zander, this thing is going to happen. The Endex is over 200. It may not be safe at your apartment. I'd like you to move in with us. That way the kids can be together. It sounds like Hannah would like that. And we're going to Arcadia soon. It's only a question of when."

"OK, I'm going back inside. I'll call you soon."

Zander had been correct about the expedited adoption procedure. When he'd explained the situation to the social worker, she was very cooperative in making it all happen quickly. "The Governor declared this an emergency yesterday. We're hoping to get some better housing for the kids. Social workers have been given the power of a family court judge, regarding adoption. Now, tell me about your boss. He's married? Does he have a house or apartment? What level of education do the prospective parents have? Can you estimate their income? Net worth? Is their house big enough so that Hannah would have her own room?"

"Some of these will be an approximation, ma'am. Yes, Matthew and Mary Frances Archer are married. Both are employed at Veritas Strategies in Brentwood, Tennessee. Both have masters' degrees. They own two houses. The primary residence is four bedrooms/four bathrooms, so yes, there's plenty of room for Hannah. Income? I'll say Mary Frances is around $39,000, and Matt with salary, bonus, and stock would come in around $600,000. Net worth? I'm not sure, but Matt is 5% shareholder of Veritas Strategies. That's worth somewhere around $200,000,000, making his part $10,000,000. I assure you, the Archers are well equipped to care for Hannah. But that's just the information for your forms. Just as important is that I am certain Hannah will be loved."

"You're serious about those numbers?" asked the astonished social worker. Zander nodded. "OK, I'd really like to get the kids out of here today. I don't want them to have to stay another night. Since the Archers are in Nashville, can you take Hannah to them?" Again, Zander nodded. "Can you get one of the prospective parents on the phone for me, so I can get some more information? I'll send the paperwork with you for their signatures. They can mail it back. Your wife isn't with you; is that correct?"

"She's at work in Nashville," Zander explained. "She works with Mrs. Archer at Veritas. You see, we all work at the same place."

"I need Dagny Fromm's signature on the application to adopt. Do you think if I excused myself for a few minutes to go to the restroom, that Dagny might *stop by* and sign the form?" the social worker asked with a wink.

"Oh, I bet she could," Zander smiled. "Shall I call Matt Archer for you, now?"

The process moved along quickly, as the social worker completed her paperwork and made the appropriate registrations with the state. Once it was official, the social worker brought Sam and Hannah into her office where Zander was already waiting, along with his parents. There were two, empty chairs for Sam and Hannah.

"Sam, we are so sorry for your loss," the social worker

began. "This is a terrible tragedy for you to endure. However, I am pleased to tell you that your cousin, Zander Fromm, and his wife, Dagny, have agreed to adopt you. They want you to be part of their family, and you will be leaving today," she said, with a smile.

"What about Hannah?" Sam demanded. "I'm not leaving her. Who will protect her? The big kids will take her food, and she'll starve." Hannah sat motionless and expressionless, as always.

"Well, here's the next good news," the social worker continued. "Hannah, the Archer family has agreed to adopt you. The Archers are friends of the Fromms, and I understand they live close to each other. Hannah, you will be going with Mr. Fromm and Sam today to your new home in Tennessee. Neither one of you will have to spend another night here. Zander, I'm entrusting you with Hannah to deliver to her parents. Also, if you will agree to give this paperwork to the Archers to be signed, notarized and returned to me, then you are free to go."

"We'll be staying with my parents here in Louisville tonight, and then we'll head back to Nashville tomorrow morning. Thank you for everything," Zander said. The adults stood and shook hands before walking to the door. Only Sam saw Hannah's big, brown eyes watching them, and he could sense her anxiety of yet another monumental change in her life.

When they arrived at the home of Zander's parents, Mrs. Fromm took charge. "Zander, you take Sam and get him scrubbed good and clean. I'll put his clothes in the washer with Hannah's. Hannah, sweetie, you come with me to the bathroom. We'll get you a good bubble bath."

"It's OK, Hannah," said Sam. "Mrs. Fromm is going to get you cleaned up. You go with her," Sam reassured her. Then, turning to Zander, he said, "I can take my own bath."

Mrs. Fromm took Hannah to the master bathroom and closed the door. She started running the bath water, checking to make sure it wasn't too hot. The whole time Mrs. Fromm was talking to her. "Hannah, sweetie, you're going to feel better after you're all cleaned up. You have such pretty hair. We're going to shampoo it and maybe put a bow in it. You know, sweetie, what would you think if we went shopping and bought you a few things. How about a new outfit so you look nice when you meet the Archers? You're probably getting hungry. I was planning to fix meat loaf and mashed potatoes for dinner, but I could make something else if you like something else better." Hannah didn't answer but sat in the warm bubble bath and let Mrs. Fromm bathe her.

After the baths, Mrs. Fromm insisted on a shopping trip to the mall because the only clothes they had was what they were wearing. Mrs. Fromm wanted the children to have some everyday clothes as well as a nice outfit for the next day when they would meet their parents.

That evening at dinner, both the children did a good job of cleaning their plates of meat loaf, mashed potatoes and green beans. When Mrs. Fromm offered them cherry cobbler with a scoop of vanilla ice cream, Zander thought he caught just a hint of a smile from Hannah.

With full stomachs and new pajamas, Zander took the children to the bedroom that had two twin beds. "Sam, Hannah, you're going to be sleeping here tonight. I'm the next bedroom down the hall, and your grandparents, Sam, are at the end of the hall. Kneeling between the beds and holding both their hands, he said, "Tomorrow, we'll drive to Nashville, Tennessee. Sam, you'll meet Dagny. She's so excited to be your new mother. And Hannah, you'll meet your new mom and dad. You're going to love them."

"How far away will Hannah and her new parents be from us?" asked Sam. "I have to look after her."

"Well, you'll like this, Sam," Zander explained. "We're all going to live together in a big, log cabin. It has a special bedroom called the bunk room. That's where both you and Hannah will sleep. I'm pretty sure you're going to like it." Sam nodded in acceptance.

"Sam, I'm going to do my best to be a good father to you, and Dagny will be a wonderful mother. Hannah, your parents are wonderful people, and I'm sure you will love them." Before turning off the light, Zander said a prayer, tucked them in and kissed them goodnight. "I'll leave the hall light on," he said. "Call me if you need anything." When he checked on them a few minutes later, both were sound asleep.

Zander found his parents in the family room, reading. "I want to thank you for everything you've done," he told his parents.

"Zander, thank you for what you and Dagny are doing for Sam. We couldn't be more proud of you and your new wife," Mr. Fromm said.

"You're changing those two kids' lives," said Mrs. Fromm, nodding in agreement.

"Your brother is having a problem, too," said Mr. Fromm. "Your mother and I are needed in California, so we're leaving in a few days. We're going to stay with your brother because the day care has closed, and there's no one to care for the children. They're having trouble out there getting people to come to work."

"Mom, Dad, do you think that's a good idea? Wouldn't it be better for them to come here?" Zander said.

"Oh, no. We're retired. We can go there. Your brother and sister-in-law have their jobs. I'm sure they'll find a new day care soon; then, we'll come back. We'll want to get down to Nashville to see you and Dagny, and Sam!"

As Zander lay in bed that night, he couldn't help but wonder about his parents and the possibility of them being stuck in California when it all collapsed. *Matt is sure it's going to,* he thought considering the severity of the situation. *This may be the last time I see my parents...ever.*

Chapter 29

Family

While Zander was busy in Louisville, Dagny and Mary Frances spent Friday night moving from Zander's apartment to the cabin while Matt made ready the spare bedrooms. Dagny had decided it best to do the move quickly before Sam arrived the next day. "Mary Frances, do you remember when I used to ask if I could still be your roommate if you and Matt got married?" Dagny asked with a big smile.

"Yes, I remember!" laughed Mary Frances.

"Well, it looks like I was right. Matt wants us all together for safety, and Zander agrees; so, we're still roommates," Dagny said and hugged her friend.

"I'm glad you're here, Dagny," said Mary Frances. "You're like a sister to me."

"Mary Frances, I'm nervous," Dagny confided. "I just got married, and now I'm going to be a mother. And I didn't get nine months to prepare! Plus, he's 10 years old!"

"Dagny, you'll be fine!" said Mary Frances. "What you and Zander are doing is amazing. You will be wonderful parents."

"If you think I'm doing something wrong, you must tell me," said Dagny. "Maybe Sam can call you Aunt Mary, and Matt can be Uncle Matt. What do you think?"

"Wow! I'm going to be an aunt!" said Mary Frances. "I'd like that very much, and I'm sure Matt will, too."

"This is all happening so fast, Mary Frances," said Dagny. "Zander says we are definitely going to Arcadia, it's just a question of when. That Endex thing is over 200."

"Yes. It's scary," said Mary Frances. "Matt says that if he's wrong, we'll just come back. It will be like we were on a vacation. Now that there're five of us, it will be harder. But I trust Matt; we'll be fine."

That night as Matt and Mary Frances lay in bed, Matt with his arm around his wife and Mary Frances with her head on his chest, Mary Frances said, "It's wonderful what Zander and Dagny are doing. And it's wonderful being your wife," she said, kissing his chest and giving him a hug. "When it seems like things can't get any better, I find out I'm going to be an aunt! But these wonderful things are happening while the world just keeps getting worse," she added with concern. Are you sure we're going to Arcadia soon?"

"Yes, even if we go and decide to come back in a month," Matt said. "I hope some miracle happens and everything improves. That would be fine with me, but I don't think so. I'm expecting we'll be away for a long time, maybe years. If it gets as bad as I fear, the best way to survive is to be alone, removed from civilization."

"Will Sam make it more difficult?" asked Mary Frances.

"Yes, but Zander says he's tough," said Matt. "Sam may turn out to be a positive."

"It's very kind of you to let him come with us," said Mary Frances.

"Dang!" said Matt. "I just realized something. Children grow. I've got clothes for you and me, Zander and Dagny. There's clothes for all of us for years, but we're not going to grow; children do. There's not time to get another load to Arcadia, besides, how do you predict how big a child is going to become?"

"Did you think of sewing supplies? We could make clothes," said Mary Frances. "Or maybe we could take in the clothes for you and Zander."

"Yes, there are sewing supplies and a sewing machine.

We'll figure it out," said Matt. "But let's not worry about that tonight. Let's get to sleep. Tomorrow is a big day, a day that I'm sure will be full of surprises." Mary Frances kissed her husband. Safe in his arms, she drifted off to sleep... completely unaware of what would happen the next day.

Bright and early Saturday morning, Zander, Sam and Hannah were on the road. "Sam, there's something we need to talk about," he began. "It's kind of awkward, but we need to discuss it. I'm your new dad, but you may not want to call me 'Dad' yet. I understand. Since I'm also your cousin, you could call me 'Cousin' or 'Cousin Zander'. And if calling Dagny 'Mom' doesn't feel right to you, just call her 'Dagny' or 'Cousin Dagny'. Just do as you feel comfortable." Sam listened quietly. "Hannah, it will be the same for you. You could call Matt and Mary Frances, 'Dad' and 'Mom' or not. It may be uncomfortable for you at first. They'll talk to you about this."

About five minutes away from Matt's cabin, Zander called. He asked Dagny to leave the front door unlocked. He also requested that she, Matt and Mary Frances wait by the fireplace. Dagny relayed the message.

"I'm so nervous," said Dagny. "What if he doesn't like me?"

"It may take him awhile to warm up to you," said Matt. "He's been through a lot, first losing his parents and then enduring the orphans' center. Extremely traumatic. Don't feel like you've done something wrong if he doesn't respond to you immediately. Give him time." Dagny nodded as Mary Frances hugged her friend.

When the front door opened, Zander slipped in alone. Closing the door, he walked to the three anxiously waiting by the fireplace. Handing Matt a manila envelope, he said, "This is for you and Mary Frances." Then addressing all of them, he said, "Everything is fine. Sam is waiting in the car. There was one problem. I'm sure Matt has explained how bad the conditions were at the orphanage interment center. It was heartbreaking. It seems that Sam has been protecting a little girl to keep the older children from stealing her food. Older kids were apparently taking blankets from the younger ones, too. She became very attached to him and wouldn't leave his side." With that, Zander walked to the front door and returned to the car. Mary Frances looked at Dagny and Matt in bewilderment.

"What did he mean about the little girl?" Mary Frances asked. "That's terrible! Who will take care of the little girl now?"

Dagny shrugged her shoulders, and Matt said, "We'll find out very soon, I'm sure."

"What's the envelope for, Matt?" Mary Frances asked. Matt smiled at his wife and put his arm around her just as the front door opened. Zander stepped through the door with Sam. Still very much a boy, it was obvious that he was growing up to be a strong man with broad shoulders. He was dressed in an outfit his grandmother had bought him the previous day, khaki pants and a blue, polo shirt. A handsome boy, his blue eyes showed a determination and maturity that had been amplified by his recent hardships.

"He's so handsome," whispered Dagny as she got her first look at her new son.

Then, out from behind Sam, peeked Hannah. All that could be seen were her brown eyes. With Sam's encouragement, she timidly emerged. A perfect, little girl in a sleeveless, white dress trimmed in blue piping stood beside him. A matching blue ribbon adorned the dark, brown pony tail hanging over her left shoulder. As Zander stood with the children, his 200 pounds dwarfed Sam, and Sam's 100 pounds dwarfed Hannah.

Mary Frances gasped when she saw the little girl. She turned to Matt only to notice there was no surprise on his face. Her mind was going at full speed, trying to comprehend the situation.

Zander and the children approached the others waiting at the fireplace. "Dagny, this is Sam," said Zander. "Sam, this is my wife, Dagny." Dagny stepped forward and slowly, cautiously touched his arm.

"Sam, I'm so happy to meet you," Dagny said. "Can I give you a hug?"

"OK, I guess," Sam said, wanting to set the example for Hannah.

Mary Frances was touched, watching her friend hold the

boy. Then, she noticed the little girl's eyes were fixed on her.

"Hannah, this is Matt and Mary Frances Archer. They're going to be your new parents," said Zander. "Matt, Mary Frances, I'd like to introduce you to Hannah."

Matt watched Mary Frances as she held both hands to her lips. Her hands were visibly trembling, and her eyes were filling with tears. Matt knelt down on one knee and said, "Hello, Hannah. It's very nice to meet you." Mary Frances dropped to both knees and slowly reached out to touch Hannah's cheek. Then she took her in her arms and held her, not wanting to let her go.

"Hannah hasn't been talking recently," explained Zander. "But she can talk very well; she just hasn't felt like saying anything. Sam can communicate with her, even without words."

Mary Frances finally released Hannah from the hug but still held on to her hands. Mary Frances looked at Matt with a look that asked, *Did you know*? She knew instantly that he did.

"And I almost forgot," continued Zander. "Sam, this is Matt and Mary Frances. And, Hannah, this is my wife, Dagny."

"Hannah, you can call me Aunt Dagny, if you like," said Dagny.

"And, Sam, you can call me Aunt Mary," Mary Frances chimed in.

"Let's all sit down," said Zander. Dagny, Sam, Hannah and Mary Frances sat together on the big, leather sofa facing the fireplace. Hannah sat with Mary Frances on one side and Sam on the other. Hannah's eyes were glued to Sam.

"Hannah needs to go to the bathroom. She's got to pee," said Sam.

"Of course, that's a long drive from Louisville," said Mary Frances. "Hannah, come with me, and I'll show you to the bathroom." Hannah stood up slowly, and Sam nodded his head. With his reassurance, she followed Mary Frances who led her to the bathroom. Hannah paused by the toilet and waited. "Oh, I'm sorry," Mary Frances said, backing out of the bathroom. "I'll just wait outside," she said, closing the door. Soon the door opened, and Hannah returned to the great room with Mary Frances.

"Who's ready for lunch?" asked Mary Frances.

Then, Dagny spoke directly to Sam and Hannah. "Are you kids hungry?" she asked them. "What do you like to eat, Sam?" Matt and Zander enjoyed watching their wives' first foray into motherhood.

"I like mac and cheese," said Sam. "Hannah likes mac and cheese, too." Turning to Hannah, he said, "No one here is going to try to take your food. And maybe we can even get seconds."

"Sam, your Aunt Mary is one of the best chefs in Tennessee," said Dagny. Mary Frances gave a smile that implied her friend may have been stretching the truth a bit. "And you can have seconds. You can have all you want."

"Thank you," Sam said, still being very formal. "We need to make sure Hannah eats enough because she's kind of skinny."

"We'll make sure Hannah gets plenty to eat, Sam," said Zander as Matt watched the conversation and smiled.

"Hannah, will you come to the kitchen and help me? We'll make lunch for everyone," said Mary Frances. Hannah took Mary Frances' hand and followed her to the kitchen. From the great room, the others could hear her explaining the preparation of macaroni and cheese to Hannah.

"Sam, while Hannah is busy in the kitchen, let me show you the bedroom where you and Hannah will be sleeping," said Dagny.

"Do we get one blanket? Or can we get two?" Sam asked.

"Sam, you and Hannah can have as many blankets as you want," Dagny answered.

"Unbelievable," Zander whispered to Matt. "He is so protective of her, and all he seems to think about is food and blankets."

"It goes to show you, Zander, how much we take for granted," Matt responded quietly so he wouldn't be overheard. "Things as basic as food and a blanket become very important if you don't have them. Those poor kids. But imagine millions of people wanting food and a blanket."

The rest of the day went smoothly with the children warming up little by little to their new parents and new surroundings. Hannah continued to stick to Sam like glue, but gradually the look on her face showed that she was realizing that no one there was going to try to hurt her. Still, however, she didn't say a word.

When it was time for bed that evening, the children put on the new pajamas Mrs. Fromm had bought. The four new parents took the children to the bunkroom to tuck them in. "You have two blankets, Hannah," said Mary Frances. "Do you think you'll be warm enough?" Hannah nodded. Everyone smiled, seeing the first glimmer of communication from the little girl.

"Let's say a prayer before lights out," said Matt. "Tomorrow's another big day. We're going to church." Matt said the prayer, then the four adults kissed both children.

"I hope you like the bunkroom, Hannah," said Mary Frances. "We picked this bedroom so you could be close to Sam. You both know where our bedrooms are, if you need us. We're close by." Then the adults all kissed the children again, told them they loved them and turned off the light as they tiptoed out.

In their bedroom, Dagny said, "Oh, Zander, he's beautiful. Did I do OK? I don't know how to be a mother. And little Hannah is precious. I was so surprised. And Mary Frances looked like she was going to faint. She is so happy!"

"He's a fine boy, Dagny," said Zander. "You did just fine. You're going to be a great mother, and so is Mary Frances. I have no doubts."

In the Archers' bedroom, Mary Frances hugged Matt and said, "I can't believe it, Matt! I was never supposed to be a mother. I was never even supposed to get married. Now, I'm both. I have a family... my perfect, little family. Matt Archer, you are an amazing man. You knew all along what was happening. I'm sure you did."

"Mary Frances, I believe that God led Hannah to Sam in that armory," Matt said. "In the midst of the chaos and heartbreak, I'm certain He led her to Sam. Sam was taking care of her, but it was more than that. When the social worker expressed to Zander that she was afraid for Hannah if the two were separated, Zander thought of us. Zander called me, and I knew immediately. Hannah needed us, and we needed Hannah."

“Matt, God sent you to me in the snowstorm, and now He’s sent us Hannah,” Mary Frances said. “And we’re an aunt and uncle to Sam, too. He’s created a family. We are a real family.

“Hannah is so perfect,” Mary Frances continued. “Did you notice she kind of looks like me? Matt, I want to know if I’m doing something wrong. I want to be a good mother.”

“You will be a wonderful mother, Mary Frances,” Matt said. “But let’s get to bed and get some sleep. It’s been a long day.” Mary Frances changed into her pajamas. Matt was already in bed waiting for her.

As she was about to pull back the covers, Mary Frances said, “I’ll just go check on her; I’ll be right back.” Matt smiled as he watched his wife sprint out of the bedroom to check on their daughter. As Mary Frances crossed the great room on the way to the children’s bedroom, she saw Dagny slipping out of her room and heading the same direction. When the two new mothers saw each other, they almost laughed aloud, but didn’t, not wanting to wake the sleeping children. They tiptoed into the bunkroom. Both children were still tucked in and sleeping peacefully. Each kissed her child’s forehead and then tiptoed out into the great room. Overwhelmed with joy, Mary Frances and Dagny hugged each other and returned to their beds and their husbands.

Chapter 30
Sunday

There are moments in every child's life that a parent always remembers like first birthday, first day of school, learning to ride a bike and graduations. And then there are the seemingly insignificant events that are treasured in their hearts as well.

Matt was just on the verge of waking up. He could hear the singing birds outside, signaling the sun had begun to rise. He could feel Mary Frances' warmth next to him in the bed. Still half-dreaming, he had the feeling of being watched. He opened his eyes to find Hannah staring at him. He smiled, instantly remembering the happenings of the day before and reached out his hand to her. She turned and bolted out of the bedroom, running back to her bed. It was an image forever burned into his memory.

"What was that?" asked Mary Frances, herself still half-asleep.

"Hannah," he yawned. "When I opened my eyes, she was looking at me."

"Maybe something's wrong," said Mary Frances, sitting up. "I'd better go check on her."

"Lie down, Mary Frances, and rest a little more. I'll go check on her," Matt said. "You were up a half a dozen times last night looking in on her. And I'm pretty sure she was just fine each time."

"She sleeps so soundly; it's hard to know if she's breathing," said Mary Frances. "It scared me the first time because I couldn't tell."

"You're not going to be one of those over-protective mothers, are you?" asked Matt, getting out of bed. He walked through the cabin to the children's room. Both were in their beds. Sam was still sound asleep. Hannah's big, brown eyes were peeping over the tops of the covers she had pulled up to her nose. Matt pointed at her and grinned. He couldn't see her lips under the covers, but the sparkle in her eyes told him that she was smiling. Matt rotated his hand and moved his pointer finger toward himself, indicating to Hannah that he wanted her to follow. She didn't move. Next, Matt held out his arms to her. She hesitated for just a second. Then, throwing the covers back, his daughter held out her arms to him. Matt bent down and scooped her up. Hannah wrapped her arms around his neck as he carried her.

"Look what I found," Matt said as he carried Hannah into the master bedroom. "Someone was spying on us, and I've caught her!" Mary Frances sat up in bed. How she cherished the vision of Matt holding their daughter!

"I'm not sure what she is," said Matt. "Maybe she's a raccoon or maybe a possum. Maybe a bobcat. I can't tell. So, we'd better hold her captive until we can figure it out." Matt put Hannah in the bed and then got in so that the little girl was between them. Mary Frances pulled the blanket up over them and looked lovingly at Hannah. "What do you think, Mary Frances?" asked Matt as he looked over his new daughter.

"I think she's a raccoon," answered Mary Frances. Then, Matt began tickling Hannah's ribs, and she started giggling. Mary Frances would treasure that moment for the rest of her life.

Dagny and Mary Frances felt completely different walking into church that Sunday morning, not only as wives but also as mothers. It was already a special place for the women; but now with the children, it was even more so. Hannah sat between Mary Frances and Sam. The new parents were impressed at how well-behaved the children were. Curious to meet the Fromms and Matt's new family, several congregants approached and eagerly welcomed the group.

After lunch, the Archers and the Fromms went shopping at Nordstrom Rack and bought more clothing for the children. Later that afternoon while Matt and Zander were busy showing Sam the steam engine, Mary Frances lost track of Hannah for a split-second. She located her by a window in the great room, gazing outside.

"There you are, Hannah," said Mary Frances. "What do you see out there?"

"Are there bears here?" asked Hannah. Mary Frances was shocked to hear Hannah's voice for the first time. She hadn't expected a response.

"I'm not sure, Hannah," said Mary Frances. "There are bears in Tennessee. We should ask Daddy. He will know."

"I think there are," Hannah said. "You know, there are good bears and bad bears. The grizzly bears are the bad ones; the black bears are the good ones." Dagny happened by just as Hannah was explaining about bears. She, too, was shocked to suddenly hear Hannah's voice.

"Uncle Zander and I went to the Smoky Mountains for our honeymoon, and we saw bears," said Dagny. "Uncle Zander bought me a little black bear. Would you like to see it?" Hannah nodded. Dagny went to her room and returned with a stuffed, toy bear.

"This is a good one because he's a black bear," said Hannah, holding the toy and checking his ears and nose.

"Would you mind taking care of my bear for me?" asked Dagny. "I don't know that much about bears, but I can tell you do."

"I'll take care of him for you," said Hannah. "What's his name?"

Dagny was caught off guard, not expecting the question. After stammering a bit, she said, "Bear. His name is Bear."

"I would have given him a better name," said Hannah, "but if that's his name, I'll call him Bear."

The three sat together at the window, discussing bears for the next 30 minutes. When the guys came back from playing with the steam engine, they were as surprised as Mary Frances and Dagny had been to hear Hannah talking.

That evening, Matt gathered Mary Frances, Zander and Dagny in the great room and sent the kids to play in the bunkroom. "Hannah certainly knows how to talk," Matt said. "I couldn't believe it when we came back from the workshop. She's a smart, little girl who can definitely talk when she wants to." Everyone laughed, delighted over witnessing the transformation.

"Now, let's discuss tomorrow since we all have to go back to work," said Matt. "Mrs. Joiner will blow a gasket when she finds out you've both become mothers over the weekend!" Dagny and Mary Frances looked at each other and cackled. "You are entitled to maternity leave, and that includes adoption. So, here's an idea. I haven't mentioned it, but Patricia Martin in HR has been working on a new program for employees. It's a week out from being operational, but very soon Veritas will have a facility for employees' children. What Zander's brother's family is experiencing is beginning to happen all over the country. It's getting harder and harder to find day care. The CEO decided it would be of great help to employees with children to be able to bring their children to work. As soon as that program starts up, I strongly suggest that we enroll Hannah and Sam."

"What about school, Matt?" asked Mary Frances. "School will be starting shortly."

"Yes, but it's likely we'll be leaving soon," Matt said. "I'd rather not put them through any more emotional trauma. They will adjust to a new school, new teachers and make new friends only to have to give up those attachments. They've had to give up so much recently."

"I see your point, and I agree. But the children must go to school," said Mary Frances.

"Yes, and they'll be doing that in Arcadia," said Matt.

"How will that work?" asked Dagny.

"I've made up a tentative division of labor chart," said Matt. "It's not written in stone, and I'm sure it will evolve, but I have Mary Frances down as the teacher." The expression on Mary Frances' face was priceless. "I already have complete textbook series. Paper, pens, every supply needed for school. That doesn't mean we won't all play a part. For example, let's say I'm better at math than Mary Frances. And let's say the children are studying calculus. I can teach that class."

"Matt, they're 8 and 10," said Dagny. "Who cares about calculus?"

"Just an example, Dagny," said Matt. "Now, about tomorrow. What if you rotate? What if Dagny goes to work on Monday while Mary Frances stays home with the kids? Then, Tuesday, Mary Frances could go while Dagny stays home. That wouldn't put such a strain on Mrs. Joiner and the others in the cafeteria, unless you girls have a better idea. And, then, the following week, the kids would go to work with us."

"Do you have a time worked out for leaving, Matt?" asked Zander.

"September, October, no later. We'll decide soon. We don't want to make the trip when it's too cold. It's going to be harder with the children. Zander, you and I could make it in two days- with the girls, probably three. But now with the children, I'd guess four days; that's if there are no problems." Everyone remained motionless, silently contemplating the very near future.

"Well, I agree the kids are doing well," said Dagny. "Sam seems to like it here, and he's loving all the guy stuff like steam engines!"

"He's a smart boy," Matt said. "I'm expecting he'll be a great help at Arcadia, especially when he gets a little bigger."

"Hannah is doing surprisingly well," said Mary Frances. "I couldn't be happier."

"And she's so pretty, just like her aunt," Dagny kidded, poking fun at Mary Frances. "It's my turn now. I get to go check on the kids," Dagny said and headed to the bunkroom. Mary Frances smiled at her friend and shook her head.

"Zander, let's go downstairs and start prepping. I want to show you the SAW and the FAL," Matt said.

Mary Frances found herself alone on the sofa by the fireplace. Turning her cell phone over and over in her hands, she decided to make a call.

"Hello."

"Hello, Mom."

"Mary Frances, how are you?"

"I'm good, Mom. Really good. How about you?"

"Not so good, Mary Frances. I'm glad you called. I've been wanting to call you."

"Is something wrong, Mom?"

"Yes ... it's George. I must apologize to you, sweetheart. I believe you. I believed you then, but I didn't have the courage to stand up to him."

"What's going on, Mom?"

"I'm so stupid to have ever married George. He's not a good man, Mary Frances. I guess you know that already. We're not getting along well. George hit me, Mary Frances. This isn't the first time."

"Mom, I'm so sorry. What are you going to do?"

"I know what I should do, but I probably won't. So, I'll just have to try harder to not make him angry. But no more about me. How are you, sweetheart? How is Matt? Is he good to you?"

"Yes, Mom. He's very good to me."

"He doesn't hit you, does he?"

"No, Mom, he doesn't even raise his voice to me. He's very kind and loving. I wish you could meet him."

"I wish I could, too."

"There's more news, Mom. Matt's friend, Zander, just adopted his 10-year-old cousin from Louisville, Kentucky. The boy's parents were killed when the water supply was poisoned. The boy, Sam, was in an orphan's internment camp in Kentucky after his parents died. He was looking after one of the other orphans, a little girl. She had grown quite attached to him. We took her, Mom. Matt and I adopted her. Her name is Hannah, and she's eight years old."

"Oh, my goodness, Mary Frances! That is wonderful! First, you get married, and now, you're a mother! Hannah...tell me about her. What does she look like?"

"She's not very big, Mom. She's thin. Dark hair, brown eyes, light complexion. She kind of looks like me at that age.

She's very smart. She wasn't speaking, not to anyone, when she first arrived. But then today, she started talking as if she'd never stopped."

"Mary Frances, you have made my day. It's unbelievable; I'm a grandma now! Maybe someday I can meet her... but the situation with George."

"Mom, did you see on the news about the disgruntled employee in Nashville who came in the building with a gun to kill people?"

"Yes, I did."

"Well, that was Veritas, Mom. That's where we work. And the man who stopped the shooter was Matt. He shot him right between the eyes. I want you to tell George that. Mother, if he lays a hand on you again, I want to know. You can tell him from me that if he does, I will send Matt to find him. Matt knows what George tried to do to me, and Matt would love the excuse to beat the crap out of him. I'm dead serious, Mom. Tell him that."

"Um... I'm going to tell him. Yes, I will tell him. Thank you, Mary Frances. I didn't protect you, but now you're protecting me."

"OK, Mom. Well, I need to go check on Hannah. We'll talk soon. I love you."

"Thank you, Mary Frances. I love you, too. I'm so sorry."

Chapter 31
The Fed Returns

"Come in, Matt," said the CEO. "Brian and the directors are here. You'll remember Ellen Gentry from the Fed, of course." Matt Archer walked in the conference room carrying a copy of the most recent Endex report. After shaking hands with everyone, he found a seat. It seemed a lifetime ago when he'd sat in the same place, the day Lynn Hanson had come in with a gun. The conference room had been completely redone and looked very different. Only four months had passed since that day.

Matt continued in his thoughts, *Time is flying by faster than I can process it. I've only been married two weeks and a father for one. And the world is going to hell in a handbasket.*

"Let's get to it, everyone," said the CEO, calling the meeting to order. With that, Matt refocused his mind.

"The Federal Reserve is with us today, represented by Ellen," continued Jim Borland. "A little later in the meeting, she will tell us about the Fed's plans for the near future. I'd like everyone to turn to page 31 of Matt's report. You'll see that what we've feared is happening. People are withdrawing cash from banks in record amounts and putting it in the mattress, so to speak. Of course, we know what the stock market has done, making new highs every day- not based on intrinsic value as investors are trying to get rid of cash. The prices of gold and silver are through the roof, too, because the smart money understands there could be devaluation and default. The not-so-smart money is just being pulled out of the banks and stashed at home. The treasury is trying to keep up with the withdrawals by shipping physical cash to the banks, but it's getting too close. We predict that the government will be forced to declare a bank holiday soon and close the banks to let the cash shipments catch up. Obviously, they would welcome any crisis as an excuse to do so, in order to avoid more panic than there is already." Ellen Gentry nodded in agreement.

The CEO turned the meeting over to Brian Eastman who continued, "Let's look at page 36, the yield curve," said Brian. "The last treasury auction didn't go well at all. Interest rates on treasuries have accelerated at rates never seen before. This, of course, will put the brakes on the economy. We are certain the GDP will be down third quarter. It's just a question of how much. The cost of money plus greatly contracted consumer spending post the water supply poisonings and the baseball shootings will greatly drag GDP this quarter. Also, don't forget that the majority of the national debt is in T-bills. Within one year, the national debt service will skyrocket as the interest rate resets to the new higher rates."

Next, the CEO nodded to Matt. "You can see the cumulative effects of all this on the Endex, bringing it to just over 200," Matt began. "Looking at some of the less traditional parts of the Endex, I'd like to point out that we are starting to see toilet paper shortages across the country. Also, we've broken 20 on the CEO vacation component. We've never had over 20% of CEO's on vacation at one time. We're now at 22%, and it's not Thanksgiving or Christmas. Vacations, toilet paper, withdrawing cash from the banks, it all adds up to... the people are starting to get it. Parts of the general population are starting to prepare for a major collapse; that's what the discerning part of the population is doing. Pages 21-35 outline the less than discerning part of the population as well as the criminal. You'll see that all levels of crime continue to rise. Pay particular attention to arson; our nation's firemen are working overtime. Also, notice that emergency room visits for mental issues are at crisis levels. If you know an ER nurse, just ask her, and she'll tell you. Of course, the question has always been, at what point do people stop going to work? In other words, when is the risk of leaving your home greater than the need to bring in a paycheck? We think we're there. Vacation requests are at an all-time high. It's not just CEO's. More and more companies are having difficulties getting employees to work. The economy is already in trouble, but if companies start closing permanently or even temporarily, the situation becomes critical very quickly."

"Thanks, Matt," said the CEO. "Ellen, share with us what you can about Washington."

"Frankly, we're scared," she said. "We've never seen anything like this. And what makes it so difficult is we don't know why it's happening. If it was Russia, we could do sanctions. If it was ISIS, we could bomb them. But it's so many different things all happening at the same time, and we can't determine the cause of most of it. No one, for example, has claimed responsibility for the water supply poisoning. It is very much feared that Russia or China may see our situation as weakness, tempting them to launch an attack- probably not militarily, but rather some type of cyber-attack to continue the erosion that's already occurring. Yes, the cash is a problem. People are withdrawing in record amounts. Of course, the money must be available because the first time a bank teller says, *I'm sorry, but we're out of money*, the lines at the banks would be 10 miles long. It would be chaos. So, money is being printed as quickly as possible and shipped as soon as the ink is dry. If the Fed can't keep up, they will be forced to close the banks to allow time for cash shipments to arrive. The NYSE is seriously considering shortening trading hours or maybe reducing trading to three days a week. The VIX is off the charts; there's never been volatility like this. While the stock market is terribly overvalued and needs a good correction, Washington is afraid of what a stock market crash would do to the population, psychologically, and on top of everything else the world is experiencing. So, the NYSE is ready to reduce trading or shut it down temporarily. Moreover, there are international problems. China moved 10 more divisions to the Indian border last night. It's likely an invasion is imminent. The fight will be over water. Both China and India lay claim to the rivers; China probably sees this as a good time to act because our hands are full here at home, and we will be less likely to intervene. Same thing in the Middle East. I just pray nothing goes nuclear. Our population is on the edge, and the news that radioactive dust would be falling on us in two days would set off uncontrollable hysteria. Bottom line, our country and the world have never faced so many problems simultaneously."

"Thank you, Ellen," Jim Borland said, gravely. "We appreciate your input."

"And we appreciate yours, Jim," she replied.

"Unless anyone has questions, I want to adjourn," the CEO announced. "I'd like to start the board meeting after a 30-minute break. I don't expect it will take long." Everyone rose, and quickly said their goodbyes.

Matt headed for his office, his mind running wild analyzing all the things that were happening and how they could manifest in the whole fabric of events. Checking his watch, he took a detour and got on the elevator. Then, stepping out on the third floor, Matt followed the sounds of children to a set of double doors. He pushed through them and almost immediately heard, "Daddy!"

"How are you doing this afternoon, Hannah?" the Vice President of Research asked his daughter as she came running up to him.

"Good," she said. "We're practicing our addition and subtraction facts. I'm good at them. In third grade, I'll start learning the times tables." Then looking around, she whispered, "I already know my twos and fives!"

Watching the room full of lively children and the three teachers who were trying to corral them, Matt lamented, *If only we could stay. I don't want to go. I want a normal life right here with Mary Frances and Hannah.* But he knew life wasn't going to be normal for anyone. His life would have to be different just to survive and ensure the survival of his family.

"I'll be finished in about an hour, Hannah," he said. "I'll come get you, and we'll find Mommy and go home." Hannah gave him a hug, and Matt retraced his steps to the meeting on the sixth floor.

"Matt, we are planning on closing Veritas Strategies... soon," said the CEO to Matt and the chief economist. "We hate it. It's heartbreaking. We have all worked diligently to build this company. But if the government starts closing banks and securities exchanges, we're out of business. Our only hope would be if the closures would be temporary."

Brian Eastman continued, "Matt, Jim and I are leaving with our families Saturday. We're 'going on vacation'. We'll stay in contact by phone and computer, so we'll still be running the company. But... we won't be here. We'll be in Montana. We're not telling you what to do, but you should consider the same course of action."

"Matt, you're 5% owner of Veritas," said the CEO. "Depending on how bad it gets and how long it lasts, your 5% could become completely worthless. I'm sorry, but we're experiencing the same loss. Brian and I have set aside enough gold and silver to restart the company, if we're able when the time comes. Again, depending on how bad it gets will also determine whether a company like this would even be needed. If events set us back to the 1970's, then, yes, the world would need a Veritas Strategies. If events set us back to 1870 or 1770, then probably not. Maybe Veritas could restart as another type of company. Regardless, you will always be 5% owner. If we can get through this, I hope we can somehow end up back here, all together again. The country will need us. We'll need each other to rebuild."

Matt was silent, touched by Jim's words and the hope they inspired. "Thank you, Jim," Matt finally said. "You hired me, and it's been a real pleasure to work alongside you. Brian, you're the smartest guy I know. I'm going to miss both of you. It's my hope, too, that we can all return for a new beginning."

That night as Matt lay in bed holding Mary Frances, he said, "There was a meeting with people from the government today; they're ready to declare a banking holiday and stock market holiday at any moment. After that meeting, I spoke with Jim and Brian. They're leaving on vacation Saturday morning..."

Matt let the news sink in before continuing. "It's time to go, Mary Frances," he said, softly. "Tomorrow will be our last day, the last day at Veritas. We're going on vacation, too."

"I don't want to go," Mary Frances said, "but I understand why we must. When?"

"I'm watching the weather," Matt said.

"This should be a good time, right?" she asked. "Thank goodness, it's cooler now."

"I'm watching for bad weather followed by good weather," Matt said.

"Bad weather? Why would you want bad weather?" Mary Frances asked.

"Don't you like to be out in bad weather?" he asked.

"Nobody does, do they?" she asked.

"Exactly," he said. "Ideally, I'd like to move at night in the rain. I want our passage from here to the drop point for the SUV to be uneventful. If it's nighttime, most people are asleep. If it's raining, people are holed up inside. So, it's a good time to move without attracting attention. After we leave the Range Rover, then we'll be on foot, walking through wilderness. There are no houses, people or vehicles to hide from. Dry would be nice for that."

"I assumed we'd just get in the SUV and drive," she said. "I never thought of it like that. We couldn't be attacked on the way, could we?"

"Probably not, but it's possible," Matt said. "The longer we wait, the closer we get to the point of chaos and the more dangerous it becomes. Eventually, towns will start barricading to keep outsiders out. Governors will block highways into their states. Criminals and desperate people will start preying on travelers."

"None of that had crossed my mind," said Mary Frances. "I love you. I want all of us to get to Arcadia safely. Do you think the long hike will be difficult with the children?"

"Yeah, I do," Matt said. "Especially Hannah. I'm afraid she's going to give out quickly, and I'll end up carrying her. Sam's strong. I believe he will do alright. Originally, I had hoped to make 12 miles a day, so we'd be camped out only one night. I've built a basecamp halfway. But now, I'm thinking it may be four days. There are lots of rock cliffs with overhangs. We'll camp under those on the first night and the third. I don't want to push us too hard because we don't want any injuries. After we're in the woods, we can take our time. There's no rush. I just worry about the children and exposure. I don't want anyone getting sick."

"I understand now why you've been taking me hiking," said Mary Frances. "I hope my feet are tough enough for 25 miles."

"Think of it as four six-mile hikes," said Matt. "We've done six miles, and you did fine. Also, if the weather is bad, we can just stay put. We'll get there, but I want to keep everyone warm and dry. So, we'll have to carry more food and water than I had originally planned."

"Will we sleep on the ground? Will we have a campfire?" Mary Frances asked.

"Yes, that's the plan. And, we'll have to carry extra food and water for the kids," said Matt. "I'll be happy if that's all I have to carry. It will be important for us to be positive with the kids. We'll need to make the hike fun. Hannah doesn't need to become overwhelmed by a 25-mile hike. She'll get discouraged."

"Yes, we can do that," said Mary Frances. "We can look for bears! ..... Are there bears, Matt? What if we find one?"

"Yes, there are bears, but you rarely see them," said Matt. "That's a good idea. Hannah will like that."

"We're going to be exhausted by the time we arrive at Arcadia, aren't we," concluded Mary Frances.

"We are, but those beds are waiting to welcome us," he said. "A nice, hot shower. A real kitchen instead of MRE's. We can sleep for three days if we want."

"Oh, Matt! There's hot water?" Mary Frances asked.

"Yes, it's a wood-fired water heater," said Matt. It will probably be best to set a time in the morning for washing dishes and taking baths because it's not constant hot water. I have to fire it up, but it makes great hot water. In fact, it's hotter than here, so we'll have to watch the kids that they don't scald themselves."

"We'll do fine," Mary Frances said. "You've prepared for everything."

"I'm concerned that I've forgotten something," said Matt. "There's an almost infinite number of possibilities of things that could go wrong. I've tried to plan for everything, but still..."

The two drifted off to sleep, Mary Frances envisioning the 25-mile hike with the children and Matt methodically going over the coming days.

Chapter 32
Last Day

Before leaving for work Friday morning, Matt called the adults together. "Yesterday, I met with Jim Borland and Brian Eastman. Their plans are to close Veritas soon. Zander, you know better than anyone about the components of the Endex and what's happening. We shouldn't wait any longer. Today, the four of us need to put in for vacation, starting Monday. We will leave sometime in the next few days, depending on the weather."

"I agree," said Zander. "I'm surprised the country is holding together as well as it is. We should go."

"I have not told you where we're going," Matt said. "That's because you don't have a need to know. It's important that no one knows our destination. I expect you'll want to make phone calls this weekend and say goodbye. I'll leave it up to you as how to handle this. Maybe you'll simply say you're going on vacation. Or, you may want to explain we're worried about the turn the country has taken and for safety we're leaving the city. In both cases, you will be asked where you're going. Think about how you'll answer that question. It's much easier for me because I don't have any family."

"My parents are with my brother and his family in California," Zander said. "I'll call them tonight and say we're going on vacation."

"I'll say we're going on vacation, too," said Dagny. "It's easier."

"Yes, me, too," agreed Mary Frances. "I'll call my mother tonight."

The workday was surreal. All four felt a combination of fear and sadness. With each and every interaction, there was an awareness that it might be the last time to ever see that person again. In the backs of their minds was the heavy, almost guilty, feeling of knowing something their coworkers did not. As the four informed others of their impending vacation, the response from a few of their coworkers telegraphed they, too, might be planning something similar.

Mary Frances and Dagny stopped by HR to make sure everything was approved for their vacation. "Do you really think we need to do this?" Dagny asked Mary Frances in the elevator.

"No, but it seems like we should," said Mary Frances. "It's what we would normally do."

When they popped in Patricia Martin's office to tell her of their vacation plans, she hugged them both. "Yes, everything is all set for you two," she said. "Matt called down to me this morning. I will miss both of you. I hope to see you again someday." Blinking back tears, she waved goodbye as they left her office.

Walking down the hall, Dagny whispered, "Oh, my goodness, Mary Frances! Mrs. Martin knows. That's not how you act when someone is leaving on vacation for two weeks."

"Dagny, I think lots of people know or are starting to know. Remember what Matt and Zander were explaining on the Endex?" Mary Frances said. "It's happening."

"Let's take a peek in the day care since we're already on the third floor," said Dagny. Both children were glad to see them. Sam, trying to act more mature, didn't run like Hannah did. The two, new mothers hugged their children and reminded them they'd be back soon to take them home. The words *for the last time* were left unspoken.

Matt had similar feelings as he said goodbye, realizing he may never see his coworkers again. When the work day ended, he took a moment to study his office, taking note of every little detail. He wanted to remember it. Then, walking down the hall with his briefcase, he recalled his first day at Veritas... six years before. Breathing deeply, he wanted to remember the clean smell of the offices. When the elevator stopped on the fifth floor, Zander joined Matt. The two men could sense each other's sadness.

Meeting on the third floor, the four comrades entered the day care where other employees were routinely gathering their children at the end of the day. Sam, always serious, and Hannah, always enthusiastic, met them. Together, the six left the third floor and exited the building, for the last time.

That evening at home, the parents told the children of the plans for a family vacation, a wilderness vacation deep in the woods. The trip would involve a hike. Hannah asked about bears. "Yes, Hannah, you might see bears," answered Matt. "We'll be staying at our log cabin in the woods."

"Another log cabin! Is it really far in the woods?" Hannah asked.

"Yes, but that's where the bears are," Matt explained. "This is going to be an adventure! We'll hike through the forest and the mountains. There are beautiful streams and waterfalls. And lots of different animals, Hannah."

"Are there mountain lions, too?" asked Hannah. "I don't like mountain lions because I saw on TV that they can eat people."

"No mountain lions," said Matt as Mary Frances gave him a look across the dining room table. "There are bobcats but no mountain lions. And bobcats don't bother people."

After dinner, Sam looked for an opportunity to catch Zander alone. "Can I ask you a question?" he said, seriously.

"Sure," said Zander. "What's up?"

"This vacation we're going on," Sam began. "Is it really a vacation? This doesn't sound like going to Disney World. Are we coming back?"

Zander looked at his son, surprised at his insight. "Let's go talk to your Uncle Matt; he's out in the workshop." Zander and Sam found Matt checking ammunition boxes. "Matt, Sam has asked if we're coming back from our vacation."

"Why do you think that, Sam?" said Matt.

"Both of you talk about the Endex all the time," Sam said. "I watch TV, too. I can see what's going on. Hannah and I were orphans because of the water department poisoning, and no one has figured out who did that. I see everything you've gotten ready for the trip, and it includes two machine guns and all this," he said, pointing to all the ammunition. "Who takes that on a vacation?" Zander looked at Matt as both men were blindsided by Sam's statement.

"Well, Sam, I want to apologize," said Matt. "I'm afraid we've underestimated you. Let's sit down and talk. Let me tell Mary Frances where we all are."

When Matt returned to the workshop, he closed the door behind him. Matt began, "Sam, I'm sorry for treating you like a child. You're not. You're very mature for your age. You are correct. It's not just a regular vacation. Your dad... Zander and I are afraid that the world as we know it may be on the verge of collapse. We have decided that it's better to be away from civilization because being away from people would be much safer."

"Uncle Matt has a cabin in the woods that's very remote," explained Zander. "That's where we're going. We'll drive most of the way, but we'll walk the last 25 miles. There's a cabin with a lake full of fish. Uncle Matt has stocked the cabin with lots of supplies. Who knows how long we'll be there."

"You're an important part of this, Sam, because you're smart, strong and very mature for your age," said Matt. "We will be depending on you a lot."

"What about all the guns?" asked Sam. "Do you think we'll need them?"

"Let's hope not," said Matt. "But if we do, it's better to have them than not. Also, Sam, I don't want you calling these machine guns. They're not. They are completely legal, semi-automatic rifles."

"I like them. They're cool. How are they different, and what do they do?" asked Sam.

"Well, this is a FAL," said Matt, pointing to a large, heavy rifle on a bipod with a round magazine. "It's a semi-automatic rifle that fires the 7.62mm X 51mm NATO round. Each magazine is 50 rounds. The 7.62X51 round is very powerful. If we found ourselves needing to penetrate cars or houses, this would do the job."

"Wow! And this one?" asked Sam.

"It's a SAW," said Zander. "This is what I used in Afghanistan. SAW stands for Squad Automatic Weapon. It's 5.56mm, so it's smaller than the FAL, but each box is 200 linked rounds. It's semi-automatic, so it also is completely legal. If we needed to control a large mass of attackers, this would do it."

"What's this one? It's much smaller," said Sam.

"That's my SIG Rattler," answered Matt. "It doesn't look like it, but it's technically a pistol. It fires the 300 Blackout round. It's subsonic so with the suppressor, it's very quiet. It has a lot more knockdown power than the 5.56," said Matt, watching Sam take it all in. "Sam, do you remember how you helped Hannah at the orphan's center?" Sam nodded as Matt continued. "That's what this is for. It's to protect you, Hannah, Dagny and Mary Frances. These are not toys. They are deadly serious. We never want to use these. We will go out of our way to avoid a fight, but if someone is intent on doing us harm, we will come down on them with such force that they will never threaten us again."

Sam looked at his father and Matt with great seriousness and asked, "Will you teach me how to use them?" Zander looked to Matt who nodded in agreement.

"We will Sam, but only if you follow our instructions to the letter. There can be no mistakes because a mistake can be lethal," Matt said.

They gathered around a table where the weapons were laid out. "First, and this is very important, *always* treat *all* weapons as if they are loaded. Even if you're certain they're not, you treat them as if they are. Do you understand that, Sam?" Matt asked. Sam nodded. "Then repeat this rule to me."

"Always treat all weapons as if they're loaded," said Sam.

"That's right," said Matt. "So, what does that mean? It means you must be in control of the weapon's muzzle at all times. You must know where the rifle is pointed. You keep it pointed down at the ground like this." Matt picked up the SIG and held it down at a 45-degree angle. "If you bring it up, you must be aware of the arc the muzzle is creating. Don't bring the muzzle up and pass it through the space of someone. It could go off; you could accidentally shoot them. Always be aware of where the muzzle is pointed." Sam nodded.

"Do you see Uncle Matt's trigger finger?" Zander asked. Sam nodded. "Do you see that it's straight? It's not inside the trigger guard on the trigger. Only put your trigger finger inside the trigger guard on the trigger when you engage the target." Sam nodded. "Let's say you're on patrol, and you trip. If your finger is on the trigger when you trip, what could happen?"

"You could accidentally squeeze the trigger, and the rifle could go off," said Sam.

"Correct, and you could accidentally shoot someone, someone you don't want to shoot," said Matt. "Lastly, we have three weapons here, a FAL, a SAW and a SIG Rattler. They all use different ammunition. Always be sure you load the right ammunition in the right weapon. If you get it wrong, you could cause the rifle to explode in your face. This one is 7.62X51, this one is 5.56 and this one is 300 Blackout. They are different. So, tell us what you've learned thus far, Sam?"

"I've learned that I must always treat a weapon as if it is loaded. I've learned to never point the muzzle in a direction that could accidentally shoot someone. I've learned to not put my finger on the trigger until I'm ready to fire. And I've learned that different weapons have different ammunition, and I cannot get them confused," Sam repeated.

"That's good, Sam," said Zander.

"Yes, very good, Sam," said Matt. "Tomorrow, we'll continue and maybe let you fire the Rattler." Sam stood proud, feeling that his father and uncle were treating him like a man instead of a boy.

"OK, let's go back to the kitchen and see what the girls are doing," said Zander, giving Sam a well-deserved pat on the back.

After the children had been put to bed, Dagny lay snuggled up to Zander as he said, "Our son is very observant."

"What do you mean?" asked Dagny.

"He understands much more than we give him credit for," Zander said. "He's already figured out that this isn't a regular vacation. He understands the world is changing, and he's guessed we might not be coming back."

"Really! And we've been trying to protect the children by telling them it was a vacation," said Dagny.

"He seems fine with it. In fact, he wants us to teach him how to fire the rifles," said Zander. "We started with some basics tonight. That's what we were doing in the workshop. Tomorrow, we're going to let him shoot some."

"Can I come, too?" asked Dagny. "I know how to shoot. Just not the kinds of guns Matt has."

"We'll see," Zander said.

Chapter 33
Shopping

At Saturday morning's breakfast table, the conversation turned to the day's agenda. "Can we get ice cream?" asked Hannah. Everyone momentarily stopped eating and looked at her.

"How can you be thinking about ice cream?" asked Sam. "We're having bacon and scrambled eggs, and you're thinking about ice cream."

"I like ice cream," said Hannah as she took a bite of bacon. Everyone laughed at her. Mary Frances smiled at her with love, marveling over the reality that she had not only a husband but a daughter.

"We need to swing by the mall," Matt said. "Also, I need to pick up some extra batteries for the Crimson Trace laser sights."

"I could be sounding like Hannah, but what do y'all think about some Martin's BBQ for lunch?" asked Zander.

"I like BBQ, too, Uncle Zander," said Hannah, and everyone laughed.

While Mary Frances and Dagny were cleaning up the kitchen, Matt approached them and said quietly, "Something has just occurred to me. Since we don't know long we'll be at Arcadia or how much the kids will grow during that period, that could become a problem. We can buy some clothes trying to predict how much they'll grow, but it's a guess. Could we make them?

My grandmother used to sew with patterns. Are either one of you familiar with those?"

"I am," said Dagny. "I'd help my grandmother with patterns. A pattern is laid out and pinned on the fabric. Then, the pieces are cut out and sewn together. You don't have a sewing machine at Arcadia, do you?"

"Actually, I do," said Matt. "I expected one to come in handy for repairing clothes. It's a brand-new machine, but it's treadle... no electricity. I also went to a fabric store several years ago and bought bolts of fabric. I had no idea what I was doing, but I did buy a variety."

"It used to be common that people made their own clothes," said Mary Frances, "but I have no experience with that."

"That's why you're assigned to the kitchen, Mary Frances," said Matt with a smile, "because that's your strength. But back to sewing. Let's locate a fabric store today and find some patterns for the kids. We'll buy shirt, pant and dress patterns in multiple sizes. Get several of them; they can be reused. Do you think that might work?"

"It'll work," said Dagny. "Patterns are very light and compact. They would be easy to carry."

"How about underwear, particularly for Hannah?" mentioned Dagny. "What are we supposed to do about bras?"

"I don't know," said Mary Frances, "unless you can make some."

"I doubt it," said Dagny. "They're very complicated. Have you ever looked at a bra closely? All those pieces and angles. They're complicated. But I did make a bikini once!"

"Can you believe we're having this conversation?" laughed Matt. "While everyone else is looting a supermarket, maybe we'd be smart to raid a Victoria's Secret!"

That afternoon after shopping and eating Bar-B-Que at Martin's on Belmont Avenue, the six returned to the cabin south of Nashville. Mary Frances and Dagny were being helped by Hannah in sorting and packing the clothes that were purchased for the children. Quickly, it was apparent that Hannah was quite smart and more aware than they realized. "Mommy and Aunt Dagny, I like all the new clothes you bought me. I really do, but some of the clothes are too big for me. Some are way too big for me! Does that mean we're going to be gone on vacation for a very long time?"

Mary Frances and Dagny exchanged glances. "Hannah, sweetheart, you're right. We may be gone a long time," said Mary Frances. "We aren't sure. But when you and Sam grow, you'll have some things that will fit."

Hannah nodded and said, "The three of us almost look alike. Maybe I'll be your size when I'm grown. Maybe I can wear some of your clothes!"

"Better than that, Hannah, we have fabric and patterns," said Dagny. "There's a sewing machine at the cabin. I can make you dresses as you get older."

"Can you knit?" asked Hannah. "I can't, but sweaters are made by knitting."

"Yes, I can," said Dagny. "That's a great idea, Hannah! Mary Frances, let's find out if Matt has yarn and knitting needles at the cabin."

That night when the Archers were alone, Mary Frances said, "Matt, I want to apologize. With being a working mother and getting ready for our journey, I've been neglecting you. I promised myself that I was going to be the best wife possible, and then I got so busy that I haven't been."

"Mary Frances, you're too tough on yourself. You're a great wife, and you're being a wonderful mother to Hannah. I don't have any complaints. We've been so busy, and this next week will be hard; I hope not too hard. But once we make it to the cabin and winter sets in, I expect more time for us. More time to relax, sit by the fire, drink some coffee, talk and make love."

Mary Frances looked toward the closed bedroom door and held her finger up to her lips. "Shhh, Matt. Be careful what you say. Little ears may be listening." Matt laughed, pulled Mary Frances to him and kissed her. "As I was saying, I've been neglecting you. I'm going to start doing a better job, and I'm going to start right now. I want to begin with a nice massage."

"I'd like that," said Matt.

"Then take off your clothes and get comfortable in the

bed. I'll be right back to give you a back rub," she said.

Matt eagerly complied. He quickly got naked, leaving his clothes in a heap on a floor. Pulling back the covers, he stretched out on his stomach and waited for Mary Frances. When she returned, she was wearing a very sexy, black negligée.

"Wow!" said Matt. "I do like this *I've been neglecting you* thing!"

"Now, be still, and let me get you nice and relaxed," Mary Frances said. Then she climbed onto the bed and straddled her husband, sitting on his butt.

As she started to rub his back, Matt sighed, "Oh, that feels so good." Neither Matt nor Mary Frances heard the bedroom door open or saw Hannah slip in, holding her bear.

"Does Daddy's back hurt?" Hannah asked. Mary Frances jumped and squealed from the surprise.

"Hannah, why aren't you in bed?" asked Mary Frances.

"I wanted to make sure you were both OK," answered Hannah. "And it's a good thing I did because, Daddy, it looks like you forgot to put on your pajamas. Why don't you go put some on? I'll turn around. I need to talk to Mommy about something."

Hannah promptly turned around as promised. Then, Mary Frances got off Matt, as he scrambled out of bed. Mary Frances had a guilty and embarrassed *I've been caught* look on her face as she reached for the satin robe. Matt quickly made it into the bathroom and closed the door, all the while thinking, *Lock on the bedroom door... I've got to put a lock on that door!*

"Mommy, I need to talk to you," said Hannah.

"Yes, what is it, sweetheart?" asked Mary Frances, wrapping the robe around her tightly and securing the belt.

"The weather is getting cooler because it's fall," Hannah explained. "You need to get some good flannel pajamas like mine. That little nightgown won't keep you very warm in the winter."

Trying to regain her status of motherhood while her daughter was advising her on nightwear choices, Mary Frances said, "Yes, Hannah, you're right. I do have warm pajamas. Your daddy bought them for me." Opening the chest of drawers, Mary Frances took out the Christmas present Matt had given her to offer proof to her daughter.

"Those are much better, Mommy," Hannah agreed, touching the soft, flannel material. Matt came out of the bathroom wearing pajamas. "You better put these on now, Mommy, so you won't be cold tonight." At a loss for words, Mary Frances sheepishly took the flannel pajamas to the bathroom while Matt did his best to suppress a laugh. Appropriately dressed for bed, Mary Frances returned to find her husband and daughter playing together with the stuffed bear.

"Why are you in our bed, Hannah?" asked Mary Frances.

"I wanted to play Bear Cave," she answered.

"What is Bear Cave?" asked Mary Frances as Matt grinned.

"Daddy taught me," said Hannah. "Bears hibernate when winter comes. They sleep all winter, and they like to sleep in caves. They find caves big enough for the whole family, and they all cuddle up and sleep together."

"How do you play this game?" asked Mary Frances as she got in the bed and covered up, Hannah now between her parents.

"Daddy, do the blizzard," Hannah said.

Mary Frances smiled as Matt started making... *SSShhhhhhsss...* noises like the wind was blowing.

"Do you hear that, Mommy?" Hannah asked, excitedly. "There's a blizzard coming! That means winter!" Mary Frances watched Hannah as she acted out the game with her dad. It conjured up memories of last December when she had been caught in a real blizzard, the blizzard that brought her Matt and now Hannah.

"Yes, I hear it! What do we do?" ask Mary Frances.

"Bear, go find us a bear cave," Hannah told her stuffed animal. She pulled him from under the covers and moved him around as if he was searching for something. "Bears are very good at finding caves for hibernation!"

"The sun's going down. Night is coming, and we've got to get out of this blizzard!" said Matt as he reached over and turned off the light by the bed.

Hannah moved the bear's nose to the edge of the covers, sticking his nose under. "Bear found a cave!" Matt made more wind noises. "Quick, everyone in the bear cave!" Hannah exclaimed as she pulled the covers up over her head.

With all three- four, counting the bear- under the covers, Hannah said, “I can hear the blizzard outside, but we’re safe and warm inside the bear cave.”

“I can’t see anything, Hannah,” said Mary Frances.

“It’s a dark cave, Mommy. You’re not supposed to be able to see. Bear caves don’t have electric lights!”

“No, I guess they don’t,” laughed Mary Frances.

“See how warm and cozy it is in the bear cave!” said Hannah.

“It’s perfect,” said Mary Frances, kissing and snuggling with her under the blankets. Then, she reached beyond Hannah to find Matt and caress his shoulder. Soon, Hannah was asleep.

“Should I carry her back to her bed?” Matt whispered.

“She is so precious. Can we let her sleep here with us tonight?” asked Mary Frances.

“If she doesn’t kick too much,” said Matt.

“Well, I can’t promise that,” whispered Mary Frances. “She’s so smart. Every day she surprises me.”

“I’ve noticed,” said Matt. “Just like her mother.”

Saturday came to a blissful end as they drifted off to sleep together. In that moment, their world was at peace. The forest surrounding the cabin was silent as the temperature steadily dropped into the forties. No one in the house was aware that in more than a dozen cities, the police and national guard were struggling to maintain law and order as riots and looting threatened civilization with destruction and chaos. The balance of good and evil was tipping.

Chapter 34
Lights Out

"When I woke up, you weren't in your bed," said Sam to Hannah the next morning during breakfast.

"I fell asleep in Mommy and Daddy's bed," said Hannah. Her mother gave her a sly grin while serving omelets to her family.

"No offense, Dagny," said Zander. "But dang, Mary Frances, you're a good cook. Everything you make is delicious."

"No offense taken, Zander," said Dagny, flipping back her hair. "*But dang*, you can't be beautiful and a world class chef at the same time! God has given us all different talents." Everyone started laughing at Dagny's drama.

"I disagree," said Matt. "Mary Frances is both beautiful and a world class chef."

"Well, yes, she's pretty," said Dagny, "but not on the same level as *moi*." The family continued to laugh at Dagny.

"Well, I think both Mom and Aunt Mary are very pretty," said Sam, "but the prettiest girl here is Hannah." The table got quiet as all eyes turned to Hannah who was noticeably blushing.

"That's a very nice compliment, Sam," said Zander.

"What do you say, Hannah?" asked Matt.

"Thank you, Sam," said Hannah, still bright red. She

was looking down at her plate, trying to concentrate on cutting her omelet. Mary Frances watched her daughter, then met her husband's eyes. Both wondered at Sam's unexpected compliment.

Seated together in church that morning, the family of six filled up a good section of a pew. The adults were well aware it was the last time to worship in that place as they sang hymns and listened to the sermon. Though the future was weighing heavily, they took comfort and found hope in their faith. The adults couldn't help but wonder what their children were thinking.

The children found comfort and security in their new family. Hannah was very grateful to have a father for the first time in her life. She so enjoyed helping her new mother with cooking. She hoped Dagny would teach her to knit a sweater for Sam. Sam was grateful his cousin Zander, now his father, had not only made a home for him but had found one for Hannah also. He was hopeful about life at Arcadia and excited over the prospect of an "endless summer vacation."

The Archers and the Fromms had much to pray about. Fervently, Mary Frances prayed, *Dear Heavenly Father, please watch over us and keep us safe and out of harm's way as we travel to Arcadia. I thank You for my husband who has prepared this place for us. I thank You for his strength, knowledge and wisdom- most of all for his love for me. I thank You for our daughter, Hannah, who You have placed in our care. She is so precious. I ask for Your help and guidance as I do my best to be a good mother. Thank You for Dagny, my best friend, and her wonderful husband, Zander. In the days ahead, we will need each other. Thank You for bringing us all together. And finally, for Sam. He's so young but so mature. I want to be a good aunt to Sam. I see Your hand at work. Whatever the future holds, I know You have brought us all together for a reason, and I trust in You. Amen.*

After church, the family grilled hamburgers and brats for lunch. As Matt was tending to the grill, Mary Frances was standing by him on the back patio. "Matt, I'm so glad everyone enjoys my cooking," she said. "I hope they'll like it when we're at Arcadia. But, I know it will be different. My goodness, our kitchen here is to die for... and a wood-fired pizza oven, too. It has absolutely everything. But what is it like there? How will I cook?"

"Well, I'm sorry, but no La Cornue range," he said. "There's no gas. But, when you get used to it, I think you'll like the range there. It's an Hergóm. I first saw one in a house in Guatemala that was so far into the mountains that electricity wasn't available. It belongs to my friend who owns a coffee finca. So, this range is cast iron. I remember it weighed 760 pounds because I flew it in on a chopper just like everything else; my friend, the pilot, needed to know how much it weighed. Typically, Hergóms are black with brass, but you know how I like blue, so I had one made in blue with brass. It's wood-fired, so it will take some experimenting to learn to regulate the temperature. It has two burners and an oven. Another cool feature is it has a 40-gallon water tank that will make hot water for the kitchen. I wasn't sure what I was doing, but my friend liked his. So, I got one. I hope you like it."

"Matt, that sounds wonderful. I'm sure I will," said Mary Frances. "It may take me a bit to learn how to cook on it since I've never cooked on a wood range. I'll probably be learning other new ways of doing things in the kitchen. With no supermarkets, I'll have to adjust."

"Yes, we'll establish new routines," Matt said. "You probably won't bake bread every day. But, when you do, I'll mill flour for you. Also, one of my jobs will be providing meat. You'll tell me what you want- squirrel, rabbit, deer and we may be able to find some razorback. I've seen signs of them, but that's a lot of meat if I kill one. We'll have to talk about preserving meat. There's always the possibility I don't bring home anything, but I can almost always catch fish. To some extent, you'll have to work with what I bring you. It will be trial and error at first, but we'll get better with practice. Then in the spring, we can plant a vegetable garden. We should be able to have fresh greens by late April. Hopefully, tomatoes and cucumbers by mid-June. There's also watercress in the streams. Watercress salad dressing is delicious. Then, there're wild mushrooms. I have enough stored food to last us at least 10 years, but I want to supplement it with fresh food as much as possible."

"Matt, this may sound crazy, but I'm excited to try this,"

Mary Frances said. "This is so very different from what I learned in culinary school, but I want to make our meals as tasty and nourishing as possible. Food is such a priority, especially for the kids because they're in their growth years."

"You'll do a great job, Mary Frances," Matt said, giving his wife a hug. "You're right, food is very important. I'm so fortunate to have you."

They ate outside on the patio, enjoying the cooler weather and the good food. "Aunt Mary, do you know how to make pickles?" asked Sam. "I really like pickles."

"Not exactly. I've never done it, Sam," said Mary Frances. "Are there pickles at the cabin?"

"Some, though not enough to last a long time," Matt answered. "But we do have a book on things like that. Pickles are just cucumbers. We will grow cucumbers, and then we can experiment with making pickles."

"That's good because a hamburger has to have pickles," Sam said, pausing to take a bite. "How about ketchup? I love ketchup!"

"Same thing, Sam," said Matt. "There's ketchup, but we'll run out eventually. We'll have to learn how to make it from the tomatoes we grow."

"Keeping us in good meals like this one will be a lot more complicated than we're used to," said Dagny looking at her friend, Mary Frances.

"Yes, like keeping us in clothes will be a lot more complicated," said Mary Frances. The two women nodded their heads, realizing many things which were so easy now were about to become much more difficult."

"Can we shoot the SIG now?" asked Sam after lunch.

"I want to shoot it, too," said Dagny.

"Hannah, why don't you and I clean up the kitchen? You can help me while they go shooting," said Mary Frances. Hannah agreed.

When they made it to the woods, Zander said to Sam, "Let's see if you can remember the rules you learned yesterday. Tell your mother the rules."

"OK," said Sam, turning to his mother. "First, treat every

weapon like it's loaded even when you know it isn't. Second, always know where the muzzle of your weapon is pointed. Make sure it's not pointed at anyone. Next, keep your finger out of the trigger guard until you engage the target. And last, always make sure to use the right ammunition."

"Good," said Matt. "Next, let's talk about pointing your weapon. Obviously, if you're pointing it at a target in a location where there's a good berm and no chance of the round flying downrange and hitting someone, then it's OK to point your weapon at the target. What if there're only woods behind the target?"

"No," said Sam, "because there might be someone in the woods or in a house beyond the woods."

"Correct," said Matt. "You must think ahead to what's going to happen after you pull the trigger. Now, let's talk about pointing your weapon at a human being. Let's say you're carrying a pistol. Let's say someone starts mouthing off and calling you every bad name in the book. You're getting mad. Should you point your pistol at them to make them shut up?"

Sam hesitated for a second then said, "No."

"That's correct," said Zander. "Do you know why?"

"I'm not sure," said Sam. "It didn't seem right somehow."

"Here's how you know," Zander explained. "The jerk is just talking trash. He isn't threatening your life. And here's something that's hard. Never get mad. Never let someone like that get you so pissed off that you become emotional. If you get emotional, you will make a mistake. What you do is back away. I don't care what he says, you should deescalate. Be calm. Don't get mad. Back off." Sam nodded. "So, let's continue our story with two scenarios. First scenario, the jerk calls you a coward but goes back to his friends. You leave, and no one gets hurt. Scenario number two, you're backing down, and he comes toward you. You're watching him, and you see him pull a gun out of his pocket. He racks the slide and points it at you. Now, what do you do?"

Sam considered it for some time while Matt and Zander watched him closely. Then Sam said, "He's not just talking now. He's threatening my life. I would shoot him."

"That's correct, Sam," Matt said. "It's easy to stand here and talk about it. You've got all the time in the world now, but you wouldn't if that really happened. Let's look at another situation. You're sitting with your parents. A man comes in and starts a fight with your father. Zander doesn't have a gun. He tries to deescalate. The man pulls out a knife and goes for your dad. What do you do?"

Without hesitation Sam said, "I'd shoot him because my dad's life is in danger."

"That's correct. You must judge instantly if a life is in danger, whether it's yours or someone else's. Once you've decided, do not hesitate. Don't try to shoot him in the leg to wound him. Shoot him dead center, and shoot him three times. If you miss, continue shooting until he's down and no longer a threat," Matt explained. "Never put the sights on something you're not going to shoot. If you make the decision to put sights on someone, it's because they're going to kill you, and you have to kill them first."

"I understand," said Sam.

"This is very serious, Son," said Zander. "It's life and death serious."

"Yes, sir," Sam said.

Matt set up the target at the base of a hill and explained why he chose that place. He went over the loading, unloading, and firing of the SIG. Then he explained the firing line and how everyone had to be behind him. The target was the life-size silhouette of a man with a five-ring target in the center of the chest.

"What weapon is this, Sam, and what type of ammunition is it chambered for?" asked Matt.

"It's a SIG Sauer Rattler; it fires 300 Blackout," said Sam. Matt nodded.

"The magazine inserts here," he said, pushing the clear smoke, 30-round mag into the magazine well and hitting the bottom with the palm of his hand to make sure it was secure. "Then, we pull back the charging handle to strip a round off the mag and put it in the chamber. Now it's live, but the safety is still on. With my finger still outside the trigger guard, I'll bring the weapon up and switch off the safety as I engage the target." With both eyes open, Matt brought the dot on the holographic sight onto the target as his finger moved into the trigger guard. “Everyone is behind the firing line. It’s safe to fire.”

Sam and Dagny flinched as three rounds of 300 Blackout spit out of the barrel and punched three holes in the target dead center. Matt lowered the weapon, took his finger out of the trigger guard and moved the safety to the *safe* position.

“It’s your turn now, Sam,” said Matt. “Don’t fire that fast the first time. Take your time. I want you to fire three rounds. Keep both eyes open as you put the dot on the target. Safety is *on*.” Matt handed Sam the weapon. Very carefully, he repeated the steps Matt had taught him. Slowly, Sam fired three times, then lowered the weapon and moved the safety to the *safe* position.

“Wow! Good job, Sam!” said Zander. “Nice, tight group!”

“He’s a natural,” said Matt. “Sam, the trigger has a reset, so you don’t have to let the trigger all the way out after firing. Just let off until you feel the click, then you can fire again. That will make it faster and more accurate, not that you can get more accurate than that.”

They took turns firing the SIG. Matt showed them how to flip down the magnifier for longer shots. Dagny did well, but not as well as Sam. “You’re anticipating the shot and flinching before you fire,” Zander explained to her.

“Let’s use the subsonic ammunition,” said Matt. “Let’s put on the suppressor, and see if you like that better.” Matt attached the suppressor to the muzzle, then handed the weapon back to Dagny.

Though the report was much quieter, Dagny still flinched. “That did help,” she said. “I just need more practice.”

“It’s OK, Dagny,” said Zander. “Your shots are still plenty good to get the job done.”

“Yes, both of you did great,” said Matt, removing the magazine and pulling back the T handle to clear the weapon. “OK, Sam, it’s not loaded. You’re going to carry it back to the house. How are you going to treat it?”

“I will treat it as if it’s loaded, even though you just cleared it,” said Sam.

Matt grinned, pleased with the training exercise. “Now, let’s go back to the house, and I’ll show you how to disassemble and clean it."

Back at the cabin, Mary Frances and Hannah could hear the firing of the gun outside. "I don't like guns, Mommy," said Hannah. "They're too loud."

"I know, sweetie, I don't like them either," said Mary Frances.

"Do you shoot guns like Aunt Dagny?" asked Hannah.

"No, I'm afraid not," answered Mary Frances. "I've never shot a gun, and it probably wouldn't be safe for me to do that. We're going to leave the guns to the men and Aunt Dagny. You and I are going to concentrate on the kitchen."

Mary Frances showed Hannah spices, letting her smell the various fragrances. "Hannah, it's amazing what happens when different spices are used on foods." Remembering the food in the refrigerator, Mary Frances said, "Hannah, let's sear some steaks tonight and then finish them in the oven in tarragon butter!"

"I like steak," said Hannah. "What's tarragon butter, Mommy?"

"I'm going to teach you how to make it right now," Mary Frances said. Mary Frances' heart was full as she taught Hannah how to cook and watched her daughter delight in it.

Later that evening, the family had a fabulous dinner of New York strip steaks finished in the tarragon butter Hannah made. Together, the mother and daughter made hollandaise sauce for the asparagus and some blueberry tarts for dessert. Hannah was very proud of her accomplishments as everyone bragged on the meal.

When dessert was finished, Matt said, "We leave day after tomorrow. We'll pack then leave Tuesday morning. I had hoped for some rainy weather, but there's no rain in the forecast for weeks. Maybe we can make it all the way by Saturday or Sunday. I'll need everyone's cellphones; we'll be leaving them here." Listening carefully, each one thought about what was about to happen and wondered how long the family would be gone-weeks or months or years.

"Let's everyone get to bed early," Zander said. "Tomorrow will be a busy day. We have the lists of what we're taking, but we want to check, recheck, and pack. All we'll have to do Tuesday is leave."

As they lay in bed, Mary Frances snuggled close to Matt. "It's so strange. If it wasn't for TV, we wouldn't know about the rioting and looting. It's peaceful here. The day Lynn Hanson returned to Veritas has been the only exception."

"We're insulated from it because we work in a nice, affluent suburb. Also, historically, Nashville hasn't had the problems many other cities have. Then, consider where this cabin is located. It's away from the city and people. It would be easy to not realize what's going on," Matt said.

"Do we really need to go?" asked Mary Frances. "I love our life, and Hannah is doing so well. She's so happy."

"I understand," said Matt, caressing Mary Frances' cheek. "But if it unfolds as predicted, people in cities will start pouring into the suburbs soon. Remember the Endex. Life will become brutal as hungry and thirsty people swarm across the landscape, looking for anything to eat and drink. By then, travel may become difficult, if not impossible. It's imperative we be in Arcadia before it gets to that point."

"Of course, you're right," she said. "I'm just wishing..."

"I'm not sure how our life will be in Arcadia," Matt said. "My hope is that we not only survive but thrive. I believe we can be happy and that our time there will be more than just getting by." Matt paused, then added, "Someday, when it's safe, I hope we can come back." Mary Frances hugged her husband. Reaching over, Matt turned off the lights.

Chapter 35
The Journey

Tuesday morning at 9:00 a.m., the journey began. Matt in the driver's seat, Zander in the copilot's seat, and Mary Frances, Dagny, Sam and Hannah in the back. The cargo area was packed with MRE's, military *meals ready to eat,* that required no refrigeration, bottled water, first aid kit, extra clothing and packs. On top, hidden under a blanket were the SAW, FAL, and an AR-15 while the Rattler was up front under Zander's feet. As the blue Range Rover pulled out of the garage and onto the driveway, Hannah said, "Don't forget to close the garage door, Daddy."

"I will shortly, Hannah," he replied. As they drove in front of the house, Mary Frances saw the sign on the front door that said ***Caution!*** *House is rigged with multiple booby traps. Nothing inside is worth dying for.* ***DO NOT*** *attempt to enter.* Matt saw his wife reading the sign as he looked in the rear-view mirror. "It may not work, but it's worth a try," he said.

When the Range Rover got to the road, Matt stopped and got out. "This will just take a few minutes," he said. Matt picked up a chainsaw he had placed by the side of the drive and walked back toward the cabin. Starting the chainsaw, he quickly dropped three trees across the drive. Then, he carried the chainsaw back to the cabin, set it inside and pushed the button that closed the garage door. Returning to the SUV, Matt had to make his way through the woods to get around the barricade he'd made by cutting down the trees. *Someone is going to have to do some work to get a vehicle in here,* he thought.

As Matt got back in the Range Rover, there was silence. Surprised at first by the sound of the chainsaw, the group quickly understood what Matt had done. "I closed the garage door, Hannah," Matt said. Mary Frances took Hannah's hand and smiled as they pulled out onto the road that would take them to safety.

"Things seemed relatively peaceful on the news this morning," said Matt. "We could use the interstates, but we're going to take the scenic route instead. Should we need to turn around, it will be easier."

"Uncle Matt," asked Sam, "is this truck a diesel?"

"It is Sam," answered Matt.

"Do you like it?" asked Sam.

"I do," Matt answered. "It gets great mileage, around 30 miles per gallon. It's also very fast, not to mention that diesel doesn't explode like gasoline does. So, it's much safer."

"Why aren't there more diesel cars?" asked Sam.

"Diesel engines are more expensive than gasoline engines," Matt said. "That makes the price of a vehicle more. But because of the mileage and the fact that diesel engines have a much longer life, I think the extra cost is worth it."

They headed north into Nashville, staying off Interstate 65. "I'll feel better when the city is behind us, and we're in the country," said Matt.

"Matt, what is that smoke?" asked Mary Frances, pointing north of the Cumberland River.

"That doesn't look good," said Matt. "Zander, turn on the radio, and scan the stations for any news. I'm changing course. Let's take a different route. We'll head west toward Waverly. Zander tuned the radio to a local station which gave reports of multiple fires in northern Nashville. They continued west for another 30 minutes, leaving the city and the fires behind.

The family stopped in Linden for Hannah to use the bathroom. Matt bought fuel even though the SUV had the range to reach their destination. He and Zander had decided to buy fuel anytime it was available, even if the tank would only hold a few gallons. Shortly thereafter, they drove over the Tennessee River bridge and then angled north and west. Crossing the Tennessee-Kentucky state line was, thankfully, uneventful.

"When is lunch?" asked Sam. "I'm getting hungry."

"Pretty soon," said Zander. "We had to change our route. Next big town is Mayfield. What do you think, Matt?"

"Sounds good to me," Matt said. "It's just a few miles ahead. Kids, get your shoes on. You, too, Dagny."

"I resemble that remark," laughed Dagny, searching the floorboard for her shoes.

The parking lot at the Catfish Corner in Mayfield, Kentucky, was packed. "This looks like a popular place," said Mary Frances.

"I'll let y'all out at the door. You can find us a table while Zander and I find a place to park," said Matt. The women and children gladly got out of the back seat, eager to stretch their legs after the morning drive.

"Zander, we need to talk privately," Matt said, slowly driving through the lot looking for an empty spot to park.

"How is this change of route going to affect our plans?" Zander asked.

"I'm not completely sure, Zander," answered Matt, "Our destination is Missouri. I'm afraid we may not be able to get out of Kentucky because of the Ohio and Mississippi Rivers. If the governors close the bridges, we're screwed. But there is a ferry at Hickman, Kentucky. I want to cross there. Do you know the area?"

"I'm familiar with the area, but I didn't know about a ferry. It sounds like a good idea," said Zander. "If we can cross there, where are we going in Missouri?"

"We're headed west into the Mark Twain National Forest. Arcadia is west of West Plains. It's in the middle of nowhere," Matt explained.

During lunch, Matt and Zander listened carefully to overhear the conversations between other customers. Some were talking about fires in Memphis and Nashville. One table was discussing governors closing state borders.

Matt and Zander approached that table and introduced themselves. “Sorry, but we overheard you talking about closing states,” Matt began. “We’re traveling, and that might be a problem for us. Can you tell us what you’ve heard?”

“Sure,” said one of the men. “I heard that Ohio and Pennsylvania have done it this morning. It’s just cars and trucks, you know, people. They’re letting the semis through. I don’t know about other states.”

“Did they say why states are closing their borders?” asked Matt.

“Yeah, it seems lots of people are trying to leave. You know how it is in the cities, all the rioting and fires. Then the poison water thing. Some people are starting to leave the cities. The governors don’t want a bunch of refugees to take care of. There’s talk that this thing is going to get bad,” said the man.

“There’s no word of Tennessee, Kentucky, Illinois or Missouri closing their borders, is there?” asked Zander.

“Not that I’ve heard,” the man said. “It would be pretty hard to enforce where the border is a land border. But for states divided by big rivers, all it takes is blocking the bridges.”

“Thanks,” Matt said. “We appreciate the information.”

The six from Nashville loaded back in the Range Rover and got back on the highway. “We left one day late,” said Matt to the women. “Zander and I have had to rethink our route

“What we learned in the diner confirms our suspicions,” said Zander. The passengers in the back listened, silently.

“OK, here’s what’s happening. States are starting to exercise control over their borders,” Matt said. “We passed through from Tennessee to Kentucky with no problem. Maybe that’s because Kentucky hasn’t closed borders yet, or maybe it’s because we crossed over on a secondary highway out in the country. Roadblocks could be going up on Interstate 24 as we speak. I’m betting that within 24 hours most states will restrict travel. We were going to travel north and cross over the tip of Illinois at Cairo then immediately cross into Missouri.

“But those two bridges could be closed by the time we get there,” interjected Zander.

“We could double back and take the Dyersburg bridge

that would get us in Missouri quicker, but that means going back to Tennessee," Matt reasoned aloud. "Tennessee may not let us back in, and the Dyersburg bridge could very well be blocked."

"Matt, can you tell us where we're going?" asked Mary Frances from the backseat. "I'm confused. Where is Arcadia?"

"It's in Missouri," Matt answered. "It's in the Mark Twain National Forest."

"Interesting," Zander said. "Why Missouri, why the Mark Twain National Forest?"

"First reason was size," said Matt. "The Mark Twain National Forest is 3 million acres. It's huge. Second was water. Lots of springs and streams. Third was low population density. I found 100 acres that was surrounded by national forest with a great spring and a beautiful trout stream. The land was far enough away from people that the smoke from our chimney wouldn't be seen."

"But how are we going to get across the Mississippi River?" asked Dagny.

"We're headed to the ferry at Hickman, Kentucky," Matt explained. "The governors might shut that down, too, but perhaps the ferry captain could be persuaded to take us across."

"How would we get him to do that?" asked Dagny.

"Offer a financial incentive," said Matt. "Make it worth his while. On the other side is Missouri, the Bootheel. Once we're in Missouri, there are no more state borders to cross. Then, it's north and west to Arcadia."

After driving another hour, the family arrived in Hickman and easily found the ferry dock. There was a *CLOSED* sign on the chain across the ferry's ramp. At first, it appeared that the ferry was tied up and the crew had gone home, but then Zander noticed the faint plume of diesel smoke coming out of the smokestack. As Matt got out of the vehicle and approached the ferry, he spotted the silhouettes of two men in the pilothouse. Stepping over the chain and the *CLOSED* sign, Matt walked onto the boat.

"Ferry's closed," called a voice from the pilothouse window.

"That's what I heard," said Matt. "Is it Kentucky or Missouri that's doing it?"

The two men disappeared from the window, then emerged on the walkway around the pilothouse and took the steps down to Matt.

"Jim Davis. This is my deckhand, Frank," said the captain of the ferry, extending his hand to Matt.

"I'm Matt Archer," replied Matt. "Nice to meet y'all."

"It's both states," said the captain. "We've received calls from Frankfurt and Jeff City to cease operations. We just got the Missouri call. The Kentucky call an hour before that. There are people who work over on the Missouri side. They're going to be separated from their families if we don't go get them. We know these people. They're our friends and neighbors. I understand what the governors are trying to do, but this is ridiculous. Several guys from Hickman work at a factory over in Missouri. Their shift is over at midnight. They'll be waiting for us."

"What are you going to do?" asked Matt.

"I'm not leaving my friends in Missouri. Those governors will never know if I make a few runs back and forth across this river. Screw 'em. Hell, they don't even know where Hickman, Kentucky, is," said the captain.

"Captain, I have a problem, and you can help me, if you would," said Matt. "My family and I are from Tennessee. We have property out in the woods in Missouri. We left Nashville this morning to go there. I understand the governors are doing this because they're afraid of ending up with thousands of refugees. But that's not us. We have a place to go. We just need to get to it. If we'd have left yesterday.... But now, we've hit this problem. Captain, could you give us a ride over to the Missouri side when you go over to pick up those men?"

"One vehicle?" asked the captain.

"One SUV, and there are six of us. Two men, our wives, and two children," Matt said.

The captain looked at Matt then over to Frank and then back to Matt. Nodding his head, the captain said, "Be here, ready to load at midnight."

When Matt returned to the SUV, Mary Frances asked anxiously, "What did he say, Matt?"

"He's going to take us. We leave at midnight," Matt

answered. Mary Frances' and Dagny's eyes met with a look that said, *Our prayers have been answered* and gave each other a hug.

"Let's check into a motel for a few hours' rest before midnight," said Mary Frances.

They checked into two rooms in the Quality Inn. "We didn't make it as far as I'd hoped," Matt told the group as they settled into the adjoining rooms. "I thought we'd be there today and start hiking tomorrow, but we'll just have to adapt. Let's rest. Take a nap, sleep if you can. Zander and I will check the TV to see what's happening."

What they saw was worse than anticipated. The TV news anchor reported, "Across the nation in almost every major city, fires, rioting and looting have broken out. Governors in the lower 48 have activated their National Guard units to restore order. With just a few exceptions, the mayors of the major cities have declared a curfew and martial law." In the background were videos of fires and looting while the names of the cities scrolled across the bottom of the screen.

The anchor continued, "Traffic in the cities is starting to look like a continual rush hour as many citizens appear to be fleeing, apparently to get away from the violence and danger. In response, the governors of 23 states have closed their borders to incoming travelers. For Tennessee and the surrounding states of Kentucky, Missouri, Arkansas, Alabama, Georgia, North Carolina and West Virginia, borders are closed. Only Mississippi hasn't closed its borders yet. Anyone attempting travel beyond your state will more than likely be met with a situation like this."

The screen changed to a man talking to a Kentucky State Trooper. Behind them was a large, blue, *Welcome to Kentucky* sign. The caption on the video read *Interstate 24 at the Tennessee/ Kentucky border*. The State Trooper was directing the traveler to turn back because the governor had closed the state. As the man walked away from the trooper and passed in front of the camera, he said, "This is illegal! They can't do this. I can drive anywhere I damn well please! They've not heard the end of this. I'm calling my lawyer!"

Turning off the TV, Matt and Zander returned to the

adjoining motel room.

Hannah was sound asleep, holding her bear, while Sam was wide awake. Mary Frances and Dagny were lying on the other bed, talking softly. “God is looking after us today, guys,” said Matt. “This ferry is an answer to prayer. Let’s set multiple alarms tonight. We can’t miss this boat. It could be the last one for a very long time.”

Chapter 36
Missouri

Though multiple alarms had been set, none rang. Unable to sleep, the men were up and ready long before the alarms were to sound. They had silenced the alarms to let the children sleep. They awakened Mary Frances and Dagny a half an hour before midnight. Sam shuffled to the SUV, rubbing his eyes, as Matt carried Hannah. She never stirred. Zander checked the rooms to make sure nothing was left behind. The night air was cool and crisp, feeling more like fall than summer. When Matt pushed the start button, the Range Rover sprang to life. Matt double-checked the gauges; the fuel tank was completely full.

Driving through the small town toward the river, no other vehicles were on the street. The only motion Matt noticed was a cat darting into some bushes. At the Mississippi River, the ferry was waiting as planned. Without stopping, they drove onto the ferry as Frank waved them aboard. Frank secured the chain behind them, and Matt killed the engine and set the parking brake. "Stay inside," said Matt. Stepping out of the SUV, he crossed the steel deck and approached Frank. "We appreciate this very much, Frank," Matt said. "I've got a little something here for you." Matt handed him a roll of bills, $1,000.

"Well, you didn't have to do that, but thanks," said Frank, pleasantly surprised.

"I'm very grateful for your help," Matt said. "Can I run up to the pilot house for a second? I want to thank Jim." Frank nodded as he threw off the hawsers that held the ferry to the dock. The diesel engine increased RPM; the ferry, with only one vehicle aboard, started across the dark water.

Matt climbed the stairs to the pilothouse. The sliding, side windows were open, and the captain was at the wheel, steering the vessel across the Mississippi. He had done it so many times that it appeared effortless, even though he was compensating for wind and current. His course would be perfect, delivering them to the Missouri side without incident.

"Captain," Matt said. "My family and I are indebted to you."

"Glad to help you and your crew," said the captain. "What's wrong with this world? They're burning down the cities. It's like everyone has gone crazy. I guess this means I'm out of a job since the ferry won't run any more. The guys I'm bringing back home will be out of a job when they can't get to work. What will become of us? At least my wife and I won't go hungry because we have a big garden and chickens. I'm really worried."

"Yes, I am, too. There's no telling how bad it will get before returning to normal. Hopefully, the ferry will only be closed a few weeks. Again, I'm very appreciative for your help. You're carrying my precious cargo," Matt said, pointing down to the SUV. "So, I have a little something for you; maybe it will help you and your wife get by in the days ahead." Matt took another roll of bills from his pocket, $3,000, and handed it to the captain.

"My goodness," said the captain. "You didn't have to do that, but thanks. We'll go to the store and buy some extra supplies with this. Good luck to you and your family. I hope you get where you're going safely, and we can all get through this."

Matt shook the captain's hand then returned to the Range Rover. A crescent moon hung in the dark sky as the ferry pushed through the slight chop on the river. The windows were down on the SUV, and Matt reached through the window and touched Hannah's hair where she lay asleep on Mary Frances' lap. Matt's eyes met his wife's, and, for a moment, the stress of the situation disappeared.

On the Missouri side, two cars and two pick-up trucks were waiting. Each vehicle held multiple people for a total of ten Kentucky men who worked in Missouri. Having heard about the state closures, the men had been concerned if they would have a way home. The ferry's red and white lights were a welcome sight as it made its way across from Kentucky. Frank lassoed the bollards, securing the ferry to the dock and dropping the chain on the deck. Matt started the Range Rover and drove off into the Missouri night.

Staying off interstates and keeping to less travelled roads, they drove through the darkness. No police were about, and there was almost no traffic. Heading west into the Ozark Mountains, the pancake-flat farmland of the Bootheel was left behind. Roads became more crooked and winding as the elevation increased. Flat, open country gave way to forest. In the back seat, Mary Frances, Dagny and the children slept, stirring briefly, then drifting back into sleep. Occasionally, there were bridges over white water rivers and Zander could see the rapids below in the moonlight as they passed over.

"We're getting closer," Matt whispered to Zander. "I'd say another 10 or 12 miles. Our sleep is off schedule, napping during the day, driving all night, so let's see how everyone is feeling. We could start the hike this morning, or we could rest all day, get a good night's sleep, and then start tomorrow."

"Sounds good," said Zander. "I'm good to go either way. My concern is for the girls and the kids. It looks like getting here may have been the hard part. We can take our time with the hike in."

The road had become progressively narrower until it became one lane with no stripes and no shoulder. Fortunately, no other cars were on the road. In the last 20 miles, the only signs of life had been a deer grazing and a possum who stood frozen in their headlights. The road, running parallel to a stream, made a sharp left to a concrete, dry ford crossing. Suddenly, a pick-up truck was in their path, blocking the ford. Gravel flew as Matt slammed on the brakes and skidded to a stop.

"Down, backseat, everyone on the floor!" shouted Matt as he scanned the road in front of him.

Two good ol' boys were standing on the concrete, dry ford, about an inch of water flowing over their boots and around the tires of the pick-up blocking their way. Both were wearing dirty jeans and wife beaters. Long hair and mangy beards along with a shotgun and pistol completed the picture. It wasn't deer season yet, and the pair had poached a deer and were gutting it on the tailgate. Matt reached up and hit the button to open the sunroof.

"They're armed, Zander," whispered Matt as the sunroof opened. "Get the Rattler. Roof's open if they start shooting. I'm backing up. I don't like the looks of them."

The headlights of the Range Rover temporarily blinded the two who were as surprised as the party in the SUV. Matt put the transmission in reverse. Watching the screen on the dash, he could look behind the vehicle without turning around. Slowly, he started to back up.

"Hey, asshole!" shouted the hillbilly with the pistol. "Where the hell do you think you're going? Stop!" Matt ignored the order and continued to back away. Zander, with the SIG Rattler at the ready, prepared to stand up in the seat and start firing if necessary. "I said, 'Stop!'" shouted the hillbilly while his buddy raised a shotgun. Zander jumped up, Rattler in hand, his waist even with the roof of the SUV.

Suddenly, a brilliant light blazed through the windshield. The pistol wielding hillbilly was aiming a marine spotlight at the SUV. All 1,300 Lumens lit up the interior of the Range Rover. Both Zander and Matt were blinded as the hillbillies started shooting.

Shielding his eyes with one hand, Matt focused on the backup cam. Gunning the accelerator, he backed up at high speed. As the Range Rover made it around the curve, Matt threw the steering wheel over hard while breaking, spinning the SUV around in the loose gravel. Throwing it into drive, he hit the gas and within seconds was up to 60 miles per hour. Adrenaline pumped through Matt's veins as he put distance between them and the attackers. By the time the hillbillies ran up to the curve in the road, the Range Rover was a faint, red taillight.

It was only then that Matt saw the windshield was shattered on the passenger side. "Is everybody in the back OK?" Matt shouted.

"Yes, I think so," shouted Dagny.

"Hannah and Sam are OK," said Mary Frances, her voice trembling. "Yes, I think we're all OK."

"Son of a bitch," growled Matt. "Damn hillbillies. They were spotlightin' deer, and we just happened to run across them. You OK, Zander?" There was silence from the copilot's seat. "Hey, Zander, are you OK?" Matt asked again.

With all the energy he could muster, Zander whispered, "I'm hit, Matt."

"Oh, my God, Zander!" screamed Dagny, jumping up and leaning over the front seat. Matt turned on the dome light as he drove, still trying to put distance between them and the hillbillies while Dagny tried to find out where Zander was hit. "It's his shoulder," she cried out.

"OK, everyone, do exactly as I say," said Matt. "We're not going to stop. I want to lose them. Mary Frances, get the first aid kit out of the back. Kids, sit down. Don't make a sound. Dagny, get his shirt off; you have to see the wound."

"Here's a flashlight, Mom," said Sam, trying to help.

Dagny tore the sleeve from Zander's shoulder. "I see it. Oh, God, he's bleeding."

"Mary Frances, find QuikClot Combat Gauze. Open it, and give it to Dagny," Matt directed. "Hang on, we're going to take a corner up here. We're still going to the same place. I'm just taking another route. Are you hangin' with us, Zander?"

"My shoulder feels like it was hit with a sledgehammer," Zander said.

"Here's the gauze, Dagny," Mary Frances said, handing the QuikClot to her friend.

"Dagny, put it on the wound and push," said Matt. "That should stop the bleeding. If you can, look behind his shoulder to see if the bullet came out."

"It's working," said Dagny. "It's stopping the bleeding." Dagny didn't realize it, but both her hands were covered in blood almost up to her elbows. Her right cheek was also streaked with blood.

"Look for an exit wound," Matt ordered. "Can you see

it?"

Sam kept pressure on the gauze while his mother carefully lifted Zander's shoulder and shined the flashlight. "I don't see anything on the back of his shoulder!" answered Dagny.

"That's what I needed to know," said Matt.

"How much further?" asked Mary Frances, anxiously.

"We've made it! There's the gate!" said Matt. "I'll jump out and unlock it. Sam, you lock it behind us. Be sure to put the padlock back through the chain and lock it. I'll drive around behind the berm. I want to get these lights off so we're not discovered."

Matt drove around a derelict farmhouse onto the back of the property. Sam locked the gate and ran, following the taillights of the Range Rover. The SUV disappeared around what appeared to be a hill. Parking quickly and out of sight, Matt ran to a camouflaged net hidden in the side of the hill. Pulling back the net, a garage door was revealed. Matt lifted the door to a spacious, concrete, two car garage. Matt drove the SUV inside and killed the engine.

"There're a couple of cots over in the corner, Sam," said Matt. "Get one out for your dad." Dagny and Mary Frances jumped out of the car to help Zander while Hannah sat terrified in the back seat.

"We're moving him over to the cot," Matt explained to the women while they opened Zander's door to help him out.

"Matt! Matt!" screamed Dagny.

"What's wrong?" asked Matt, trying to sound calm. "Don't yell. We don't want a passerby to hear."

"Zander's leg!" she cried, trying to be quiet. "There's another wound in his leg!"

Matt ran to the passenger door. Instantly, it registered that the bullet that came through the windshield wouldn't have hit Zander in the shoulder.

Zander was white as a sheet as Matt picked him up. Taking every bit of strength he had, Matt carried his friend to the cot. Zander was drifting in and out of consciousness. "Mary Frances, get his boots off him. Dagny, get scissors!" Matt ordered as everyone tried to help. Together, they cut Zander's pants off and found an entry wound and exit wound in his left thigh. "It's bleeding, but not terribly," said Matt. "Mary Frances, more QuikClot!"

"I think it missed the major artery because it's outside his femur," said Matt. "I don't want to put a tourniquet on him, but we have to stop this bleeding immediately. Sam, get blankets. They're over there. He's getting shocky on us."

Quickly, they were able to stop the bleeding from both wounds to his thigh. Covering Zander to keep him warm, they finally sat down exhausted. Looking out through the open, garage door, they saw light; it was morning. Scanning the room, Mary Frances panicked for a second as she'd forgotten about Hannah who wasn't in sight. Checking the back seat, she found Hannah quietly crying. Mary Frances held her closely, assuring her that Uncle Zander was going to be alright.

Catching his breath, Matt calculated their next move. "Sam, Hannah, I need you two to sit with Zander while I talk with your mothers. OK?" The two children pulled up folding chairs next to a sleeping Zander. Mary Frances, Matt and Dagny walked outside into the sunshine of the fall day.

"I'm not a doctor, but I know that bullet must come out of his shoulder. Otherwise, it will get infected for sure. I have some supplies here. I have lidocaine and syringes. I have hemostats and sutures. I've never done this, but I believe I can. Then, we must irrigate the wounds and put on antibiotic dressings. We must do that now. Next, we'll need antibiotics; the problem is they're at the cabin." Mary Frances and Dagny listened intently.

"After we get the bullet out and treat the wounds, then I need to go to the cabin and return as quickly as possible with the Levaquin. It will probably be two days before I can get back. That's not fast enough, but it's better than no antibiotic at all. Zander won't be able to move for several weeks at the very earliest. We will stay here for now and let him heal. The weather is good, and it's dry here in the garage if it rains. When he's able, we'll continue on to Arcadia." Matt watched the women to see if they were understanding or if they were too much in shock for his words to sink in. He couldn't tell if the women were fully aware of the gravity of the situation.

Matt wondered if Zander would make it. The wounds

were severe. This was completely beyond his medical ability. The antibiotics were two days away, providing Matt could cover 50 miles in that length of time. What was in Zander's favor was that he was 28 years old and strong.

"We should get started," Matt said. "Who can assist me?"

"I can," said Dagny, without hesitation.

"Sam, you take the SIG. You know how to use it. You stand guard. Hide behind the bushes up by the house. I doubt those guys from last night will find us, but I want you standing guard anyway. If you see them, come tell us." Sam nodded and left carrying the SIG.

"OK, let's get set up. It's important that everything is completely sterile. He's survived the gunshots. It's infection we're worried about now," Matt said as they began preparations.

Matt kneeled by Zander who barely opened his eyes when he felt Matt by his side. "Buddy," Matt said, "here's the plan. That bullet is coming out of your shoulder. We're going to numb you up real good, so it doesn't hurt too bad. Afterward, we'll dress it. Then, you'll just have to rest and heal and drink lots of water.

"A few hours after the bullet's out, we'll make you walk around to prevent blood clots in that leg. We've got plenty of MRE's so I want you to eat as soon as you feel hungry. We even have your favorite, Bar-B-Que." Zander managed a weak smile. "We're going to get you well," Matt said. "You can rest as long as you need."

"OK, buddy, sorry I got hit," Zander whispered, weakly. "I'm really messing up our schedule."

"No, you're not. We're fine here in the garage," said Matt. "It's fall, nice weather. Cool at night. Good sleeping. Your job is to rest. After we get you fixed up, I'm going to run up to the cabin and bring back some Levaquin for you, some antibiotics to help you get better quicker. I'll only be gone a short time. So, you and Sam can hold down the fort while I'm gone."

"Everything seems ready, Matt," said Dagny.

Zander smiled a faint smile and nodded, not opening his eyes. The area around the wound was disinfected. Matt filled a syringe from a vile of lidocaine and, pushing the needle in all around the bullet hole, numbed the wound. Mary Frances couldn't watch; she decided it best to take Hannah outside. Matt could hear them talking about bears outside the open garage door as he took the hemostat and pushed it down into the wound channel, prodding until he felt the bullet. Zander moaned as Matt tried to get ahold of the bullet, the lidocaine not completely stopping the pain. Finally, on the sixth try, Matt pulled out a .38-caliber projectile.

Matt and Dagny irrigated the wound that had started bleeding again from the prodding. Matt carefully removed the damaged tissue around the wound, then sewed up the hole with a number 2 suture. Finally, he dressed the wound with an antibiotic-impregnated dressing. "Dagny, you have to change this dressing every 8 hours. When I get back, we'll see how it's doing." Dagny nodded her understanding.

Then, Matt went to work on Zander's thigh. He repeated the process, minus the bullet extraction. Matt couldn't help but wonder where the bullet had ended up; probably lodged in the passenger seat of the Range Rover. The thigh wounds were irrigated with sterile saline solution. The damaged tissue was abraded, and sutures were put in place. Sterile, antibiotic dressing were applied just like on the shoulder. It was done. Matt was exhausted, having run on adrenaline for hours.

Having rested for 10 minutes, Matt gathered the family. "I have to get medicine for Zander. I'll be back tomorrow afternoon. Sam, close and lock the garage door tonight. Drape the camo net over it. I don't think most people would ever see the door. During the day, the door can be open, but I want you on guard duty. Dagny, you tend to Zander. Make sure he drinks a lot. Get him up three or four times a day. Watch the wounds after he walks. If they break open and start bleeding, you know how to stop it. Mary Frances, make sure everyone is fed. There's another cot in the corner so Dagny can sleep next to Zander. Mary Frances, you and the kids can sleep in the Range Rover. I'm just taking my pistol. I'm leaving the SIG with you, Sam."

Matt said his goodbyes and stood in the open garage door. It was noon. "Matt, you're so tired," said Mary Frances. "Shouldn't you rest first?"

Matt motioned her out of the garage away from the others.

"Mary Frances, I would love to rest, but I can't. I'm worried about Zander. He needs those antibiotics as quickly as I can get them. I'm trying to be positive for Dagny and Sam, but his wounds are serious. So, I'm going. I'll rest a few hours at the cabin, then come right back. At one time, I could have done this in two days. I'm not sure if I'm still that fast. But I'll be back as quick as I can. I hate to leave you and Hannah, but I'm the only one who can do this. You should be alright for a couple of days. I love you so much. I'll be back soon, and we'll all get to Arcadia."

Matt took off through the woods as Mary Frances watched him disappear into the trees. As he moved through the forest, driving himself to make four miles an hour, his mind calculated that by dark he might make 22 miles. He'd almost be there. He wondered how long he could keep up that pace through the woods. He hadn't slept in over 24 hours and was already exhausted.

Remembering a rock overhang that was about five miles from the cabin, he wondered if he could make it that far by dark. Matt bulldozed through the forest, finally reaching an old, fire trail that hadn't been used in years. Though overgrown, it was easier than pushing through the woods.

At the garage, Dagny watched Zander sleep. Mary Frances assessed the various MRE's. Later, she and Hannah walked out around the hill and found Sam sitting on a log behind some bushes, watching the gate. "Are you doing OK out here, Sam?" asked Mary Frances.

"Yes, Aunt Mary," Sam answered.

"I'll bring you some food in a little while," she said. Hannah stood by her mother, watching Sam with the SIG slung across his chest. Mary Frances watched her and thought, *How much trauma can these children endure?* As she and Hannah walked back to the garage, Mary Frances told her daughter they should stop and pray. Together, mother and daughter prayed for Zander to get well, prayed for Sam on guard duty, prayed for Dagny as she nursed Zander and for Matt as he hiked 50 miles through the wilderness to bring Zander medicine.

"Mommy, I've been asking God to help you and me, too," said Hannah. "Sometimes, I don't think I help very much. I want to. You make sure everyone has enough to eat. And Aunt Dagny is helping Uncle Zander. Daddy does all kinds of things. Sam is guarding. I wish I could do something."

"Oh, sweetie," said Mary Frances, hugging her daughter. "You do help. Your just being here helps me. And you're getting bigger every day. Very soon, you're going to be able to do all kinds of things to help." The two walked hand in hand back to the garage.

Together with Dagny, Mary Frances helped get Zander up and walked him around the garage. It wasn't easy because he weighed what the two women weighed together, but they did it. When they got him back in bed, Zander was hungry. Mary Frances and Hannah got busy preparing an MRE dinner. Mary Frances asked Hannah to take Zander's food to him. Then, she had Hannah take food to Sam.

Time crawled for the inhabitants of the garage as the hours of watching Zander, checking on Sam and preparing meals dragged on. Mary Frances did her best to keep Hannah occupied and distracted. When the sun started to set, Sam came inside after camouflaging the entrance and closing the door like Matt had told him. It was completely dark inside the garage, except for the flashlight. Sam knelt by his father's cot, feeling the need to be near his parents for a little while. It had been difficult to be alone all day. Mary Frances put down the rear seats in the Range Rover and spread a blanket for herself and the children. Dagny got in her cot next to Zander and switched off the flashlight.

Twenty miles away, an exhausted Matt collapsed on the sandy ground under a rock outcropping. He got out a meatball and marinara MRE and devoured it. Not even taking time to build a fire, he lay down in the sand and in 15 seconds was sound asleep.

Chapter 37
Alone

Matt never awakened until the sun came up. He climbed to his feet, aching all over from having slept on the ground. He started coughing. *Damn it, I can't get sick now,* he told himself. Knowing it was only three miles to the cabin, Matt found new strength and ran.

Reaching his first goal, Matt arrived at the cabin. *If only I could snap my fingers and magically transport everyone here,* he thought. He grabbed the Levaquin, some extra in case it was needed, three water bottles and a handful of candy bars. It was tempting to stop and rest, but the urgency of the situation demanded he keep going. Within 10 minutes, Matt was on his way back, eating a candy bar. The sugar gave him a burst of energy. Throughout the day, he kept his mind focused on only one thing... getting back to the family.

Zander woke several times in the night, crying out in pain. Dagny comforted him and felt his forehead for fever. Sleeping in the back of the SUV wasn't the best, but Mary Frances and the children were so tired they slept straight through the night. When morning came, Sam opened the garage door and all were surprised to see the sun. It was already 8:30. The new day began like the previous one had ended, with caring for Zander and Sam standing watch.

During the morning, Zander was awake from time to time and seemed to be improving. Dagny tended to his needs, seeing that he drank plenty of water, walked and ate a little. By afternoon, Zander's condition began to change. He started to show signs of fever and slept almost constantly. Dagny wiped his brow and chest with a wet cloth to cool him. *Hurry up, Matt, and get back here with the antibiotics!* pleaded Dagny, silently.

Watching Zander suffer was difficult for everyone. It was a blessing that Sam was outside standing guard and didn't have to witness it. When she wasn't preparing food, Mary Frances prayed, checked on Sam periodically and tried to keep her daughter busy. Around mid-afternoon, Hannah started asking where her father was and when he would be back. Mary Frances answered the best she could, but Hannah kept asking. Outside, around the hill and by the road, Sam vigilantly kept watch. While no one spoke of it, panic began to set in. With Matt gone and Zander unconscious, they all were worried.

Around 4:00 in the afternoon, Sam heard a vehicle pass by. Listening closely, it seemed to stop just past the farmhouse. Slowly, Sam made his way to the overgrown hedgerow that separated the road from what used to be the yard. Sam worked his way through an opening in the hedgerow and stopped in his tracks, seeing the pick-up parked on the side of the road. Though no one was in sight, obviously someone had just parked the truck. Sam climbed back through the hedges and emerged in time to see two men disappear around the old farmhouse, heading toward the hidden garage.

Mary Frances, Dagny and Hannah sat in the garage on folding lawn chairs, monitoring Zander for any change. Mary Frances was calculating distances and time in her head and wondering where Matt was when footsteps were heard outside the garage door. The three looked up; their hearts stopped at the appearance of two men in dirty, wife beaters and jeans. Both were armed.

"Well, well, well. What do we have us here?" laughed Darrell, the one with a pistol. "Hey, Cletus, it looks like I did hit him!"

Cletus laughed, exposing several missing teeth. "I told

you they wuz 'round here someplace," he said. "This here place is all built in under the ground."

Mary Frances, Dagny, and Hannah were paralyzed, their hearts pounding with terror.

"Well, girls, with your man out of commission, it looks like me and Darrell is gonna have us some fun," said Cletus.

"Cletus, I think they's sisters," said Darrell. "I'm likin' the one on the right. You can have that other one."

Dagny and Mary Frances almost became ill, realizing what the two men had in mind. Dagny looked to the corner where the guns were but determined she couldn't get to them before they shot her. Hannah moved closer to her mother.

"Bein' brothers, we likes to share. So's when we's done, we gonna swap 'em. We believe in sharin'," said Cletus.

"Amen!" Darrell chimed in.

"You're going to have to kill us first!" Dagny shouted at the men.

"Don't think so," said Darrell. "If you ain't cooperative... no, more than cooperative... If you ain't enthusiastic, we'll just do the little girl, too."

"And I'll shoot your old man," said Cletus. "Looks like he's about done for anyway. You got to shoot him yesterday, Darrell. My turn today." Both men laughed.

"Ready for some fun?" drooled Cletus. "I'm goin' first!"

Dagny and Mary Frances were completely helpless. The instinct was to fight back, but they couldn't bear Zander or Hannah to be harmed. Hannah started crying, and Mary Frances held her.

Cletus started for Mary Frances when two quick and deafening explosions filled the concrete room. Mary Frances gasped as the hillbilly's undershirt turned bright red, and he crumbled to the floor. She instinctively covered Hannah's eyes. Darrell turned toward his brother as two more explosions rocked the room; his chest disintegrated just like his brother's. Mary Frances screamed as the two writhed on the concrete floor, choking on their own blood. It was only then that they saw Sam standing just outside the garage, SIG Rattler in hand.

Dagny ran to Sam and hugged him as she cried. Mary

Frances held Hannah as they both sobbed. Dagny turned to the two dying on the concrete. Writhing in agony, gurgling sounds came from their throats as they choked on their own blood. Their long hair and dirty beards were blood soaked as they fought for every breath. Each lay in a pool of blood that grew bigger as the two pools connected. The smell of cordite hung in the air.

"My God, how long does it take for them to die?" cried Dagny. "Shoot the bastards again, Sam!"

"No, Mom. It's a waste of ammunition, and someone might hear more gunshots," said Sam. "Let them suffer."

Dagny stepped around the blood and to Mary Frances and Hannah, then guided them around the gruesome scene and on outside to Sam. "Take them to safety, Sam. If anyone heard the shots, more people might come. Go into the woods and hide. I'm going to get a rifle and stay by your father."

Sam led Mary Frances and Hannah to the tree line, and Dagny grabbed an AR-15. Pulling back the T-handle, she chambered a round. Sitting on the cot beside Zander, she held the rifle with her right hand while wiping her unconscious husband's brow with the left. At last, the two on the concrete were dead and still.

Only two miles away, Matt feared he'd heard gunshots. He wasn't sure. Matt's legs were screaming, but he resolved to go even faster. He'd done this before when he'd been in the Army. Ranger school taught him that there was always more deep down inside him. *You can always do more than what you think you can. Never stop. Never quit. Drive on.*

Sam had hidden Mary Frances and Hannah in a depression in the forest. A boulder on one side and a log on the other made them invisible to anyone who might be nearby. Sam lay close, behind the log. His position gave him a view through the trees to the garage door. His 10-year-old brain struggled with the responsibility of his situation. While formulating a plan to pull the two bodies from the garage, Sam heard footsteps in the woods behind him. His heart pounding, he made eye contact with Mary Frances and Hannah, then put a finger to his lips. Switching off the safety, he brought the SIG around and faced the footsteps. Sam aimed the holographic sights toward the sound of footsteps, keeping his finger off the trigger... but ready. Suddenly, Matt appeared in the sights. Sam raised the muzzle and switched the safety back on. “Uncle Matt!” he called out.

“Matt!” cried Mary Frances, jumping to her feet. She and Hannah ran to Matt and threw themselves against him, sobbing with relief and joy. Though he was wet with perspiration and his clothes were filthy, they didn’t notice. “Oh, Matt! Thank God, you’re back. It was terrible!” cried Mary Frances.

“What happened?” asked Matt, trying to figure out why they were in the woods and so upset.

“The two that shot my dad came back,” said Sam. “They were going to hurt Mom and Aunt Mary and Hannah. I killed them.”

Dumbfounded by what he’d just heard, Matt asked, “Is everybody OK? Where are Zander and Dagny?”

“Mom and Dad are in the garage,” said Sam. “We’re all OK.”

“Come on, let’s get this medicine in your dad,” Matt said as he led the group out of the trees and toward the garage.

“Matt!” cried Dagny. “You did it! Thank God!” Matt saw Dagny seated next to Zander, holding a rifle. Then, he saw the carnage on the concrete floor.

“You did this, Sam?” Matt asked in disbelief.

“Yes, sir,” answered Sam.

Matt was overwhelmed with emotion. Then, he took the boy in his arms and hugged him. Matt looked at Sam and asked, “Are you alright, Sam?”

“Yes, sir,” answered Sam. “I knew what to do. I didn’t have a choice.”

“How did they get here?” Matt asked, looking at the bodies on the concrete.

“In the truck. The same one as last night,” said Sam. “It’s parked out on the road.”

Matt took the Levaquin out of his pocket. “Here, Dagny. One pill every 12 hours, starting now. You all stay here while Sam and I move the truck off the road.” Then, stepping in the blood, Matt fished through the dead man’s pockets to find the keys to the truck.

Sam and Matt ran around the hill and to the gate. "Sam, close and lock this as soon as I get the truck in." Matt ran to the truck and drove it back through the gate; Sam locked it behind them. Back at the garage and out of sight from the road, Matt said, "Sam, you've got to help me drag those bodies out and get them in the truck."

"They were going to hurt my mother, and Aunt Mary, and Hannah. They were going to rape them. That's why I killed them," Sam explained.

Matt put his hands on Sam's shoulders and looked him straight in the eyes. "You did the right thing, Sam," he said. "I am forever in your debt. I should have been here to protect them, but I wasn't. You did it for me and your dad. Thank you." With a pensive smile, he nodded to his uncle. Sam knew he'd done the right thing, but it was reassuring to hear Matt say so.

"OK, Sam, let's see if we can drag this scum out. They're big. Lifting them into the bed of the truck will be difficult. We may have to use a ramp."

"There's some plywood in the garage. We could use that," Sam replied. Averting their eyes, the women and Hannah focused their attention on Zander while Matt and Sam dragged the corpses out of the garage. Both men were over 250 pounds and couldn't be lifted into the truck bed. Having to use a ramp, they eventually rolled the two bodies onto the truck; it was still difficult. Covering them with a tarp, Matt finally could rest.

"How's my buddy doing?" Matt asked, kneeling by his friend.

"I feel like hell," Zander answered weakly, his eyelids barely opening.

"He's been running a fever since yesterday," said Dagny.

"Is he drinking enough water?" Matt asked.

"Yes, I've seen to that. He's also been walking some. He doesn't like to, but I make him," said Dagny.

"Is he urinating?" asked Matt.

"Yes, I'm peeing, Matt," whispered Zander. Dagny looked at Matt and grinned. Matt chuckled.

"He's going to be fine," Matt said. "It's just going to take time. And we have plenty of that."

"Matt, you need to get some rest," said Mary Frances. "We have to keep you healthy. I can't believe you walked 50 miles in two days!"

"I can't either," said Matt. "I'd really like to take off these boots, and lie down. Sorry, I'm so dirty. I was only at the cabin for 10 minutes, no time for a bath. We're going to have to find some water around here."

"We'll worry about that later. Rest now," Mary Frances said, kissing her husband on the forehead.

"Mary Frances, I have to get rid of that truck and the bodies," said Matt. "Can you wake me up around midnight?"

"Oh, no! You can't leave us again!" cried Mary Frances.

"I have to," said Matt. "Their families will start looking for them. They can't be found here. About 10 miles away is a big cliff. I'm going to push the truck off that cliff. Chances are no one will ever find them. But just in case, there can't be any connection to us."

Hannah joined her parents, kneeling by her mother. "Don't leave again, Daddy. We're scared without you."

"I have to, Hannah," he answered. "But I'll be back tomorrow morning. Besides, Sam is here. He will take care of you." Hannah nodded.

"Daddy's right, Mommy," Hannah told her mother. "Sam is very brave, and he will protect us until Daddy gets back."

Before Hannah finished talking, Matt was sound asleep. Midnight seemed to arrive instantly as Mary Frances woke him. Shortly thereafter, he drove the pick-up with the two bodies out the gate with Sam locking it behind.

Thirty minutes later, Matt was at the cliff. He'd not seen a single car the entire night. Putting the truck in neutral and giving it a push, Matt jumped away from the pick-up as it rolled forward and over the edge. A few seconds later, Matt heard the crash as the truck hit solid ground at the foot of the cliff. Then, there was silence. Surrounded by darkness, Matt turned in all directions. Could anyone have heard the crash? He reminded himself that one reason he'd chosen the location was low population density. Hardly any people lived in the area. He concluded that no one had heard and that the way the world was going, no one would care about a couple of good ol' boys gone missing. Matt started walking. In a few hours, he would be back in a cot and sound asleep, too tired to care. *Only 20 miles tonight, and I got to drive 10 of it*! he thought, laughing aloud.

Chapter 38
Rest

Matt awoke to the sound of Sam talking... something about a mattress. At first, it seemed like a dream. Opening his eyes, Matt saw Mary Frances and Hannah working on dinner. Matt had slept all day. Dagny was in a lawn chair by Zander's cot, holding his hand. Matt caught the faint whiff of cleaning solution. Sitting up and swinging his legs over onto the floor, his bare feet felt the cold concrete. Scanning the garage, he noticed his SUV and then a large dark spot on the floor. Remembering what had happened the day before... or was it two days before? It appeared the blood was gone.

"Good morning, sunshine," said Mary Frances. "How do you feel?"

"Much better," Matt replied. "It's amazing what a little sleep can do for you. Looks like y'all have been busy."

"Yes," said Mary Frances, sitting by her husband. "Sam found an old well behind the house. With a rope and bucket, he started bringing us water. We scrubbed the floor."

"Good God, I need a bath," said Matt. "I never expected to be living in this garage, so I never planned for running water. Thank goodness, I stored some drinking water here."

"No, you don't smell very good," said Mary Frances, "but I'm so happy that you're back, I don't care."

"How's our boy, Zander, doing?" asked Matt, looking toward Dagny and her sleeping husband.

"Better, it seems," Dagny answered. "He's not as hot. The fever may have broken."

"That's good news," said Matt, looking to Mary Frances and stretching his aching body. "Where are the kids?"

"Sam took Hannah to the bathroom," said Dagny. "He takes her out in the woods and finds her a good place, then he walks away and turns his back."

"She doesn't like doing it in the woods. She says she's not a bear and would much prefer a human bathroom," Mary Frances laughed. "But she's adapting, as we all are."

"I think camping is fun," came a weak voice from Zander.

"Hey, you're awake," said Matt. "How are you feeling?"

"Better, I think," he answered softly. "I didn't have to pee until I heard y'all talking about it. Now, I've got to go." Carefully, Zander moved his feet to the floor and slowly sat up with Dagny's help.

"I'll go with you, buddy," said Matt. "I've got to use the facilities, too." Matt helped his friend to his feet. Zander put his good arm around Matt's shoulder, and slowly, they shuffled out of the garage into the cool, open air.

"Daddy!" cried Hannah as she and Sam came out of the woods. "You're awake!" she cried, hugging him.

"Uncle Matt, did you see what I got for you and Aunt Mary?" asked Sam.

"No, I didn't," answered Matt.

"It's a new mattress," said Sam. "Well, it's pretty old, but it's a mattress. I found it in the house. It's in the corner in the garage. You and Aunt Mary can sleep there. Mom and Dad have the two cots next to each other, and Hannah and I can sleep in the back of the Range Rover. I found some old burlap bags that I stuffed with moss for pillows, too."

"That's great, Sam," said Matt. "You are quite resourceful! We're going to stay put for awhile until your dad gets stronger. That will make sleeping a lot better!"

The family ate dinner together for the first time since the restaurant in Hickman, Kentucky, before taking the ferry across the Mississippi. To Mary Frances, it seemed months ago, not days. Then she thought back to her life in Tennessee, to working at Veritas, to meeting Matt. It seemed like that was decades ago, but it all had been in the past year. And now, here they were, somewhere in the Ozark Mountains of southern Missouri, living in a garage.

"Ready for a fine dining experience?" Mary Frances laughed as she read the description on the MRE package. "I've worked very hard on this chicken with egg noodles creation we are enjoying tonight."

"I like it, Mommy," said Hannah. "It's pretty good."

"Bar-B-Que is better," said Zander as they all laughed. The sun was starting to set, and the slight breeze brought crisp air in the garage.

"I'm going to make us a kitchen table tomorrow," said Sam. "On the back porch of the house, I saw some wood I could use. There are some old chairs, too."

"You're wonderful, Sam," said Dagny. "What would we do without you!" Hannah looked at Sam with admiration as did the others. Everything would have been completely different without him.

"That sounds great, Sam," said Matt. "Be careful. None of us can be running around by the road where someone passing by might notice. Fortunately, there are no close neighbors and very little traffic. People around here know this as an old abandoned farmhouse, and we want to keep it that way." Everyone nodded their heads in agreement as they continued eating.

"Y'all have done a great job of getting the garage cleaned up," Matt complimented the group. "Sam's found a mattress and a well. Tomorrow, we'll make this place more comfortable, and Sam has some good ideas for that. I have a question for everyone. Who would like to take a bath?" Joyous cries of agreement erupted.

"I've never been so dirty in my life!" said Mary Frances.

"And our clothes are terrible!" cried Dagny. "It's embarrassing!"

"But, Daddy, there's no bathroom!" said Hannah.

"I chose this area because of all the streams and springs. They're everywhere. There's one about half a mile through the woods. We could go there tomorrow afternoon, wash clothes and take a bath."

"That sounds wonderful, Matt!" said Mary Frances, and the rest agreed.

"There's just one thing," Matt said. "The water is cold. Most of these streams are spring-fed. That means the water is crystal clear and clean, but it also means *cold*."

"I don't care," said Dagny. "I want a bath!"

"Zander, you're not strong enough to walk that far yet," said Matt. "Not tomorrow, but soon. I don't want to leave you here alone, so we'll go in groups."

As they went to sleep that night, it felt good to look forward to the next day.

Cooler days and much cooler nights brought that feeling of fall, and the leaves started to turn. Soon, bright reds and brilliant golds began appearing in the green foliage. Having a fire would have been welcomed, but Matt vetoed it. A campfire could be seen or smelled; they couldn't risk being discovered.

Days turned into weeks as they lived in the garage while Zander recuperated. Mary Frances did the best she could with MRE food. Slowly, a routine was adopted that included a bath every other day. The family noticed that without a normal routine of work, school and church on Sunday, it was difficult to determine the day of the week. The days ran together.

There was plenty of time to discuss life at Arcadia and the jobs each would have. Matt assigned the job of timekeeper to Dagny. She was to maintain the calendar, notifying everyone of upcoming holidays, birthdays and celebrations. She had started that job at the garage and announced one evening at dinner that they were nearing the end of October. They had been in the garage for six weeks.

Life wasn't easy in the garage. A 25-mile hike sounded more appealing everyday as they looked forward to life in Arcadia. Each afternoon Hannah would ask about the cabin, and as Matt would describe it, everyone listened. "Daddy, is there a real bathroom in Arcadia?" she asked. "I don't like going in the woods like a bear." Everyone laughed and agreed with Hannah's assessment.

"Yes, there are three bathrooms in the cabin," Matt said.

"I'm not sure why I did it that way. I had no idea there would be six of us when I built the cabin; it felt right. Now, I'm glad I built it that way."

"We are, too," laughed Dagny. "With three girls and one bathroom, the guys would still be going out in the woods with the bears!"

"Maybe... maybe not, Dagny," kidded Matt. "My cabin, my rules. So, as I was saying, there are three bedrooms with three adjoining bathrooms. The two, downstairs bedrooms have fireplaces. The one upstairs is the bunkroom. It's really cool because it's up in the loft. That's where you and Sam will sleep, Hannah. It has a bathroom with a shower."

"No bathtub?" asked Hannah. "I like bubble baths."

"We have a tub in our bathroom, Hannah," explained Matt. "You can use it anytime. And I know how much everyone loves ice-cold baths, but there's also hot water when I make it."

"How's that work, Uncle Matt?" asked Sam.

"To make hot water, I build a fire in the water heater. We'll need to find a time that works for all of us, so we bathe every day at the same time when the water's hot. Kids, you must be careful with the hot water because it's hotter than you're used to, and you could easily burn yourself. Don't just turn on the shower and jump in. Adjust it carefully."

"Are the toilets regular toilets?" asked Hannah.

"They are, and we have running water from the spring that's up the hill from the cabin. The water runs all the time, and you may use as much water as you like. But, toilet paper is another issue. We must not waste toilet paper. Hannah, I'm talking to you. A lot of toilet paper is stored at Arcadia. It may look like a lot, but we don't know how long we'll be there. We must conserve. But if we must, I have several thousand, Yellow Pages phone books that make pretty good toilet paper although that's not flushable."

"Yellow Pages phone books?" questioned Sam. "What's that?"

"A long time ago before we googled everything, we looked up phone numbers in books," explained Matt. "The pages make good toilet paper, especially when you don't have the real thing.

Should we use up the phone books and toilet paper, then we're looking at gathering moss."

"Ew!" exclaimed Hannah in surprise.

"That's right, Hannah. Let's not be wasteful," Matt said. "I understand that women use more toilet paper than men, but we can't go to the store to buy more."

"What do you mean?" asked Hannah. "Why do girls use more toilet paper than boys?"

Looking at his daughter with complete seriousness, Matt was at a loss for words. "You will need to talk to your mother about this," he said, having been caught off guard by the question. Then, turning to Mary Frances, he added, "Your mother will explain it to you." Mary Frances eyes widened as Dagny chuckled.

One day Mary Frances asked a question about the kitchen. "There are two, the inside kitchen and the outside," Matt explained. "The inside kitchen has a wood-fired cook stove, oven, and its own built-in water heater. It has running water. I installed a Norcold refrigerator that runs on 12 volts. It will take some experimenting with our electrical usage. All the lights are LED, and I've tried to conserve in every way possible. Plus, we have a steam engine, water turbine, and solar panels to make our own electricity. With the size of the battery bank, I think we can use the fridge 24/7. I also put in ceiling fans because I like sleeping with the breeze. But back to the kitchen, I hope you like it, Mary Frances. I hope you'll be able to continue your fantastic cooking." Mary Frances smiled at her husband and then patted Hannah's hand. "Then there's the outdoor kitchen," Matt continued. "It's attached to the house in the back, kind of like a screened-in porch that's part kitchen, part living room. There's another cook stove outside, and another kitchen table with six chairs. Because it's hot in the summer, we won't want to heat up the cabin with the cook stove. People used to have summer kitchens for that very reason."

"Is there heat and air-conditioning, Uncle Matt?" asked Sam.

"The heat for winter comes from the cook stove in the kitchen, the wood burner in the great room, and the bedroom fireplaces. There isn't regular air- conditioning like you're used to, but I did build in a series of ductwork below the basement floor. No compressor like in regular air-conditioning because that would use more electricity than we have. A blower pushes air through the buried ductwork to cool it, then through the cabin. I also have a couple of dehumidifiers to bring down the humidity. Between the ceiling fans, my version of air-conditioning and moving the cooking outside, I think we'll be comfortable."

Zander continued to get stronger and could hike to the stream for a bath without assistance. Matt kept focus on the weather. One night at dinner, Matt said, "What do you think, Zander? Do you feel strong enough?"

"Yeah, I'm ready, Matt," answered Zander. "We don't have to do the entire 25 miles in one day."

"That's right," said Matt. "We could do it in three or four days. But, we're in November now. Sometime this month we're going to get a solid week of rain, and then it's going to get cold. I want to get us to Arcadia soon. I also want to get there to find out what's going on in the world. There's no cell reception here. There's no radio reception. We've been out of touch for six weeks. Let's pack tomorrow and leave the next day." Everyone agreed. The sense of anticipation changed everyone's mood as they looked forward to finally getting to their destination. They were ready.

That night as the lights were turned off and everyone drifted off to sleep, Dagny held Zander's hand as they lay on the cots together. In the back of the Range Rover, Hannah scooted over next to Sam. Not saying a word, she was aware of the warmth of his body and the sense of safety being next to him. Mary Frances lay in her favorite position, her head resting on Matt's chest with his arm around her. Matt put his lips next to her ear and whispered softly, "In a few days, we'll have our own bedroom again." Mary Frances squeezed her husband and snuggled even closer.

Chapter 39
The Hike

Matt led the way, setting a slower pace for the benefit of both Zander and Hannah. He kept a watchful eye to see how well they were holding up as the miles ticked off. The group remained quiet, even though it was doubtful anyone was in the area. Matt walked point because he knew the way. He made Sam rear guard and explained how Sam's job was to stop from time to time while the group moved on ahead, waiting to make sure no one was following. Mary Frances, Dagny, Hannah and Zander were in the middle. Matt carried an AR. He let Sam keep the SIG because he was obviously very proficient with it. The other weapons were left at the garage to be retrieved another time.

The autumn leaves had completely turned two weeks before and were now falling rapidly. Every puff of wind brought another wave of dry, brown leaves from above. Walking quietly was almost an impossibility. But the sound of feet swishing through the leaves wasn't the only thing making noise.

Hannah kept lagging behind to walk at the rear with Sam. She also wanted to talk. Finally, Matt allowed it. Being with Sam and talking to him distracted Hannah from focusing on the miles. Zander moved slowly but steadily. Each time Matt checked, he'd nod that he was OK.

Stopping for lunch beside a stream, Matt said, "I wish I

had my fly rod. I'd catch some trout, Mary Frances. You could make us trout almondine for dinner tonight."

"Soon, Matt. When we get there, you can bring me trout any time," she said. "I know at least a dozen ways to prepare trout."

"Nothing against MRE's," said Dagny, "but trout almondine makes my mouth water."

It was around 4:00 in the afternoon when Matt stopped the family for a short rest. "I'd like to make an announcement," he said. "Y'all have done a great job today, far better than I'd anticipated. Just over that ridge is the basecamp. That's halfway. We've covered 12 miles today." Later, Matt wondered if he should have waited to tell them because Hannah started to think about how far she'd walked, and there was some complaining on the last mile. Soon enough, they arrived at the wilderness basecamp Matt had built several years prior in preparation for just such a time.

"Cool! This is like a little fort!" exclaimed Sam. There were two lean-tos made between three trees. The lean-tos were at a 90-degree angle to each other, forming two sides of a square. An L-shaped wall completed the other two sides of the square. A gate made of small saplings was the entrance. A center circle of stones made the fire pit for warmth and cooking. Inside the lean-tos were log beds, roughly queen size, that were elevated about a foot off the ground. Also inside was firewood, already cut and dry.

"Zander, lie down and rest. Hannah, lie down with Uncle Zander and help him rest. Sam, you can help me get a fire going. I'll show you how to use a ferro rod. Mary Frances and Dagny, you can start on dinner," Matt said, opening the door to the stockade as everyone filed into the basecamp.

"Nice basecamp, Matt," said Zander.

"This will be good," said Mary Frances.

"And the fort will keep the bears out," said Hannah.

Soon, the fire was going, and dinner was ready. Matt prayed thanking God for the MRE dinner and for the impressive distance they'd covered. After dinner, Matt and Mary Frances walked outside the camp and found a rock outcropping in the forest where they had a view above a wooded valley. The air was getting quite cool as the sun was setting, and Matt put his arm around Mary Frances.

"We did great today," Matt said. "Hannah did very well. I'm surprised actually."

"I think the key is letting her talk," said Mary Frances. "And she likes to talk to Sam. It's interesting to watch. He just listens."

"He does. He's so protective of her," said Matt. "Do you think it's OK to put them in the same bedroom at the cabin? They're young, not old enough for us to worry."

"I think it's OK for now," Mary Frances said. "But someday we may have to separate them, if they'll let us."

Matt smiled then continued, "Mary Frances, I'm so pleased with how well we're working together as a group. The unit cohesion is impressive."

"Unit cohesion?" asked Mary Frances, skeptically. "Do you mean that we all get along well, help each other and don't fight?"

"Exactly," said Matt. "I was concerned about that when we decided to include Zander and Dagny, but they're great. Even the kids fit right in. That Sam is quite the young man."

"After that day in the garage when you were gone... we all have tremendous respect for Sam," said Mary Frances, quietly.

"And then there's you and me," said Matt. "We don't seem to get aggravated at each other at all, much less fight."

"You've never done anything to upset me," said Mary Frances. "And if you ever do, I've already forgiven you." Matt considered his wife's words.

"I don't know what to say," said Matt, seriously. "I know I get bossy and order you around sometimes."

"You do, but that's OK," she said. "You do it because you love me. I remember when you rescued me in the blizzard. Soon, that will be one year ago. You were a little bossy. 'Get in the car! Where are your boots? I'm taking you home with me!' I was more scared than angry. But, I quickly understood you were just trying to help me. Honestly, I never get mad at you."

"How in the world did I get so lucky?" asked Matt.

"I don't think it's luck," said Mary Frances. "I believe God made us for each other."

Matt hugged his wife, and then kissed her. Together, they slowly returned to the basecamp.

Zander and Dagny were talking to Sam. Zander was commending him on the job he'd done that day. "You did well on read guard, Sam. Remember to keep your muzzle down at a 45-degree angle. Always listen behind you."

Then the conversation moved to their last name, Fromm. "Sam, our last name is German. It means honorable, capable and trustworthy. You have been all those things. We're very proud of you."

Sam nodded. "Thank you," he said. "I think about my parents... my parents before you. I miss them, but I know I'm lucky you came to the armory that day. So is Hannah."

"Someday, Sam, when you're ready, we'd like to hear about your parents," said Dagny. "Maybe that will happen this winter when we're sitting around the fire, talking."

About that time, Matt and Mary Frances opened the gate to the stockade. Matt threw some more wood on the fire as Mary Frances said, "Time for bed, Hannah. You're sleeping between Daddy and me tonight." Hannah got up from Zander's and Dagny's bed where she'd been sitting with Sam. She smiled at Sam as if to say, *I'll be right here close to you.* Soon, everyone was under blankets, grateful to be done for the day with a roof over their heads. Each secure in their own thoughts and prayers as the fire crackled, warming the occupants inside the lean-tos.

Only a spiral of smoke rose from the ashes of the fire as the first light of morning made its way into the dense forest. Matt slipped out of bed, careful not to wake Mary Frances and Hannah. Using the ferro rod, he had the fire going again in just a few minutes. He saw his own breath while working on the fire, calculating the temperature had dropped into the 30's. Leaving everyone to sleep, Matt walked back to the rocky point where he and Mary Frances had stood the night before. Low, gray clouds covered the sky from horizon to horizon. Immediately, Matt sensed rain.

Everyone was huddled around the fire when Matt returned. "I walked out to the point," he said. "It looks like rain. Let's get packed up and on our way. There are several rock bluffs between here and Arcadia. If it starts raining, we can take shelter under one of the rock outcroppings."

"Dang, it's cold this morning!" Dagny declared.

"I was thinking the same thing," replied Mary Frances, rubbing her hands together.

"It's November," Matt said. "So, it's time for it to get cold. That's why we want to get to the cabin... before it starts snowing! We're farther north than Nashville. And there's elevation here. We're going to get colder weather than we're used to."

Soon, the family was back on the trail in the same configuration as the previous day. Hannah and Sam were bringing up the rear. Zander and Dagny were in the middle. And Mary Frances had moved up behind Matt.

"Like mother, like daughter?" laughed Matt as Mary Frances started asking him questions about Arcadia. Mary Frances stuck her tongue out at Matt, realizing she'd done the very thing that Hannah had done. Matt laughed even more.

The group made good time until the wind picked up around 11:00. The branches high in the trees bent and swayed under fast-moving air. Looking up, fine drops of rain began to hit their faces.

"Let's go! There's a cliff up ahead!" Matt shouted to those behind him. Just as it started to rain harder, they made it to the rock overhang of the cliff where a boulder provided more refuge from the wind and rain.

"Sam, come with me. Let's drag some downed wood under cover before it gets wet. Everyone else, stay here and stay dry," Matt ordered. "Leave the SIG here, Sam. No need to get it wet if we don't have to." The heavy rain held off about 10 minutes, just enough time for them to drag some firewood into the dry. Then, the rain started coming down in earnest.

"Why do you like the ferro rod, Uncle Matt?" asked Sam as they worked on getting a fire going. "Why not use matches?"

"I can start thousands of fires with this one rod; it doesn't matter if it gets wet because it's a lot hotter than a match. Especially on a damp day like this, a ferro rod is better," Matt said. Soon, the fire was burning brightly. Matt and Sam rolled six, large rocks around the fire and made everyone a seat. They all sat around the fire warming their hands as the rain fell outside the natural shelter. Thanks to the boulder, they had a good windbreak and were somewhat protected from the storm.

"Well, girls and boys, we may be done for today," said Matt. "This feels like it may do this for hours. How are you feeling, Zander?"

"I'm doing OK, Matt," said Zander. "My shoulder is feeling pretty good. My leg hurts. I guess it's because of the walking."

"Guys, I'm sorry. I'd hoped that we might make it today, but I don't think so now," Matt said. "Sorry it's taking so long. I promise when we arrive, the first thing we're going to do is rest."

"No, the first thing we're going to do is thank God for getting us there," said Mary Frances. "Next, we're going to rest. Then, I'll prepare a feast. And then, we're going to thank God again."

The afternoon passed slowly, and the night even more slowly. The rain didn't cease until midnight. They slept against each other in one group, wrapped as best they could in wool blankets. Matt and Sam kept the fire going all night for warmth, but the cold ground crept into their bones; and no one slept well. By morning, everyone was exhausted. Matt guessed Arcadia to be six miles away. They moved much slower than they had the previous two days. Even Hannah was too tired to talk. Zander never complained, but his leg felt like it was on fire.

After only one hour, Matt gathered the family together. "I'm too tired to keep going," said Hannah.

"That's what I want to tell you," Matt said as they stood around him in the wet, cold forest. Each saw one another's breath in the morning air. "We've almost made it. Everybody's very tired. Zander's leg is killing him. We wish we had warmer clothes. We're all cold and exhausted. But what I need each of us to do is reach down deep inside yourself and find the will to keep going. Do not give up. We're almost there. Say to yourself, *Never Stop, Never Quit, Drive On*. Say it over and over and over. Keep putting one foot in front of another. Now, let me hear you!"

Slowly and quietly, almost in a whisper, the group started repeating, *Never Stop, Never Quit, Drive On.* Then a little louder, *Never Stop, Never Quit, Drive On,* over and over until they were almost shouting, *Never Stop, Never Quit, Drive On*! They were still repeating it an hour later when they crested a ridge, and Arcadia came into view.

The cabin sat nestled in the autumn foliage and pines. The lake in front reflected the blue sky and autumn colors of the trees around it. Tears running down her cheeks, Mary Frances hugged Matt and Hannah to her. Spontaneously, Dagny, Zander and Sam hugged each other. The final quarter of a mile didn't seem to exist because they could finally see it. Home.

Chapter 40
Arcadia

Reaching the steps of the cabin's front porch, Mary Frances fell to her knees, giving thanks. Then, Hannah knelt by her mother. One by one, the family followed suit, all giving thanks for guidance and protection on the journey. And finally, expressing thanks for achieving their final goal... Arcadia.

In time, they rose to their feet. Instinctively, Mary Frances found Matt's hand while Dagny found Zander's. Then, Hannah ran to Sam and took his hand. Together, the family climbed the wooden stairs onto the porch. Turning around, they paused to gaze at their surroundings. Across the lake were the Ozark Mountains, painted in the warm colors of autumn. When a gust of cold wind blew across the lake, brightly colored leaves fluttered to the ground. Matt reached in his pocket and found the key that he had carried all the way from Nashville. He unlocked the front door.

Slowly, the family entered the cabin and were enveloped in its warmth. Surrounded by wood... the log walls, the beams above and the plank floor, the great room welcomed the pilgrims. Directly ahead was a large wood burner anchored before a massive, stone wall. Three, leather sofas formed the heart of the great room, placed in a cozy and familiar arrangement in front of the wood burner. No one spoke as Matt guided them toward the sofas. Then opening the door of the wood burner, he struck the ferro rod to the kindling that was already in place. A fire sprang to life. Mesmerized, the family began to feel warm for the first time in days, feeling comfort for the first time in weeks. Looking around the cabin and at each other, emotions overwhelmed them.

"Matt, it's beautiful," said Mary Frances, trying not to cry. "We're home."

"We're home again," said Matt, "for the first time."

"This is a great cabin, Uncle Matt," said Sam. Everyone nodded, unable to find the words they were feeling.

"I'll get the water heater going," said Matt. "It'll take about 30 minutes, then each of you can take a nice, hot bath. Be careful because it makes very hot water. Mary Frances, would you help Hannah so she doesn't burn herself? I'll be right back, then I'll show everyone the rest of the cabin." He disappeared around the stone wall to go outside to fire the heater. Sitting perfectly still as if in a church or library, everyone remained quiet.

Returning a few minutes later, Matt said, "Zander, Dagny, your bedroom is this way." Matt gestured to them. They followed him into a small but cozy bedroom with a stone fireplace. There was a window in the exterior, log wall. A queen-sized bed made of logs was covered in a Hudson Bay blanket with another one folded at the foot of the bed. Dagny reached out and touched the bed, imagining how good it was going to feel. Then, she walked around to one side of the bed and picked up a framed picture on the night table.

"My family! My parents and my sister!" Dagny said. "How?" she asked, shaking her head in disbelief.

"Facebook," Matt said. "You have that picture on Facebook. I thought it might make the room feel more like home."

"Look, I have one, too," said Zander, picking up a framed picture from the other night table. He studied the photograph of his family with affection. "Thanks, Matt. I've accepted I may never see them again. We can share this with Sam. He never got to meet my brother. Wow! This means so much." Tears filled Zander's eyes.

After the moment subsided, Matt motioned them to a door by the fireplace. "And here is your bathroom," he said.

"My goodness, Matt! A bathtub and a shower!" said Dagny. "This is so nice."

"You'll find clothes in the chest of drawers and in the closet," said Matt.

"Clothes? But how?" asked Dagny.

"That's why he asked about our sizes. He bought them for us and brought them here in the helicopter with the last load," Zander explained.

"Let's show the kids to the bunk room," said Matt as they walked back to the fire where Mary Frances was sitting with the children.

"Mary Frances, our bedroom is beautiful! The bed! A fireplace!" Dagny said on the verge of tears.

"Hey, guys let's go up the stairs to the bunk room," said Matt. Everyone followed Matt up a flight of wooden stairs made of roughhewn logs to a loft that was over the kitchen. There were four, twin beds and two chests of drawers. Sam and Hannah leaned over the railing, looking down at the great room.

"This is cool," said Sam. "It's almost like a tree house!"

"I'll teach you how to make paper airplanes," said Zander.

"Paper airplanes?" Sam replied. "What's that?"

"You'll see. I've got lots of things to teach you," said Zander with a smile.

"Through this door is the bathroom," Matt said.

"This is my bed," said Hannah, indicating the bed closest to the bathroom door. "And this is your bed, Sam!" she said, assigning him to the bed next to hers.

"Feel free to look around... this is your home," said Matt. "Hannah, this is your chest of drawers. You'll find clothes inside. And, Sam, that one is yours. Now, if you will excuse Mrs. Archer and me, I'd like to show her to our bedroom."

Matt and Mary Frances left the others behind while Hannah expressed delight over the peaked roof in the bunkroom. When they got to their bedroom, Matt opened the door and held it for Mary Frances. Entering, she scanned the room, looking at the log walls, the stone fireplace and the bed. It had a headboard and a footboard made of rustic, pine logs. A framed picture drew her to the night table. It was a photo of her mother and father.

"I hope you like it. I took it out of your photo album and made a copy at Walgreens," Matt explained.

"I love it! Thank you," she said and gave Matt a kiss. Then, he showed her the fireplace and the bathroom. "Thank you, Matt. It's beautiful. We will all be safe here. I can feel it. Although it was an awfully hard journey, I understand why you did it this way. We will be safe. And we will be happy here."

Matt took his wife to the kitchen and gave a tour of everything from the stove to the copper pots and pans. "Matt, it's amazing! I feel like I've gone back in time 200 years; but they didn't have LED lights then, did they. What a combination of old and new!"

Matt explained the stove and said, "When you get ready to cook, you'll need to light the fire at least 30 minutes before. When it gets really cold outside, we may decide to keep it going all the time. Let me help you at first, until you get the hang of it. Wood storage is out the back door and so is the summer kitchen."

"Matt, we are so blessed," said Mary Frances, stunned. "I wonder what's going on in the rest of the country."

"We have satellite TV, Mary Frances," Matt said. "Let's turn it on and see. I hope it's still working. Some of the channels might have gone off the air. On second thought, I'm afraid to turn it on in front of the children. They've been through so much."

One by one, they all took a hot bath and put on clean clothes. Matt and Zander, both looking rough after not shaving for over a month, were much improved after their turns in the bathroom. The women had never enjoyed shampooing their hair as much as they did that day.

Mary Frances stepped into the great room, feeling almost radiant. "Hot water and soap! That was the best! Life is going to be normal again."

Dagny came out of her bedroom with something in her hand. "Mary Frances, did you look in the drawer in the bathroom? Makeup! Look! Lipstick! It's even the right shade!"

Matt smiled at Dagny's discovery. He wanted everyone to thrive, so he'd gone to great lengths to add little luxuries that would make life feel more normal.

The four adults were relaxing in the great room in front of the fire waiting for the children to come down from the bunkroom. Something outside the window caught Mary Frances' eye. She rose and looked out into the late afternoon. "You won't believe this! Matt, come look!"

Matt hurried to the window and looked out to see falling snow. The wind was blowing hard, stripping more leaves off the trees. A combination of leaves and snowflakes were falling to the ground. Dagny and Zander joined them at the window to watch the landscape from the warmth of the cabin. "We made it here just in time," said Dagny. "I've never appreciated being clean and warm so much in my entire life!"

Mary Frances cuddled up to Matt. He put his arm around her as they enjoyed watching the snow come down. "I remember the last time I got caught in a blizzard," she said. Matt gave her a hug.

Sam and Hannah came down the stairs. "What handsome children!" said Mary Frances as they joined their parents.

"And what clean children!" said Zander.

"Did you see it's snowing outside?" asked Sam.

"Yes, we did," said Matt. "How were your baths?"

"Mine was great," said Hannah. "I like being clean! Mommy adjusted the water for me. And she explained the toilet paper thing so I understand now.... I think."

The adults smiled, and Matt said, "Just don't waste it, Hannah."

Matt showed Mary Frances the food storage downstairs. She was surprised, but not totally, because she had begun to expect the unexpected from her husband. The basement was a warehouse full of supplies. Part of the basement was even deeper than the rest and extended beyond the footprint of the house.

Matt demonstrated how to light the wood stove in the kitchen. Thirty minutes later, Mary Frances was cooking. The family dined on beef stroganoff, mashed potatoes, broccoli and cookies for desert. As the weary family sat around the fire that night, enjoying the comfort of the leather sofas and the crackle of the flames, Matt said, "There's only one order for tomorrow. Sleep in! Sleep for as long as you want. Y'all have done great.

Tomorrow we rest! We deserve it!"

Mary Frances and Dagny took the children to the bunk room. Hannah first, the kids each changed into pajamas in the bathroom. Afterward, their mothers tucked them in bed, pulling the blankets up to their chins. "This bed is so comfy, Mommy," said Hannah. "I never want to sleep on the ground again." Matt and Zander climbed the stairs to the bunk room. Together, the children said their prayers. Then, their parents kissed them each goodnight.

Matt turned off the LED's in the kitchen and in the great room until the only light was the firelight shining through the glass of the wood burner door. "I'm serious about sleeping in, guys... for as long as you want," Matt said. "All that has to be done tomorrow is check the electric system, see how much electricity we've used today and get the water turbine going to make more power."

Once Matt and Mary Frances were in bed, she cuddled up with her husband and said, "Hannah is so right. I've never felt a bed that feels this good. I hope I never have to sleep on the ground again."

"I'm sorry you all had to go through that," he said. "I didn't expect the trip to be so difficult. But, it also means others are going to have to work very hard to find us, and no one knows where we are. I believe we're safe."

"You're amazing... *my* amazing husband," said Mary Frances. "I want to show you how much I love you, but I can't tonight. I'm so tired I can hardly move. In a day or two, I'll show you."

Matt laughed softly, "I'm worn out, too, sweetheart. There will be plenty of nights to make love. Sweet dreams. I love you." In less than a minute, the entire cabin was sound asleep.

The next morning, Matt was the first up. Being quiet so as not to wake Mary Frances, he looked out the window at the snow. It was a light, first snow of the season- about a half an inch. Matt carefully closed the bedroom door behind him as he pulled on his robe. After restarting the fire in the great room, he fired up the kitchen stove to make coffee. While waiting for the stove to warm, he decided to watch TV. Pushing buttons and pressing *mute* on the remote control, he brought up the cable TV menu. The satellite was still working. He moved the menu to the news stations. The first one he selected was off the air. Moving to the next one, it was off, too. Finally, he found a working channel. What Matt saw shook him to his core.

Unmuting, but only turning the volume to barely audible, Matt moved closer to the screen. With fires burning in the background, the news anchor showed city after city on fire. Then, the screen switched to Washington, D.C., with the camera on the White House. The White House was on fire. Surrounded by firetrucks, firefighters were trying to get it under control. The reporter said the Capitol building had burned the previous day. The Government had been moved to an undisclosed location three days prior.

The news program then switched to a reporter who explained that Goliath, the largest company in the world who also owned most of the computer servers, had experienced some type of malfunction. Banks, hospitals, schools, cities, power companies, water companies, trucking companies and stores all used the Goliath servers. When Goliath went down, so did everyone who used their servers. The chaos that ensued was catastrophic. Massive lines formed at banks as people converged to get cash. The banks were overwhelmed with the withdrawals, forcing the government to close all the banks. Across the world, mobs of customers stormed banks to get their money, breaking out windows and forcing bank employees to open the safes... only to find them empty.

Because the world was computerized, all stores closed... including supermarkets. State governors had assumed control of their individual states six weeks before, declaring martial law and controlling ingress and egress with National Guard and State Police. Power outages were happening all over. The chaos made workers afraid to leave their homes. Without the men who knew how to operate the complex equipment at the power plants, they just shut down. The army had set up perimeters around nuclear plants and had permanently detained the workers to prevent a nuclear meltdown if not operated correctly. All cell service was out of operation. The massive fleets of semi-trailer trucks that kept the country supplied with all goods from food to gasoline had practically stopped. People were quickly running out of food. In cities across the country, people were fighting over dwindling food supplies. The anchor concluded by saying that while the number of casualties was unknown due to the chaos and breakdown in communications, it was estimated that five million had already perished. Matt turned off the television.

Stunned, he sat in silence. Throwing another log on the fire, he returned to the kitchen to add more wood to the cook stove. Matt crept back to the bedroom and quietly opened the door, then got back in bed. He lay beside Mary Frances, staring at the wooden beams in the ceiling overhead, trying to comprehend what he'd just seen on TV. The reality was that he did understand it. *It's happening. It's just like we predicted... even with a black swan, the Goliath servers. I knew they owned most of the servers, but I hadn't considered how vulnerable that was. It's happening as we predicted. Five million dead. And that's just the beginning. It'll be 250 million or more in the US and who knows in other countries. This is real.*

"Matt, are you awake?" Mary Frances asked.

"Yeah," Matt answered.

"Is something wrong?" she asked.

"I turned on TV," he said. "It's happening. What we feared is happening. There's five million dead already, and it's only beginning. It was horrible, Mary Frances. Washington, D.C., is on fire. The White House is burning."

"Oh, Matt," she said. "It's getting worse not better."

"No, Mary Frances, it's getting *much* worse," he said. "It looks like we're going to be here a very long time."

Over the next week, Matt turned on TV from time to time when the children were playing outside. He shared what he'd seen with Mary Frances, Dagny and Zander but not the children. One by one, stations went black until eventually the television was silent. The last casualty reports, which were only estimates, were 50 to 75 million dead.

Matt had a ham radio and a satellite phone that didn't

operate off cell towers. When he called Jim Borland and Brian Eastman in Montana, they were overjoyed to hear from Matt's and Zander's crew. Matt was relieved to learn the Montana group had made it to their retreat and without incident. Jim and Brian had no new information to share but agreed to a weekly call time to stay in touch. The contingency plan was to use the ham radios if the sat phones ceased to function.

Matt also called Switzerland. Fredèric, Sophia and sons were safe at their farm in the mountains and were doing well. According to Fredéric's contact at a European data base company, the Goliath servers had been accessed through the payroll program. Even though the servers were separate for security purposes, they were still connected to Goliath for the employees' payroll. That was how the hackers got in. Switzerland had dynamited the passes, cutting itself off from the world. The Steiners were doing fine, but the rest of Europe was in chaos.

Day by day, the family at Arcadia adapted to a new life. Matt gave out assignments and duties, adjusting the details as needed. School started for Sam and Hannah as Mary Frances took on the new role of teacher. Bringing in food for the family, Matt began bow hunting and fly fishing. What used to be a pastime was now a regular part of life. Mary Frances used the fresh meat and fish he brought in to add variety to the freeze dried and dehydrated foods that were in storage. Zander and Sam learned about all the systems at Arcadia, electrical and hydro. There was a two-year supply of firewood already on hand, but soon the men began the endless job of cutting more as Zander got stronger. Dagny kept the time on the calendars Matt had preprinted at the cabin. Every birthday, every anniversary and every holiday was celebrated. As Dagny experimented with sewing projects she discovered the knitting needles and yarn in storage. Hannah was thrilled to begin her knitting lessons. Work and school brought the comfort of normalcy with Sam and Hannah surprisingly enjoying their lessons. The family rested on Saturday and worshipped on Sunday.

At first, the lack of electronics seemed strange; but gradually, everyone adapted. Matt had amassed a library of over a thousand novels and dozens of board games. After the evening meal, the family would gather around the fire and talk, play board games and then read for pure pleasure. Surprisingly, television was hardly missed.

Thanksgiving was celebrated in high fashion even though Matt had been unable to kill a turkey. So, he hiked to the stream with his fly rod and caught trout. All along, he had told Mary Frances she'd have to fix what he brought her. He just wished he could have gotten her a turkey.

At the table, Hannah stared at the platter of fish. "Isn't today Thanksgiving? Don't we have to eat turkey at Thanksgiving?" Sam nudged Hannah under the table.

"Not if you don't have a turkey, Hannah," Dagny said, finding humor in the situation. "Isn't that right, Matt?"

"New traditions, Dagny," Matt responded with a grin. "We'll have lots of them."

"Well, I like this new tradition!" said Sam.

When a December snow confined everyone indoors for several days, Matt brought out the games. There were several games that were new to Sam and Hannah... they had never even heard of them. The family played checkers, Monopoly and cards. After the kids went to bed, the adults played pinochle. Matt and Mary Frances beat Zander and Dagny. Matt found it so funny he had to call Fredéric and Sophia in Switzerland. Considering it afterwards, Matt thought, *How crazy is this? The world is falling apart while I'm on a sat phone talking to a man in Switzerland who's also sitting in a cabin in the snow. And we're talking about pinochle.*

On Christmas Day, the family celebrated the birth of Jesus. Zander and Sam had cut a pine tree. It stood in the great room, decorated with the same ornaments Matt used the Christmas before at his Tennessee cabin. Mary Frances made turkey and dressing, freeze dried of course. Everyone was pleasantly surprised at how tasty it was.

Hannah asked sincerely, "Why didn't we have this at Thanksgiving?" Sam nudged her under the table again as everyone laughed.

During the meal, Matt noticed Mary Frances' bracelet. "You brought it!" he said, touching her wrist.

"Yes, of course," she replied. "I had to have my Arcadia bracelet in Arcadia!"

When Christmas dinner was over, Matt slipped out of the room and returned with five boxes. "I have gifts for everyone," he said, handing them out. Each was delighted to find a watch inside. "These aren't quartz. They're mechanical, so they have to be wound," he explained.

"What do you mean, *wound*, Uncle Matt?" asked Sam.

"Quartz watches use batteries; these don't. Mechanical watches run off springs. You have to wind the spring every day," explained Matt. "There won't be batteries again for a very long time."

"Cool," said Sam. "I like new technology."

They all thanked him and apologized for not having gifts to give. "You are all gifts to me," Matt said. "Each one of you. When I started planning this place years ago, I expected it would be only me. But that would have been terribly lonely. I'm so glad you're all here."

That night in bed, Mary Frances lay under the covers watching the fireplace. Matt lay behind her, his arm wrapped around her and his body pressed against her.

"Do you remember where you were one year ago?" he asked. "And do you remember what we were doing?"

"Yes, of course I do, Mr. Archer," she said, savoring his warmth as he held her.

"We should do that every Christmas," he said. "Let's make it our tradition."

"I thought you'd never ask," she said, turning to him.

Mary Frances touched her husband's face, framed by the firelight as it flickered on the ceiling above. He kissed her. They made love, slowly, then passionately. Outside, it had begun to snow. While the world was in chaos, there in Arcadia, it was warm and safe and peaceful.

That was the first Christmas at Arcadia. It would be four more Christmases before the family would see Tennessee again.

Chapter 41
Forty Years Later

Autumn arrived late in Tennessee, the leaves not changing until well into October. By Thanksgiving Day, the last leaves, though not as brightly colored as a few weeks before, were still hanging on. The blue sedan with a smokestack protruding from an opening in the trunk headed south down a recently oiled and chipped road. The Nashville traffic was heavier than normal that morning. A total of 10 cars had been passed since leaving home.

"Isn't this road nice, since it's been resurfaced," commented Hannah. "That big machine that runs on steam does such a good job. Maybe our street will be next."

"Is the entire family supposed to be there today?" asked Sam.

"I think so. Mom has been cooking for a week," said Hannah. "Three turkeys and, of course, trout. Why is it we have trout, Sam? I can't remember."

"The first year... your dad couldn't kill a turkey. He must have hunted for three days but never saw one," Sam explained. "So, he went fishing and brought your mother trout instead."

"That seems vaguely familiar," Hannah said.

"What do you remember about those days?" asked Sam. It was a topic that always came up at Thanksgiving.

"My memories," she said, "are more feelings and images

than specific events. I remember the place I was taken after my mother died. I can see the gymnasium. I still hear the children crying. Someone took my blanket, and you got it back for me. And, I remember the first time I walked in the cabin with you. Everyone was staring at me."

"And the trip to Arcadia?" he continued.

"Bits and pieces," Hannah said. "Our parents were talking about riding on a boat across a river, but I don't remember doing that."

"You were asleep when we crossed," Sam said.

"I remember a lot of yelling. Mom pushed me down on the floor in the backseat and lay on me. I was scared," Hannah continued. "We slept in Dad's blue truck in the garage. I remember being very scared again, but I'm not sure why. And I remember that long hike to the cabin. I was so tired and so cold!"

Sam listened to his wife recount memories of a time 40 years before. He clearly remembered that terrible day at the garage. He was glad she didn't.

"I remember getting to the cabin and how good the hot shower felt," said Sam.

"Oh, who could forget that ice-cold spring we bathed in at the garage!" Hannah exclaimed, thinking back through four decades. "And you'd even go with me into the woods to use the bathroom in case there were bears around. I like to remember lying on my bed under the log beams of the bunkroom ceiling. With you there, I felt so safe. That's what I remember most... you were always protecting me and taking care of me." Sam nodded, keeping his eye on the road as he drove.

"Sam, I've never loved anyone but you," said Hannah. "From the first moment, I saw you... I think I loved you. I was only eight years old. Is that possible, Sam, to fall in love as a child?" she asked. Sam smiled.

"I loved you from the first moment I saw you, Hannah," Sam said. "I can't explain it. I just did. When we came back here, there were other girls who made it known they were interested in me, but none of them ever mattered. It's like you were made for me."

Hannah blinked back tears and looked out the window at

the passing landscape of trees and fields as Brentwood was left behind, becoming less town and more country. "You know, Mom told me it was the same for her. She met Dad when she ran off the road in a snowstorm. He found her and took her home. She said she loved him immediately from that moment."

"How does that work?" asked Sam. "It's not that way for everybody."

"No, it isn't... but if it is, you are truly blessed. It's a gift from heaven," Hannah said. Sam reached over and took her hand.

Turning off the newly paved road, Sam was forced to slow down. The deteriorated pavement included sections that were completely missing. He slowed to only five miles per hour as he navigated the labyrinth of pot holes. "Uncle Matt and Aunt Mary have moved to the cabin for the winter, just like always," said Sam.

"Every year," Hannah said. "They love the cabin. I do, too. It's very important for them to be there for Thanksgiving and Christmas. Sam, could we have a cabin down here in the country someday? The children are grown now. Wouldn't it be fun to have a bunkroom for the grandchildren?"

"I think that's a great idea," said Sam. "I'll start working on that, and we'll see." After several miles of potholes, the blue sedan turned up a gravel drive that wound through the trees and finally emerged in front of a log cabin. There were cars and pick-up trucks parked in a line along the side of the drive. Children were playing happily everywhere.

"There's Mom!" said Hannah, pointing to a woman standing by the front door. It was Mary Frances Archer. Over the years, her appearance was almost unchanged. The obvious difference being the pony tail over her left shoulder was silvery gray. Two little girls were jumping around her and hugging her leg. She hadn't gained a pound in 40 years and still looked attractive in her red plaid shirt and blue jeans.

"Mom!" shouted Hannah, running up the sidewalk with Sam close behind. The two women embraced affectionately. Hannah had grown to be almost the same size as Mary Frances. For years, they had been able to share clothes. Mother and daughter looked lovingly at each other as Mary Frances gently touched her daughter's hair and smiled.

"Where's Dad?" asked Hannah.

"Hi, Sam," said Mary Frances, hugging her son-in-law. "He's out in the barn with some of the grandkids. Becky had her baby, a girl. Your dad's showing her off. Becky's a good momma."

"Who had a baby? Becky?" asked Sam.

"Becky, one of our draft horses," said Mary Frances. "It's so common now, but who would have dreamed draft horses would be in such demand. I don't know if we'll sell her or keep her. It's tempting to keep her, but we have a list of people wanting to buy draft horses. Our doctor friend down the road will want her, I'm certain. Let's go find your father, then I need to get back to the kitchen."

When the three entered the barn, they were met with the sight of several children reaching through the boards of the stable to pet the new foal. She had four white stockings and a white blaze on her face. Grandpa looked on.

Matt Archer looked much the same. A life of hard work had kept him thin; the only differences were the lines in his face and the dark hair now gray. Hannah ran to her father and hugged him a long time.

Cars and trucks kept arriving as more family gathered. When Zander and Dagny arrived, everyone ran to greet them. Matt kidded Zander saying, "Zander, when are you going to get that house painted? It looks terrible." Matt knew full well that the paint had come in, and the project was complete.

Matt had set up heavy, wooden picnic tables in the back. Hoping for good weather, they had it that day. Mary Frances insisted the tables be arranged in a large *U* so the entire family was eating at one table.

When the turkey and trout were served, Matt rose and gave thanks. As he prayed, Mary Frances stood by his side. She didn't bow her head but looked out across the yard full of people, all her family. Tears came to her eyes as she spotted her 12 children, then Zander's and Dagny's three children. Counting spouses and grandchildren, a total of 79 people shared that Thanksgiving Day. As Matt thanked God for the blessings of that year, Mary Frances silently thanked Him for 40 years of blessings. She reached down to the gold, spiral bracelet on her wrist, the one Matt had given her all those years ago, and thanked God for constantly being with them through every trial they had encountered.

While heads were bowed, a little girl with dark, brown hair and brown eyes, looked up and watched her grandmother. Mary Frances smiled and gave her a wink. Mary Frances listened to Matt's prayer and then smiled again at the little girl and thought, *She looks just like me!*

The End

ABOUT THE AUTHOR

This is LL Fox's second novel. *The Blue Gate*, his first novel, is available on Amazon. Follow LL Fox on Facebook and check out his website www.llfoxbooks.com.

Attention book clubs. There are discussion questions for both *The Blue Gate* and *The Endex* hosted at www.llfoxbooks.com.

Printed in the USA
CPSIA information can be obtained
at www.ICGtesting.com
LVHW022156271223
767609LV00022B/184/J

9 781087 879505